**Praise for the previous works of
Robert Westbrook:**

*"Westbrook . . . possesses a masterful sense of
narration."*—Washington Post Bookworld

*"What a marvelous novel—and a pleasure to read a
mystery that is both suspenseful and funny."*—Margaret
Truman

*"Westbrook delivers . . . mercilessly witty social
satire."*—Publishers Weekly

"Exciting, funny, and entertaining."—USA Today

"Robert Westbrook is a real talent."—Eliot Roosevelt

Also from Robert Westbrook

Ghost Dancer
A Howard Moon Deer Mystery

WARRIOR CIRCLE

A Howard Moon Deer Mystery

Robert Westbrook

A SIGNET BOOK

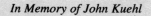

In Memory of John Kuehl

I am grateful to Michaela Hamilton, my editor, and to those who read various drafts of this book and offered wise suggestions: Ted Chichak, Gail Westbrook, and Me'l Christensen. A special thanks to Deputy Marshal/Medical Investigator Bill Hubbard of Red River, NM, for his attempts to educate me in the ways of law enforcement.

Power Animals

Silver Bear had a slight stutter.

"It is the wi . . . wi . . . *will* of the Great Spirit that we should meet together on this night of the Green Corn Moon."

He took a breath, grateful he had not mangled moon into *moo . . . moo . . . moon*. He got through the rest without a hitch:

"Oh, Great Spirit, you have caused the silver orb to shine with brightness upon our hearts. We thank you for all these favors as we walk the Medicine Path together. Oh, Great Spirit, come into our Warrior's Circle and let the dance begin!"

Black Wolf and Coyote-That-Sings began beating the great drum, making a rhythm like a heartbeat, sending a bass pulse deep into the forest and upward into the night sky above Bear Lake. It was close to midnight, and the full June moon had just risen over a snowy peak—the Green Corn Moon, as the Indians call it. The bonfire near the drum leapt with dancing flames that reflected against the black and red war paint on the men's half-naked bodies. There were seven warriors present at the ceremony. Silver Bear, Owl Dancer, Dog-Running-Free, Dreaming Lion, and Cosmic Turtle chanted and danced in a circle around the bonfire as Black Wolf and Coyote-That-Sings continued to beat the drum. Each of the warriors summoned his personal power animal to come forth and enter him, to guide his journey tonight.

The ceremony was very ancient—at least, this is what they had read on the Internet website, which was their source of authentic native ritual, www.shaman/rules.com. For when these particular warriors weren't busy being Indians, they led quite different, pale-face lives. One was a TV producer, the others an architect, a real estate developer, a once-famous rock musician, a scion of the wealthiest family in town, the owner of the most chic restaurant in San Geronimo, and finally a cop. They were a men's group. All of them, for different reasons, had felt something lacking in their lives, an emptiness at the center of their manhood, a lack of ritual and meaning. So they gathered once a week on Wednesday nights to discuss male issues, and they held occasional special ceremonies in the woods, as they were doing tonight, earnestly borrowing from the native culture their great-grandparents had even more earnestly tried to destroy.

The seven men had fasted for three days to prepare for tonight's ceremony. In the morning, they had hiked all day up a steep trail high into the San Geronimo Wilderness to Bear Lake, their stomachs rumbling, two of them carrying the huge drum suspended from a pole on their shoulders, the others with backpacks full of war paint, loincloths, feathers, fur, and animal masks. At sunset, the entire group had ingested the Sacred Medicine, peyote.

The black waters of Bear Lake, the bonfire, the drums, the chanting, the full moon rising overhead—it was a good night to throw off the modern world and step into a more ancient realm, a consciousness that was strangely familiar and seemed to have been waiting half-asleep in the corner of each man's mind. Of the seven, six were having a fine time connecting with their wise inner-savage. But the seventh, Cosmic Turtle, was having a rough night. He was the ex-musician, and he wasn't exactly certain when he had begun to feel like the odd man out. Occasionally he had the distinct impression that the others were giving him weird looks. *Hey, I'm just being paranoid!* he told himself. His mouth was dry, his tongue felt like a swollen cactus, and he didn't know what was wrong with him.

After a while Cosmic Turtle had to stop dancing and sit down away from the fire. He was definitely feeling very strange. It must be the drug, he decided. Yet peyote was a natural high, part of the Medicine Path to higher consciousness. He tried to reassure himself that he was only shedding his ego, feeling a little naked right now without his personality to keep him warm. This was only a transitional moment, something he needed to experience on his journey to becoming a Man of Power.

Meanwhile, things were getting out of hand around the bonfire. Without warning, one of the warriors began to howl: *Yee-e-eowl! . . . Yee-e-eowl!* It was Coyote-That-Sings, but in this instance, he seemed to Cosmic Turtle more like Coyote-That-Has-Just-Gone-Over-the-Top. And now, by God, someone was passing the wooden bowl of peyote his way. It was Owl Dancer, in all his paint and feathers, who had come over to where he was sitting. Cosmic Turtle felt a wave of nausea. The hideous tubercles of dried cactus looked to him like the shriveled penises of some extinct race.

"Cosmic Turtle, take some Sacred Medicine, my brother—it will guide your journey."

"No, thank you, Owl Dancer," he managed to reply. "I'm just sitting here doing some work on myself. I'm going to be fine . . . hey, you didn't bring any Pepto-Bismol, by any chance?"

Owl Dancer shook his head sadly, rising to leave. "May the Great Spirit be with you."

"And you too, Owl Dancer."

What bullshit! Cosmic Turtle thought to himself with unexpected clarity. It was as if the curtains had parted and he saw what a joke this was, playacting Indians, then driving away at the end of the weekend in their Land Cruisers and BMWs. Cosmic Turtle's real name was Gary Tripp, and he was an aging baby boomer who had ridden the waves of his generation. Once upon a time—it seemed like a dream now—he had been the keyboard player for Headstone, a San Francisco band that had several top-forty hits in the early seventies before disappearing from the charts of human memory. Later, Gary had paid some dues—tax troubles, drug rehab, and a few other things as well. He had gone through EST, Jesus, and Zen Buddhism; now he was a family man and a male warrior. *And I still don't know jack-shit!* he thought to himself grimly. It was remarkable; he had spent his entire life always searching, but never finding.

Gary stood up, lurched toward the bushes, and threw up. This was getting to be pretty scary, feeling sick like this miles from nowhere in a remote wilderness area with a full moon overhead and a bunch of half-naked men pounding on a drum. The other guys were really going wild now. A few had stripped off the rest of their clothing and were dancing around the fire, stone naked, screaming and yowling. The TV producer and the architect were putting more paint on each other's bodies. The real estate developer had discovered a new language, and he was talking in tongues. Gary found his teeth were chattering, and he feared he might need to throw up again.

He thought he'd better go down to the lake. Splash some water on his face. Make the world real again. He managed to walk on rubbery legs down to the dark water where the giant moon floated upside down. As Gary watched, some creature broke from below the black surface and swam toward the reedy bank. It was a large rat, causing him to shiver. He felt he had to get somewhere safe before he went mad. He walked farther along the bank to the far side of the lake and found a small strip of gravelly beach. Across the lake the bonfire flared, and the drumming had become more raucous, a hint of salsa creeping into the beat. Far away, the shriek of a predatory bird pierced the night.

All the fire had gone from Gary Tripp's belly. He fell to his knees, shivery with fear. His forehead was burning hot and icy cold at the same time. He leaned forward toward the surface of Bear Lake, cupped water with his two hands, and splashed his face. The water felt good—cold and substantial. The moon, undulating on the surface, was disturbed by his motion, breaking into silver fragments. He was about to splash himself again when he saw the reflection of someone coming up behind him.

Gary turned and saw two malevolent eyes regarding him through an animal mask. The eyes were frightful, barely human, not of this world. But when he lowered his gaze, he saw something that was certainly of human making, and it worried him even more: a small, snub-nosed revolver in a gloved hand. It was the glove—a white latex surgical glove—that made him understand that this was serious business.

The masked figure gestured with the barrel of the pistol for Gary to come. It was Death standing before him, here to take him away. "But you can't do this, you mustn't break the Circle!" Gary whispered hoarsely, for his voice failed him.

But Death only laughed at his feeble protest. Gary felt the cold hard gun pressed against the back of his head, an irresistible summons. As he was marched from the bank of the lake into the nearby woods, he gazed sadly upward at the moon for the last time. He felt so entirely insignificant, like a small fluttery insect about to meet its end on a midsummer's eve.

Did it matter? Did anything really matter? The two shots, when they came, one immediately after the other, were hardly more than little plips of sound, barely audible beneath the deep manly beating of the drum.

PART ONE

———⊶∞∞⊷———

DISAPPEARING WOMAN

1

Howard Moon Deer was in postcoital heaven when his world fell apart on a wet Tuesday night in mid-August. It came when he was least expecting it, when he was a snug and sated satyr: the sound of rain outside his cabin, skin against warm skin, his arm nearly asleep beneath the weight of her head, his nose nestled in her tangled strawberry-blond hair. This was about as blissed-out as a native could be—post-Columbus, at least, and severed from anything resembling roots. But then, unexpectedly, Aria Waldman disengaged and sat up in bed.

"I've got to go," she said quietly, almost to herself.

Dreamy and half-asleep, Howie lay on the pillow and pretended to be an octopus. He slipped one of his muscular guy legs over her two more delicate lady legs and wrapped both his arms around her waist, encircling her. He only wished he had a few more tentacles to hold her and stroke her and pull her back into their love nest.

"Howie, honestly . . . I've got to go."

"You're always going," he muttered. "Why?"

"I've got work to do. A story I'm finishing."

She had succeeded in snagging the attention of his hormone-soaked brain. Reluctantly, he glanced at the bedside clock. "At eleven-thirty at night? Can't it wait until morning?"

"Do I ever ask you if *your* work can wait until morning when you and Jack are off playing detective?"

With little warning, something unpleasant had begun. A tit-for-tat exchange in the battle of the genders, a war Howie didn't completely understand.

"Stay," he protested. "Forget work. Forget everything. It's raining outside, and there's nothing sadder than post-*coitus interruptus.*"

Then, without warning, she exploded. "Goddamn it, Howie! Stop making this so hard for me! You don't own me. I don't have to answer to you every time I need to do something. So get off my back, will you?"

"It wasn't your back I was on," he pointed out.

Howie sat up in bed. She was a volatile woman, Aria Waldman. Volatile and voluptuous, he thought ruefully. From the beginning, it had been a tumultuous affair, full of ups and downs, tears and reconciliations. These explosions would happen out of nowhere, and he really didn't know why. She kept him guessing. Perhaps that was part of the attraction.

"Let's start this again," he suggested calmly. "Can't you finish your story tomorrow? Look, I was all psyched up for you to stay the night. I even bought some lox and bagels for breakfast. And you know, when an Indian goes kosher, it's a sign of serious lust. . . ."

He was trying to be funny. "Make a woman laugh and she's halfway to your bed" was Howie's motto. But not tonight clearly. Tonight his humor only rubbed her the wrong way.

"I really *hate* it when you get so clingy!" she cried. "You're smothering me, Howie, and I simply refuse to feel guilty for doing my job! I'm a workingwoman—you always knew that about me. And if I can't come and go without you making such a big deal about it, I've got to stop seeing you."

Clingy? That was certainly an unattractive way to put it. Was it clingy to expect her to stay the night when she had told him she would? Howie wasn't at all sure what was going on. He put a hand gently on her shoulder, to comfort her, to reconnect. But she stood up violently.

"For chrissake, just let me go, Howie!"

He really didn't know what he had done wrong. Aria had been odd and moody all evening, even while they were eating the gourmet candlelit dinner he had cooked earlier. Then they had made love passionately, full of greedy lust for one another, and he thought the moodiness was gone. Now Howie studied her as she walked around the room in search of her clothing. Aria Waldman was certainly a pleasant sight au naturale, reddish-blond hair, long-legged, and rosy-complexioned. A tad plump, perhaps, but interestingly so—Renoir was the word that generally came to mind, though tonight she might just as well have been a Jackson Pollock, a study of abstract motion making an unexpected exit from his bed. Howie had a dull sense of having missed some vital piece of information. With a discreet motion he moved the sheet to cover his limp, dejected manhood.

"Aria, talk to me. There's obviously more going on here than some article you're writing."

She shook her head. "This is my fault!" she said bitterly, refusing to look at him. "I should never have allowed myself to get sucked into a relationship. I never *wanted* a relationship at this stage of my life. Don't you understand? I'm just too busy for it!"

"Busy?" Howie was struggling now to contain his own anger. "I'm busy just like you are. I have a job, I'm trying to finish up my Ph.D., I've got a zillion things to do. But we're not robots, Aria— this is real life passing us by. *Our* lives. It's not just some stupid career ladder we're climbing."

She turned on him. "Oh, yeah, that's easy for you to say! You had all those cushy scholarships to fancy schools. Christ, they *paid* you to go to Dartmouth and Princeton! . . . that's been *real* tough for you, hasn't it? But I always had to make it on my own. I'm not some minority-of-the-month, like you are. There's no one to pick up the pieces if I fall."

This was hitting below the belt. It hadn't been so easy for Howard Moon Deer, a Lakota Sioux who grew up in an Airstream trailer on a reservation in South Dakota, to win those "cushy scholarships," as Aria called them.

"Look," he said, trying to calm things down, "Of course I understand if you have work to do. You only need to give me a little warning, that's all. When you came over for dinner tonight, I was expecting you to stay."

She looked so brittle, Howie was afraid she would shatter.

"Well, I'm sorry," she told him, jaw clenched, her lips barely moving. "I'm wrong, you're right. I'll be a nicer person tomorrow, I promise."

"Hey, what's going on here?" he demanded. But she only sighed and shook her head. There had been times in his life when he thought he had love all figured out, but the older he got, the more he realized he barely had a clue. Moodily, Howie watched as she dressed, stepping into a pair of bikini panties that had a design of red chile peppers on them—cute but they were falling apart, the elastic separating from the cotton material. Aria was a slob when it came to underwear, a trait he had always found strangely endearing. He watched her strawberry thatch of pubic hair disappear from view. It was exquisite, his own personal Bermuda Triangle that had spun his compass in a big way. She was dressing quickly now, almost violently; he could tell from her body language how upset she was. In a moment, she would start to cry. The signs were all too familiar, the way her face was flushed and her shoulders had gone all rigid, and how she steadfastly refused to look in his direction.

"You just put your T-shirt on inside out and backward," he observed.

She stopped dressing and saw that Howie was perfectly right. She took a deep breath. "That's because you're making me *so* uptight," she managed, her voice rising. "I mean, Christ! Just lying there *watching* me!"

"Well, where do you want me to look?"

"Anywhere but at *me*!" she shouted, bursting into tears. The floodgates had opened, as he had been expecting. "I hate to be . . . *studied*!"

He hated to see her cry. His instinct was to comfort her, but he knew from experience that at this point in the cycle, it would only make matters worse. So Howie obliged her by burying his head in the pillow. He wondered if it was his fault they always seemed to end up fighting. Or was it hers? Was he being some kind of insensitive male brute for trying to keep Aria Waldman in bed, rather than encouraging her to fulfill her career goals at eleven-thirty at night? All these questions swirled in his brain, like water gurgling down a drain. Howie was twenty-eight years old and starting to feel awfully discouraged about the gender game. Love wasn't easy in the postfeminist jungle; sometimes it seemed like Tarzan was still swinging through the trees, but Jane had taken a powder. It made his head ache just to think about it. His mind wandered to the soothing sound of rain falling outside his cabin. He could smell the wet sagebrush, visualize the huge expanse of desert and mountains, the harsh rugged landscape of northern New Mexico. It was a stormy summer night full of thunder and lightning, the rain slapping hard against the windows. Wouldn't it be nice, he thought, if men and women could be as natural together as nature?

Howie looked up from his pillow to find Aria standing by the door, ready to leave. She was still sniffling, but refusing to look his way. He watched her, feeling confused, awkward, and hurt. But he didn't want to let her leave like this, not while they were still fighting. So he rose from the bed, turning discreetly to hide his maleness while he stepped into a terry cloth robe. He approached her for one more try.

"Look, I guess I'm a gorilla when it comes to love," he admitted. "So probably I'm doing this all wrong. But I'm your friend, honestly. I don't mean to smother you, or keep you from your work, or any of those bad things. I'm just a little slow, that's all. So you gotta help me and tell me what you want."

She turned his way, finally, her face all red with tears and exasperation. But then her will seemed to collapse, and everything about her softened. "Oh, Howie! What am I going to do with you? You're not even vaguely a gorilla. You're the nicest man I know . . . it's me, *I'm* the one that's all wrong! You should give up on me, really."

"But I don't want to give up on you."

"Then you have to give me some time. I'm a little confused right now. It's not you . . . there are a lot of things going on in my life. Just be patient. Okay?"

He smiled wearily, battle-scarred. "Of course. Look, we'll talk tomorrow."

She took his hand and held on tightly, as though she were a swimmer tossed at sea, and he was a buoy that she must cling to or be swept away.

"You're such a good guy!" she said impulsively.

Good guy? Howie didn't want to be a good guy. He wanted to be a dashing, virile, romantic figure she couldn't look at without melting into a puddle of girlish butter. Probably she saw the disappointment in his eyes because she kissed him quickly on the lips. Her mouth was warm, and Howie felt his last ounce of resistance ebb away. *All right, I'll be a good guy,* he thought. *If that's what you want from me.*

She hesitated a moment longer. Was she going to say she loved him?

"By the way, that was a fabulous paella you made tonight. You really are the King of Saffron Rice."

Well, at least it was something, he supposed.

Howie watched from the doorway as Aria pulled out of his driveway in her powder-blue Jeep Cherokee. A jagged bolt of lightning filled the night sky, turning the landscape magnesium-white for just an instant as she drove off into the rain. In the flare of light, he saw her turn a final time and wave good-bye. It was an image he would try to reconstruct in his mind afterward. Was she crying, or was that only water from the sky streaming down her windshield? He could hear the muffled sound of her car stereo—she was playing Puccini's final opera, *Turandot,* which he had given her for Christmas. The music grew fainter, and then she was gone.

Howie turned and faced his empty nest. It wasn't much, Howie's cabin, only a single room twelve feet by sixteen, a guest house that belonged to a larger estate. There was a kitchen alcove, a bathroom about the size of a phone booth, and many windows looking out on the desert and nearby mountains. Maybe romance went more smoothly if you had more room. He had papers and books piled up in disorderly stacks everywhere—on the floor, the small dining table, the kitchen shelves, even the bathroom. The latest draft of his unfinished Ph.D. dissertation, "Philosophical Divisions at the Top of the Food Chain," lay scattered across his crowded desk alongside a laptop computer and a half-eaten bag of blue corn tortilla chips. Theoretically he was a graduate student at Princeton University in the field of culinary psycho-sociology, but he had allowed himself to get waylaid in New Mexico these past couple of years.

Howard Moon Deer took a mental snapshot of himself as he stood surveying his world, a kind of spectral photograph that produced a clear image of who he was—a portrait of a scholarship Indian who had wandered too far from his South Dakota roots and now, as a result, belonged nowhere. An Indian without a tribe. A big man with wide cheekbones, a round, moonlike face, large, dreamy brown eyes—too dreamy!—and the flattish nose of his people. His long shiny black hair fell clear to his waist, usually tied in a ponytail, but hanging loose and wild tonight in honor of lust. *So this is me!* Howie thought dismally, not impressed. He was too intellectual, too indecisive, and too damn poor!

"Hell with it all!" he said wearily.

There was a tremendous crack of thunder, sharp as a gunshot, as Howard Moon Deer turned off the light and shuffled to his solitary bed.

He woke in darkness at some lonely hour before dawn. The rain had stopped and the room was still, except for the sound of his own heart beating. He wasn't certain what woke him. Then, as he lay staring at the ceiling, he heard the faint sound of Italian opera somewhere outside his cabin. It was Puccini, unmistakable, soaring and romantic. As Howie listened, the music identified itself more concretely. It was *Turandot,* Luciano Pavarotti singing "Nessun Dorma."

Howie yawned with pleasure, since he liked opera. It took a moment for him to realize how odd it was that Luciano Pavarotti should be singing outside his window at this hour. He sat up in bed and glanced at the glowing numbers on his digital alarm clock. It was 3:23 A.M., very puzzling.

Howie decided he'd better investigate. He slipped into his terry cloth robe and his Birkenstock sandals, found a flashlight on a shelf by the front door, and walked outside. The stars overhead were reflected in puddles of water on his gravel driveway. The air was pungent with the scent of damp sagebrush. To his surprise, he saw two glowing red taillights standing motionless a hundred feet down the road. He could just make out the shape of Aria's Jeep Cherokee.

Lighting his way with the flashlight, Howie walked quickly along the muddy road toward the car.

"Aria!" he called. "Are you there?"

He stepped in a deep puddle and almost lost a sandal, wishing he had thought to put on more substantial shoes. As he approached the Jeep, the music grew louder. The sound was eerie, like phantom voices singing to the sagebrush. Howie broke into a run the last twenty feet, his Birkenstocks flapping and splashing through the puddles, now fearing that something was terribly wrong. Luciano Pavarotti was soaring toward a dramatic climax on the car stereo as Howie came up to the car. The engine was running, the driver's door was hanging wide open. But the Jeep was empty.

"Aria!" he called again. There was no answer. As Howie stood dumbfounded in the mud staring at the abandoned car, the engine shuddered and died. The music kept soaring, unstoppable. Howie slipped into the driver's seat and saw that the gas tank had run empty. He turned off the cassette player, and the silence that followed seemed huge, an engulfing vastness of summer night. The key was in the ignition, attached to a polished turquoise stone along with Aria's house keys. He flicked the ignition off, causing the headlights to die and the red-and-green-glowing dashboard lights to extinguish as well. Now there was darkness as well as silence.

None of it made any sense at all. Howie stepped out of the Jeep. "Aria!" he shouted. "Aria! . . . Where are you?"

Still there was no answer. Only a restless wind through the sagebrush and the Jeep engine gurgling itself to sleep.

"Aria!" he cried more loudly, cupping his hands to his mouth. He stepped away from the car and turned in four directions, repeating the ritual. He called to the north, the south, the west, and the east. But Aria did not answer.

It had been a clueless night from the start, and Howie was now completely mystified. Why in the world would she abandon her car late at night in a thunderstorm? He walked slowly around the Jeep, inspecting the tires, wondering if she had had a flat. But the tires appeared to be fine. He was inspecting the front left wheel when the beam of his flashlight caught the glint of a metal object that had fallen beneath the chassis of the car. At first he thought it might be an engine part that had somehow come loose, but when he moved closer and knelt near the wheel, he was dismayed to see it was a pistol.

Howie picked up the gun carefully and held it with distaste. It was a hard, nasty thing, heavier than he would have imagined, a snub-nosed revolver partially covered with mud. Howie did not like guns and knew very little about them. Kneeling in the mud, he forced himself to inspect the gun more closely. He opened the swing-out cylinder and saw that there were three live bullets still in the gun and three chambers that were empty. He sniffed the barrel. At some point, and not so very long ago, someone had fired this weapon, leaving behind a lingering acrid smell of smoke and death.

2

Howie stood in the muddy road in the predawn darkness, holding the small, snub-nosed gun loosely in his right hand. He gazed upward to the cold puzzle of bright New Mexico stars overhead and wondered what he should do next. The stars told him nothing, so he stuffed the gun into his dressing gown pocket and walked quickly back along the road in the direction of the main house, where his landlords lived. The gun banged against his leg as he walked, a heavy burden uncomfortable in his pocket.

Howie lived on a fifty-acre estate, renting his small guest house from Bob and Nova Davidson, a couple he had met several years ago in Paris. Howie had been in Europe on a research grant, but Bob and Nova had only come to play; Nova's father owned a chain of department stores in California, and this allowed them the luxury to be free spirits. They were artists—"trust fund hippies" was the pejorative phrase in San Geronimo. Certainly it was morally reprehensible to have so much money so young, without doing a thing to earn it, but Howie liked the Davidsons anyway. The main house was a full ten-minute walk from Howie's cabin along a path that meandered in a deliberately semi-aimless manner through the sagebrush. This is where Howie headed now. With the exception of his own cabin, Bob and Nova's was the closest place where Aria might have gone after abandoning her Jeep.

There was a hint of steel-gray dawn above the eastern mountains, which rose sharply upward from the desert plateau a few miles away. This far northern corner of New Mexico was violently beautiful, not a gentle land, not for the faint of heart. The storm had cleared, and the translucent sky had become an inverted fish bowl of stars, darker in the west than the awakening east. The air was thin and insubstantial, for the San Geronimo valley rested at an altitude of seven thousand feet, with the surrounding mountains rising abruptly to elevations of thirteen thousand feet. Somewhere in the distance a rooster crowed. Howie jogged along the uneven path, down into dry arroyos and up along the tortured mesas, past cacti and sagebrush and cottonwood trees.

Bob and Nova's home stood on a fast-moving stream, the Rio San Geronimo, in an oasis of green vegetation and huge old trees, the entire complex surrounded by an adobe wall. Howie entered the compound through a back gate in the wall. Because of the stream, the Davidsons were water-rich. There were flower beds, roses everywhere, a hot tub, large metal sculptures in odd places among the shrubbery, and a stretch of well-manicured lawn that flowed toward the house. Everything smelled fresh and new now after the rain. To Howie, the landscaping looked more like New England than New Mexico, but of course true Yankees would never be so fanciful. The house itself was a free-form, sprawling adobe structure that was composed of odd shapes, mostly curves and semicircles, with a roof supported by huge natural timbers that had been brought down from the local mountains and stripped of their bark. Neither the Spanish nor the native Pueblo people had ever lived in adobe homes like this; this was a progressive wing of "Santa Fe style." Adobe might be the traditional building material of the Southwest, but it took rich Anglos to play with it, treating mud and straw like it was nutty-putty, bending it into fantastic shapes.

Howie walked across the lawn and called to a second-floor tower window: "Bob! Nova! Hey, wake up!" A moment later, Nova opened the window and peered down at him. She had thrown on one of Bob's denim work shirts, open at the throat, her long red hair flowing down her shoulders. She gave Howie a freckly, sleepy smile.

"Well, well," she said speculatively. "Are you up early or out late?"

"I'm looking for Aria," he told her. "I thought she might be here."

"In bed with Bob and me? *He* would like that, but I'm afraid I'm not quite so avant-garde."

"Well, it's very strange. She left my cabin about midnight, drove off in her Jeep, but she only got a hundred feet down the road. I woke up a little while ago when the rain stopped. I could hear her car stereo, so I went out to investigate. The engine was going, the lights were on, but she wasn't there. She wasn't anywhere."

Nova regarded Howie shrewdly. "So did you two have another one of your fights? Is that it?"

"Sort of. Not really."

"Well, is it sort of? Or is it not really?"

Howie sighed. "She blew up, said I was being clingy. Keeping her from her career just because I wanted her to stay the night with me. We made up before she left, though. But that's not what I'm worried about now."

"Look, I probably shouldn't say this, but I'm going to say it anyway. Let her go, Howie. You'll find the right woman one day, I know you will. But to be honest, I never thought it was Aria."

Nova meant well; she was Howie's self-appointed big sister and never hesitated to offer life instruction for him. But he wasn't really in the mood for a protracted discussion about his love worries through an open window at dawn.

"I'd better keep looking," he told Nova with a friendly wave.

"You need to stop chasing these princess types, Howie—they'll only cause you grief!" she called after him. "You should find yourself a nice intellectual. Someone you can discuss books with. I even have someone in mind. She's very sweet and quiet, an English teacher, recently divorced. . . ."

"My libido's going crazy just thinking about her," he called back, in motion. "Tell her to save herself for me!"

This was an old subject between Howie and Nova. According to Nova, he had "a princess problem," since he always went for "the babes" (as she put it). Nova was deeply suspicious of women who were too attractive, and probably she was right. Howie was the first to admit that he was very immature when it came to love, but he was horny and young and romantic, at the mercy of strong forces. What was worse, he *wanted* to be swept away.

"Howie, listen to me. You're creating your own pain . . ."

But Howie had developed a sudden case of deafness. He kept waving and headed across the lawn to the back gate through the adobe wall. But he stopped just before he left the compound and turned toward the hot tub, which was covered at the moment with blue canvas. The hot tub was an unusual shape, built from concrete and natural rock to resemble a mountain grotto, with a small waterfall at one end. For Howie this was a tub with memories, as it was here, last September, that he had met Aria Waldman for the first time.

The first glimpse he ever had of Aria was spectacular. It was Bob's birthday party, his fortieth, a huge and ironic event, a party on a sunny Sunday afternoon in September. Howie was sitting in the water with a group of laughing people when a movement to the left of his vision caught his attention. It was Aria in the act of lifting a multicolored chenille sweatshirt over her head. She was braless. First the left breast, then the right popped into view. They were memorable breasts—suggestive, graceful, somehow corresponding to Howie's inner platonic ideal of precisely what a breast should be. Howie was wearing dark glasses—only dark glasses, nothing else—which enabled him to get a better peek than he might have done otherwise. It wasn't hip, of course, to stare at people while hot-tubbing nude, and even with his dark glasses, Howie was too much the gentleman to direct more than a few sideways glances her way. Still, he managed to get a quick snapshot of her: flat stomach, an intriguing belly button, positively peachy skin, and many interesting curves. The sweatshirt came free of her head, and she shook loose her strawberry-colored hair with a laugh. Then came her jeans and underpants, and in a moment she was naked, stepping into the grotto near the artificial waterfall, oo-ing and ah-ing a little with the hot water.

Howie smiled vaguely in her direction and then looked away politely. There were nearly thirty people in Bob and Nova's backyard, half a dozen in the pool itself—most everybody naked, squealing and running back and forth from the steaming tub into the icy stream, the Rio San Geronimo, a dozen feet away. It was a luscious afternoon, unforgettable, with a certain Maxfield Parrish glow to it, a golden September light playing about the lawn and trees. When Aria stepped into the pool, two bodies away, Howie had been in the middle of a conversation with an older man about whether New York or Los Angeles was currently the more progressively postmodern artistic city. Under different circumstances Howie might have enjoyed this conversation, but now he continued with it absentmindedly. He forced himself not to look, but he found he was distracted by the attractive woman nearby. A short time later, when he decided he might risk another glance in her direction, she was gone. Howie was disappointed and, at the same time, relieved. He was still getting over an affair with a woman doctor that had ended in June. Howie was starting to wonder if love was more pain than it was worth.

Then half an hour later, he encountered Aria again, this time swimming in the river—floundering was perhaps the more accurate word, for the Rio San Geronimo was only ankle-deep. Bob had constructed a makeshift dam with a few fallen trees, creating a sort of swimming hole, but one had to stretch out to fully submerge.

The current moved Aria close to where Howie was soaking. She was the first to speak:

"So are there any fish in here?"

"A few trout. But they're awfully cagey, very hard to catch. Bob and I have tried a few times. Mostly it's an excuse to sit on the bank and guzzle a six-pack of Guinness."

"You live next door, don't you?"

"In the guest house. My name's Howard Moon Deer."

"I know. I'm Aria Waldman."

She reached out of the water to shake his hand, which seemed absurdly formal and funny, both of them naked. She laughed at the silliness of her gesture and then turned modestly onto her stomach, the crack of her ass protruding just above the waterline, twin islands in a rushing sea. Howie sat next to her, the water swirling about his chest.

"Aria Waldman?" he wondered. "I know—you're the reporter for *The San Geronimo Post.*"

"You've seen my byline, huh?"

"Sure. I remember the piece you did on the guy who was embezzling money from the public schools. What was his name?"

"Albert Martinez. He was the business manager of the school district. He managed to steal nearly thirty grand over a five-year period before the cops got him."

"*You* were the one who got him. That was a pretty neat piece of investigative reporting."

"Well, he annoyed me, stealing from the kids here. Public schools in New Mexico are bad enough without crooked bureaucrats feeding from the trough."

"So what are you writing now?"

"Oh, this and that," she said vaguely. "I'm sure it's not nearly as interesting as your detective work."

He raised an eyebrow at her. "Someone's been telling my secrets, I see."

"Oh, I know *all* about you, Howard Moon Deer," she said coyly. "As a reporter, I get to be as nosy as I like. It's an occupational prerogative."

"Is it?" Howie laughed. "So tell me—who am I? I'm still trying to figure that one out myself."

"All right, then. Howard Moon Deer, Lakota Sioux. Got shipped off the reservation when he was a teenager because he was so wonderfully smart at school. Won a scholarship to a fancy prep school in Vermont, then Dartmouth, and finally Princeton for his postgraduate work. At present struggling somewhat to finish his Ph.D. dissertation in sociology, which seems to be taking him forever. . . ."

"I'm in the cultural anthropology department, actually," Howie corrected.

"Sounds very impressive anyway you look at it. No wonder it's taking our Mr. Moon Deer such a long time to finish his thesis. And, of course, he has found a few distractions along the way. He likes to ski. He's a great cook. And most intriguing of all, he's working at the moment as a private investigator, assistant to a big shot cop from California who retired to New Mexico and started a detective agency here."

"I'm not a real private eye, honest," Howie told her, laughing. "It's only a very part-time job for me, helping Jack Wilder with some investigative research now and then. We met by accident and became friends, and I definitely need the money. It's sort of like working your way through school as a waiter."

"Only you're working for a man who nearly became the police chief of San Francisco. And I don't believe for a second that you're only doing it for the money. I think you're *much* more of a romantic than that, Howard Moon Deer. My sources tell me you fell hard for Alison Hampton, the daughter of your last client."

Howie could only sigh. Aria was starting to cut too close to the bone. That was the problem with women—they always seemed to have his number. Aria even had all the specifics.

"So where's Alison now?" she asked.

"In Africa. She's a doctor, you know, an OB-GYN . . . she went off to Ghana to help with the AIDS crisis there. She's very idealistic."

"Yes, I met her once," Aria mentioned. "Not only is she idealistic, she's smart, she's rich, and she's terrifically good-looking too."

Yes, and she's gone, gone, gone, Howie thought glumly. He put his head back in the cold water for a moment, suddenly weary. Aria was studying him with her jade green eyes. The stream moved over her body like a transparent plastic wrap.

Suddenly she smiled at him. It was a nice smile, mischievous and very astute, and he couldn't help sitting up and smiling back. Their eyes met and they laughed. They both knew, at that exact moment, that they were about to have an affair.

3

Eventually, on that golden afternoon in September—Bob's naked birthday party—the river water started to feel cold. Howie and Aria found their clothes and dressed. Strangely, nakedness had seemed completely natural in the hot tub and river; it was only now with their clothes on, standing on the shore, that the erotic possibilities danced in the air between them.

"Bob told me there are some old Indian petroglyphs nearby," Aria mentioned.

"They're very ancient, quite interesting, actually. Would you like to see them?" Howie offered. "It's a ten-minute walk."

"I'd love it."

Howie led the way from the walled backyard into the seclusion of the desert, both of them knowing very well that anthropology was not the true purpose of this walk. There was a late afternoon glow on the land. Autumn is always the most lovely time of year in New Mexico. In the distance, the mesa tops seemed more red in color than he had ever seen them before, the earth more vibrant, the shadows more mysterious—walking with Aria sharpened his perceptions, made his heart go pitter-patter. They descended along an old trail into a steep canyon, a dry arroyo that was littered with huge boulders fallen from some ancient cataclysm. A raven flew overhead, flapping its wings with a whoosh of air. Howie took Aria's hand to help her navigate a rock, and then, experimentally, he kept holding it gently as they walked. She did not pull away.

"Well, there they are," Howie said, pointing up the side of a cliff. "They were probably done by the Anasazi around the thirteenth century, but no one knows for sure."

The petroglyphs were etched into the rock a dozen feet from where they stood. There was a stylized lizard, several antelope, a circular pattern that resembled the symbol of infinity, and a stick figure of some ancient human. Howie and Aria stared at them for some time in silence.

"I'm trying to visualize the past," she said finally, full of the mystery of this ancient place. "I wonder what life was like in this valley seven hundred years ago, when some artist made these etchings in this rock?"

"There probably weren't any hot tubs back then," Howie assured her. "No art galleries, no sushi bars, and probably very few yuppies."

"I bet they were a beautiful people, the Anasazi," she said wondrously.

"Actually, they were short and unhealthy and generally they died very young. It was a brutal life."

"Was it?"

"I'm afraid so. But you can think of them as noble savages, if you'd like."

"I've always been big on noble savages," she admitted.

Her eyes were bright. She was standing so close he could smell the clean lovely scent of her skin. On impulse, Howie leaned forward and kissed her lips. He felt her body relax into his embrace. Her mouth opened and they touched tongues. The past two hours had been foreplay enough, and soon they quickly shed their clothes. They used a rock for their bed, a huge flat boulder that was smooth and warm from the sun, sensual against naked skin. It was lizard-sex, cheerfully amoral. "A truly cinematic screw," Aria said months later, nostalgically recalling their beginnings. "Yes, we really got our rocks off," Howie joked. And they did, copulating under the huge desert sky just as the sunset was exploding bright colors into the west.

Later, when the sky was a dark turquoise and the first stars had begun to shine, they walked hand in hand back across the desert to Howie's cabin and made love again, this time in between the coolness of sheets. Close to midnight, Howie staggered out of bed long enough to cook them an omelette stuffed with odds and ends from his refrigerator—scallions, tomato, an avocado, and a bit of Jarlsberg cheese—washed down with some Romanian chardonnay, Monsieur Henri's selection, cheap but dry and drinkable. They ate naked in candlelight, ravenously hungry, and then, giggling, returned to bed.

Such was their promising beginning, and Howie expected great things. But when he phoned her the following afternoon, she apologized and said she was working on a story, she had a deadline— she was just too busy to see him that night. Howie was very understanding. Sure, he told her, he knew all about deadlines. So what about the next day? Dinner perhaps, then a movie? She said she'd have to call him about it tomorrow, because right now her schedule was so tight it was hard to say. Okay, Howie told her. But the following day she did not phone, and he wasn't so certain they were an embryonic couple after all. He decided not to call again himself but to wait. Maybe he had misread the signals, it wouldn't be the first time. She had his number. What the hell.

A week went by and he didn't hear from her. Howie decided he'd better forget it. Go fish some other river; maybe some other maiden would float down naked into his life. Then late one afternoon he was doing his bachelor routine, shopping for dinner at the Good Earth Co-Op, the main health-food market in San Geronimo, when he saw her again. He had just bought organic greens for a salad, a boneless, skinless, free-range chicken breast, a few pesticide-free red potatoes, and finally (a reward for such healthy living) a carton of Ben and Jerry's Purple Passion sorbet. As he was leaving the store, he stopped to read the bulletin board, which was always entertaining. San Geronimo had a large New Age population, recent immigrants who had come to New Mexico in search of the latest installment of the American dream: peace and happiness, perhaps even the meaning of life. There were announcements for crystal-healing workshops and hypnosis to get in touch with your inner-child. Someone was advertising psychic surgery, another person healed with magnets. A women's group was forming "to heal the scars inflicted upon us by men." Quite a few of the flyers were devoted to worshiping "the goddess." None of these events was inexpensive.

"Oral sex!" Howie heard over his shoulder, an intriguing remark. He turned to see Aria Waldman, dressed in tight jeans and a flannel shirt, looking very cowgirl sexy, holding a brown paper bag with her organic groceries sticking out the top.

"Oral . . . uh . . ."

"Look."

She was pointing to a flyer he had missed. *"Aural Sex!"* it read. "Discover the love-colors compatible with your aura! Aural couple counseling by appointment only." There was a phone number for a woman named Shambala who charged a mere $75 per half hour for her wisdom of the ages.

"So what color is *your* aura?" she asked him.

Howie laughed. "Believe it or not, I don't know. I've never had it read."

"Oh-oh! And here I figured you for a good New Ager, Howie."

"You know, with your bag of groceries and mine, I bet we could get something cooking," he suggested. "Are you hungry?"

"I'm starved," she admitted. "Your kitchen or mine?"

"Either way," he told her.

"I'll follow you home," she said.

And she did just that, following him back to his carnal kitchen where they passionately simmered far into the night. Afterward, Howie liked to date their real beginning from this second night together, when the conversation flowed along with wine and other juices. They talked for hours. So many personal anecdotes to tell, though Howie realized later that he in fact had done most of the talking. They saw a lot of each other after that, and for a time, Howie thought that this was the start of something big in his life. But Aria continued to be elusive. It felt so right between them, yet there was no steady progression toward real intimacy. As the months passed, Aria became very busy again and she seemed to be holding him at arm's length. They began having their fights, infrequently at first, but then more often. Her career as a journalist clearly came first. She was a modern, independent woman, of course, and Howie understood this—after all, he liked to think of himself as a modern, independent man. Yet it was disappointing. The sex continued to be extremely inventive, if not downright pornographic. But after a while, he felt almost as if he were being used as a kind of impersonal physical therapy, a way for Aria to release tension, work up a good sweat, and get back to her job with renewed vigor. Sometimes he feared a good strenuous game of racquetball would satisfy her just as well.

By spring, the affair was starting to feel schizophrenic. Either they were having a great time, or they were fighting—there was nothing in between. To Howie, it felt like there were two separate Aria Waldmans inhabiting one body, and he was never certain which one he would encounter on any given night. The Bad Aria was obsessed with her work and treated their affair as a kind of side dish to the main course, lovely when there was time for it, but not essential. Often this Bad Aria phoned at the last minute to stand him up. She couldn't come to dinner after all, or go skiing or hiking with him because there was always too much work. Howie was so furious at one of these cancellations, he threw a casserole pot of coq au vin against his kitchen wall. Sometimes she didn't even have the grace to cancel, but would simply not show up, or arrive three hours late. Then they would fight and tear at each other hopelessly for hours. How could she be so inconsiderate? he shouted. And she always came back with her classic line that he was smothering her. That she had to be free, that you never knew where a reporting assignment would take you, and sometimes there wasn't a phone nearby to call. Some freedom, he complained, to be the absolute slave of a career! It was ironic: Men were supposed to be the heart-attack corporate stress junkies, not women, but somehow they had traded gender roles. He had become the advocate for feelings, for taking time to sniff the flowers, for love. But that was modern romance, he supposed, completely topsy-turvy.

Howie truly suffered over their fights. But then, just when he was fed up and ready to call it quits, the Good Aria would appear and tantalize him, sometimes for days and weeks at a time. The Good Aria was wonderfully smart and funny—key ingredients of sexual attraction for Howie. She was so much fun to be with, those times when she was really with him: the most vivid and blazingly intense woman he had ever known. They didn't discuss books, as Nova seemed to believe he wanted to do with women. They played. The Good Aria, in fact, taught him how to relax and let go of his own preoccupations. And, of course, the sex was great; it might be racquetball for her, but for him it was incredible. It wasn't her body, per se—in truth, he had known prettier women than Aria Waldman. It was her energy. She broadcast waves of erotic energy that he found irresistible. Sometimes he felt almost mad with longing for her.

So Howie tried his best to make it work with her. He knew that relationships weren't easy these days and that one had to work at love, like mining for coal or building a hydroelectric dam. So he worked at it. He worked at better communication, telling deep, personal things about himself, hoping that she would get deep and personal in return. But she was evasive. She smiled mysteriously, she piqued his curiosity, but he was always left with the maddening sense that he did not really know her at all. The mystery made her romantic and desirable, but it tortured him to his very soul.

He learned certain facts about her, naturally. She had grown up in Westport, Connecticut. She said her father was a successful advertising executive who commuted each day into Manhattan, but then he died quite young and life became difficult financially for her family. She went to the public high school in Westport, she lost her virginity in the eleventh grade to a boy named Eric, she went to Smith College and later attended the Columbia University School of Journalism. She had always planned on being an investigative reporter, but then on a summer trip to Santa Fe, she ran into a major detour in her life: a man. An attractive Englishman who ran an art gallery.

Aria married, and wasted nearly seven years of her life until she eventually discovered that the attractive Englishman was boring and selfish. So she left him. This unfortunate detour had the consequence of leaving her an unemployed ex-housewife in Santa Fe, New Mexico at the age of twenty-eight, rather than a star reporter on *The New York Times* or *Washington Post*. She was off the career track in a serious way, and when she tried to get back on, the only job she could find was on the tiny *San Geronimo Post* in a desolate, northern corner of the state. But it was something, at least, and Aria hoped to use the job to catapult herself to bigger things. She had been in San Geronimo for a year before Howie met her, and she was starting to wonder when her break would come. Apparently a woman had to do years of penance for a stupid early marriage.

So that was the story of her life, a brief capsulized version upon which she was reluctant to expand. It was odd how little she had told him—he saw that now. As Howie walked back by himself from Bob and Nova's house to his own small cabin, he felt an overwhelming sense of failure, that he had somehow screwed up another relationship.

Dawn was inching up over the mountains, a burst of crimson bleeding up San Geronimo Peak. Howie continued walking past his cabin onto the gravel road to see if Aria's Jeep Cherokee was still where she had abandoned it. The Jeep hadn't moved. It stood in the road in the gray early morning light, an enigma, a question mark. Howie could not imagine a single possible scenario that made a shred of sense. It was as if a flying saucer had come down and spirited Aria Waldman away.

"There must be an innocent explanation," he said aloud to the dawn. But then he felt the gun weighing down his dressing gown pocket, and he knew, in his heart, that there was not.

4

Howie used the telephone on his bedside table, punching in the familiar sequence of numbers, digits that had once been his mainline connection to romance. He should have thought of this earlier. Certainly Aria would pick up and give him some simple explanation of what had happened. But the phone rang, and she did not answer. He got her disembodied voice instead, her machine telling him to leave a message after the beep.

He spoke into the tape: "Aria, this is Howie. Look, I've found your car down the road, and I'm a little worried. So please give me a ring when you get this message, just to let me know you're okay."

He put down the phone and sat on the edge of the bed, fingering the revolver in his dressing gown pocket, trying hard to think. What now, he wondered? After a while he rose and put the gun into a filing cabinet that contained seven years of notes for his Ph.D. dissertation. Then he dressed in a pair of old jeans, a T-shirt, a faded flannel shirt that he wore loose over his jeans, and ancient sneakers with holes in the toes. This was Howie's basic uniform, the wardrobe of the nouveau American Indian, as he liked to tell his friends. He had one more idea to try before he started sending out distress signals, one final place to look. There was a new house several hundred yards across the desert: an odd, modern house that had appeared suddenly last fall. It was a long shot, but this was the closest neighbor after Bob and Nova, and perhaps Aria had wandered there.

* * *

Howie walked overland across the sagebrush. The sun had burst free of San Geronimo Peak, ushering forth a sparkling fresh August morning. The desert was as green as an English moor after a summer of monsoon rain, a carpet of stubby grasses and sturdy little flowers. Howie stepped around rabbit holes and ant hills and small cactus. The sun beat down on him, gathering strength as it rose in the sky. As he drew closer to his new neighbor, he saw that it was an unusual house for New Mexico, the wrong color even— stark white, rather than the traditional adobe-brown, two white blocks stacked one atop the other. There were tall, narrow windows that looked out onto a straight line of freshly planted trees. Perhaps in time the house would blend into the surrounding landscape, but at the moment it had the appearance of total disconnection, a mirage that had appeared in the desert out of thin air, and might vanish just as easily in a blink of an eye. There was a new dark green Toyota Land Cruiser in the driveway, the high-end choice of rich city folk who came to places like San Geronimo to live out their four-wheel-drive fantasies.

Howie came to a stop at a high white cement wall that enclosed the backyard. He could hear someone swimming laps in a pool on the other side of the wall, but there was no sign of a gate.

"Hello!" Howie called.

The swimming stopped. "Who's there?" answered an unseen male, friendly but cautious.

"I'm your next-door neighbor. From across the desert a bit."

"No kidding?" said the voice vaguely.

"I was wondering if you'd seen a woman, about five foot six, reddish-blond hair, late twenties, quite pretty—she left her car on the road near my cabin a few hours ago, but I can't find her."

There was a pause as the swimmer absorbed the information. Then, "What exactly do you mean, you can't *find* her?"

"She's disappeared. It's the damnedest thing."

"A disappearing woman, huh?" Howie heard the man climb out of his pool and sigh. "Must be an epidemic! I've lost a few of 'em, myself. Three ex-wives, and that's just for starters."

"Have you seen her?"

"Late twenties? Good-looking? . . . no, I'm afraid not. But offhand, she sounds like heartbreak."

"Well, thanks anyway. Sorry to bother you."

Howie was starting to walk away when the man called to him:

"Hey, wait a second! Let's talk about this. Men need to stick together when it comes to the opposite sex."

"Thanks anyways—it's probably just a misunderstanding," Howie assured him.

Howie was about to walk away when a gate he had not previously noticed opened in the wall. He found himself facing a thin, fortyish man who was wearing nothing but an obscenely small green European swimsuit and a Rolex watch. He was bald on the top of his head but hairy everywhere else, one of the hairiest individuals Howie had ever seen standing erect on two legs. There was a carpet of curly black hair covering his arms, chest, legs, and back. His eyes were close together and deeply inset; his face was long and pale, a little goofy-looking, framed by a dark five o'clock shadow even though it was early morning.

Suddenly the man smiled. "Hey, I know you!" he said.

Howie had to admit, his neighbor looked oddly familiar too, though it took a moment to make the connection.

"I've seen you too. You're . . ."

"Denny Hirsch," he said, offering an elaborate brother-to-brother handshake: interlocking fingers and thumbs, the whole jivey ritual. "You've been in my restaurant. You're that Navajo, aren't you? . . . Spread Eagle, is it?"

"Moon Deer," Howie replied, a touch indignant. "Howard Moon Deer. And I'm Lakota, actually."

"Of course! I've seen you with Aria Waldman."

"That's who I'm looking for. Aria."

"*She's* your disappearing woman?"

Howie nodded. Denny was the owner of the Blue Mesa Café, San Geronimo's most chichi and expensive restaurant. The food was New Mexican *nouvelle,* enchiladas that cost a mint and bore little resemblance to their poor Hispanic roots. Denny could be seen most nights wandering through his establishment dressed in a white double-breasted tropical suit, floating from table to table with silky charm.

"I didn't realize we were neighbors," Howie said.

"We weren't, until a short while ago. I built this place last year, but I only moved in two months ago. Come on in, Moon Deer. I'll make us up some tea."

"No, I don't want to bother you. And if you haven't seen Aria, I'd better be on my way."

"No, don't go. I dig Aria Waldman. She did a story on the café a few months back, about a program we started to give food to the homeless. It drives me crazy, you know, how much food gets wasted in restaurants—it's better to give it away than see it rot in the walk-in . . . she spoke about you, of course."

"Did she?" This surprised Howie.

"Look, I sense a relationship problem here. I've been through this, I swear to God, I can't tell you how many times. She broke up with you, right? That's why you say she disappeared?"

"It was only a fight," Howie said reluctantly. "It's a little complicated."

"Come in, come in!"

Howie was uncertain about this conversation; unlike the average paleface, Indians are naturally reticent, not quite so keen to vomit out their personal problems to passing strangers. Nevertheless he followed Denny into the backyard. There was a narrow lap pool, the turquoise water glistening in the morning sun, and two white deck chairs set beneath a white umbrella. It was a strangely sterile backyard, geometrically arranged, not a flower out of place. Howie settled into one of the deck chairs without actually leaning back, preparing to keep this brief.

"Can I get you a cup of tea?" Denny asked.

"I'd prefer coffee," Howie replied.

Denny shook his head sadly, as though Howie had just requested a syringe of heroin. "Oh, no, no . . . I don't keep caffeine at home! I have to serve it at the café, of course, but it's a terrible drug, so harsh on the system. Why don't you let me get you some peppermint tea instead? It'll help you have a nice morning bowel movement."

Put in such an alluring manner, it was difficult to say no. While Denny went inside the house to prepare tea, Howie noticed for the first time that soft piano music was coming from hidden speakers, a single chord, as bland and healthful as herbal tea, played over and over and over again with several hundred violins swelling in the background—Yanni, the Liberace of the New Age. Denny returned with the tea, sat on the edge of his deck chair, and regarded Howie with a sappy smile.

"You're going to laugh, Moon Deer, but I've got to tell you something. I really honor your culture. All my life I've wanted to be a Native American!"

Howie didn't laugh, but smiled tolerantly. "You're attracted to a life of third world poverty, is that it?"

Denny laughed uproariously. "Oh, no! . . . of course it's a terrible thing what the white man did to Native Americans, how we absolutely raped your culture. But even though you're poor, you have spiritual values—and isn't that far, far better than mere material wealth?"

Howie kept his tolerant smile firmly in place.

"Look," Denny said, lowering his voice, "the thing that really bothered me growing up in America was that there was never any sense of initiation, no ritual to help a boy become a man. You know what I'm saying? I grew up on Long Island—my father used to come home on the train from the city every night and collapse with a martini in front of the TV. And that was it, *that* was the only initiation I ever got into manhood. But you native people—you pass on your traditional wisdom one generation to the next. You take boys away from their mothers when they're twelve or thirteen, you put them in a mentorship program with a circle of men, it's just so fantastic!"

Howie nodded, but didn't want to get into it. A hundred years ago, the white men were making jewelry from the genitals of Howie's murdered ancestors; soldiers from the Seventh Cavalry had been known to cut the vaginas from Sioux women and turn them into handbags. But palefolk were sentimental creatures; they got very misty-eyed about the things they destroyed: pristine forests, rivers, buffalo, and the native people who once inhabited this continent. To Howie it was like Hitler in his old age, had he won the war, saying to his grandchildren: "Oh, those Jews! Weren't they a lovely people!"

Denny looked away from Howie's hard and steady gaze.

"Anyway, here I am going on and on, and naturally you're upset about Aria," he said with an empathetic sigh.

"When's the last time you saw her, Denny?"

"Oh, it's been since June, early July, a while anyway. But I want you to know, I feel your pain, Moon Deer, I really do. My second wife—my God, she broke my heart! You know what she did? She ran off with a *woman*! Now, that hurt. *That* really made me feel like some sort of slug. The way I see it, as men, we're in this very difficult, transitional phase. For twenty, thirty years, women have been making themselves strong and independent. But men, it's like we're dinosaurs, we're only just beginning to respond to the challenge of feminism . . . have you ever thought of joining a men's group, Moon Deer?"

Howie put down his half-finished cup of tea, preparing to make his escape.

"I'm not much of a joiner, I guess."

"Really? That's too bad. I'm part of a men's group, and it's saved my life, I swear to God. Just to have other men to talk to. In this society, guys have been taught to isolate themselves, repress their feelings. But I've been learning to give myself permission to *feel,* Moon Deer. To weep when I need to. To embark upon the long journey of reclaiming my fierce masculinity."

Howie smiled and rose from the deck chair. "Sure," he said vaguely. "And, now, speaking of journeys, I need to go home. If you do see Aria, I'd appreciate it if you'd give me a call. I'll leave my number."

"You bet. And look, Moon Deer—I'm going to give you a piece of paper with an address on it. Tonight just happens to be our weekly Wednesday night men's group meeting. I really think you should stop by and share this transitional time, this pain that's happening in your life right now . . . no, let me finish. I can see the skeptical expression on your face, and believe me, that's how all of us were in the beginning. But I tell you, it's really very casual, our group. We don't have any agenda or philosophy. There's no leader, we simply try to be honest and talk about some of our concerns. We discuss gender issues, personal matters, bullshit, anything . . . You know, Moon Deer, there are no accidents in this universe, and I have this odd feeling that you didn't walk across the desert this morning for nothing, that your Medicine Path and our Medicine Path are destined to intermingle."

If Howie had gotten more sleep last night, he might have made a good reply. As it was, he only smiled vaguely. He took a pad of paper and a pen from the coffee table next to Denny's deck chair and wrote down his phone number. Then he accepted the address that Denny jotted down for him.

"Seven o'clock," Denny said. "Think about it, Moon Deer. It's a great group of guys, some of the real movers and shakers in San Geronimo—it may surprise you a little who's there. This could be an experience that'll change your life."

"I'll think about it," Howie agreed, making his escape out through the high wall into the relief of open desert.

Howie walked home quickly across the sagebrush, fearing he had wasted precious time. He came to Aria's abandoned Jeep Cherokee and was surprised to see a San Geronimo County Sheriff's car parked alongside, it's blue and red emergency lights flashing on top. A plainclothes deputy was bending inside the open door of the Cherokee, examining the glove compartment. He straightened and turned when he heard Howie's footsteps.

"You saved me the trouble of a phone call," Howie told him. "I was about to call the police."

"Were you?" The cop was skeptical. He was a slight man, wiry, not tall, a middle-aged Anglo with a sad, haggard Abraham Lincoln sort of face. He wore crisp designer jeans, a blue short-sleeve polo shirt with a Ralph Lauren insignia on the breast, and a gun bulging on his hip. He regarded Howie glumly.

"I live just down the road," Howie told him. "My name's Howard Moon Deer."

"So what do you know about this vehicle?"

"It belongs to my girlfriend, Aria Waldman. She left my house around midnight last night. She drove off, and this is as far as she got, apparently. I can't imagine what happened. I woke up about three-thirty a.m.—I heard her car stereo going. I came out to investigate, but there was no sign of her. I've been looking for her ever since. I just got back from my neighbor's house, to see if she had wandered over there."

It had been on the tip of Howie's tongue to mention the revolver he had found on the ground, but there was something in the way the sad-eyed sheriff was regarding him that made him decide to keep this information to himself—at least for the moment, until he had a better idea of what Aria was involved in.

"You're saying this woman is your girlfriend?" the cop repeated ponderously. "Did you have a fight with her, Howard?"

"Well, yes, we did fight, actually. But we worked through it by the time she left. Why do you ask?"

"Let *me* ask the questions here. So the two of you had a fight, and then she vanished. Is that your version of the evening?"

Howie nodded, not liking the word *version*. "Yes. But like I said, we made up before she left."

The cop sighed with all the weariness of a weary world. "You know what I think, Howard? I think you're a domestic abuser."

"I'm not!"

"Let's cut to the chase, my friend. Probably you were drinking last night, so when you started fighting, things got a little out of control. You got angry, didn't you? Real angry. Maybe you didn't mean to do it, but you hurt her. You knocked her around real good. You can tell me the truth, Howard, because I'm a guy who understands these things."

Howie shook his head. "No, it wasn't like that. We had a small quarrel, we made up, then she drove away. That's all."

"You expect me to believe that? She drove away and just vanished, huh? Leaving an eighteen-thousand-dollar car in the middle of some lonely dirt road?" His voice was rising.

"I know it sounds odd."

"*Odd?* Oh, you can do a lot better than that! Believe me, it'll go much better for you, my friend, if you tell me the truth. A lot of things can happen in a moment of anger, and if I can testify in court how broken up you were when I found you, everybody will be sympathetic . . . the only question I have is how *badly* did you hurt her? Did you kill her, maybe? Have you been out in the desert right now burying her body?"

This was getting crazy. As he spoke, the cop wandered lazily from where he had been standing by the Jeep and began to circle Howie, like a vulture circling its prey. Howie felt drops of sweat moving down his forehead, and it wasn't from the growing heat of the August morning.

"You're straining my patience, Howard," the cop whispered into his ear, standing behind him. "I hate it when people lie to me. It offends my fundamental sense of decency."

"I'm not lying. Why should I lie? I was about to phone the police."

"*About to phone the police!*" he said with a sharp laugh. "Oh, that's good. That's a real classic . . . 'Oh, Sheriff, I just buried my bitch-girlfriend in the desert, would you come and arrest me, please?' . . . Is that what you were going to say?"

"No."

Without warning, the sheriff lashed out at him. Howie felt a sharp blow to the kidney. It took him by surprise, and his legs collapsed beneath him. For a slight man, the deputy packed a wallop.

Howie knelt on the hard ground, gasping in pain. When he was able to look up, he saw the sad-eyed cop was standing above him, breathing hard, his gun in hand, the barrel pointing at a spot just above Howie's left eyebrow. Howie felt a wave of nauseating fear.

"Now, you listen to me, Howard Moon Deer, and listen good. There's just you and me out here, no one to help you. So either you tell me what happened, or you're going to get shot resisting arrest. Believe me, no one's going to give a shit about one less Indian. Nod if you're getting my drift."

Howie nodded.

"Now, what did you do with her?"

"Nothing. We said good-bye and then she drove away. That's the entire story."

Howie prepared himself for a bullet through the forehead. Would it happen so quickly he wouldn't even know he had died? But there was no bullet, just a boot. He saw it coming, the sheriff's boot rising swiftly, kicking against the side of his head. The world flashed brightly, and Howie fell backward into the mud. He lay in a world beyond puzzlement, disconnected from all things except hard pain.

Then the cop was hissing at him: "You give me any more trouble, boy, I'm going to kill you for sure. You understand what I'm saying? So if you see Aria Waldman, you give me a call right pronto. You just phone the department and ask for Sheriff Lou Snider. You got that?"

Howie nodded. The name surprised him, for this wasn't a deputy, it was *the* sheriff, the elected head of the San Geronimo County Sheriff's Department. Snider turned abruptly and walked away. Howie groaned, he curled into a soothing fetal position on the ground and listened to the cop car drive off. This had turned into an exceptionally bad morning. Sensitive New Age Guys were bad enough, but when it came to a real horror show, there was nothing quite like the Angry White Male.

Howie sat up slowly, experimentally. It was only as he was stumbling to his feet that it occurred to him to wonder what Sheriff Snider, an important man, had been doing in this far corner of San Geronimo County, and why he seemed so particularly interested in Aria Waldman.

5

Mid-morning on Wednesday, ex-police Commander Jack Wilder knelt in his garden, groping with his hands along the vines of his plants for ripe tomatoes. He was dressed in his old gardening clothes: bib jean overalls, a long-sleeve work shirt, floppy wide-brimmed straw hat to protect him from the sun, his wraparound dark glasses perched on his nose. He was a stout man in his mid-fifties with a well-trimmed beard and curly gray hair that had grown longer and more unruly in retirement. His wife, Emma, liked to call him her shaggy Irish bear. Howie, his assistant, said he was starting to look like Jerry Garcia come back from the dead. Jack knew very well that he was starting to cut an eccentric figure, paying less attention to his appearance these days than he should, but after all, that was one of the joys of country life. Letting it all go.

Jack stood up to move down the row from one tomato plant to the next. Then suddenly he was falling, sprawling forward onto the ground.

"Christ!" he cried. He had just tripped over a basket full of vegetables that was in his way. A stupid mistake, a lack of concentration. Jack broke his fall with his hands, narrowly avoiding a rake. So damn undignified! He was glad, at least, that no one was around to witness his humiliation except Katya, his German shepherd guide dog, who had seen plenty of these accidents before. But now there was a new problem. His dark glasses had come off during his fall, and he didn't know where they were. He felt vulnerable without his glasses, strangely naked. He forced himself to

approach the problem calmly, to feel around on the ground in a methodical fashion, inch by inch. All of this was a further humiliation. Sometimes it seemed inconceivable to Jack that only five years ago, before going headfirst through a car windshield in a bungled drug raid, he had been one of the most important police officials in the city of San Francisco. He'd had cars at his disposal, boats, even helicopters. Not once in his wildest dreams had this self-important person, his past self, ever imagined that he'd one day become a farcical figure in a small town in New Mexico, a blind Elmer Fudd in bib overalls tripping over baskets and feeling the damp ground for his lost glasses.

After a five-minute search, Jack felt his glasses underneath a zucchini leaf. He was covering his dead eyes when he became aware of a car pulling into his driveway. It wasn't Howie—Jack knew the sound of Howie's car very well. Katya wagged her tail and gave a friendly bark. In a moment Jack heard children's voices, and he smelled patchouli oil . . . now, *that* was a smell to take him back!

"Jack Wilder?" It was a woman's voice with a slight Texas accent. A young woman, he decided, from the lack of timbre.

"Yes, that's me," he told her grumpily. He remained kneeling, hoping his glasses were not crooked on his nose, and that he had managed to cover up all traces of his recent fall.

"I'm Mary Jane Tripp. I saw your ad in the newspaper. I'm sorry I didn't call first, but to be honest, I've been going back and forth in my mind whether I really wanted to come to you or not. And then I was in the neighborhood, and I just thought . . . anyway, these are my kids. Sativa and Indiga . . . say hello to Mr. Wilder, girls . . . and this little guy, this is Bud."

She was speaking too loudly, almost shouting. It was an odd fact, but many people spoke to the blind as though they must have problems with their hearing as well. Jack was accustomed to it. The children meanwhile were unruly as little weeds, running about and shouting at each other. Jack rose to his feet and debated whether to chance walking unaided from the garden. He knew his way; normally, on his own, he wouldn't think twice. But he didn't want to risk another fall in front of a stranger, especially a potential client.

"My dear, if you would just give me a hand, please, and lead me to the picnic table beneath that cottonwood tree . . . do you see it? We can talk over there."

He felt her hand encircle his arm; not so often these days that a young woman touched him. Mary Jane sent her children to play down by the stream that bordered Jack's property, then she guided him down the row of vegetables, out the garden gate, and to a picnic table in the deep shade.

"So what can I do for you?" he asked.

"My husband is Gary Tripp. Do you know him?"

"Gary Tripp? Didn't he disappear in the mountains back in June? I believe I read about him in the paper."

"You can read the paper? I guess that's a rude question. . . ."

"Not at all. A very practical question. There are people who are kind enough to read to me," he explained. "Now, if I remember, your husband was on a camping trip and somehow he managed to get separated from the rest of his group and got lost. At one time, Search and Rescue had nearly a hundred volunteers combing the mountains for him."

"They stopped searching a few weeks ago. Everyone says he's dead."

"Well, what has it been—seven weeks now? That's a long time to be missing up in those mountains."

"No, I think he's dead too," she said, more loudly. Over the course of the conversation, her voice had been growing in volume.

"Mrs. Tripp, please—I can hear you just fine. I'm blind, not deaf."

"Oh, my gosh! I'm sorry!"

"Don't be. Now, what can I do for you?"

Her voice dropped nearly to a whisper: "I think they killed him."

"They? Who is they?"

"The Warrior Circle. That's the men's group Gary was in. Now they're saying they own my ranch, the Hemperware business, everything . . . you've got to help me, Mr. Wilder. I just don't know where else I can turn!"

The young woman was upset, close to tears.

"Perhaps you'd better tell me about this," he said gently.

She took a deep breath and began.

She was not a sophisticated woman, only a country girl from a small town in Texas. She had met Gary ten years ago when she was seventeen and he was in his early forties, down on his luck, working in a rockabilly band, playing little towns throughout the Southwest, traveling in an old school bus. Even down on his luck, Gary was a glamorous figure to her, a once-famous musician in the early-seventies band Headstone. Gary had seen the world, he had lived briefly in a house in Malibu, he had met Bob Dylan, he had even had an affair with one of the Beatles' ex-girlfriends. For Mary Jane, he was an exciting window onto a wider world, and it more than compensated for the age difference between them. They hooked up, lived in Colorado for a while, then moved to New Mexico eight years ago.

Five years ago, after becoming disillusioned with a radical Jesus cult, Gary joined a men's group in San Geronimo that called itself—pretentiously, Jack thought—the Warrior Circle. Mary Jane hadn't liked this much. It took Gary away from her and the kids one evening a week as well as the occasional weekend. But then had to admit, it had done wonders for him. Four years ago, Gary had started Hemperware, a business that dealt with natural hemp products—shirts, sandals, hats, even hemp shampoo and toothpaste. The idea was that distributors would throw Hemperware parties, convince their friends to become distributors as well, and the whole thing would work like a chain letter, a kind of spontaneous green revolution. The business was successful, and suddenly the Tripps had money to burn. Three years ago they bought an old ranch, eighty acres out in the desert about an hour's drive west of town. Everything was looking up. And then in June, Gary had vanished during one his male-bonding camping weekends. Yesterday, to her surprise, one of the men came to her house and informed her that it was the Warrior Circle which actually held the paper on her ranch as well as the Hemperware business, and that she had three months to find a new place to live.

"And you had no idea of this financial arrangement?" Jack asked.

"Gary took care of everything like that. I guess I'm sort of a space case. All I've done the past seven years is raise the children—but that's a job too, don't you think?"

"A very important full-time job," Jack agreed.

"That's why this has come as such a shock. I mean, naturally I *assumed* we owned our house and the business."

"Tell me, who exactly are these men in the Warrior Circle?"

"I don't know."

"You don't *know*?"

"I guess that sounds crazy, but it was sort of like a secret society. That's what Gary told me. He said it was a private, spiritual part of his life, and that if he talked about it, it wouldn't be so spiritual anymore. He said that men needed someplace where they could really open up and trust one another, and they could only do that if they agreed to a vow of silence."

"And you went along with this?"

"Well, Gary called the shots, you know." Her tone held a mixture of frustration and regret. "He was older, he knew so much more than me. Or at least, that's what I thought. He was like my father."

"I understand. But look, Mrs. Tripp, you're telling me that he spent at least one evening a week with these men for five years—surely in all that time, he must have occasionally talked about what went on?"

"Well, not much. I guess every now and then a few things slipped out—you know, funny things that had happened. But Gary always called the guys by their Indian names."

"What sort of Indian names?"

"Black Wolf, Coyote-That-Sings, Silver Bear . . . I don't remember them all. I thought it was sort of silly, these grown-up guys playing Indian."

"All right. Now, who came to see you? To tell you that you had three months to leave the ranch?"

"Zor McCarthy. He's an architect. He owns Solar Revolution—maybe you've heard of them. They make those houses out of straw bales and weird materials like that."

"So obviously he's part of this Warrior Circle. Had you ever met him before?"

"Yeah, a couple of times. He always throws a big Christmas party. But I never knew he was one of the guys in the group."

"I see. Now, Gary disappeared when exactly?"

"June twenty-third."

"And this architect, Zor McCarthy, waits nearly seven weeks to inform you that the men's group owns everything you thought belonged to you. Did he say why he waited so long?"

"He said all the men felt bad about it. They'd tried to give me a little time to mourn Gary without having to think about practical things."

"Did he show you the warranty deed? Any papers at all?"

"Uh, no. I didn't think to ask."

Not a very clever young woman, Jack thought. "Now, Mrs. Tripp, you said earlier that you believed your husband had been murdered. What made you say that?"

"Because I don't trust those guys, not any of them. And it's just not fair what they're trying to do to me," she said angrily. "Anyway, I'm sort of psychic, you know. I read Tarot cards."

"Uh-huh," Jack managed, keeping a neutral expression. "You don't trust those guys, as you say, yet you've only met one of them, Zor McCarthy. Can you give me any reason for your mistrust?"

"Because Gary wouldn't just vanish like that," she said passionately, refusing harder logic. "It doesn't make sense."

"We have very rugged mountains in this part of New Mexico, Mrs. Tripp. Eleven, twelve thousand feet . . . accidents can happen."

"They killed him, I know they did. I just feel it."

"But *why* would they kill him? What motive would they have?"

"So they could take over the business, of course. And get the ranch."

Jack pursed his lips, wondering how he might best send Mary Jane Tripp on her way, leaving him to his peaceful garden and the lovely summer day. The children's shrill voices filled the air. A fight was breaking out down by the stream.

"Mommy, Bud splashed me!" cried one of the girls.

"Bud, don't splash Sativa," Mary Jane called mechanically to her son.

"Mommy! He did it again! Tell him to stop!"

Jack listened to the children's tears and the mother's ineffectual attempts to restore peace. He felt sorry for the young family, but wasn't at all certain he wished to get involved.

"Mrs. Tripp, tell me something. You say that Hemperware, your husband's business, sold natural hemp products. Has Gary been growing marijuana on your ranch?"

"Oh, no! I mean, well, maybe just a plant or two for our own use. It's a medicinal herb, you know. Very healing. But the hemp clothing and stuff, that all came from other places—Gary didn't actually make them himself, he was just the distributor."

"You're positive he wasn't selling any homegrown?"

"No, you don't understand Gary. He'd give away a little stash now and then to his friends, but he'd never, never think of selling sacred medicine! Gary was a very free person, you know. Very spiritual."

Jack sighed. "Well, Mrs. Tripp, I'm not certain if I can help you," he told her. "I have a very small private investigations company—I'm blind, of course, and I only have a part-time assistant, so I have to confine myself to a few special cases where I believe I might be useful. Frankly, in this instance, I think what you really need is a good attorney, not a detective. You need to get a copy of the warranty deed and have your attorney go over your husband's papers very carefully to see who really owns what."

"But it's not right that they should get my house! I don't care about the business so much, but I *love* that old ranch . . . I know Gary wouldn't leave me and the kids without anything. You've got to help me, Mr. Wilder."

Jack sighed. "Well, I'll tell you what. Let me spend a few days looking into this, and I'll get back to you. Once I establish the facts, I'll be able to advise you a little bit better than I can now. At the very least, I may be able to recommend a good lawyer in town."

"Oh, thank you so much, Mr. Wilder! Look, I'm kind of broke right now, but I have my checkbook. . . ."

"Oh, no, that's not necessary," he told her quickly. "Let me see if I can be useful in this matter first before you give me any money. Unfortunately, I don't think this is the sort of situation where I can be of much help at all."

To Jack's embarrassment, she came around from her side of the picnic table to give him a hug and kiss on the cheek. He turned awkwardly at the wrong moment, and the kiss landed directly on his lips.

"You're a good man, Jack Wilder," she said fervently. "You're one of God's angels."

Jack couldn't help but smile. In his entire life, no one had ever called him an angel before.

"Just don't expect any miracles," he warned.

6

Howie pulled into Jack's driveway in his ancient two-seater MGB convertible shortly before noon. The MG was a rattly old car, dark green, dented, the canvas top patched with silver tape. Howie was feeling fairly dented and patched together himself at the moment. He had showered vigorously and changed clothes, but the acrid smell of violence seemed to cling to his nostrils. A pretty young woman with long brown hair and three barefoot children in tow was just leaving as he arrived. The mother wore a kind of gypsy outfit—a loose flowing skirt and blouse that hinted at a lack of underwear. She gave Howie an appraising look, a sort of hippie-chick-seeks-a-father-for-her-children kind of look. It worried Howie just a little. Then she and her kids piled into a dusty old Volvo stationwagon and drove away. The rear end of her car was covered with advice in the form of slogans and stickers. ARMS ARE MADE FOR HUGGING, said her rear end. LEGALIZE MARIJUANA . . . LOVE ANIMALS, DON'T EAT THEM! Howie smiled despite his bruises. It was somehow reassuring to glimpse a bygone era of peace and pot. There were times in San Geronimo when you felt the world had stopped circa 1973.

Howie walked slowly up the path to Jack's house, passing between two huge, sleepy cottonwood trees. Jack's wife, Emma, had inherited the property from a maiden aunt a number of years ago, when she and Jack were still living in California. They had fixed it up during summer vacations, always planning to retire here, little suspecting how soon that retirement would come. The house was over a hundred years old, a rambling two-story adobe. Like

Howie's landlords, the Wilders had a stream running through their land, creating an oasis of tangled green. But whereas Bob and Nova's land was well-organized, almost Japanese in concept, the Wilder's property was a chaos of growth. The flower beds were a jungle of daisies and wild roses; hollyhocks and flowering vines climbed the adobe walls of the house. Halfway up the path, Howie spotted Jack sitting at his picnic table near the vegetable garden. Howie changed direction and limped that way.

"So who's the hippie mom I saw driving away just now?" he asked.

"Her name's Mary Jane Tripp. A possible client." Jack looked up from the table, focusing his black glasses on Howie, like two radar screens probing a possible midair collision. "What's wrong with you?"

"How can you tell something's wrong?"

"You're limping, and there's a martyred tone of self-pity in your voice. Self-pity is not an attractive quality, Howie."

Howie's mouth fell open in outrage. "Self-pity! In the past twelve hours, Aria and I had a blowup for no good reason that I can tell. She drove off, then I woke up a few hours later and found her Jeep abandoned a hundred feet down the road with the tape player blasting and a pistol lying on the ground. Since that ungodly hour, I've been looking for her everywhere. I've endured a half hour of male bonding with my neighbor, a SNAG of the first degree, and I've been beaten up by a sadistic sheriff . . . all before my morning coffee! So don't give me any shit about self-pity, Jack!"

Jack scowled. "Do you have the gun?"

Howie slipped a green day pack from his back, unzipped the top, and handed Jack the pistol he had found by Aria's car.

Jack ran his hands over the shape of the metal. "It's a Smith & Wesson .38 revolver."

"You can tell that just by feeling it?"

"Of course. It's one of the most popular handguns ever made. This one feels like an old model." Jack sniffed the barrel, and his expression changed. "It's been fired recently."

"I know."

Jack sighed and put the gun down on the table.

"Just for the record, what's a SNAG?" he asked.

"A Sensitive New Age Guy. A very scary breed, Jack. They're always making goo-goo eyes at you. Looking deep into your soul and talking in very gentle-gentle voices. This particular SNAG, my neighbor, even tried to get me to come to his men's group meeting tonight!"

"A men's group?" Jack asked, raising an eyebrow.

"I'm afraid so. If you weren't such a gender dinosaur, Jack, I could probably get you an invite too. We could both get in touch with our fierce masculine nature, maybe even do a little beating on a drum."

Jack seemed puzzled by Howie's tone. "I'm curious. Why are you so down on men's groups? I imagine they could be helpful for certain men at certain times."

"It's New Agers—goo-goo eyes are only the start, I'm afraid. They listen to horrible elevator music by people like Yanni. And if that's not bad enough, they have no sense of humor. Beware of people who don't have a sense of humor, Jack—they're the source of most of the problems in the world."

Howie was prone to such grand philosophical statements. But Jack didn't seem to be listening. "A men's group, you say?" he repeated aimlessly. "A gun on the ground . . . and then a cop beats you up. Well, we'd better go over this from the top."

Howie spent the next hour telling Jack the saga of his sad Tuesday night and Wednesday morning. Jack listened with concentrated interest, making Howie go over several points.

"You say Aria left to work on a story she was writing—did she say what the article was about?" Jack asked.

"No. She often works odd hours, Jack. And she doesn't like to discuss what she's writing."

"So this *wasn't* odd, then? That she should get up and leave you at eleven-thirty at night saying she had to work?"

Howie considered this. "Well, it *did* feel odd, not the fact that she left to work, but the way she did it. Usually, she gives me some advance warning. She'll say she's coming for dinner, but she can't stay late because of some deadline. But last night . . . she seemed preoccupied all evening, sort of moody, and then she just sprung it on me."

"And she didn't explain?"

"Aria rarely explains," Howie said dryly.

"Did you sense she was meeting anyone? That she had some sort of rendezvous planned for later in the evening?"

"I don't think so," Howie replied, discouraged. "But who knows?"

Jack fell into a brooding silence. He sat for a full fifteen minutes without speaking. Howie was accustomed to these silences and waited patiently for the oracle to resume speaking. You never knew where Jack might end up after such periods of meditation; he might suggest a new recipe for chicken soup, or have a case totally sewn up.

"Listen, I'm worried about the gun," Howie said at last, interrupting Jack's meditation. "I got such bad vibes from Sheriff Snider, some instinct made me hesitate to tell him about it. But there's going to be hell to pay, withholding evidence like that."

Jack seemed to wake up from his trance. "Leave the gun with me. I'll make a few phone calls and get you off the hook. Meanwhile, I have some chores for you to do. . . ."

Jack sent Howie off to perform several investigative deeds and gather more information. When he was alone once again in his garden, Jack felt a wave of dissatisfaction. He wandered inside the house, through his kitchen to the living room, holding the .38 revolver loosely in one hand. The story Howie told him was disturbing, though he couldn't quite decipher its meaning. In the past few months, Jack had begun to regret his impulse to start a small detective agency in San Geronimo. It had seemed like a harmless idea at the time, a way to keep mentally active, and as long as he had an assistant like Howard Moon Deer to do the actual legwork, he didn't see why his blindness should get in the way. But recently he had come to dread the bits of human misery that occasionally came his way: *My wife is cheating on me, my partner is robbing me blind, will you please find out if my son is taking drugs . . . and while you're at it, if you can dig up any dirt on Joe Schmo down the street, I'd love to run that bastard out of town and take over his business!* Lord, it was depressing! Jack had an increasing desire to simply sit in his garden, the sun on his face, and let the world slip by.

Emma was at work—she held one of the two paying jobs at the San Geronimo Public Library. The house was empty and still, engulfed in the languid summer magic of mid-afternoon. Katya was snoring in her usual napping place by the fireplace, a grandfather clock ticked ponderously in the living room. Jack paced restlessly, knowing his way through the familiar surroundings. Finally he sat down in front of the Steinway upright in the living room, setting the revolver on the piano bench next to him. He opened the cover and felt the cool touch of ivory, the geometric puzzle of raised and flat keys against his fingertips. The piano was one of those things he had always wished he had time to study back in the days when he was a busy police official; now at last there was world enough and time, but he hadn't made much progress. Jack caressed the keyboard and located middle C—from here he could usually orient himself and launch forth with some blues or boogie-woogie. He wasn't exactly Ray Charles, he hit a lot of wrong notes, but he found it soothing to play.

Jack played the blues this afternoon in honor of Howie's romantic troubles. Personally, Jack was glad he had been young at a time when the sexes seemed to like each other a good deal more than they did today; the sixties, when Jack was a young man, had been a time of sexual coming together, rather than falling apart. Thinking about Howie and Aria, Jack's fingers gradually slowed and came to a stop on the keyboard. He reached next to him on the bench and picked up the Smith & Wesson.

A gun. So hard and heavy, such a deeply familiar object in his hands. Terrible memories flitted through his mind. Dead cops. Dead outlaws. Pools of blood, smoke and darkness. Jack Wilder shivered as the ghosts of friends and enemies—some that he had killed himself—walked briefly from their graves.

But this wouldn't do. He had to get a grip on himself. All this nostalgia and moodiness was a self-indulgence that a blind man could not afford. He ran the index finger of his right hand along the metal casing near the trigger guard until he felt the small indentation of where the serial number had been stamped. He tried to make out the numbers by tracing them with his fingernail, but they were not easy to decipher by feel. He thought the first number was a six, but then again it might be an eight. The figures were simply too small for a blind man to make out with any degree of accuracy. He was not on the ball today—he should have asked Howie to read them for him. Now he would have to wait for some seeing-eye help. Jack brought the barrel to his nose and inhaled the aroma of burned gunpowder. Lord, it was a smell that brought back memories. . . .

"Jack!" said a voice close by, speaking very carefully. "Put the gun down!"

It was Emma, and beneath her surface calm there was terror in her voice. Jack had been vaguely aware of her car driving up and the kitchen screen door opening, but he had been so involved in his labyrinthine thoughts that he hadn't considered what this would look like. He lowered the barrel from his nose.

"I wasn't expecting you," he told her.

"I forgot a book I need for the literacy program I'm doing at five. I have to get right back. Jack . . ."

"Emma, honestly, I'm much too practical and ornery to shoot myself. Believe me, I may be an old goat, but I have all four hooves on the ground."

"Then, you weren't . . ."

"This is a gun that Howie brought me today, and I was sniffing the barrel hoping to determine when it was fired last. Actually, you can do me a favor and read me the serial number."

Emma sighed. She knew Jack was telling the truth but she worried about him anyway, sensing deeper currents.

"Jack, you need to keep talking to me. I know for an active man, it hasn't been easy for you to adapt to your new situation."

"Emma, please, I'm fine. Just tell me the serial number."

She took the gun reluctantly. Emma Wilder was a gray-haired woman, a little stout from Jack's cooking, but to Jack, in his blindness, she was forever young. It was hard to believe that thirty years had passed since he had courted her, a slim and pretty girl who had come to San Francisco from the Midwest to run a small bookstore in Northbeach, where he, a uniformed cop with a taste for poetry, used to stop in for thin volumes and conversation. She had never entirely approved of his profession, and she still hated guns.

She read the serial number off for him, and he memorized the number quickly. Memorization was an essential part of blindness. When Emma left the house to return to the library, Jack pondered his next move. He hated to deal with the San Geronimo police. It was incredible, but in the years he had lived here, the local justice system had not managed to solve or prosecute a single serious crime. If a suspect was miraculously apprehended, in every instance the case was thrown out of court due to some amateurish procedural error—often tainted evidence or bungled medical reports, or just plain corruption. Unfortunately, New Mexico was the poorest state in the union—a third world country, for all practical purposes, and the extremely low salaries to pay law enforcement did not entice qualified people. Jack found it all very frustrating. As for forensics, the entire state was back in the 1940s. A simple matter such as checking fingerprints was a nightmare, for the Department of Public Safety in Sante Fe, which administered these things, had invested in an inferior AFIS—Automated Fingerprint Identification System—whose software was not compatible with the FBI or the NEC computers used in other states. As a result, the New Mexico AFIS often rejected pristine prints, and it sometimes took six to eight weeks simply to get a result.

Jack found these things intolerable, and he avoided local law enforcement whenever possible. Yet he must do something about the gun that Howie had found. After some thought, he phoned Captain Ed Gomez, who was in charge of the San Geronimo substation of the New Mexico State Police, the only police outfit in town Jack considered semiprofessional. As he expected, the captain was only politely interested in Aria Waldman's disappearance and the .38 revolver that had been found—guns were a dime a dozen in this part of the world, Aria had not been missing long enough yet to stir official concern, the state police were understaffed, and few disappearances were investigated anyway. This was fine with Jack. The purpose of the call was only to cover his and Howie's collective rear ends, so that no one in the future might accuse them of withholding evidence or obstructing justice.

Next, Jack made a more useful phone call to an old FBI friend in Denver, to request that the Smith & Wesson's serial number be run through the vast National Criminal Intelligence Center, the NCIC computer. The change in Jack was astonishing as he set himself in motion with these small investigative chores. He was no longer some clownish Elmer Fudd tripping over baskets of vegetables in his garden; he was on a case again, a man with a purpose.

7

The town of San Geronimo boasted a tri-cultural population of 11,310 souls. Tri-cultural was a word bandied about in New Mexico tourist literature to imply a happy commingling of ethnic groups. In San Geronimo the division was as follows: Spanish, 61 percent; Pueblo Indian, 12 percent; and Anglo, 27 percent. The Spanish had a monopoly on the political power, the Anglos had pretty much all the money in town, and the Indians possessed shit little except their reservation, 90,000 acres of stunningly beautiful land. There was no happy commingling. Howie suspected you would need to travel to South Africa in the last days of apartheid to find a place in which the ethnic groups kept a greater separation from one another.

The heart of town—the lost heart, at least—was a pretty old Spanish plaza whose shops sold T-shirts and Indian art of doubtful authenticity. (The real heart today, in fact, was Wal-Mart, a few miles away, where the old-timers gathered on benches facing the parking lot to gossip with their friends.) Encircling the now touristy plaza, there was a quaint historical district where all the buildings, by command of the town fathers, were required to look like old adobes and be painted a sandy brown, even the McDonald's and Pizza Hut. This was an exhausting illusion to maintain, such unmitigated quaintness, and after a few blocks the realities of modern America returned with a collective sigh of relief. The roads to the north and south of town were dominated by the usual strip malls, gas stations, fast-food chains, supermarkets, motels, and auto dealerships.

After leaving Jack, Howie drove downtown through the plaza into the historic district. Parking was always a problem in these narrow, congested streets, but he managed to find a spot on Don Orlando Street next to the Kachina Art Gallery. He put a pocketful of quarters into the not-so-quaint meter, then walked down the road to the New Wave Café, an old adobe building directly across the street from *The San Geronimo Post*. The café had a well-shaded garden, where the newspaper crowd like to gather. Howie had often met Aria here for lunch or a cappuccino after work.

Jack had sent Howie out with two chores. His first assignment was to learn what Aria had been working on recently at the newspaper, whose toes she might have been stepping on with her investigative journalism. San Geronimo was a community with all the usual small-town corruptions, and then some—in the nearly two years that Aria Waldman had worked on the local paper, she had exposed a series of municipal sins, small and large, earning herself some influential enemies. It was possible, Jack suggested, that someone she was investigating was less than enthused about the prospect of being exposed on the front page, and had decided to make Aria vanish to insure that this did not happen. It seemed, at least, a reasonable place to start looking for some rhyme or reason to her disappearance—if indeed there *was* a rhyme or reason to what had happened. Jack cautioned that Aria might have fallen victim to a random crime against a woman late at night. And, of course, there was always the possibility that she would simply reappear at any moment with a totally innocent explanation of what had happened, although as each hour passed, it was becoming increasingly difficult to imagine what that explanation might be.

The second chore Jack wanted done today was for Howie to learn as much as he could about Gary Tripp, the ex-musician who had vanished on a men's group camping trip in the mountains earlier in the summer. Jack wanted Howie to go through all the old newspaper accounts and find out who exactly had been present on the camping trip; statements would have been given to the authorities by the men involved, and most likely the newspaper would have a list of their names, perhaps even notes from old interviews.

Both errands involved the newspaper, and after some thought, Howie had used the phone at Jack's house to reach a young intern on the *Post,* Heather Winter, and ask her to have lunch with him this afternoon at the New Wave. Heather was a journalism student from UC Berkley who was taking a year off to get some practical experience. Howie had never actually met the intern, but over the past months he had spoken to her a number of times on the phone. Heather shared an office with Aria and had helped with research on a number of stories, so she seemed like someone who might prove helpful.

Howie was the first to arrive; at least he saw no woman at a table by herself who looked as if she expected him. The café was busy with a lunch crowd, and there was only one free table remaining in the entire restaurant—it happened to be the outside patio table where Howie and Aria had most often sat. *Their* table. He sat down with nostalgic angst beneath a colored umbrella in a chair that faced the *Post* building across the street. Some tourists at the next table gave him a worried look and then glanced quickly away. His left cheek was starting to swell from finding itself on the receiving end of Sheriff Snider's boot; he was clearly an Indian who had been in a fight, a class of persons to be avoided.

"My God, you look awful!" cried Sarah, the pretty English waitress, appearing at his table.

"I had a small accident," he admitted.

"Oh, Howie!"

There was nothing quite so warming as the gush of a woman's sympathy. When you could get it.

"I'm waiting for someone," he told her bravely. "So I won't order yet. But I wouldn't mind a few Advil, if you have them."

"Two?"

"Four, please. You see before you a wounded man."

Howie was sitting in a semi-stupor when he became aware of a pale young woman with short dark hair and huge eyes who was standing in front of him, regarding him solemnly through round, rimless glasses, the sort that John Lennon had once made famous. She looked about twelve years old, an undernourished waif who was dressed in baggy unisex clothes, loose black cotton pants, a floppy old T-shirt, and black Doc Marten boots. It was the refugee look.

"Heather?" he asked cautiously.

"What did you do to her, Moon Deer?" she said angrily.

"What do you mean, what did I do?"

"You heard me. I know all about your fights—I guess you don't like women to have opinions of their own, do you? Such a big blow to a fragile male ego!"

"You think I knocked her around?" Howie asked in astonishment.

Heather's gaze was level and cool; for a scrawny unisex waif, this lady was not to be messed with.

"Why else would she go into hiding?" she asked. "She's frightened of you, I guess."

Howie was flabbergasted. The way she was looking at him, Howie couldn't help but feel generically guilty. Guilty for all the times he had mentally undressed women in crowded restaurants. Guilty of being a lustful male beast. But he was not guilty of beating up Aria Waldman.

"Look," he managed, "you're all wrong about me. Why don't you sit down, and we'll talk about this."

"Okay, I'll sit."

Howie managed a wry smile, hoping to disarm her with charm. But Heather wasn't buying it. She sat on the far side of the table, as far from him as she could, and seemed prepared to kick him in the balls at the first hint of any macho nonsense. Most likely she had taken some woman's self-defense class and could beat the shit out of him just as easily as the sad-faced sheriff had this morning. Howie was starting to feel like a punching bag to the world.

"The side of your face is swollen, Moon Deer," she observed. "Aria fought back, didn't she?—well, good for her!"

"Aria didn't do this. These particular scars came from a crazy cop a few hours ago."

"You're saying you're a victim of police brutality?" In Heather's cosmology, the world seemed neatly divided between sadistic brutes and selfless victims. "What happened?"

"He judged me in advance, just like you have," Howie told her pointedly. "He assumed I get my kicks abusing women."

"And you're telling me you don't?"

"Listen carefully. Aria said good-bye, I kissed her good night, then I went back to bed. I woke up a few hours later, found her car down the road, and I've been trying to figure out what happened ever since. That's the entire truth."

Heather studied him with deadpan eyes through her rimless glasses, like he was a bug on a slide. "I saw Aria yesterday afternoon," she said finally. "She came into the office to pick up some blank computer disks, and we talked for a while. She told me you're a . . . well, she said you're a sweet guy but she needed her independence."

"You see?—I'm a sweet guy." Howie was glad for the testimonial.

"But she said she was planning to break up with you."

"What?"

"That she didn't want a relationship right now. That you were squashing her. Keeping her from doing the things she needed to do."

"Well, we had a fight, sure. But she didn't break up with me," Howie said helplessly. "Jesus! I've never tried to squash her independence!"

"Men do it without even noticing," Heather assured him. "Anyway, let's get back to this cop you say beat you up."

Howie sighed. "He was *not* so sweet, I'm afraid. I was walking around the neighborhood a bit, and when I got back, I found him searching through Aria's Jeep. I live on a private road, not exactly a main thoroughfare, so I can't figure out what he was doing there. He just appeared out of nowhere."

"You hadn't called the cops?"

"I was planning to, but no, I hadn't gotten around to it yet. I wanted to investigate a little on my own first."

"So who was this cop?" she asked, still skeptical.

"It was Sheriff Lou Snider. I've seen his picture in the paper, but I didn't recognize him until he told me his name."

The name seemed to surprise her. She opened her mouth to say something, then changed her mind. Finally she shook her head. "You're *sure* it was Sheriff Snider?"

"I'm sure. What's on your mind, Heather? You seem to know something about him?"

"I know he's our county sheriff, that's all. And that a lot of people in San Geronimo think he's a sleaze, though no one's ever been able to prove anything against him. Look, if you're telling me the truth, Moon Deer, I'd like to write a story about this."

"I thought you were an intern, not a reporter."

She shrugged. "I do a bit of everything. Even a story now and then, if I can come up with something. So let's start from the top with Sheriff Snider. When exactly did he become abusive?"

"Whoa! Hold on, Heather. I'm sorry, but I just don't have time at the moment to help you expose police brutality in New Mexico. All I'm interested in right now is finding Aria."

Sarah, the waitress, appeared at their table, and they stopped to consider their choices for lunch. Heather asked for the vegetarian chef's salad, and Howie ordered a tofu burger—he would have preferred a real cheeseburger, dead cow with fries and fat, but he felt Heather was just starting to soften a little and he didn't want to come across as a barbarian carnivore.

"Look, let's call a truce," Howie suggested after they ordered. "You must have some idea what's been going on in Aria's life recently—*I* sure don't. I'm only the boyfriend."

"But what if she doesn't *want* you to find her? Have you considered that?"

"Look, at this point if she never wants to see me again, that's cool. All I need is some explanation of why she should leave her Jeep near my house like that, and for her to tell me that she's okay."

Heather lit a cigarette, an unfiltered Camel, and expelled smoke into the afternoon air. "All right," she said finally, "how can I help?"

"I want to know what stories Aria's been researching the past few weeks. She's turned up a lot of dirt in this town, and there's a possibility that she found out something that was dangerous for her to know."

Heather frowned. "Doesn't she tell you about her work?"

"Not much. She said once that if a writer talks too much beforehand, the energy isn't there when it comes time to sit at the computer and actually string sentences together. She put the subject pretty much off-limits."

"Well, a lot of writers feel that way. Aria is very secretive about her work-in-progress."

"Surely not with her colleagues on the paper?"

"*Especially* with her colleagues on the paper."

"How about the editor? He must know what she's been doing?"

"Don Jolly? Not particularly. He's always given Aria pretty much a blank check to go after whatever interests her. She insists that's the only way she can do good work."

"What about her computer?"

"What about it?"

"Won't it have all her notes and story ideas on the hard drive?"

"Not her office computer. She's erased all her personal files."

"Has she? How do you know that?"

"Because *I* use her computer. As an intern, I don't rate a terminal of my own, so Aria lets me use hers—after she's off-loaded everything personal from it first, of course. She hardly ever comes into the office anyway, particularly the last month or so. She does all her writing at home on her laptop and e-mails in her stuff."

"I didn't know that. I'm surprised Don allows it."

"Well, why not? She's the big star reporter, and she definitely delivers the goods. Besides, we're overcrowded in the office and having a few people like Aria send in their stories from home frees up space."

"So you're telling me you don't have a clue what she's been working on recently?"

"Well, read the paper. This past month, she's pretty much been concentrating on youth issues—the crappy local schools, gangs, drugs, the fact that there isn't anything for young people to do in this town but get in trouble. In the edition coming up, she has a piece on underage drinking. I've read it. She names all the bars and liquor stores in town where minors can get served without much hassle."

"She actually lists these places in the article?"

"You bet."

"That's going to make some people unhappy, isn't it?"

"Maybe a little. Of course, Aria's investigation was unofficial, so these places won't actually get fined. Probably they'll tighten up for a few months, then it'll drift back to the way things have always been."

Sarah brought their food, giving Howie a moment to ponder what Heather was telling him. Perhaps Aria's disappearance was connected with her job on the paper, but perhaps not. It seemed very difficult to determine, and a huge task to run down all the articles she had researched over the past six months, all the people she might have offended.

"Tell me something, Heather. I remember a while ago, Aria and I were talking and she said that sometimes you helped her with research."

"That's right. When she gets real busy, sometimes she'll throw me something to do."

"What's the most recent thing you helped her with?"

"Well, there hasn't been anything for a few weeks. She's been sort of distracted, I haven't even seen her much in the office, like I said. I guess the last thing she asked me to do was research Gary Tripp. He's the musician who got himself lost in the mountains back in June."

Howie felt a shiver of interest. But he kept his tone casual. "Gary Tripp. I remember the story. Did she ask you to research him before or after he got lost in the woods?"

"It was about a week before the camping accident."

"*Before?* You're sure about that?"

"Of course I'm sure."

"So why was she interested in him then?"

"She didn't really say. But I guess she thought there was some story value there—a musician who was big in the early seventies goes through a lot of ups and downs and then reinvents himself in New Mexico, sort of thing."

"But Aria didn't . . . *doesn't* write human interest stories," Howie said, correcting himself. He didn't want to start speaking about Aria Waldman in the past tense, not yet.

Heather shrugged. "Sometimes she asked me to check out things without telling me why. I was always glad to do it—it's a lot more interesting than proofreading and writing up wedding and funeral announcements, the usual stuff they give me."

"So what did you find out about Gary?"

"Nothing earth-shattering. I managed to get my hands on a copy of his first album with Headstone, the one that was a hit—it was pretty good actually. I spoke to a few people who knew him, found out some stuff about his Hemperware business. Apparently he went through some hard times in the eighties. Drug problems, hassles with the IRS. He joined a few cults and tried different things. Then ten years ago he hooked up with a Texas woman, got married, had a bunch of children, got a successful business going—he seemed to be doing all right."

"Did you interview Gary himself?"

"No. Aria asked me not to. She didn't want him to know she was interested in him, and that made it a little more difficult for me."

"So what else did you find out?"

"Not a whole lot. I have my notes back at the office, if you're interested, but it was sort of a bust."

"Did you show your notes to Aria?"

"Of course. She said it wasn't really what she was after, but it didn't matter. I had done fine, and I should just forget about it."

"Really?" Howie said thoughtfully. "And this was *before* Gary went camping?"

"I've told you that twice now. About a week before."

"Sorry, but it just seems strange to me. If it's all right, I'd like to come back to the *Post* with you and read through all the old newspaper accounts of the camping trip where he disappeared. I'd like to know who was with him."

"He was with a men's group," she said distastefully. "I'm sure we have their names somewhere. Most of them gave statements to the paper."

"Good. Let's go try to find 'em," Howie urged.

8

After lunch, Howie walked with Heather across the street to the *Post* building, a single-story mud-colored structure that was trying hard to look like an old adobe, though, in fact, it had been built within the past ten years and was constructed from cement and brown paint. The paper came out every Thursday, and it was the lifeblood of the rural community in a way that would be difficult for a city person to imagine; this was where the people of San Geronimo turned eagerly each week for the latest gossip, scandals, employment opportunities, used refrigerators, real estate, what movies had come to town, who had died, how the high school basketball team was faring in the state play-offs, and—above all—the cranky letters to the editor, which most readers turned to for entertainment value immediately after the front page.

Howie followed Heather through the reception area, past a large open room full of desks and computers, and into a small reading room at the rear of the building. Heather helped him get settled in a green armchair with a stack of newspapers—the *Post* kept six months of old issues before putting them onto microfilm. She gave him her notes on Gary Tripp and went off to do her own work. Howie yawned vigorously to clear his head and then started to read.

The story about the lost camper was the headline of the Thursday, June 25 issue, though the incident itself had occurred on the night of the full moon, Tuesday, June 23. "CAMPER MISSING IN SAN GERONIMO WILDERNESS," cried the banner across the top of the front page. As of press time Wednesday night, June 24, several dozen volunteer members of San Geronimo Search and Rescue in conjunction with the New Mexico State Police had been searching the remote area near Bear Lake for Gary Tripp, who was described as a local businessman and musician, ex-keyboard player for the legendary seventies band Headstone. Tripp had been reported missing late Wednesday afternoon by Misha Ballantine, a TV producer. Ballantine, who was part of a growing segment of the New Mexico population who commuted to Hollywood, said that a small group of men had been camping together at the lake, where they were "doing a vision quest." On Tuesday night, the men had separated in order "to meditate, pray, and spend some quiet time alone," so it was not immediately clear how or even when Tripp had become lost. At dawn, the vision questers returned to camp, and no one thought it particularly odd that one of their group should be late. Perhaps he had simply lost track of time, after all that praying and meditating. By around nine o'clock, however, Ballantine and his friends had become mildly worried. They decided they'd better search for their missing member, and they divided up and began to comb the rugged terrain. By noon, Gary Tripp had not returned to camp, nor had they found any sign of him. It was at this point that Ballantine volunteered to hike down the mountain and summon Search and Rescue, while the remaining five men continued looking for Gary. As of press time, a state police helicopter had joined the search, but bad weather was moving into the area, hampering their efforts. The article concluded with the fate of Gary Tripp still in limbo. There was some advice from the head of San Geronimo Search and Rescue—a periodontist in everyday life—on how hikers might avoid such mishaps in the future. Always take a compass along, said the periodontist. Never hike alone. Bring plenty of water, matches, and a large plastic garbage bag that can be put over your head and used as emergency shelter if things get really bad.

A week later, the *Post* still had Gary Tripp on the front page. This time the story, written by Aria Waldman, centered on the huge rescue operation of nearly a hundred volunteers, which had so far been unable to locate the missing camper. Unfortunately, the San Geronimo Wilderness was a vast, mountainous area, densely forested and filled with an assortment of dangers—deep ravines, unpredictable weather, even bears, just to name a few. It was the sort of place where someone might wander off and disappear forever. By the second week, many in Search and Rescue were privately expressing their doubts that Gary would be found alive; Bear Lake was above ten thousand feet in altitude, and the temperatures at night sometimes dipped down to the single digits Fahrenheit, even in June.

By the third week, the story of Gary Tripp had moved to the rear of the paper. It was a sad fact, but one or two hikers died in these mountains every year—hunters in particular were prone to fatal mishaps, and of course many of the New Agers in town said it served these murderers right, instant karma paid in full. Gary Tripp's story was all too common; some died in unseasonal snowstorms, others fell off cliffs, many people simply got lost. After three weeks, the search for Tripp was officially ended with more warnings given out to future campers to enter the rugged wilderness reserves of northern New Mexico with proper caution and respect. A reporter for the *Post*, Steve Westrom, managed to have a word with Misha Ballantine at the tiny San Geronimo airport just as the TV producer was about to take off alone in his private Cessna for L.A. Ballantine found comfort in the fact that his friend Gary died "while doing what he loved to do, during a vision quest when his consciousness was at its fullest peak of self-realization." Before soaring off to Hollywood, the producer remarked that Gary was "a brother who had fought the good fight and had traveled the hard journey toward becoming a true man."

Comforting words, certainly. As Howie continued to read, the sky grew dark and he heard distant thunder, the sound of the daily summer afternoon monsoon storm drawing near. After the newspaper stories, he turned to Heather's five pages of notes on Gary Tripp. The lost camper had been born in Santa Rosa, California, on March 21, 1947. His mother was a piano teacher, his father an Episcopalian minister. Gary inherited his mother's gift for the piano and his father's interest in sin. He started his first band when he was thirteen; at seventeen, in 1964, he moved to San Francisco and rode the wave of the sixties through all its drugs and glory. He was twenty-three when the band Headstone burst out of the Bay Area and achieved a brief two years of fame. It must be difficult, Howie imagined, to be rich and famous so young and then have all the rest of your life to live as an anticlimax. Gary had fallen into the usual hell of has-been rockers, drug problems, issues to resolve with the IRS, but he seemed to have come out of it fairly well toward the end of his life. He had a wife and children and a business that was doing well.

As Howie read, rain began to fall outside, drumming softly on the pavement and roof. He settled more comfortably into the armchair, his eyelids dropping. Suddenly he smiled, remembering an afternoon last February when he had gone skiing with Aria at San Geronimo Peak, the local resort. The memory assaulted him, entirely out of context, a fragment from the good times they had shared.

And what a luscious day it had been! A bright blue sky after nearly two feet of new snow had fallen. They were both good skiers, and all morning they had dived down into the steep trails, making dreamy zigzags through the fresh powder, skiing fast and free. It was a feeling close to flying, to soar down the side of a white mountain. This day of skiing had come during a period in which they were fighting a great deal, so it stood out in sharp relief. One of the sweet times, what their affair might be always if only Aria would relax and stop obsessing so much about her career.

Sometime in the afternoon Aria said she needed to pee, and he had led her off the trail into the forest, deep into the untracked snow, where one thing soon led to another. It took inventive minds to have sex on skis. Aria stood with her snow pants down around her ankles, holding on to the branch of a fir tree for support; Howie slipped his skis between hers and entered her from behind. He felt magnificent, like a wild stag in the forest. Then he gave in to a wild impulse; just as she was coming to a climax, he reached between her legs to the ground, scooped up a handful of virgin snow, and pressed it against her clitoris. She screamed with surprise, perhaps even pleasure. They came together, snow dribbling down her legs as her body arched and convulsed. Afterward, they collapsed laughing into a deep snowdrift, snow everywhere, in their underpants, down their backs, in their hair.

Sitting in the green armchair in the newspaper reading room, Howie vowed that when he found Aria again, he would do whatever it took to make things right. He would be sensitive to her need for independence, but convince her—gently—that feminism should not imitate the worst aspects of a totally debunked lifestyle that hadn't worked for men any more than it would work for women. She would see the light, they would have a second chance;

they would ski forever down white, perfect slopes. But meanwhile, the rain made such a restful sound outside the building that his eyes grew heavier and finally closed. He fell asleep with a goofy smile on his face and a bulge in his pants.

It was late in the afternoon when Heather Winter came back into the reading room and found Howard Moon Deer asleep in the green armchair. Her first reaction was to be annoyed, but when she studied Howie more closely—the goofy smile, the bulge—a primal urge took place within her, a wave of heat that traveled like magic from her brain down her body, all the way to her black Doc Marten boots.

Howie opened his eyes to find Heather gazing at him through her round rimless glasses. Something—he was not certain exactly what—had changed drastically in her attitude toward him.

"I'm sorry. I fell asleep," he muttered stupidly.

"You must be exhausted. I didn't mean to wake you up."

He sat up and rubbed his eyes. "No, I can't sleep now. I have too much to do. I've got to find Aria."

"I made that list for you," she told him. "The men who were camping at Bear Lake. I hope it's helpful, Howie."

"Me too," he said.

She gave him the list and turned away. "If I can do anything," she offered, her back to him. "Anything at all, just let me know."

She walked dramatically from the room. Howie was already studying the list and missed her passionate exit. There were six names on the piece of paper:

> Misha Ballantine
> Zor McCarthy
> Chuck Hildyard
> Denny Hirsch
> Louis Snider
> Shepherd Plum

Howie was so startled by the list that he straightened up in the armchair, wide awake now. He recognized all the names except the last, Shepherd Plum. Misha Ballantine was the TV producer he had just been reading about; Zor McCarthy was the solar architect Jack had mentioned, the one who told Mary Jane Tripp she had three months to get out of her house; Chuck Hildyard was a real estate agent whose large office on the main street in town he had often passed. And was it possible that Louis Snider was really the same Sheriff Snider who had used him as a punching bag this morning? A cop in a men's group? It seemed like an odd group of men indeed.

But the name that interested Howie the most at the moment was Denny Hirsch, his hairy neighbor across the desert who had invited Howie to the men's group meeting tonight. It seemed suspicious that one of the members of the so-called Warrior Circle should live so close to where Aria had disappeared, while a second, Sheriff Snider, had appeared at her abandoned car without being summoned. Howie rose suddenly, put the newspapers back on the shelf, gathered his things, and walked quickly from the building. There was a pay phone on the porch outside. He tried Aria's number one more time, praying she would pick up and answer, ending this mystery with a simple hello. But there was no hello, no end to the mystery, only her voice on the answering machine.

Howie put down the receiver with a sinking feeling, afraid he had a grim evening ahead of him. From an investigative point of view, there didn't seem to be any choice. He decided he would have to attend the Wednesday night men's group after all, meet the guys and find out what they were all about. Maybe he would get something out of it. He had to acknowledge that when it came to gender issues, he could use some help.

9

At seven o'clock that night, Howie pulled into the circular driveway of a modern two-story pseudo-adobe home, 147 Hollyhock Terrace, the address Denny Hirsch had given him for the men's group meeting tonight. This was the swanky part of town, just off the road to the ski resort, a neighborhood of second homes, rarely occupied, that belonged to the fancy set who came to San Geronimo a few weeks out of the year to enjoy the clean air, the mountains, and the arty ambience. When people in town complained that San Geronimo was becoming just like Santa Fe, they usually had neighborhoods like Hollyhock Terrace in mind.

Howie edged past a Toyota Land Cruiser and parked behind a white BMW convertible that had a sticker on the rear bumper: LIVE SIMPLY SO THAT OTHERS MAY SIMPLY LIVE. It was possible that no irony was intended; it was Howie's theory that the Me Generation in its ruthless pursuit of self-enlightenment was incapable of irony. He stepped from his ancient MG, which looked like a beat-up old shoe alongside such fine automobiles, and walked along a flagstone path to the front door. There was a smell of rain in the air and distant, dreamlike flashes of lightning over the mountains. He rang a chiming doorbell and waited to be admitted into the realm of male bonding.

Denny answered the door, dressed in black jeans and a loose black long-sleeved shirt that was open two buttons in the front to reveal his manfully hairy chest. He gave Howie a solemn, heartfelt handshake and gazed intrusively into his eyes, eyeball to eyeball, guy to guy.

"Moon Deer, how *are* you?" he asked warmly, keeping hold of Howie's hand. "I'm *so* glad you decided to come!" Then he squinted at Howie's face. "My God, it looks like you got kicked by a mule!"

"The mule happened to be the sheriff of San Geronimo County. I believe you know Sheriff Snider. I found him lurking near my house this morning after I left you."

Denny's mouth fell open. "Lou Snider? *Lou* did that to you?"

"A short, wiry guy with a sort of droopy Abraham Lincoln face?"

"That's Lou, all right . . . oh, no! This is *really* disturbing." Denny sighed, shaking his head. He did in fact look extremely upset. "Lou's a wonderful man, I have to tell you this. Just wonderful! But sometimes he gets overwhelmed by all that negative cop energy he has to endure as part of his job. He loses touch with the love and gentleness that's inside of him."

Howie smiled vaguely and pulled his hand free. "Is this lovely, gentle man going to be here tonight, by any chance? I'd like to bash his face in."

"Oh, Moon Deer! Don't even joke about things like that! Come on, let me introduce you to Misha." Denny took Howie forcefully by the arm and led him into the house. "Misha's my guru, I swear to God—he knows everything, that man. Absolutely everything!"

Misha Ballantine, the man who knew everything, was the owner of the house. He stood in the middle of his vast living room talking on a cell phone and waved hello to Howie without breaking off his thought.

"David, I lu . . . lu . . . *love* you, bro, you know that," he was saying ardently into his small plastic device. "But if Paramount wants that much money for one week on a goddamn su . . . su . . . soundstage, I say, the hell with them—let's do the whole shoot at Malibu." The producer paused, and with an obvious effort he got a grip on his stutter: "I know a fabulous house right on the beach; it belongs to a dear, dear friend of mine. We'll have natural light, and those studio bastards can stick it up their collective ass . . . come in, come in, Moon Deer! I'll be right with you! . . ."

The living room was impressive. A few acres of rain forest had died so that Misha might have lovely hardwood floors and gleaming shelves for his books, stereo system, and huge TV-VCR complex. There was Oriental art on the walls, some of it pornographic—a goddess with six arms was sitting on the lap of a hairy, slathering male monster, a deity for whom Howie felt a certain empathy. There was a nice jade Buddha near the huge stone fireplace, and wide windows looking eastward toward San Geronimo Peak. Misha himself was a short man, deeply tanned, brown as a nut, fiftyish with a shiny bald head, bushy eyebrows, and a short well-groomed beard.

"Look, David, I gotta go, I got company . . . right, screw those sons of bitches; if they don't want to play ball, that's their hard luck . . . give my love to Shanti . . . God, I hate Hollywood bullshit!" he cried dramatically, punching the off button of his cell phone. "They're all so phony in California. That's why I live in New Mexico."

"Isn't it a hell of a commute back and forth?" Howie asked politely.

"Well, sure. But at least I get some peace and quiet up in the Cessna. A chance to meditate and work on myself, just me and the sky."

Howie liked that. *Up in the Cessna.* He'd have to let that one fall off his own tongue one day, in the unlikely event he was ever rich and famous. "You produce television shows, I understand?"

"Well, infomercials. Frankly, I couldn't stand the hypocrisy of doing anything else—I mean, if it's the money you're after, why pretend you're Fellini? Personally, I'm a realist. My theory about dealing with Hollywood is take the moola and run. The place is absolute poison, believe me. I'm planning to retire as soon as I can, get out of that damn rat race!"

"And live the simple life here in San Geronimo," Howie agreed.

There was something in Howie's tone that made Misha pause and look at his guest more closely. Denny took the opportunity to clear his throat unhappily.

"Uh, Misha, it looks like our Lou has gone on one of his little rampages. He knocked Moon Deer around a little this morning."

"Di . . . di . . . did he?" Misha asked sharply, his stutter now returning. "You know, I love that man! And it just saddens me so much to see him regress!"

"It saddened me too, frankly," Howie admitted. "He beat the shit out of me."

Misha took a deep breath. "Tell me about it."

"My friend Aria Waldman disappeared somewhat mysteriously last night," Howie explained.

"Yes, yes, Denny told me about that. And I'm *extremely* disturbed to hear it."

"I was coming back from Denny's house, and I found Snider standing by Aria's Jeep. He seemed to think I was some sort of monster of a domestic abuser, that I had beaten up on her and frightened her away. That's what he accused me of, anyway. Then suddenly he just went crazy. He started kicking and doing some heavy abusing himself."

"And he's been making so much progress recently!" Denny said mournfully.

Misha sighed. "Can I tell you a secret, Moon Deer? Lou's the sweetest individual you'd ever care to meet, but he has a few unresolved issues that he's working through. Frankly, he came from an abusive family. His father was a cop in Oklahoma, and a very violent man—he used to beat up Lou's mother. Lou broke down one night, crying when he told us about it. You remember, Denny?"

"Oh, I remember!" Denny said solemnly. "We were *all* crying by the time he was through."

Misha continued: "So if Lou suspected even for a moment that you were a domestic abuser, Moon Deer, it would have pushed all his buttons. It's because of his natural chivalry, you see—the thought of you beating up a woman must have made him go temporarily berserk."

"To tell you the truth, I'm a little surprised a cop would join a men's group," Howie mentioned.

"Oh, no, no, no, don't say that!" Misha objected. "Cops are people who are deeply attracted to the warrior path. Sometimes they don't even know it consciously, but that's why they join the force—the good ones anyway. It's a certain vision of what it means to be a man. An archetype, don't you see? To strap a gun on your waist and go out into the world to fight for justice."

"Like the knights of old," Denny added.

"Lou is definitely our resident knight of old. He joined us, what?—six or seven years ago now. He came looking for answers, a new definition of what it means to be a modern man. He was tired of the old answers, all that macho posing and bashing of horns," Misha said, smiling earnestly. "There's no need for men to compete, you know. We need to cooperate, and forge a new paradigm of brotherhood."

"I'm still going to smash his face in the first chance I get," Howie mentioned.

Misha nodded wisely, pursuing his lips. "You know, maybe that's a good idea. A man has to honor his anger, after all. And frankly, I think Lou could use a fist in the face to wake up to himself. Don't you think so, Denny?"

"Oh, absolutely. You know, the Zen masters in Japan often used to beat their students. Sometimes it's that element of shock that's just what's needed to bring us to a satori, that big hot flash of understanding."

"Sort of like the sound of one hand clapping," Howie agreed. "Only in this case, it's one hand coming swiftly through the air."

While they were talking, two other men arrived. Howie was introduced to Zor McCarthy, "*the* solar architect" Denny proclaimed, an elfish-looking man with a narrow face, bright eyes, and long dark blond hair in a ponytail. Next came Shepherd Plum, a gaunt, tall man of indeterminate age and sexuality. Shep (as everyone seemed to call him) looked like a vampire to Howie; decadent, refined, pale-complexioned, with dark circles under his eyes.

"Lou's not coming," Shep said. His voice was strangely low, a basso profundo. "I saw him this afternoon in town. He was running around looking stressed to the max. I'm not sure what's going on with him, but he said he's going to be busy tonight."

"Too bad!" Misha said, frowning. "Chuck isn't coming either— he phoned a little while ago. Well, let's get under way . . ."

Shep, Denny, Zor, and Howie arranged themselves on a gathering of sofas near the fireplace, a platter of banana bread on the coffee table nearby, while Misha stepped into the kitchen to make a big pot of tea. When he returned, the session began.

"Well, Moon Deer, I was hoping you'd start tonight, tell us a bit of what you're going through right now," Misha said warmly. "I understand from Denny that you're having wu . . . wu . . . woman troubles." Misha paused, he took a deep breath, then he resumed: "My God, we all know what *that's* like, don't we? To get the shaft, the pain of rejection! I want you to know, Moon Deer, you're not alone—all of us in this room have experienced this, haven't we? We deeply empathize."

"Misha, don't you think woman rejection is the *real* start of a warrior's journey?" Denny asked, before Howie himself could respond to the problem of his own love life. Hell, he'd just had a little tiff with his girlfriend and the pain of rejection wasn't all *that* bad. "In a sense, Mother has to slam the door before the child can start on the long process of becoming a man," Denny went on. "I remember my first divorce. . . ."

Howie was starting to think he wouldn't have to bare his male soul after all; with this group, the problem was more how to get a word in. But then Misha interrupted.

"Denny!" he gently chided. "Let's let Moon Deer talk."

Howie had been dreading this moment. Luckily, he was saved again, at least temporarily. Shepherd Plum raised his hand and gave everyone a wounded look. "Look, *I* have something I really need to work on tonight," he said sullenly. "And I didn't get to speak last week either."

"Now, Shep, you had the hot-seat three entire evenings in July," Misha said, his patience straining.

"I don't mind if Shep wants to begin," Howie managed to interject. "Honestly, I would rather just listen tonight anyway. Sort of wade into these waters gradually."

"Well, go ahead, then, Shep," Misha agreed reluctantly.

To Howie's embarrassment, Shepherd Plum burst into tears, slobbering like an infant, and proceeded over the next hour to unload the most amazing shitload of woes that Howie had ever heard.

From what Howie could gather, Shep was married to a woman named Krista; they had two children, girls—Lhasa and Veda—but over the past few years, Shep had been involved in a secret cyber-affair with another woman, Ursula, who lived in Dallas. The computer era, it seemed, had opened up a whole new bag of tricks when it came to sex. Howie hoped he had all the facts straight, because they were complicated: in this cyber-affair, Shep (who was forty-two) pretended to be a blond, seventeen-year-old cheerleader named Cathy. For her part, Ursula (who was thirty-six) had posed as a twenty-two-year-old guy, a stud by the name of Frank. With computers, anything was possible, and for a while Frank and Cathy had a hot and perfect cross-gender time of it, enjoying cyber-sex in the backseats of automobiles while their puppet masters, Shep and Ursula, pulled the strings—or rather, punched the keys and moved the mice that made things cook.

This was Phase One of the odd affair, and it lasted for over a year. Phase Two began when Cathy confessed that she was really a forty-two-year-old man; Frank, not to be outdone, admitted that he was in fact a thirty-six-year-old woman. This brought a new dimension to the relationship, a rush of cyber-truth, and the affair continued for a while with their gender roles reverted to normal . . . if there was a normal in any of this. Eventually they had to see each other in the flesh. Ursula left her live-in boyfriend in Texas and moved to New Mexico; she was a nurse, she got herself a job at the local San Geronimo hospital, and the two lovers set about turning cyber-sex into real sex—in their case a difficult transition. After some initial problems of impotence, they decided to resume their original cross-sexual roles: when they met for their clandestine sessions, Shep put on a dress and a blond wig—he became Cathy—and Ursula dressed herself up as Frank. Perfect! It seemed to them both that they had conquered space, time, and gender limitations.

But now there was a crisis: Krista, Shep's real-time wife, had found out about the affair, and she was threatening to leave him.

"She knew about the dress, the wig, *everything*!" Shep wailed. "It was so humiliating! She tried to make me feel like a pervert, like some transvestite, when it's really very simple, don't you think?"

Misha, Zor, and Denny thought it was simple; Howie was not so sure.

"Personally, I think it's very good that this has finally come out into the open," Denny said calmly. "Krista needs to accept you for who you really are, Shep. And most importantly, *you* need to accept yourself for who you are."

"I disagree. I don't think you needed to tell Krista zilch," Zor objected. "It's your life, not hers, and she doesn't own you . . . don't you think so, Moon Deer? If Shep wants to put on a dress and have a cross-sexual encounter, what business is it of hers?"

"Well, she *is* his wife," Howie said cautiously.

"Wait a second! Time out!" Misha called. "There's another issue here—how in the world did Krista find out about this? Did *you* tell her, Shep?"

Shep shook his head and lowered his eyes. "Someone sent Krista a photograph in the mail."

The room fell silent. "Wha . . . wha . . . *why* didn't you tell us this in the bu . . . bu . . . beginning?" Misha asked finally, his stutter returning with a momentary vengeance.

"I don't know, the whole thing has just been so upsetting." Shep buried his face in his hands. "It was a photo of me and Ursula . . . me in my dress and wig. I was so ashamed!"

"The photo came in a letter?"

"Just the photograph by itself, no letter. Krista showed it to me. The postmark was San Geronimo."

Howie had the impression of odd looks being exchanged between Misha, Denny, and Zor.

"Is it blackmail?" Zor wondered. "Do they want anything?"

Shep only shook his head woefully. "I don't know."

"This is entirely unacceptable," Misha said firmly, and for the moment, he did not appear to be such a warm and understanding New Age guy. "But let's leave this now and go on to other things. Moon Deer, I would hate for you to go away from here tonight without dealing with your pain. Why don't you tell us about your breakup, what you're *feeling* right now."

"Misha, I just don't know what I'm going to do about this!" Shep cried, not happy to see the conversation move on to other pains, other problems.

"Shep, I said drop it. We'll deal with this later, okay?" Misha's voice had become cold steel. Shep lowered his eyes and nodded. Howie sensed some currents going on in the room that weren't so nice and friendly. But then Misha became once again all warmth and understanding. "Moon Deer," he said, "won't you share with us?"

The men all turned toward Howie, their eyes shining so full of manly sensitivity that Howie really couldn't say why he suddenly felt a chill, as though he had stepped into a clearing full of cannibals, and he was the main course.

An hour later, Denny walked Howie to his car. The clouds were moving quickly overhead, hiding then revealing the moon. It was a wild night. A warm wind blew, there were sudden flashes of lightning, and a few fat raindrops splashed against the ground with the promise of more to come.

"So what did you think?" Denny asked hopefully. "A great collection of guys, isn't it?"

"Oh, great," said Howie dutifully.

"Wait until you meet Chucky Hildyard—he's just a wonderful human being. And Lou. I know you two got off on the wrong foot, but sometimes that's the best way to start a real friendship. It's like you can cut through all the bullshit and move on to the heart of things. Don't you think?"

Howie smiled enigmatically.

"Look, you really made a big impression on Misha, Moon Deer. He thinks you have true potential."

"He said that?" Howie was surprised. In fact, during the past hour he had meandered, obfuscated, and downright fibbed when talking about his relationship with Aria, revealing very little indeed. He simply did not share these men's compulsion to tell all.

"Misha says you're repressed, obviously. You need to give yourself permission to let your feelings out, Moon Deer. I know it's scary, but you should honor your pain, it's there for a reason. . . . Look, as it happens, this Saturday we're doing a weekend intensive up in the mountains, and Misha's asked me to invite you along. He thinks it could be very important for you, really give you a chance to make some important breakthroughs."

"I'm into breakthroughs," Howie agreed. "But what's a weekend intensive?"

Denny smiled mysteriously. "Oh, it's *everything*. It's the path, the sacred journey that leads to the discovery of our ancient selves. I can't tell you more than that. Or I *could*, but you wouldn't understand yet."

"Denny, I'd need to know a little more about it."

"Well, think of it as a camping trip. We're going to leave early Saturday morning and spend two days climbing San Geronimo Peak. Literally and figuratively, if you see what I'm saying."

"I'm not quite sure I do. A figurative mountain climb?"

"Of course! Life is a metaphor! You climb a mountain, and it can mean nothing . . . or it can mean *everything*, depending on your attitude. You'll have to see for yourself."

This was seeming a little fuzzy to Howie, but then a lot of New Age thinking struck him as fuzzy in the extreme. He settled into his car and was about to turn on the ignition. He peered up at Denny's face through the open window.

"Tell me something, Denny. This blackmail thing with Shep—if it *is* blackmail, that's pretty serious. Who do you think sent that photograph to his wife?"

Denny shrugged impatiently. "Oh, Shep, he always gets involved with these melodramas! He comes from this old San Geronimo family, old money, you know. He's a good guy, don't get me wrong, but sometimes he's awfully self-indulgent!"

"Still, he didn't send that photograph of himself in drag to his wife. Someone's trying to make serious trouble in his life."

Denny sighed. "Well, we'll just have to see. I know it sounds crazy, but with Shep, just about anything's possible."

Howie studied Denny, still trying to penetrate the obscurity that seemed to shroud these men. "There's some bad shit coming down in the men's group, isn't there?"

"What do you mean?"

"First one of your guys, Gary Tripp, gets lost and dies on your weekend intensive. Now someone's sending poison pen letters to Shep's wife. What's going on, Denny?"

Denny squatted so he was at eye level with Howie inside the car. He lowered his voice: "Look, Moon Deer, a men's group is an organic thing, we go through ups and downs just like everybody else. It was a tragedy what happened to Gary, and that's why we're looking for someone to fill his place. There *are* some risks up in those mountains, I won't kid you. But no one ever becomes a warrior without confronting risk. That's just the way it is—risk nothing, gain nothing. As for Shep, like I told you, we'll just have to see if he's making up this whole thing or not. He likes to be the center of attention, and . . . well, he has a rich fantasy life."

"Are you saying Shep's lying about the photograph that was sent to his wife?"

Denny sidestepped the question. "Look, Moon Deer, I'd like to see you in the Warrior Circle, I really would. I think it would be great for your personal growth, and good for us too, frankly. The Circle's gotten awfully inbred the last few years, we could use some fresh blood."

"Fresh blood?" Howie wondered out loud. It seemed an unfortunate choice of words under the circumstances.

"You know what I mean. Fresh ideas. Fresh pain, even. I guess that sounds funny, but if I have to listen one more time to Shep talking about his cyber-affair, I think I'll scream! So you'll join us this weekend, won't you?"

"Well, it depends," Howie told him. "Can I let you know in the next day or so?"

"Of course. But it depends on what?"

"On whether I find Aria Waldman or not."

10

Aria Waldman lived in a rented A-frame house on a winding road in the foothills east of town. The place was originally the vacation home of a Texas family, built ten years earlier from some platonic blueprint of vacation cabins in mountain resorts everywhere, from Lake Tahoe to Maine. There were severely sloping roofs, lots of windows, and a redwood deck; architecture that was once the latest word in American upward mobility, but cheaply constructed and already starting to fall apart. Aria had always made fun of the place, but the rent was reasonable and she liked the location. The house stood on a steeply wooded slope at an altitude of nearly eight thousand feet; she had a magnificent view of the San Geronimo valley spread out before her, and the vast San Geronimo Wilderness area behind her, thousands of acres of forests, mountains, and lakes.

After leaving Hollyhock Terrace, Howie drove up Aria's mountain road with his creaky windshield wiper parting the curtain of water that had once again begun to pour from the night sky. He had no precise reason for coming here; he was simply drawn to Aria's habitat. His evening with the men's group had left him restless and dissatisfied. He had found out very little from them, nothing to shed any light on Aria's strange disappearance. At best, male bonding had no great interest for him; female bonding was Howie's thing, and he was feeling some serious angst on that score.

He pulled up next to the garage at the rear of Aria's house just as a flash of lightning illuminated the A-frame and the forest behind it, making everything look for an instant like a photographic negative, reversing white for black. There was no car in the drive-way. When the lightning subsided, there was nothing but darkness and rain and trees shaking in the wind. Howie made a dash up the outside stairs to the redwood deck. He knocked on the front door for good form, but as he expected, there was no answer. After a decent wait, he found Aria's hide-a-key beneath a potted geranium on the deck—not a creative hiding spot, but people in rural New Mexico didn't worry much about burglary. A moment later Howie stepped inside, out of the rain.

The living room was dark, but Howie sensed wrongness immediately. He ran his hand over the wall, found the light switch, and all the wrongness sprang brightly into view. The room had been trashed. Chairs were overturned, the coffee table was on its side, magazines and books were scattered on the floor. Howie moved cautiously into the kitchen–dining-room area where the destruction continued: more overturned chairs, pots and pans and cans of food pulled from cabinets. The refrigerator door had been left open with a trail of produce spilling out onto the linoleum, like the innards of some beast.

Howie stood amid the rubble, wondering what it could mean. The main bedroom was an upstairs loft, an alpine balcony overlooking the living room below. He walked up the stairs, fearful of what he would find. Aria's clothes were everywhere, yanked from drawers and hangers in the closet. There were clothes that Howie recognized, jeans and sweaters and dresses from past moments of their affair. Clothes that Howie had at various times unzipped, unbuttoned, and undressed from her body; clothes that now looked somehow dead and violated. The mattress had been pulled from the box spring and was sagging against the wall. In the upstairs bathroom there was more mayhem still—vials of pills and creams and dental paraphernalia in the sink, an upset laundry hamper, a shredded box of tampons on the floor. Howie had never seen a home reduced to such a frenzy of destruction.

He had to stop for a moment just to breathe. Ever since he had discovered Aria's abandoned Jeep, he had tried to tell himself that there must be some innocent explanation; now, with the trashing of her house, the possibility of innocence was gone forever. He returned downstairs into the living room and on through to the spare bedroom that Aria used as a home office. Here there were papers on the floor, drawers yanked from the desk, an upturned wastebasket, a blizzard of stamps and envelopes and paper clips scattered everywhere. But there was no sign of Aria, nor the object he was hoping to find: her home computer, a small but expensive laptop she had bought as a present to herself last Christmas. Aria belonged to a new class whose most intimate daily dealings, personal and professional, might be found on her hard drive; Howie very much wished to learn these secrets. He spent the next three minutes searching through the rubble for the computer. It wasn't there.

At the end of all his searching, he felt an overwhelming emptiness. It was hard to believe that this was the same snug and orderly house where he had spent so many evenings: candles lit, soft music on the stereo, the delicate smell of food drifting from the oven. And, of course, Aria, dressed or undressed (she had a nonchalant way of walking around stark naked), carrying wine and glasses up the steep stairway to heaven, as Howie jokingly called her bedroom loft. Howie retraced his steps, turning off the lights in each room. He stood in the darkness of the high-ceilinged living room remembering happier times that he had spent here. This was when he noticed a red light blinking on the Formica counter that separated the living room from the kitchen area. It was Aria's answering machine. Howie walked over to it and pressed the play button. There were eight messages on the tape. Six had come from Howie himself. He stood and listened to his own voice through the tiny speaker. His voice sounded horribly dorky, he thought, changing in tone from casual to increasingly anxious as the day had progressed.

Message number three was from Heather Winter, at 11:43 A.M: "Hey, Aria, it's Heather. Look, I just got a call from Howie Moon Deer. He seems to be worried about you. Don't you *hate* that, the way men act like they own you? The minute you're off doing something on your own, they get that uptight proprietorial tone. Anyway, I thought I'd give you a call and see what's up. I'm meeting him at the New Wave for lunch—the last thing I'm in the mood for today, but he sounded so pathetic on the phone, it was hard to say no. So give me a call. I'll be in the office until about five."

Howie steamed as he listened to this. *Uptight proprietorial tone indeed!* But message number four was more disturbing still, left at 12:23 P.M. It was a man. Apparently a man who knew Aria so well he did not feel it necessary to leave his name. The message was short, but intimate:

"Hey, kitten, it's me. . . . Hey, where the hell *are* you? Pick up, if you're there, will you . . . look, I gotta run. Give me a call when you can. *Ciao,* pussycat."

Howie was stunned. He played the message several times, his heart sinking with each repetition. *Hey, kitten, it's me.* What sort of creep talked to a woman like that these days? *Ciao, pussycat!* Along with the words, there was a tone of sexual familiarity, the insinuating banter of lovers. The whole structure of Howie's life, all that he had assumed to be true, was suddenly shaken. *Pussycat, indeed!* Could there be any doubt about it? Aria had been cheating on him! He was so shocked, he had to sit down for a moment on the floor. Was this the real reason Aria was always so busy, particularly at night? If so, it seemed to him desperately unfair. He had tried so hard to make their relationship work, but apparently he had been playing against a stacked deck: she had clearly not been making any serious effort in return. Howie was dizzy with anger. He stood up and played the message one more time, listening carefully to the man's voice. He was certain he was right: this was a lover calling, no casual acquaintance. Not only that, the voice was somehow familiar, though he could not quite place it.

Howie needed fresh air. He relocked the front door behind him and slinked out into the night feeling like a roadkill. How could he have been so stupid? He hadn't suspected a thing! Outside, the rain had slowed to a wet drizzle. The night was densely black and lonely, a smell in the air of gusty wind and fetid leaves. Howie made his way slowly down from the deck to the lower level, where he had left his car. Heavy with defeat, he slid into his MG and started up the engine. He was thinking of Aria so hard that he had half swung around in the driveway before he realized he hadn't turned on his headlights. He pulled the knob, and two beams of white light ignited the nearby forest. He was so startled, he nearly screamed.

A dozen feet away, peering at him through the branches of a tree, he saw a face frozen in the headlights. It was an odd face, unfamiliar. It took Howie a moment to register the details: a man in his late forties or fifties. A big face, not handsome, but flabby, somewhat bovine. A secretive face that was as startled to be seen as Howie was to see it, the heavy mouth hanging open in surprise. The man's skin appeared sickly, washed-out in the unflattering glare of the headlights. Howie absorbed all these impressions during a single second of stunned time as he and the man stared at one another in mutual astonishment. Then the stranger seemed to free himself from the spell that was holding him in place. He turned and scrambled up the steep hill, heading deeper into the woods.

It all happened so quickly, it might have been a dream, except for the heavy sound of footsteps in the underbrush. Howie scrambled out of his car. "Hey!" he shouted. "Come back here!"

Howie left his headlights on and rushed up the hill into the wet forest after the retreating figure. It wasn't easy going. The ground was slick, an obstacle course of fallen limbs and thick growth. He made his way through a tangle of aspen, piñon, and scrub oak that tore at his hands and legs as he climbed. The light through the trees was confusing him the farther he got from his car, ghostly beams and deep shadows crisscrossing the woods. He could see very little, but he ran after the sound of footsteps ahead of him. A branch slapped him hard in the face; he tripped, picked himself up, and kept going up the incline. Just when he thought he was getting nowhere, he saw the outline of a figure directly ahead of him. The man was a giant, towering above him—but, of course, he had the higher ground. The stranger had stopped and was waiting in ambush.

All of Howie's adrenaline was pumping hard. "I got you!" he shouted. It was a bold taunt, but premature. With a grunt, the man raised a muddy tennis shoe and kicked violently against Howie's chest. Howie saw the shoe coming and managed to grab hold of it with both hands. He yanked hard, and tried to pull the giant's leg out from under him. But the steep terrain was against Howie. The shoe he was pulling suddenly came off in his hands, and Howie felt himself falling foolishly backward. He reached out wildly trying to find some part of the man that he could hold on to; for a second he seemed to have caught hold of a piece of clothing, but then the cloth gave and Howie tumbled backward down the hill. He rolled a dozen feet and came to a hard stop against the trunk of a fir tree. Howie lay gasping in pain, scratched and bloody and wet. *I'm really not cut out for a life of violence,* he thought wearily as he heard heavy footsteps disappearing into the woods.

He sat up slowly, entrapped in a world of pain. He felt so utterly battered, both emotionally and physically, that it came to him only gradually that his efforts had not been completely in vain. For he held in his lap two tangible trophies of the chase: a huge muddy tennis shoe, the largest tennis shoe he had ever seen. And a small black carrying case, whose strap had somehow become entangled around his wrist. The case was familiar to Howie. It contained Aria's laptop computer.

11

It was past one in the morning when Howie pulled into Jack's driveway. He was wet, muddy and bruised, and triumphant. For the moment, testosterone had cleared his soul of Aria's betrayal, like Liquid-Plumr flushing out clogged pipes. Real pain seemed a welcome relief after the more complex black hole of suddenly finding oneself cuckolded.

The Wilder house lay sleeping in the restless shadows of a huge old cottonwood tree. A half-moon had broken through the clouds above San Geronimo Peak, throwing a silvery light on the vegetable garden. Howie climbed out of his car and limped along the path toward the house, carrying his retrieved booty, a soggy tennis shoe in one hand and Aria's laptop in the other. Katya was the first to hear his footsteps on the path, and she let out a friendly bark from somewhere inside the house. Howie called up to a second-floor window: "Hey, Jack, it's me! Wake up!" When there was no response, he picked up a pebble from the path and threw it against the upstairs window. Unfortunately, he threw too hard. There was a tinkle of broken glass. When a guy was in a macho mood, it was hard to rein in his stallions.

"What the hell is going on down there?" he heard Jack shout angrily.

"It's me. Howie. I've got to speak to you. Sorry about the window."

The lights went on in the upstairs bedroom, an indication that Emma was stirring as well. Katya barked more excitedly, sensing something out of the ordinary. Howie waited by the back porch.

He was strangely exhilarated, pumped full of life, all his senses tingling. The night was beautiful, and he was alive. He kept reliving the fight in his mind, seeing the foot coming at his chest, remembering the way he had grabbed at the tennis shoe. He knew now exactly what he should have done. He should have reached higher and grabbed the man's ankle, not his shoe. Still, he hadn't done too badly. Howie couldn't help but feel a little wonderfully heroic about his brawl, now that it was over.

Emma turned on the porch light, opened the back door, and gaped at Howie in astonishment.

"Howie!" she cried. "Did you crash your car?"

"Just a small wrestling match with a giant," he told her modestly. "Sorry about the window," he said again.

Jack appeared in the kitchen wearing a gaudy blue and green silk dressing gown that made him look like a Chinese emperor.

"What's this about a car crash?" he growled. "Is Howie hurt?"

"He's bleeding in a few places," Emma answered. "But I sense he'll live."

Howie liked Emma Wilder. She was an attractive, down-to-earth woman in her early fifties. A bit feline, a mama cat—that seemed to suit her, Howie always thought. All in all, there was something very comfortable and nice about Emma Wilder, an intelligent woman who was entirely natural. Living in New Mexico, she had gradually lost her city ways; she had stopped wearing makeup, she rarely went to the hairdresser, she dressed in casual country clothes. The nicest thing about being married to a blind man, she always said, was that she didn't have to worry about her appearance anymore.

"Well, tell us! For chrissake, what happened, Howie?" Jack was asking impatiently.

"Jack, he's soaking wet . . . let him change first. Howie, you can use the downstairs bathroom to get out of those clothes. I'll give you one of Jack's old robes to wear while I put your things in the dryer. . . ."

"Emma, he's a big boy. Stop babying him."

"You're all big boys," Emma assured Jack. "And if some woman wasn't there to baby you, God knows how you'd survive!"

Howie sensed he could write a dissertation about what Emma had just said, the gender roles implied. But not right now. After hearing the gory details of Shepherd Plum's cross-sexual cyber-

affair, there seemed something frankly reassuring about a traditional marriage. Jack, the old bear, shuffled toward the stove.

"I'll put on coffee," he grumped. "Emma, you'd better get a
broom and dustpan and clean up that broken glass upstairs before
the cats cut their feet . . . Howie, that damn bit of foolishness is
coming out of your salary!"

"I'll get it fixed tomorrow," Howie promised. He took a quick
shower, tossing his muddy clothes outside the bathroom door and
receiving an old terry cloth robe in return. He found a tube of first-
aid ointment and a box of Band-Aids in the medicine cabinet and
did his best to doctor the worst of his most recent round of abra-
sions. Fortunately, none of the cuts was deep.

He stepped out of the downstairs bathroom to find a huge turkey
sandwich and a mug of black coffee waiting for him on the kitchen
table. The Wilder kitchen was a low, cluttered room with crowded
shelves and pots and pans hanging on hooks from the vigas overhead—the natural wooden beams that hold up ceilings in traditional adobe homes. The kitchen had a kiva fireplace at one end,
an ancient (but very workable) gas stove, a refrigerator that
hummed and gurgled, and a heavy round oak table that was cluttered with plants and spices growing in various pots. Howie sat
down at the table and tore into the turkey sandwich. He always felt
strangely peaceful in Jack and Emma's kitchen, like he was a kid
visiting mythical grandparents that he had never actually had.

"All right, now, tell us what happened," Jack insisted, his patience at an end.

"The guy was a monster, Jack. He must have been six foot six.
He had this strange pale face. My adrenaline was really pumping.
And yet, you know, it was wonderful in a way to pit myself against
a real adversary rather than the usual psychological shadowboxing
I generally do."

"Howie, I'm going to slug you myself in a minute," Jack interrupted. "It's nearly two in the morning, and I would like to get
back to bed, thank you. So start from the beginning, please, and
stop wasting my time."

Howie popped a last bite of sandwich into his mouth and then
launched forth on a detailed account of his afternoon and evening,
starting with his conversation with Heather Winter at the New
Wave. He told all: How he had found his fierce masculinity at the
Wednesday night men's group meeting. How he had lost this

aforementioned fierceness on hearing the disturbingly intimate *ciao, pussycat* message on Aria's answering machine. And finally, manhood regained—his epic wrestling match with the giant on the hillside behind Aria's A-frame house.

While Howie spoke, Katya lay stretched out under the table nearby, her long ears perked forward, praying for any falling crumbs from the table. From the porch came the sound of Howie's wet clothes being tossed in the dryer. And on the table rested the two items that Howie had managed to keep as proof of his David-Goliath encounter: Aria's laptop in its black leather carrying case, and the tennis shoe, a muddy old Nike with the laces dangling, a curled toe, and a defeated air.

Jack sat at the kitchen table listening intently, his expression blank, his eyes obscured by his dark glasses. Emma sat next to Jack, with more sympathy showing on her face. Howie spoke for nearly an hour, and then he waited for Jack's response. At the end, he felt like a patient who has blurted out everything to his doctor, all the symptoms of a terrible disease; now he wanted a prognosis. Tell me what it means, Doc? He waited for Jack to put together the pieces of the puzzle. But Jack just sat there and looked as stumped as Howie.

"So? What do you think?" Howie prodded.

Jack shook his head. "What do I think? Christ, Howie—you've certainly managed to get yourself into a mess!"

"The man you fought with on the hill—you've never seen him before?" Emma asked with kindly concern.

"Never. I don't have a clue who he was. I must have surprised him while he was trashing Aria's house."

"I wonder if he found what he was looking for?" Jack asked vaguely.

"Well, he took her laptop," Howie said. "He wanted that, obviously."

"Perhaps," said Jack. "But we can't assume it was the main object of his visit." He started banging a coffee spoon softly against the wooden table. "This men's group," he said finally. "Do you think they're on the level?"

The question surprised Howie. "Sure, why not? But it depends on what kind of level you mean. There's a lot of psychobabble that goes on in an arty little town like San Geronimo. Men's groups, women's groups, crystal healing, psychic surgery. There are a lot of wounded souls out there, Jack, all of them looking for big answers. Of course, it's the Anglos mostly who are into the self-help thing—for one, they've bought the whole advertising campaign, that human beings are supposed to be fabulously happy and healthy, just like a toothpaste commercial on TV. The Spanish and the Indians have a more mature understanding of what life is really about, if you will forgive me for saying so. And anyway, they're working too hard, and they don't have enough money to pay for gurus. If they have problems they just drink themselves to death."

"Yes, yes. But what about this Warrior Circle? What's your gut feeling about them?"

"Well, they obviously believe in what they're doing, finding their true male identity, and all that. Who knows—maybe we should all be spending our lives looking for our inner-warrior. But there's something about them that worries me. I can't quite put my finger on it."

"Put your finger on it, Howie."

Howie tried. "It was just a vibe in the air, it made me uncomfortable. Maybe they have too much money."

"You think truth seekers need to be poor?"

"No, just the opposite. When you're poor, God knows, there's not much time to seek anything more than your next meal. But these guys . . ."

Howie's voice trailed off. He wanted to be fair. He didn't like them. They were the sort of people he would avoid like the plague in his own social whirl because they weren't amusing and he found their philosophy self-serious and second-rate. But this still didn't account for the chill he had felt in their presence.

"I don't know," Howie said finally. "You would have had to be there, Jack. On the surface, they all pretend to be so full of love and understanding, they talk to one another in these very gentle voices. But it seemed totally phony. I forgot to tell you—Shepherd Plum, the guy who looks like a vampire, someone sent a photograph of him in drag to his wife. It doesn't appear to be blackmail so much as someone trying to cause trouble. But the thing is, I had a sense that *any* of the other guys could have done it."

"Who do you *think* did it?"

"I have no idea. Maybe it was the crazy sheriff, or the real estate agent I haven't met yet. But you asked me what I felt, and that's it. They make their New Age goo-goo eyes at you, but you just know they'd stab you in the back in an instant."

"Howie, let me get you a bowl of soup," Emma suggested, fearing he wasn't up to this lengthy cross-examination in his battered condition.

"Emma, stop it! Howie hasn't stopped eating since he came in the door," Jack said curtly to his wife. "He can have soup later. *After* we find out what's so special about Aria Waldman's laptop computer."

Emma returned to bed, even Katya fell asleep under the kitchen table, leaving Jack sitting impatiently by himself waiting for the results. Jack had absolutely no rapport with the computer age. He was of the wrong generation; back in his cop days, he had had several assistants to take care of his cyber needs. Tonight it was irritating for him to wait on a kid who seemed to be tap, tap, tapping away on a keyboard forever with no appreciable results.

"Aha!" Howie said meditatively from time to time.

"Aha, what?" Jack requested. "What have you found?"

"Not much yet. I'm trying to figure out her password. Aria has WordPerfect. It's an antique as far as software goes. DOS, you know. But I still can't get in without a password."

"DOS! Sounds like a form of syphilis," Jack sighed.

"Well, she has Windows too—that's how she sends e-mail, but there's not much in there. Let me just try something. . . ."

When there were no immediate results, Jack settled more deeply into his chair, extending his legs in front of him, his grisly gray beard resting on his chest. Time passed in silence as Howie tried to find the key to Aria's private cyber world. It was absorbing work, and Howie did not realize Jack was asleep until a small snort escaped his nostrils. Katya was snoring as well from her position on the floor, joining her master in a symphony of deep sleep.

Howie stared at the screen in frustration, caught in a great electronic nowhere, unable to get beyond the C-prompt. He tried hundreds of possible passwords, from Aria's birthday (9/25/69) to her favorite chocolate, Godiva. He typed in words of things she liked: wine, Sundays, *Casablanca,* saxophones, jazz, the Beatles, sex, Tolstoy, *sushi*, Miles Davis, cunnilingus, Greta Garbo, and many other possibilities. He tried countries she had told him she wanted to visit someday—Greece, Spain, Thailand, New Zealand, Tibet.

He tried anagrams of her name spelled in different ways and anything else he could think of too. But the response was always the same: "Bad Command or File Name." In short, no access.

Then around four o'clock in the morning, he typed in his own name after the C-prompt: *Howie.* Suddenly there was a chatter of information, a flare of graphics, and he was inside her files. He had penetrated her security. *He* was the password! It gave Howie a moment of serious pause. In the past twenty-four hours he had come to realize that he did not know Aria Waldman very well. Yet he must have meant something to her, after all.

As Howie brought up the files from her hard drive, he had a disturbing sense that he had been granted access to a hidden recess of her brain. It was a violation of her privacy, of course, and he felt suitably embarrassed. Nevertheless, he kept reading until dawn touched the panes of the kitchen window with a cold, mystic gray. He read the terrible words that danced in front of him on the blue screen, and by the time the sun rose above San Geronimo Peak, he had a pretty fair idea why someone might wish Aria Waldman to vanish forever.

12

Howie allowed himself to be kissed awake. It was a long gorgeous kiss. This is more like it, he thought dreamily. Aria had returned, and everything was all right again between them.

Such a sweet, lingering kiss! But he didn't remember Aria having whiskers on her mouth.

"Yaw!" he cried, opening his eyes. Katya was licking him with her long tongue, wagging her tail hopefully.

"You are a disgusting dog!" he told her, sitting up, wiping his mouth with the back of his hand. But he regretted his words when he saw the rejected look in her brown doggy eyes. He had to scratch behind Katya's velvety ears until she cheered up again. The wounded of the world needed to stick together. "Good doggie!" he said to make amends. "Lucky, lucky doggie—you don't have to worry about romantic disappointments. You're fixed!"

"I'm sure that could be arranged for you too, Howie. If you're really so ready to pack in your libido."

It was Jack, seated in a dark corner of the living room near the grandfather clock. Jack could be very quiet when he wanted to be, and Howie hadn't seen him. Howie was stretched out on the couch, unable to remember when he had transported himself here from the kitchen. He felt tired and old and used up. No wonder no one wanted to kiss him except a dog. He sat up painfully and yawned. Morning light was streaming in the living room window, an assault on his eyes.

"I feel awful," he said. "What time is it?"

"Nearly nine-thirty. Emma's already left for work. I'll get you some coffee. Then you can tell me what you found on the computer."

Howie followed Jack into the kitchen and settled himself back at the round oak table with a mug of coffee. The aroma was deep and expensive, for Jack was a true coffee snob; he had beans mailed to him each month from a little Italian store in the North-beach section of San Francisco.

"Well, there was a lot of stuff in her hard drive," Howie began. "Notes for research, ideas she's been mulling over for various articles, e-mail. It's going to take a while to read everything carefully. Last night I concentrated mostly on what she's been up to this summer."

"The files are dated?"

"Naturally. Whenever you save a computer file, it gets assigned a date, even a time of day—as long as you have the day and time installed correctly in your setup, of course."

"Go on."

"Well, like I say, there was a lot of research for her work. Gangs in the schools, some local highway project where most of the money seems to be ending up in the contractor's pocket, stuff like that. But Aria's main interest the past few months has been the proposed Chamisa Mall on the south side of town. She's gathered a lot of material about it. It's supposed to be a huge deal, the very first covered shopping mall in San Geronimo, complete with a new hotel, a conference center, and a parking lot for five thousand cars. The modern world seems about to arrive on our rural New Mexican doorstep. The local environmental groups are dead set against it, of course. There's been talk about Chamisa Mall for a few years, but it looks like they'll actually break ground this summer."

"I remember Emma reading to me about this," Jack said. "But refresh my memory. Who's actually building this thing?"

"The financing comes from a California outfit that calls itself—get this, Jack—Karma Konstruction with a K. Very cute. But cute or not, it's serious out-of-state money, about $40 million worth. And guess who their point man is here in San Geronimo?"

"Howie, you woke me up in the middle of the night, and I didn't get much sleep, either. I don't feel like guessing."

"It's Chuck Hildyard, the warrior who couldn't make the meeting last night. He's a real estate agent, as you'll remember. This men's group has a strange way of popping up everywhere, don't you think?"

"Aria was investigating him?"

"You bet. She's been digging deep into the whole Chamisa Mall deal. There's been a series of delays, getting the necessary permits from the town council, environmental impact studies that needed to be done, that sort of thing. But the big thing that was holding up the project was securing the necessary water rights. All politics in the Southwest come down to water eventually—man is greedy, man wants to build, but Mother Nature has the last word after all. As I'm sure you know, there's been a moratorium in San Geronimo on new commercial water hookups for two years while a bunch of supposed experts try to figure out how much water we actually have in our underground aquifers. But despite the moratorium, the San Geronimo Water Board is apparently about to issue an exemption for Karma Konstruction so they can start building. . . . Now, here's where it starts to get interesting. According to Aria, Chuck Hildyard slipped a $20,000 dollar bribe to Joe Corazon, the head of the water board, so he'd expedite matters. Aria also suspects that the palms of our town mayor have been similarly greased, though not quite so handsomely. The mayor's brother, who owns a fleet of bulldozers, has been promised the job of preparing the site, and no one in the town council is going to walk away with entirely empty pockets."

"And Aria was about to expose all this in the *Post*?"

"Absolutely. She was still gathering proof, of course. This will be a huge story when it breaks, and she knew she'd have to back up every word."

"How far away was she from getting her story in print?"

Howie shrugged. "I can't tell. It seems to me that a lot of what she says is speculation, but she may have some proof that I don't know about. Now, guess who happens to be the president of Karma Konstruction, this California corporation that wants to bless our small community with a shopping mall?"

"Misha Ballantine," Jack answered quickly.

Howie blinked. "You got that too easily. It must have been the word karma that tipped you off."

"It was more the fact that Ballantine commutes to California. Are all the men involved?"

"Yep, the entire Warrior Circle. According to Aria, Misha is the president, Chuck Hildyard the treasurer, Denny Hirsch the secretary, and the board of directors consists of Zor McCarthy, Shepherd Plum, Louis Snider, and Gary Tripp. Of course Gary's probably building shopping malls in heaven right now, so he may not share in this particular pie after all. The way I see it, our male warriors decided to honor their greed and manifest some serious wealth. This is a very New Age concept—you can be rich if only you give yourself permission to *feel* rich inside. It's hard to feel manly these days in America unless you have a vault load of cash, so you'll be glad to know, Jack, that it's only your inner doubt and psychic negativity that's keeping you from becoming the next Bill Gates."

"I'll keep that in mind," Jack assured him. "Now, what else did you find out from Aria's laptop?"

"There's trouble in our male-bonding paradise, I'm afraid. A big falling out. Apparently the prospect of so much money has created some divisions among our warriors."

"I see. And how did Aria learn all this?"

"I'll get to that in a minute. She's been keeping separate files on each of the seven men, by the way, including Gary Tripp—though his particular file hasn't been updated for a while. They're quite a bunch of warriors. Do you want to hear about them?"

"Yes, yes. Just tell me, Howie."

Howie made himself some toast and scrambled eggs while he told Jack what he had read. Aria hadn't managed to discover the precise inner workings of Karma Konstruction, for instance, if the men all had equal investments and shared equally in the profits, but it did appear to be a cooperative effort to a remarkable degree. Karma had supplied the money to Gary Tripp to start his Hemperware business, and also to Zor McCarthy, who designed and built solar homes on spec and sold them at a profit. According to Aria, Karma had also financed Lou Snider's run for sheriff three years ago, and it must have been nice for the boys to have the law on their side. The first hint of trouble began when Denny Hirsch wanted to use some of the group money to start a new restaurant, a sister café to the Blue Mesa, but Shep and Misha were both against the idea, fearing that new restaurants often failed and this could be a bad investment. Denny sulked for a month afterward. Then Shep and Chuck Hildyard wanted to start a fancy spa for men, a New Age retreat up in the mountains on an old thousand-acre ranch that was for sale—there could be a huge profit in such an undertaking, they argued. But Misha, Zor, Denny, Lou, and Gary all nixed this idea quickly. Too expensive to get started, they said, and anyway they were overextended financially with the Chamisa Mall project in the works.

First there was quibbling over money, then there was betrayal: One afternoon Shep came home unexpectedly and found his wife, Krista, in bed with Gary Tripp. Gary apologized like crazy; his morals, he said, had been forged back in the sixties during his rock 'n' roll days. What could he say? He was a stray dog, that's all, who needed to seduce every female in the neighborhood. So Shep should be understanding, not take it personally just because he had screwed his wife. Unfortunately, Shep *did* take it personally, and for several weeks it seemed if the Warrior Circle were to continue, one of them would have to resign. Eventually Misha brought about a reconciliation between the two men during a heavy weekend intensive, a men's group camping trip in the desert, but it was never quite the same again between Gary and Shep.

Then there was more serious trouble. Misha found out that Gary was stealing, cooking the books on his Hemperware venture in order to keep more than his share of the profits. This was a blow against the very communal fabric of the Warrior Circle, the philosophy of true brotherhood. Aria was not certain how Misha found out about Gary's betrayal, but the Wednesday-night meeting that week was apparently full of storm and high drama. At first Gary denied everything, then he collapsed weeping on the floor, begging for forgiveness and, most of all, a second chance. He had unresolved problems from his childhood, he claimed. Old insecurities that caused him to grab for more than his fair share in life. Obviously he needed to do more work on himself. But with some love and understanding from his brothers, he promised never, never to do it again.

A vote was taken, for the Warrior Circle was a democracy in which a consensus was necessary for any action. Everyone voted to give Gary a second chance except Shep, who had still not entirely forgiven Gary for the episode with his wife. Misha took Shep aside and talked to him almost an hour. Finally Shep and Misha came back into the room, and another vote was taken. This time it was unanimous, Gary was back in the Circle. There was a lot of hugging and weeping—even Shep wept, embraced Gary, and let go of his anger. But it was a week later that Gary disappeared on the camping trip to Bear Lake. Aria suspected, of course, that this was no accident at all, that Gary had been killed by either Misha or Shep. She had no proof, but she believed these men were certainly capable of murder and that the so-called disappearance after such a violent quarrel was far too suspicious to accept on face value.

"Anyway, this is just a synopsis," Howie said. "Aria's obviously been working on this for months, and there are hundreds of pages of notes, a lot I haven't read yet."

Jack was nodding. "Interesting . . . but now let's cut to the chase, Howie. Who was Aria's informant? She couldn't possibly have learned all these details unless someone inside the Circle has been feeding her secrets."

Howie's face lost all expression. "It's the sad-eyed Sheriff Snider."

"Lou Snider? *He* was Aria's informant?" It was difficult to surprise Jack Wilder, but he seemed surprised now. "But why? Why should he tell her all this?"

"Because guys say a lot of things when they're lying in bed with a woman. Postcoital indiscretion, you know. You'd think a sheriff would be more careful, but of course Aria's a smart lady and she spent six months pumping him. Pumping a lot of things, I guess. I finally recognized that Sheriff Snider was the *ciao-pussycat* voice I heard on her answering machine. Unfortunately, *he* was the pussycat in this particular relationship. She mined him pretty good, slowly and carefully, over a long period of time, like a prospector chipping away methodically at a promising vein of ore. And he went along with it because he had the hots for her."

Jack was silent for some time. "I'm sorry, Howie," he said finally. "This can't have been pleasant news for you to read last night."

Howie tried to pass it off with an ironic shrug. But he knew the gesture was wasted on Jack, and fraudulent as well.

"Well, yes, it definitely sucks," he admitted. "I feel like some kind of slug squashed on the bottom of someone's shoe. But I take consolation from the fact that it wasn't really personal. I think Aria honestly preferred me. But all those evenings when she wasn't seeing me, she was seeing the sheriff. They also had quite a thrilling e-mail correspondence back and forth, some of it fairly randy. I'm a little sorry for Snider, actually—an older guy like that, a sexy younger woman. He fell for her hard, got involved big time. But for Aria, it was only business, I think. She was after the story of her life and ready to do whatever was necessary to get it. It's funny, Jack. I always suspected that Aria was the sort of woman who cared more for her career than romance, but I never realized just how ruthless she . . . *was*. You notice I'm speaking about her in the past tense."

"I notice," said Jack.

"Well, here's my theory. I think Aria was poking her nose into something very big, finding out a lot more than she should know about a $40 million real estate deal and a corrupt water board and the mayor and the town council, all of them receiving hefty bribes. So she was abducted and probably killed to keep her from exposing all this on the front page of the newspaper. As for my big one-shoed stranger last night—no wonder he wanted her laptop! I bet he was hoping to destroy all her notes about Chamisa Mall."

"And Sheriff Snider?" Jack asked. "What was he doing at Aria's Jeep on Wednesday morning?"

Howie shrugged. "I don't know. Offhand, I don't think he was the one who made her disappear. Why would he return to the scene of the crime?"

"Perhaps to pick up something he had dropped earlier by accident?" Jack suggested. "His gun, for instance?"

"But you told me it was an old gun, Jack, almost an antique. Wouldn't a cop have something newer, fancier?"

"Not necessarily. Not if he wanted to use a gun that wouldn't link him to the crime."

Howie rubbed his temples with both palms, trying hard to concentrate. "I think maybe one of the guys in the men's group found out about Aria and Lou and decided that Aria was a liability that needed to be disposed of. Denny could have done it easily. He lives just a few minutes away. I don't pretend to know exactly how he arranged it, but if he had flagged her down that night, she would have stopped. She knew him, and wouldn't have been afraid. Until it was too late."

"But what about Joe Corazon at the water board? Or the mayor, or anyone on the town council?" Jack asked. "Or, in fact, anyone who has an economic stake in seeing Chamisa Mall get built? You don't want to limit your suspects prematurely, Howie."

Howie shook his head bleakly. "I guess Aria was making herself a whole shitload of enemies, wasn't she? You know, Jack, I wish I could decide if she was some kind of noble crusader, or just a very ruthless lady who got carried away by her own ambition."

Jack and Howie sat quietly for a few minutes, both of them pondering different possibilities.

"Well," said Jack after a while. "This is all speculation, which is interesting. But we need more facts. Fortunately, we have ourselves a client of sorts. And I think we might start by paying her a visit."

13

The Tripp ranch was a forty-five-minute drive due west of town, far into the badlands of empty desert, a vast scorched landscape of red rock mesas and twisted ravines. This was rattlesnake country. Buzzards flew overhead, the sun beat down unmercifully. It was a land where if you stayed too long, you could start imagining flying saucers floating down onto distant mesas. A land where if you didn't bring enough water, or you were careless in any way, you could soon be dead.

Howie glanced at his watch as he bounced through a dusty arroyo. It was high noon in the Valley of Death. Jack refused to ride in Howie's MG, saying it was too small and dangerous, so he and Jack were riding in the Wilders' second vehicle, a red four-wheel drive Toyota pickup truck—Truck Two, as Howie liked to call it, since about a year ago he had driven its predecessor, Truck One, off a cliff in Colorado. Mary Jane Tripp had given him directions over the phone, but they were not like directions anyone would give a person in Princeton, New Jersey: set your odometer, drive 37.4 miles west on Highway 12 from town. You will see a nameless, trackless dirt road on the right; you'll recognize the road by a Taoist yin-yang symbol painted on a rock fifty feet from the highway, as well as the fact that it hardly seems to be a road at all, more like a bumpy goat track going nowhere. If the road is too good, or you don't see the yin-yang symbol, turn back—you're on the wrong road, the one to the old copper mine, and there are a bunch of rednecks living there who will probably shoot you for sport.

So Howie was relieved when he saw the familiar black and

white Chinese symbol painted on a rock: yin/yang, life/death, man/woman, the great dance of opposites. From this marker, the directions were simple—go slowly so you don't bruise your kidneys, and after about fifteen minutes of jolting and jerking and bouncing, you'll probably find the ranch. The Toyota lifted a plume of dust in its wake as Howie maneuvered the bone-jarring terrain. He had to admit, there was a fine macho feeling in driving a pickup truck through such wild and empty land. This was guy stuff, as good a way as any to ignore his intense emotional pain over Aria. He almost wished there was a rifle in the gun rack instead of the furled umbrella that Jack kept there.

They rounded the backside of a mesa that was shaped like a boat—a desert ship plowing a sandy sea—and came to an old ranch house that stood in a surprising oasis of green. The house was a rambling wooden building painted white with windows outlined in dark blue trim. There was a windmill in the front yard, a propeller mounted on a tall metal derrick, dead still in the breathless summer day. It was a retro-dust bowl kind of farm, something you might have found in Oklahoma during the Great Depression, except for an odd assortment of hippie artifacts—an old school bus painted in psychedelic swirls that was sitting in the weeds of the driveway, a string of Tibetan prayer flags dangling over by the vegetable garden. As they drove up, Howie saw a woman working in the garden. She was wearing a broad-brim straw hat, cutoff jeans, and a man's shirt that had once been blue but now was faded and smudged with earth. She turned and watched them approach, her long straight brown hair flowing over her shoulders. There were three naked young children playing in a plastic wading pool near the Tibetan prayer flags. The woman put down a shovel and walked loosely over to where Howie had parked. Howie had seen her before at Jack's house yesterday, but he hadn't really had a good look at her then.

"Hi, I'm Howie Moon Deer," he told her.

"Cool," she replied.

Howie stepped out into the fierce noonday sun and squinted at her. She had cracked lips and gray eyes. A pretty country woman, mid-twenties, deeply tanned, organically hippie, everything about her an imitation of a lifestyle from a quarter century ago—a style that had, in fact, been dying out just about the time of her birth. Up close, Howie noticed dark circles beneath her eyes. Probably it wasn't so easy to live way off in the desert, alone with three kids and no man. Her eyes seemed full of worry and some undefined hunger as they scanned Howie. Jack stood in the yard next to Howie trying to get his bearings, his dark glasses scanning the unfamiliar surroundings, taking in impressions through all his senses except his eyes. Howie took Jack's elbow and gently turned him toward Mary Jane.

"Hello, Mrs. Tripp," Jack said. "Perhaps we can go inside out of the sun? I have a few things I'd like to ask you."

"You've decided to take my case, then?"

"Yes, I think so."

She led the way through a screen door into a large old farm kitchen, shouting at one of the girls, Sativa, to keep an eye out for her younger brother. The kitchen walls were a fly-spattered green, and there was a cast-iron cooking stove that must have been seventy-five years old. Howie led Jack to a Formica-top table, where they sat on kitchen chairs that were sticky from children's fingers. Mary Jane got them cans of organic kiwi-lime soda from a refrigerator that was nearly as old as the stove.

"This seems to be quite a spread, Mrs. Tripp, from the way Howie described it to me while we were driving up. How many acres did you say you own?"

"About eighty . . . of course, that's *if* I really own them, and they don't belong to those men."

"To be honest, my information so far is that the Warrior Circle seems to be a kind of investment co-op, as well as a men's group. Apparently, there's a common fund they're able to draw on for various projects, such as your husband's Hemperware venture. If this is true, they may very well own the business, perhaps the ranch as well. We'll just have to see. However, if they conspired to murder Gary, as you suggested yesterday, I can imagine filing civil proceedings against them—after the criminal case is concluded, of course. It might be a way for you to keep the ranch. Do you understand what I'm saying?"

"Yeah, I think so," she said uncertainly. "Kind of like that civil suit against O.J. Simpson, where he had to sell his golf clubs and things to pay off what's-their-names?"

"Exactly."

Mary Jane Tripp flashed Howie a hopeful smile, like everything was going to be fine now. Howie smiled back cautiously.

"So let's get back to why you believe someone killed Gary," Jack suggested.

"Well, I just can't imagine it otherwise. I mean, Gary went into the mountains a lot; he knew his way around up there. He wouldn't just wander off and get lost, even if he was tripping on peyote."

"Wait a second. What's this about peyote?"

Mary Jane bit her lower lip; she looked as though she hadn't meant to let this slip out.

"Mrs. Tripp . . . Mary Jane, please, you need to tell me everything you know. I can't help you properly unless I have all the facts."

"They call it Sacred Medicine," she said sullenly. "Hell, I like to get stoned too, but I don't pretend it's some big holy deal."

"Yes, I understand. But how do you know the men were taking peyote on the night Gary disappeared? I thought you told me that he rarely discussed his men's group activities with you."

"I knew because he was fasting for three days before the camping trip, just drinking water and eating a little fruit. I thought maybe he wasn't feeling well, so that's when he told me he was getting himself cleaned out so he could do some Sacred Medicine."

"This makes everything more difficult, I'm afraid," Jack said unhappily. "If Gary was hallucinating on psychedelic drugs . . . well, it's much more likely that he *did* get lost or suffer some sort of accident. I'm sure you can see that."

"But Gary was used to tripping," Mary Jane objected. "Sometimes we'd all pop acid and drive down to Albuquerque just to see a movie or something. He could maintain, no problem."

Jack exhaled a small sigh of dismay. While they were talking, one of the naked children, a little boy with long blond hair, came running into the kitchen, giggling from some game he had been playing with his sisters. He stopped and stood by his mother, studying the strangers with his intense blue eyes.

"*That's* Howie Moon Deer—he's an Indian, isn't that cool?" Mary Jane said in a singsong preschool voice to her son, indicating Howie. The little boy seemed fascinated with Howie. "I think he likes your ponytail," Mary Jane said with a smile.

"Well, it's traditional with my people," Howie explained, trying to maintain a strictly anthropological tone. Meanwhile, the little boy lifted his arms toward Howie in supplication; it was a take-me, be-my-father, give-me-any-attention-at-all sort of gesture that made Howie very nervous.

Mary Jane giggled. "He wants to sit in your lap."

"Well, sure. Upsy-daisy," Howie agreed, lifting the child into his lap. He was a cute little thing, certainly, three or four, round as a cherub, his little pecker hanging free as the summer breeze. Howie just hoped he was housebroken.

"Poor Bud, he sure misses his dad," Mary Jane remarked with a sigh.

Howie bounced the child on his lap and made some funny faces, but tried not to appear too much at home in the role.

"Mary Jane, tell me—did Gary keep a home office here?" Jack asked, butting into the domestic scene.

"Well, sure. It's out in the barn, back behind the house. He converted an old tack room into a place where he could do his Hemperware stuff. It's just the way he left it—I haven't had the heart to go in there much, except once or twice trying to find the checkbook and things."

"Do you mind if Howie has a look around?"

"No, that's okay. But what are you looking for?"

"I don't know," Jack replied. "Something. Anything to go on."

"I'll get the key," she agreed. "Do you want me to go with Howie, to show him around?"

"No, Mary Jane. Howie's extremely resourceful on his own. I think perhaps it's better you stay with me and chat."

The barn was a dusty five-minute walk from the house. Howie passed a small duck pond and a corral where two llamas were munching contentedly on alfalfa. A large sheep dog appeared and accompanied him, sniffing at his heels. From the front yard, he could hear the shouts and cries of children's voices. An idyllic country setting, yet to Howie there seemed something sad here, stagnant, separate from real time and motion.

It was a classic red barn with a hayloft, though the paint was now faded and cracking. Howie used the key Mary Jane had given him to open the office door to the converted tack room at the side of the building. He expected a messy, chaotic room to fit with the dust-bowl ambience of the rest of the ranch. But Gary's home office was modern and bright with a sleek Danish-looking desk, a comfortable swivel chair, an expensive desktop computer, and a laser printer. There were framed posters on one wall from various political initiatives to legalize marijuana in California and Oregon. Another wall was crowded with old black-and-white photographs from Gary's glory days as the keyboard player for Headstone. In the photographs, four lanky, long-hair guys stood onstage along-side mountains of instruments, amplifiers, and speakers. Howie assumed that Gary was the one behind the stack of electric pianos, organs, and synthesizers; he had a mousy-brown mustache, hair to his shoulders, a feral face.

On the floor near the desk, Howie discovered several cardboard boxes stuffed full of hemp products. There were sandals, hats, T-shirts, dresses, and cute kitchen aprons with huge green marijuana leaves printed on the front. It was amazing how many things could be done with nature's most all-purpose weed. In another corner of the room, he found a box of hemp cosmetics—shampoo, conditioner, body lotion, and Maui Wowie Toothpaste. Howie couldn't resist opening a tube of the toothpaste and dabbing a little on his tongue. The taste was unexpectedly fruity, a subtle hint of papaya and pineapple mixed with a more pungent touch of resin. Not bad, but did it fight plaque?

Howie wasn't certain where to begin his search, or what indeed he was looking for. He decided to start with the computer, since he had been so successful cyber-sleuthing on Aria's laptop. But he got nowhere with Gary's fancy setup. For one, it was a Mac, and Howie was almost completely Mac-illiterate. A password seemed to be necessary to get things going, but in this case, he had no idea where to start. After ten minutes, he gave up on the computer, fearing it was hopeless, and started to search through the desk drawers instead. There were stamps and envelopes, rubber bands and paper clips. He found a list of suppliers, the various small cottage industries that produced the different hemp products that Hemperware distributed. The sandals came from a small town in Iowa, the T-shirts from Washington state, the dresses from Watsonville, California, and so on. There was another list of the people who actually distributed the Hemperware line around the country, a growing pyramid with Gary Tripp at the top.

Howie found a small stash of smokable hemp in a carved wooden box, but this was the extent of suspicious contraband. There was a nice stereo system in the office with a CD collection that was heavy on the sixties, with all the Jimi Hendrix and Cream you'd ever want to hear. A bookshelf contained some mystical reading—shamanism, astrology, natural healing, and all subjects dealing with Tibet. But there was nothing here to give any indication that Gary's disappearance and presumed death was anything other than what it appeared, an unfortunate camping mishap. Nothing even that mentioned the controversial Chamisa Mall.

After going through Gary's things for nearly forty-five minutes, Howie was about to give up. Then he noticed a small spiral-bound book that had fallen behind the desk. It was Gary's engagement calendar for the year, published by some outfit that called itself Candidly Cannabis; for each week of the year, there was a different color photograph of a positively lethal-looking marijuana bud. Howie glanced through June, the month leading up to Gary's disappearance. There were notes to call various Hemperware suppliers and distributors whose names Howie recognized from the lists he had read. Everything on the engagement calendar seemed to do with business, except a dental appointment, and one afternoon appointment in town to have a tune-up done on his car. And then on Friday, June 19, Howie came to an entry in Gary's now-familiar handwriting that made him freeze: "Aria Waldman, 4:30." That was all it said, not a word more, no indication of what was to happen at this appointed hour. Had Aria come to the ranch to interview him, gathering her endless research material on the Warrior Circle?

Howie was closing the engagement calendar when a folded piece of paper fell out. It was a sheet of white paper that had only two words written on it, a name in capital letters at the top of the page, laser printed by a computer: DONALD HICKS. It was not a name that Howie recognized from the Hemperware lists. It seemed odd, a single name on a sheet of paper tucked away importantly in an engagement calendar. Howie refolded the sheet and took both it and the book with him, locking the office door behind him as he left. He found Jack and Mary Jane still at the kitchen table in the main house. Jack stood up as Howie came into the room.

"Well, we'd better get going, Mary Jane. Thanks for your time."

"Do you want me to give you a retainer check now? Frankly, I'm a little broke, but I could manage maybe a hundred dollars or so. . . ."

"No, no, you'd better hang on to your cash, Mary Jane. We'll send you a bill when we're a little farther along."

"So did you find anything helpful?" she asked, turning to Howie.

He shook his head. "Not really, not anything I can make any sense out of. Have you ever heard the name Donald Hicks?"

She shook her head. "Dan Hicks, I know. The musician from the seventies. But I don't know any Donald."

"If it's okay, I'd like to take Gary's engagement calendar with me. There are some entries I'd like to check out."

"Well, sure. As long as you bring it back," she said.

Mary Jane walked Jack and Howie out into the yard. "Look, when you come back with Gary's book," she said to Howie, "why don't you let me cook you dinner? I know all about you single guys—you probably live on pizza and frozen food."

Howie smiled evasively. "What makes you think I'm single?"

"You just have that single-guy look," she said.

This was worrisome, since he had been womanless now for only a day and a half. Was it in his eyes? Something new in his posture? A lonely crease in his forehead? Horny hormones secreting from his pores?

Howie helped Jack into the Toyota and fired up the engine. Mary Jane stood in the driveway in front of her house, her children gathered around her, her girls on one side and her little boy on the other. They made quite a picture of the postmodern frontier, Mary Jane and her Tripp-lets, the kids all blond and shaggy. As Howie watched in the rearview mirror, they each raised an arm in choreographed motion, as if on the count of three, and waved good-bye.

14

Heading eastward back to town, the highway cut through the empty desert, straight as an arrow. Howie pointed the pickup toward San Geronimo Peak, the tallest mountain in this section of the Sangre de Christo range—a holy mountain, according to some, that rose from the desert like some giant fat Buddha squatting on the earth. Up until early July, the top of the Peak had been white with snow, but now in August the snow was finally melted, showing the craggy rock underneath. In the vastness of the sky and vista, the little red Toyota truck seemed hardly to be moving as it traveled seventy-five miles an hour toward the distant town that sat at Buddha's feet.

"Well, I didn't learn much either," Jack was saying as they drove. "An ignorant young woman, I'm afraid, with little interest in the world outside her ranch and children. She says she's never heard of Chamisa Mall. Or Aria Waldman. She *had* met each of the men in the men's group when I mentioned their names, but only at barbecues and parties. She thought they were all 'kind of cool,' unquote, except for Shepherd Plum, who she thinks is weird. And that's about the extent of her not-so-vivid impressions."

"Did you ask about Gary's affair with Shep's wife, Krista?"

"Yeah. She had never heard of Krista, but she wasn't entirely surprised to learn of the affair. She and Gary had an arrangement, apparently. Neither of them believed that marriage means you absolutely own somebody—that's the way she put it. So they gave each other a certain amount of freedom."

"How about Mary Jane? Did she have affairs?"

"Why? You interested, Howie?"

"Jack!" Howie cried, outraged. "Believe me, I'm only interested in Mary Jane Tripp as a client, in a completely objective fashion."

"Uh-huh. Anyway, she says not. Running the house and taking care of three kids seems to consume all her time and energy. But I sense she's looking for help, domestically speaking."

"Well, she should put an ad in the paper, then," Howie said huffily. "Personally, I'm not a candidate for instant fatherhood. As far as I can see, this afternoon's been a bust."

"Nothing's a bust. This is what detectives do, Howie, most of it very boring stuff, checking out possibilities, ninety-nine percent of which don't lead anywhere at all. The peyote angle is interesting, though. Getting high in the high country could be a dangerous proposition, even for an experienced tripper like Mr. Tripp."

"So you're thinking Gary wasn't murdered after all?"

"I don't think anything yet. I'm gathering information, that's all. Some people have an open marriage; what you and I need to have, Howie, is an open mind."

"And where precisely would you like our open mind to travel next, Jack?"

"Chamisa Mall."

"But there's nothing there yet. Only an open field."

"That's all right. We'll use our imagination." Jack laughed suddenly, for he had an odd sense of humor that erupted from time to time. "We'll go on a little shopping trip to Sears, I think. Actually, I need to buy a new weed whacker . . . an imaginary weed whacker!"

Jack was really tickled by this image, for some reason. But Howie was not. He drove in silence, trying not to think about the three cute children who still seemed to be waving to him in the rearview mirror.

Howie was wrong about the site for Chamisa Mall; there was more than an open field there. An hour later, he maneuvered the pickup truck through the snarled mid-afternoon traffic of San Geronimo to an overgrown parcel of land that stood between Wal-Mart and a miniature golf course. This was the unscenic part of town that had sprouted up during the past ten years, what the locals called the South Strip, several miles of gas stations, fast-food outlets, and strip malls. Howie pulled off the highway into a deeply rutted dirt road that led to a padlocked wooden gate. Beyond the gate stood an old abandoned house that was surrounded by a grove of tall apricot trees. Weeds grew up around the house, and the windows were shuttered. Apricots lay rotting on the ground next to empty beer cans and broken glass, signs that this abandoned place had been used for parties. The property was nearly thirty acres, the last undeveloped land to be found on the south end of town, a vestige of a more languid past.

"So start describing," Jack said.

It wasn't always easy to be Jack Wilder's eyes, but Howie did his best. "It's run-down now, but it must have been very pretty here at one time. Sort of genteel shabby. I'd say the house was built by an Anglo—it's an old wood frame house, more like something you'd expect to find in Vermont than New Mexico. The apricot trees are huge. They've been here a long time, Jack. Kind of a shame to see a big old orchard like this cut down for a shopping mall, but I guess that's what you palefolk call progress."

Jack wanted an apricot, so Howie walked over to the gnarly branch of a huge old tree and pulled a few loose. Apricot trees grew well in San Geronimo, though the fruit itself only appeared every four or five years, during those rare seasons when there was a mild spring without a late freeze. There were at least forty trees in this old grove, but Howie could still see a corner of Wal-Mart through the branches at the north end of the property. There was something depressing about an old estate like this that had gone to ruin. He walked back to Jack and put two ripe apricots in his hand.

"I've always loved apricots," Jack said slowly as he bit down. "They make me think of midsummer hot days in August back when I was a kid."

"Want me to fill you up a bag? They're just rotting here, Jack."

"Maybe another time. Well, let's get going."

"We came here just so you could eat a few apricots?"

"Sure, why not?"

Howie was leading Jack back around the padlocked gate when he noticed an old mailbox that had collapsed on a rotten wooden pole, fallen over into the brush. There was a faded name on the side of the mailbox, and Howie stepped over broken glass to investigate. The name was painted in neat black letters, still legible: DONALD HICKS.

"Hey, Jack, I've found something interesting. Apparently someone named Donald Hicks lived here, God knows how long ago. It's the same guy I asked Mary Jane about—I found his name on a piece of paper inside Gary's engagement book."

"Yeah?" said Jack vaguely. He stood for a moment thinking. "Let me examine this piece of paper, please."

"What are you going to do? Read it? . . . I'm sorry. I didn't mean it to sound like that. . . ."

"Just get it for me, Howie."

Howie walked back to the Toyota, pulled the folded sheet from the book, and brought it to Jack. Jack unfolded the paper and ran his hands carefully along both sides of the page. Howie stood watching him with fascination, unsure of what Jack thought he was doing.

"Donald Hicks? Those are the *only* two words?" he asked.

"That's right. They're in capital letters, and they look like they were written by a laser printer."

"Where exactly are they on the page?"

"They're centered near the top."

Jack handed the paper back to Howie. "Put this away carefully, please. I'm sorry we had to touch it at all. I think it's a blackmail note."

Howie's mouth fell open. "That," he said, "is *not* a logical deduction."

"Sure it is. Look, Howie, the note is folded in thirds, as if it had been fitted inside an envelope. I think Gary received this in the mail—only two words, a name, but one that he would obviously know and perhaps be startled, even afraid to receive."

"But where's the blackmail part of it?"

"Well, perhaps that was to come later. The first part of any blackmail scheme is to instill fear, to let your victim know that you know something they don't wish to have revealed. Where exactly in the engagement book did you find this, Howie?"

"It fell out from somewhere in the middle."

"Somewhere in the middle . . . well, that makes it this summer most likely. Put this together with the photograph that Krista Plum received of her husband Shepherd in drag and I would say that one of our men is playing some very nasty tricks on the others in the group. Now we need to discover what exactly this name, Donald Hicks, indicates—what secret it threatens to reveal."

"You deduce that, do you?" Howie asked skeptically. Personally, he suspected Jack was making a big deal out of very little.

"Yes, I deduce that. Provisionally, at least. We won't grasp onto this thought like it's the Holy Grail, but we will use it as a tool—a crowbar, so to speak, to move our imaginary rock."

"Great. And now would you like me to take you to imaginary Sears so you can buy your imaginary weed whacker?"

This time Jack didn't laugh. He shook his head impatiently. "No, we don't have time for that. Howie, you need to make a phone call. I want you to accept that invitation you've received to climb San Geronimo Peak this weekend."

Howie groaned. "Jack! Tell me you're kidding!"

"I'm not kidding at all. A little chanting and beating the drum—it'll make a new man out of you, Howie."

It was already mid-afternoon, nearly three-thirty, when Jack and Howie finally stopped for lunch at Alicia's Burrito Wagon, a dilapidated old trailer with window service and picnic tables in a shaded field behind a supermarket—a modest place, but it happened to have the best burritos in northern New Mexico. While waiting for their order, Howie used Jack's cell phone to reach Denny Hirsch at the Blue Mesa to say yes, by golly, he'd love to be included in the weekend men's group metaphorical climb to the top of San Geronimo Peak. Howie struggled to sound pleased at the prospect, but in return Denny wasn't nearly as gushingly enthusiastic as he had expected.

"Well, sure. Okay, Moon Deer," was all he said. "It still seems to be on, I guess."

"Is something wrong, Denny?"

"Oh, just a lot of hassles. The Circle's not at a real high point right now, but we've weathered these things before. You know how it is. Even warriors have their human side every now and then."

"And here I thought you were all enlightened beings," Howie said. Unfortunately, anything as nuanced as sarcasm was apparently lost on Denny at the moment. He only sighed.

"We try. Lord knows, we try," he said wearily.

"Denny, what's going on?"

"Nothing, nothing," he said, speaking double. "But, you know, maybe it's good that you *are* coming. Frankly, we need a jolt of some new positive energy."

"We can all cleanse our auras together," Howie suggested. "A sort of New Age laundry day."

Denny actually laughed at the joke. His enthusiasm was definitely on the rise, and in a moment he sounded more like his old self again. He told Howie to bring warm clothes and water, but not to bother about a tent, sleeping bag, or food, for they were going to rough it and live off the land. They planned to carpool to the parking lot at the bottom of the mountain trail—real men, it seemed, conserved gas—so Denny would pull by Howie's cabin bright and early on Saturday.

"Just how bright and early?" Howie asked.

"Four-thirty."

Howie absorbed this bleak information. "A.M.?" he asked cautiously.

Denny chuckled. "It's going to blow your mind, just how much you're going to learn this weekend, Moon Deer!"

"I'm counting on it," Howie assured him.

15

After their late lunch, Howie drove Jack back to his house, reclaimed his MG, and went home. Jack said he had some thinking to do, phone calls to make. It was time to set up an appointment with Captain Ed Gomez of the state police, time to swing into high gear. Howie's assignment tonight was to make a more thorough inventory of the information on Aria's laptop, for last night he had been reading quickly and skipped many of the files. Jack was in a brisk, organizational mood. "Make a written summary, please," he told Howie. "I want to know everything that Aria Waldman was thinking. *Everything!*"

Good luck, Jack! Howie thought bleakly. Personally, he would settle for just a few clues and hints as to what had been going on inside his girlfriend's mind. As long as he had been in motion, busy with Jack and the investigation, he seemed able to stave off depression. But driving back alone to his cabin, thoughts of Aria overwhelmed him. He found her Cherokee still sitting in the middle of the dirt road where she had abandoned it so mysteriously on Tuesday night, and he stopped simply to shake his head and wonder. Everything about the Jeep seemed to reflect Howie's own ambiguity. Did he owe anything at all to this woman who had cheated and caused him pain? Should he just leave the car unattended on the road to be vandalized?

In the end, he couldn't bear to see the Jeep looking so sad and neglected, so he decided to move it into his front yard. This required some maneuvering, since the tank was out of gas. First, Howie drove home, and cut off a section from the garden hose that lay curled up on his back patio, then he returned to the car and si-phoned off about a gallon of gas from his tank into hers. This seemed vaguely intimate, an exchange of vital fluids; it made him nostalgic for happier days when the vital fluids in question had not left the taste of gasoline on his tongue.

By the time he had finished all this jockeying back and forth, it was past seven o'clock. There would be another two hours of fad-ing light this time of summer, and Howie decided to make a more scientific search of the desert near where Aria had vanished. He began at the spot where she had left her Jeep and walked in slowly expanding circles outward for about a hundred feet, carefully ex-amining the ground beneath him as he went, doing his best to empty his mind of all the angst and ambivalence he felt about Aria Waldman. Unfortunately, it had rained several times since Tuesday night, occasionally raining hard, so there was no possibility of finding footprints. But the desert was not empty of signs that hu-mans had come and gone. He found a bottle cap of Grolsch beer, a buffalo head nickel, a ballpoint pen, and a champagne cork. Howie had a memory of this particular cork—he had shot it off like a rocket across the desert from a frosty green bottle of Moët & Chandon earlier in the summer one evening when he had been strolling with Aria in search of a romantic place to watch an espe-cially fiery sunset. The memory cut like a knife. He picked up the cork and threw it violently, as far as he could off into the desert again.

He spent nearly an hour walking slowly outward searching hard for clues, however slight. Close to eight o'clock, he made a small archaeological find, a pottery shard—garbage from an earlier era, perhaps Anasazi. It seemed that man was an animal inclined to litter, even pre-Columbian man. The light was fading, so Howie reversed course and moved more quickly back toward ground zero, his starting point, hoping to find something he had missed. Then, nearly back to where the Jeep had stood, he caught a glimpse of something brassy yellow that was half buried in the dirt. He reached to pick it up. It was an empty bullet casing. Howie sniffed the shell and thought he could detect a slight scent of burnt gunpowder, but he wasn't certain. Of course, you often found spent bullet shells in the desert; people came out to these remote places to shoot up targets and old bottles.

He held the empty cartridge up to the setting sun, trying to imagine its brief violent history. Finally, Howie slipped it into his jeans pocket and walked quickly back to his cabin.

By ten o'clock, Howie's eyelids were waging a losing war with gravity. He sat at his desk with Aria's laptop open in front of him, reading the words on the screen. He had tried to make himself snug. There was a Shostakovich string quartet playing on his CD player, a glass of cheapo Chilean red within easy reach of his hand. The wine was probably a mistake, adding to his growing grogginess, but a man without a woman needed comfort. The Shostakovich, however, was starting to sound like four cats having a quarrel. Howie stood up, stretched, and put on some Vivaldi instead, bright cheery morning music, hoping his body might be fooled into waking up.

He found several files that he had not read yesterday. The most interesting had to do with the New Mexico State Engineer, a man by the name of Ernest P. Anaya, whose approval was needed for any project as large as Chamisa Mall. According to Aria's notes, Chuck Hildyard and Misha Ballantine were worried about Anaya, who had a reputation for being an honest man, as well as having a slightly leftward leaning, antigrowth point of view. So they had set Sheriff Snider loose to see what dirt he could find on him, if there were any skeletons in his closet. For several months last spring, Snider had used his detective skills as well as the power of his office to dig and dig . . . but alas, the guy came up clean. This did actually happen every now and then.

Then the sheriff turned his attention to Ernest's older brother Gilbert, a Catholic priest, and here he struck gold. It seemed that Gilbert had once worked in a parish in Oklahoma where he had been accused of sexually molesting several choirboys. The church, which was expert at hiding such matters, shipped Gilbert off to a special treatment center for sexually disturbed priests; a few years later, rehabilitated, they quietly slipped him into a diocese in Albuquerque. All this happened a number of years ago, but if Gilbert's past came out, it could still cause a scandal. Lou Snider had believed this could be useful leverage, that Ernest P. Anaya would do quite a lot to keep his brother's history secret, for the brothers lived within a mile of one another and they were close. At the moment, it appeared that the state engineer was inclined to give his approval to Chamisa Mall, so perhaps the threat of revealing

Father Anaya's old sins would not need to be made. But it was nice to have the ammunition ready, just in case.

Howie was astonished that Aria had managed to pry all this information from her amorous sheriff. They were lovers, of course, and pillow talk for a man could be nearly as seductive as sex itself, a chance to unwind and blab to his heart's content. But still, Aria was a reporter, and he must have known how ambitious she was. She seemed surprised herself that Lou had been so forthcoming, and at the end of the file, she had written some notes to herself speculating why:

"Lou's cracking, drinking heavily most nights we're together. The man's set to self-destruct. Two months ago it took me days of work to get a few morsels of info. Now he's positively throwing his sins at me. He told me the other day he was raised Catholic, and I can see it still inside of him, eating away, the confessional urge. Naturally, I've told him that if I ever finish this story, I'll use it in such a way that he won't be traced as the source. But we both know that as a practical matter, this can't be done. It's strange, but I don't think he particularly cares. If I was one of the Warriors, I don't think I'd be sleeping very easily right now. He's going to bring down everything around their heads—Karma Konstruction, Chamisa Mall, the men's group, the works. I've never met a man so eager to embrace his doom as poor, tragic Sheriff Lou Snider."

Howie read these words with a heavy heart. "Damn it, Aria!" he thought angrily. "*You* were too eager to embrace your own doom! Did you really think you could sleep with the enemy and live to tell the tale?"

At close to eleven, Howie turned off the laptop, unable to read any more. It was like closing a part of Aria's brain, all that he had left of her, and he felt suddenly lonely without her words on the screen. He couldn't remember ever feeling quite so weary in body and soul. He poured himself another glass of wine, but it was starting to taste sour, and it only succeeded in making him even more depressed. He wondered if Aria walked through the door right now, what he would do. Would he take her back? *No way!* he said to himself grimly. But then he imagined the fantasy scene in more tantalizing detail: how sexy she would be, her enigmatic smile, the warmth of her lips. The truth was that he would take her back in an instant! It was pathetic, really, what a fool he was for her still!

When Howie couldn't bear his thoughts any longer, he stripped off his clothes, turned off the lights, and climbed into bed. Just as he was falling asleep, it occurred to him that Aria's laptop was a dangerous little box of secrets that some people might very well kill for. He should get up and hide the thing, at least. Maybe even copy the hard drive files onto a floppy disk, a backup in case of trouble.

Hell with it! he thought indulgently. *Someone who's feeling as rejected and emotionally despondent as I am shouldn't have to get up out of bed when he's nearly asleep!*

He would take care of the laptop tomorrow, when he found the energy to start again.

Howie woke with his heart thumping. There was someone in the room standing next to him in the darkness, someone breathing hard with booze on their breath. Scotch, Howie decided, deciphering the alcoholic fumes. He was trying to decide what he should do when he felt cold metal pressed against his right temple, the barrel of a gun.

"I want it," the voice said. It was a familiar voice, and Howie knew very well what *it* was. He felt awfully stupid. He had understood the danger, yet he hadn't even bothered to lock his front door.

"Hey, Sheriff," Howie said, managing to keep his voice from shaking, but barely.

"Where is it?" the voice repeated sternly.

"The state cops have it," Howie lied.

The barrel jammed harder into his temple. "I want that laptop computer. So what I'm going to do is this. I'm going to count to five, and if you haven't told me where it is by then, I'm going to shoot your dumb brains out, then I'll simply tear your cabin apart until I find it. One . . ."

"Whoa! Lou, listen to me. . . ."

"Two . . ."

"We're brothers. Almost. We're going to go camping together this Saturday, for chrissake!"

"I don't camp with dead men. Three . . ."

"Okay, okay! The computer's on the desk!"

Howie felt the gun barrel pull away from his temple. Sheriff Snider walked backward carefully and turned on the desk lamp. A yellow light flooded into the room revealing Howie's situation more clearly. It didn't look good. Snider's face was even more glum than the last time Howie had seen it. He held the gun pointed toward Howie as he unplugged the laptop and picked it up with his free hand. Then he stepped back to the bed and pressed the gun once again to Howie's right temple.

"I hate killing people," the sheriff said gloomily. "Their faces come back to haunt you, usually around four a.m. Yours will too, I'm sure."

"Then don't do it," Howie forced his dry lips to say.

"Gotta do it. You read Aria's notes. You know too much. Better close your eyes, Moon Deer. It'll go easier that way. Take a moment or two to prepare yourself, if you want."

Howie's mind raced and raged, searching for some way out. But he couldn't think of a thing. He felt about as helpless as a person might be. This was really it, the big moment. Howie was trying to come up with some fast-talk fast when the night exploded. He felt it first as a physical wave, a whoosh of sound. Then there was a thunderous roar and a flash of light outside the cabin. His front windows seemed to implode, blown apart by some cosmic wind, flying glass everywhere.

Was he dead? Was this what you saw when someone shot you in the right temple? But the sheriff seemed confused as well. He cried out in surprise and ducked instinctively. Then he backed slowly away from the bed toward the glassless window.

"Son of a bitch!" he said. "My car just blew up!"

"*I* didn't do it, believe me," Howie told him earnestly.

Lou Snider turned back to Howie, studying him coldly. Howie knew his life was hanging in a precarious balance, but he saw a flicker of hope.

"Look," he said, "you can't get away with killing me now, not if you have to leave your bombed-out car outside. They'll know it was you. So why don't you just take Aria's Jeep and get out of here before my neighbors walk over to see what's wrong. Her key's right behind you in the abalone shell by the front door."

Sheriff Snider kept staring at Howie. *Will he, or won't he?* Howie wondered. It seemed like this could go either way. At last the sheriff lowered his gun.

"I liked Aria Waldman," he said unexpectedly. "You know, I really liked that girl."

Under the circumstances, Howie resisted the temptation to say that these days a woman of nearly thirty was *not* called a girl. "What happened to her, Snider?" he asked.

The sheriff only shook his head. "What happens to anybody?" he asked vaguely. Then he reached for the keys in the abalone shell and walked out the door.

Howie didn't push his luck. He waited until he heard Aria's Jeep drive off before he stepped carefully out of bed, doing his best to avoid the broken glass. He found his Birkenstock sandals and walked to the front door. Outside was a fiery ruin of twisted metal, the remains of Lou Snider's county car sitting in his driveway, sending a plume of black smoke into the night sky. Farther down the road, the red taillights of the Cherokee were disappearing into the distance.

Howie picked up his telephone to call Jack, smiling at the thought that Lou wasn't going to get very far in a Detroit guzzler on less than a gallon of gas.

16

Two black New Mexico State Police cars were the first to arrive. Howie stood in his doorway watching them speed in his direction from a long way off across the desert, their blue and red emergency lights popping and flashing, making a strangely beautiful light show in the night. The sirens grew louder, there was a crunching of gravel, an opening of doors, then three men in black uniforms stepped self-importantly from the two cars.

"Sweet Jesus!" said one of the troopers, surveying the smoky remains of Sheriff Snider's county vehicle. Three sets of official eyes turned suspiciously toward Howie.

"Faulty wiring?" Howie suggested. But they were not amused; this was serious stuff, as serious as stuff got in San Geronimo. While they were talking, Jack arrived in a separate car in the company of Captain Ed Gomez, the head of the San Geronimo substation of the state police. Gomez walked in a circle around the destroyed car, examining it from several angles, then he nodded curtly to Howie. They had all worked together before. The captain was a tall, dignified man in his mid-fifties; Howie always thought he looked like an Hispanic Clark Gable, except for his sour expression and leathery neck. He was a dry man, arid as the desert. Dry wit, dry skin, and dry conversation.

"We found the Cherokee on the north side of town," he said. "Ran out of gas. No sign of Lou, though. Too bad. We'll get him in the end. Just hate to drag out the pain."

The captain stayed in the front yard to secure the crime scene. Howie guided Jack around to his back patio, since the inside of his cabin was in shambles and did not offer much hospitality. He set Jack down on a canvas chair, and then perched himself on a low adobe wall.

"Did he get the computer?" Jack asked.

"Yeah, I'm afraid so."

"You made some backup files, I trust?"

Howie sighed, but there was nothing to do but admit the truth. "Jack, just as I was falling asleep, it occurred to me that Aria's laptop was a real time bomb, if you'll excuse the expression. In the morning I was planning to copy everything from her hard drive onto a few backup disks, but I hadn't gotten around to it yet."

"So Lou got everything, then? And we got nothing?"

Howie had to agree that this was the situation. It was almost as if Aria had been made to vanish a second time, along with all her words and research.

"I still don't understand how Lou's car just exploded like that," Howie said. "Will they be able to tell if it was a bomb?"

"Of course. Explosives leave behind specific chemical residues. Most bombers don't know this, but generally about ninety-five percent of an explosive device survives the blast—in small pieces, of course, sometimes *very* small pieces, but a good crime lab can do wonders with fragments. Right now, Ed will be trying to make a secure perimeter around the car so in the morning they can do a proper search. But I have to tell you, Howie, it's very strange *when* this device exploded."

"I can assure you, it happened just in the nick of time for me!"

"Yes, yes. But car bombs are generally set to go off when the ignition is turned on, or by remote control. The idea is for one to be *inside* the car when it explodes, not for the bomb to go off at some random time of night. If it *was* random, of course."

"It was close to midnight, as far as I can reconstruct it," Howie said. "Of course, I wasn't exactly looking at my watch."

"Well, there you see the oddness of this. Midnight in San Geronimo is a very quiet time, even for a sheriff. On a normal night, Snider would have probably been in bed asleep. So if the bomb was set to go off on a timer, why then? And if it was on a remote control, then the perp would have been nearby, probably watching—maybe he followed Snider here, I don't know. But why destroy the car when Snider was inside with you?"

"Maybe it was an electronic screw up?" Howie suggested. "A

timer that wasn't working right. Or maybe it was just meant to be a warning."

"A warning?" Jack reflected, pursing his lips thoughtfully. "Well, we'll just have to see."

Howie slept on Jack's couch for what remained of the night, since his own cabin had been turned into an active crime scene. At ten the following morning, Friday morning, they had arranged to meet with Captain Gomez at the San Geronimo state police substation, an ugly cement-block building that stood next to a Texaco station on the south side of town.

Law enforcement in San Geronimo was a confusion of too many cooks in a very small kitchen—this was how Jack usually put it, at least. In descending order of competence, there was the New Mexico State Police, a small organization—there were only 452 troopers in the entire state, but they were "quite professional." (Jack's assessment.) From here, things went downhill fast: the San Geronimo County Sheriff's Department, led by an elected sheriff, which had jurisdiction throughout the county but not, theoretically, within the actual town. That honor fell to the San Geronimo Police Department, which ruled the town with a fine combination of macho bravado and ineptitude—the most recent scandal concerned the money from the town's parking meters, which had a strange way of disappearing without a trace. Next came the San Geronimo Pueblo Tribal Police, who had jurisdiction on the Indian reservation but little actual power to do much except hand out speeding tickets and keep the tourists off the sacred parts of their land; when an actual felony occurred on Indian land, it was handled by a federal agency, usually the FBI or the BIA—the Bureau of Bashing Indians Around, as it was called locally. To complete this law enforcement stew, there was also Fish and Game and the forest rangers assigned to caretake the national forest, both of whose agents carried side arms and could make arrests under certain conditions. Considering that San Geronimo had a population of eleven thousand, this seemed an absurd number of agencies to be bumbling about, often getting in each other's way. Jack generally did his best to avoid all of them, but when an official encounter was necessary, he preferred to go to Captain Gomez, whom he considered the best of the lot.

The captain's office was a small room with a desk and a window looking out onto a bleak parking lot and a revolving Texaco star. Jack and Howie sat on uncomfortable plastic chairs facing the captain. They were all groggy from lack of sleep, speaking in low growly voices. Jack had phoned Gomez on Wednesday afternoon to report Aria's disappearance, but as Jack had expected, no investigation had been mounted. The explosion last night, of course, made this case suddenly top priority. Now Jack wanted Howie to go through the whole story in detail for the captain's benefit, starting with Tuesday night. How Aria had left his cabin, Sheriff Snider's unexpected appearance on Wednesday morning, the men's group, Chamisa Mall, the saga of the laptop computer—Howie did his best to tell it all in more or less chronological order. It seemed that each time he told this story, he told it a little bit better; yet with each retelling, it felt as if Aria herself slipped further away. The smart, sexy, funny, deceitful woman who had slipped irrecoverably from his bed on Tuesday night with so little explanation.

As Howie spoke, Ed Gomez occasionally reached inside his desk drawer for a giant bottle of Extra Strength Tums, passing the bottle around to Jack and Howie. Howie liked the peppermint taste. He had consumed nothing since the burritos late yesterday afternoon except red wine and coffee, so it was pleasant to feel the Tums at work doing their heroic best to mop up the acid debris of his stomach.

"I knew that Lou was a bad cop—I just didn't know how bad," Ed said mournfully when Howie finally came to a stop.

"Tell me about Lou Snider," Jack urged.

"Well, he was a detective with a sheriff's department in Nebraska for about fifteen years. Had a wife and family, I understand. Then he got wounded, shot in some police action—I don't know the details. He was put on medical leave for six months, had nothing to do but sit around and watch TV. Apparently all that time to mull over his life was not a happy experience for Lou. When he was well enough, he resigned from his job, left his wife, his kids, and came to New Mexico. He was down in the southern part of the state for a while, and then he moved up here about six years ago. He was doing construction work, building houses with what's-his-name, the solar architect."

"Zor McCarthy?" Howie asked.

"Right. The Sun King. Then three years ago he ran for county sheriff with a lot of money behind him for ads, radio spots, even TV. His big competition was the incumbent, Sheriff Willy Moreno, who was even more of a sleaze than Lou. There were several well-publicized rapes back then where the perps walked due to Willy's total nonchalance, so all the women's groups were against him, of course. Lou used that issue, promising to make crimes against women a big priority. Still, he only won by a squeaker. And that's pretty much all I can tell you. Lou and I have always tried our best to have as little to do with each other as humanly possible."

"Did you know he was a member of a men's group?" Jack asked.

"Yeah. I suppose that was a little unusual for a cop, but I always considered that to be one of the better things about Lou Snider, all in all."

"And Lou was camping in the mountains back in June when Gary Tripp disappeared?"

"Yeah. Lou was on that camping trip. It's starting to seem like too many people have disappeared around here. Lou volunteered for the search team, I remember. That was a huge rescue operation, but this land can swallow people up, I've seen it happen before."

"Of course Gary's disappearance might not have been voluntary," Jack suggested.

"Homicide? Well, maybe," the captain said unhappily.

"If the body was buried, it would explain why you never found him. Did you think to drag the lake, by the way?"

"Yeah. But you know, some of those little mountain lakes are deep. So it wasn't really conclusive. The idea of murder was never seriously considered at the time—we were more concerned that he might have accidentally drowned."

"They were all high on peyote," Jack remarked.

"Were they? . . . no one told me that, but I guess it doesn't surprise me too much."

"So you found nothing?"

"Nothing . . . well, there was just one little thing. But nothing major, really."

"I'm always interested in little things," Jack said.

"Then, hold on a second." The captain rose from his chair and left the office for a few minutes. He came back with something in the palm of his hand. "One of my people found these in a grove of trees about fifty feet from the lake." Captain Gomez opened his hand to reveal two brassy yellow bullet shells. "They're .38's. At first I was interested, but you know, a lot of people go up to remote wilderness areas to try out their guns. With nothing to match these with—no slugs, no body, no gun—they don't have a lot of relevance."

"I can match them," Howie interrupted. Ed's eyes and Jack's dark glasses turned his way. So much had happened that Howie had forgotten all about his find yesterday evening in the desert. Luckily, he was wearing the same jeans. He reached inside his pocket, pulled out the spent bullet shell, and gave it to the captain.

Ed Gomez set the three empty cartridges side by side on his desk. They were identical.

17

Sheriff Lou Snider's house was in the sagebrush to the west of town, designed by Zor McCarthy, the self-styled Sun King of solar architecture.

It was a straw bale house, the latest architectural rage in San Geronimo County—a house constructed with straw bales piled one on top of the other to create the basic form, then sealed with plastic to prevent rot, then covered with plaster to give the illusion of a conventional exterior. The house faced due south with a front of slanting glass that took maximum advantage of every ray of sunlight. In this part of New Mexico, building codes were lax and there were hundreds of avant-garde dwellings like this, but generally they were inhabited by counterculture types, not cops. Lou's house was completely self-sustaining, "off-the-grid," as people said here, which meant he got his utilities directly from Mother Nature. Howie thought it was pretty nifty. The roof was shaped to work as a cachement system. It collected the rain and snow that fell from the sky and funneled it through various filters down into a cistern below and to a pond in the living room that was stocked with talapia, a warm water African fish, providing dinner as well as water. Solar panels provided electricity; the toilets worked without water and were self-composting, turning human waste into fertilizer for the garden. There was no pollution, no waste—except perhaps the life of the man who had lived here.

Howie drove Jack to the house after leaving the substation. A lot of different people were busy looking for Sheriff Snider, and there was a state police car in the driveway with an officer sitting inside, just in case the sheriff should return home. Captain Gomez had made a few phone calls so that Jack and Howie could look around. The matter was sensitive, politically and legally, for no one was quite ready yet to ask a judge to issue a search warrant against the sheriff of San Geronimo County; there was a feeling that it would be a lot less painful for everyone if Lou simply showed up and explained himself. Perhaps a search warrant would be sought later in the day, but meanwhile it didn't seem like a bad idea to turn a blind eye, so to speak, and allow two civilians to case the joint.

"You'll be on your own, Jack, if some lawyer ever makes an issue about this," Captain Gomez had cautioned. "You'll just be two P.I.'s who broke the law. You'll probably lose your license."

"I understand," Jack said.

"Meanwhile, I'll be curious as hell what you find in there."

And so the officer in the driveway pretended to be asleep in his squad car when Howie and Jack arrived. Jack used a thin blade on his Swiss Army knife to tumble the lock on the front door.

"You have many hidden talents, Jack," Howie assured him.

"Don't I? Now, start describing, Howie. I don't want to stay here longer than we need to."

Howie stepped inside a spacious living room of odd shapes and angles. "A nice house," he said. "More attractive than you'd think it would be from the outside. There's a lot of plants and sunlight, an inside garden, even some interesting artwork on the walls. The furniture is handcrafted, plenty of natural wood, expensive one-of-a-kind stuff. Our sheriff has good taste, as well as the money apparently to buy what he likes."

"You say that like you're surprised. You think that just because a man's a cop, he has to be an ignoramus?"

"No."

"Yes you do. Don't be such a culture snob. As for the money, we already know that our warriors have not exactly taken a vow of poverty. Obviously, the men's group thought it was a good idea to have Lou Snider run for sheriff—I'm sure they financed his campaign and made it worth his while to be their personal cop. What else do you see?"

"A huge CD collection. Mostly jazz . . . I'm envious. He has just about everything Miles Davis ever recorded. Billie Holiday, Bill Evans, Thelonious Monk, Charlie Parker. . . ."

"Howie, we didn't come here to drool over his CD collection. Let's get to work, my friend. I'm afraid we're running out of time."

Fifteen minutes later, Howie found a trapdoor beneath a beautifully woven Afghan rug in the master bedroom. The bedroom was a hard place for Howie because he kept imagining Aria here, pumping Lou for information and getting pumped in return. Up to now the interior of the house had revealed nothing: expensive, tasteful, orderly, yet empty of personal knickknacks and clues to the inner man. Then, while Howie was staring gloomily at Lou's king-size bed, Jack tripped on the Afghan rug, pushing back a corner of it, and nearly breaking his neck in the process. Distracted by romantic anguish, Howie had not been paying proper attention to Jack—sometimes he almost forgot that Jack was blind, that in unfamiliar surroundings he needed someone to actively look after him. Howie helped him to his feet and was pulling the rug back in place when he noticed a thin crack in the hardwood floor. Curious, he moved Jack to one side and then pulled the rug back all the way. The crack was a trapdoor with a handle at the far end.

The door was counterbalanced, and it opened easily, revealing a flight of wooden steps that disappeared into the darkness below. It was cleverly designed, and Howie suspected there must be a light switch nearby. He probed with his hand inside the opening until he felt a toggle. The room below sprang into view, a windowless cellar perhaps fifteen feet by twenty that was more a bunker than a basement. Howie told Jack to stay where he was, and then he climbed downward. Jack waited impatiently for Howie's report, but for some time there was only silence.

"Well? What's down there?" he asked finally.

"It's kind of sad," Howie replied, his voice muffled, as though he were speaking from inside the stomach of a whale.

"Sad?" Jack repeated with irritation. "I'm not interested in *sad,* Howie—what I want is factual information, please."

"Major Louis Snider lived heavily in the past, I'm afraid. It's all down here."

"*Major* Snider? What are you talking about?"

"He was a major in some elite special force in Vietnam. There are a lot of photographs on the walls, Lou in camouflage clothes, his face blackened. Lou with some of his army buddies . . . he's made notes when they died. PFC Richard Arlen, Landing Zone

Columbus, July 2, 1969. Corporal James Tanner, An Khe, January 17, 1970 . . . it goes on and on, Lou's private war memorial. My God, all these guys look so young! . . . oh, Jesus, here's a photo of Lou with a severed head in one hand and a knife in the other! Yuck, he's holding the head by the hair. Right next to that, there's a picture of a woman and two children on a lawn in front of a house, possibly the wife and family he left back in Nebraska. This whole place seems to be a bunker of personal regrets . . . and then there's the arsenal."

"Let's hear about the arsenal," Jack demanded.

"Well, there's a little of everything. Military pistols, a machine gun, a few rifles . . . also some very lethal-looking knives that I don't think were designed to mince onions, Jack. And then there's a box of grenades."

"Live hand grenades?"

"I think so. Would you like me to pull a pin and find out?"

"That won't be necessary. Describe the rest of the bunker to me. Is there furniture? A desk?"

"No desk, just a single armchair and a lot of candles. There are wax drippings on the cement floor. I can picture Lou sitting in the armchair brooding over his personal dead while the candles burned down."

"Not a very healthy picture. Are there any papers?"

"Some. Here's a box of letters . . . 'Dear Major Snider, Thank you for taking the time to write such a moving letter about my son Ralph. It helps a little to know that he died quickly, without pain, in such an important mission as you describe. . . .'"

Howie fell silent. His silence lasted so long that Jack called down, "Are you okay?"

"Yeah, fine," Howie answered. But he was not okay. With the weapons and the photographs of dead soldiers, Howie was starting to feel very eerie, like he was standing inside a tomb. He turned in a slow circle, his eyes scanning the mementos that had been mounted on the dank cement walls. There was a musty American flag with holes in it—bullet holes, Howie imagined. There were black-and-white photos of Vietnam war atrocities. Burned bodies. Severed limbs. Howie looked more closely and saw that some of the atrocities were domestic, forensic photographs of old crime scenes, perhaps from Snider's years as a sheriff's detective in Nebraska. But why would anyone want to surround himself with so much death? Were they old cases that Lou liked to revisit from time to time?

Howie was taking a last look around when he noticed a snapshot of Aria. She was standing in the desert smiling at the camera, looking happy and free, wearing a San Geronimo Art Association T-shirt that Howie had bought her one night after they'd gone to an art opening together. Lou must have taken the picture, for Howie had never seen it before. It's significance in Lou's personal crypt was unavoidable. Howie had already faced the probability that Aria was dead, but this was more concrete. An inescapable conclusion, as Jack liked to say. Howie felt hope draining out of him like blood flowing from a wound.

"Howie! What's going on down there?" Jack called.

"I just found a photograph of Aria."

"Well, Howie, you knew she was seeing him," Jack said more gently. "This shouldn't come as a surprise."

Howie climbed halfway back up the wooden steps and stood in the open hole. "It's not the sex. I mean, hell, when it gets right down to it, who cares who's sticking whose weenie where? I don't care, I really don't, not anymore . . . but this bunker, Jack, it's like a mausoleum. With Aria's picture here, I figure it must mean . . ." He let the sentence fade off, unfinished.

"That she's dead? It's only her photograph down there," Jack reminded.

"No, this is real death down here. You should see it, Jack. It's Lou Snider's memorial to death. I think Lou killed her. Oh, I'm sure he did it very mournfully, with lots of regrets. But he killed her anyway, and for the same reason he was going to kill me. She knew too much."

"That's because he told her too much."

"Well, sure, but it's the same thing in the end. How could he afford to leave her walking around?"

"Howie, come on out of that hole. You're getting yourself all worked up over imaginary things, and it's time to get out of this house anyway."

"I'm okay," Howie told him, climbing up from the trapdoor. "Why should I care about a woman who was screwing around and got herself killed because she was so ambitious she took all kinds of stupid chances? I don't feel anything anymore, I really don't."

This didn't sound like Howie, but Jack let it pass. Just as they were leaving the house, Howie said he'd be a minute—he needed to use the bathroom. Jack waited in the living room, listening for several minutes to the sounds of Howie throwing up into the toilet behind the closed bathroom door. Then the toilet flushed, and Howie came out.

"You okay?" Jack asked.

"Sure, I'm okay. So stop asking. I've never felt so goddamn okay in my life before."

Jack shook his head, glad for once that he could not see.

18

Go home, Jack had said. Get someone to fix your broken windows, then get yourself some sleep. You're overwrought and overtired and not much help to anyone the way you are now.

It was three in the afternoon by the time they were finished at Sheriff Lou Snider's home. Howie was in a dangerous mood. He dropped Jack off at his house, but instead of returning home himself, he decided to make a detour to the Blue Mesa Café. The café was on the edge of the historical district in a house that had been built by an eccentric Russian artist who had arrived in San Geronimo via Paris in 1923. There were large, airy rooms with high ceilings and French windows that opened onto a formal courtyard with a fountain in the middle. Howie had come here often with Aria. Romantic dinners in the courtyard with the fountain gurgling and the waiters and waitresses coming and going with silvery trays of food and good bottles of wine. Howie paused, looking at the places where they had once sat—empty chairs and tables that were imbued with memory. He forced himself to turn away.

He found Denny Hirsch in the kitchen in the midst of some major difficulties with his chef. The restaurant was closed at this hour, and they were really going at it. The chef was an excitable, elfish little man dressed in kitchen whites and a baseball cap; he kept waving his arms, complaining that he couldn't produce a suitably *nouvelle* menu in the wilds of New Mexico unless he had the proper gastronomical supplies.

"Where are my chanterelles?" he was screaming. "Where are my cèpes and morels?—I'm going to have a nervous breakdown!"

Denny was listening patiently, nodding from time to time with the expression of a man who had been in group therapy and wasn't afraid of real emotions. He was dressed casually for a boss: rubber flip-flops, baggy shorts, a Grateful Dead T-shirt, dark glasses dangling around his neck on a braided string.

"René, I want you to know that I hear you, man—I really *hear* you," he said earnestly. "When people talk, there's nothing they can't work out together. I've spoken to Santa Fe, and your mushrooms are on the truck along with the radicchio and the softshell crabs. Everything will be here by four o'clock. I promise."

"*Four o'clock!* And you think I'll be able to open at six. Are you trying to kill me, Denny?"

"I'm trying to *validate* you, man. We're in this together."

Together or not, Denny seemed awfully glad to see Howie, who offered a way of escape from the kitchen.

"Moon Deer!" he cried. "Just the man I want!"

There was darkness in Howie's soul; so much darkness that he was able to pull off a perfect imitation of love and light, almost as good as Denny's imitation. They gave each other a heartfelt Hollywood hug and then stepped into the courtyard.

"You seem to be having a bad afternoon," Howie mentioned. "I just dropped by to see if the hike was still on for tomorrow."

"Yes, it's on—just barely, but we're going to do it, by God. We decided we really need to make some spiritual interconnections right now. Lord, what a day this has been! What a week! What a *life*!" Denny cried, on the edge of hysteria.

"Have you seen Lou?"

Denny shook his head. "I just can't understand what made him flip out like that. I know what happened—the state cops have been all over us asking questions. Like a men's group must be some weird, evil cabal! Isn't it awful, how people are so afraid of things they don't understand?"

"Speaking of things that are hard to understand, Lou was getting ready to kill me last night," Howie pointed out.

"You mustn't take it personally, Moon Deer. Lou . . . he has problems, you know."

"I sensed that," Howie agreed.

"And then I understand, some bomb went off? His car *exploded*?"

"It just went boom," Howie said. "Do you know what this is all about, Denny? Why anybody would plant a bomb in Lou's car?"

Denny shook his head again, helplessly. "I'm like totally clueless, I kid you not. I'm just a guy who believes in love and peace and everybody getting along together. I don't know. Maybe I'm a dreamer."

"Dreaming's great. But who planted the bomb?"

Denny brought his hands together in front of his lips in a prayerful gesture. He lowered his voice: "This is the worst part. Personally, I think it was Chucky. But I may be wrong."

"Chuck Hildyard? I haven't met him yet. But why Chucky?"

"Chucky and Lou are going through some intense negativity right now, I'm afraid. We're all trying to help them work through it. But *nada*. It's like melodrama time."

"But what's the melodrama about? I don't understand."

"Welcome to the club!—*none* of us understands! The only thing I can think of is that love and hate, they're just so closely related. You dig what I'm saying?"

"I can certainly dig that. And Chucky and Lou . . ."

"They go way, way back. They love each other like brothers. But when brothers fall out, it's a real monster."

"You're saying Chucky and Lou knew each other before the Warrior Circle?"

"Oh, yeah. Since 'Nam," Denny confided. "Look, this is something I shouldn't be saying because neither of them likes to speak about it. It's just so painful, you know. Memories like you and I can't imagine. They were in some special squad together. They had to go behind enemy lines and do horrible, horrible things! They've both come a long way, getting in touch with their spirituality after all that violence. That's what makes it so tragic, their falling out now."

"But they're going camping tomorrow?"

"Well, not Lou—not unless we can find him and talk some sense into the guy. Nobody knows where he is right now. But the rest of us, you bet. I just spoke with Misha on the phone, and we all feel that this weekend retreat is absolutely essential under the circumstances, to regain our center. I hope *you're* still planning to come, Moon Deer?"

"I wouldn't miss it for the world."

Denny nodded wisely. "So I'll pick you up at four-thirty?"

"I'd better come to your house, Denny. My place is in shambles, and I may not sleep there tonight. But yeah, four-thirty on the dot. I'll be there."

"Great! This weekend is going to be *mondo fabuloso,* man!"

"*Mondo* to the max," Howie agreed. To seal this sentiment, they clasped hands, the elaborate shake of soul brothers. But Howie held firmly to Denny's hand and would not let go. "Look, I don't want to leave on a bummer," he said, lowering his voice. "But tell me—do you *really* think Chucky could have planted that bomb? It would take a certain amount of technical expertise, don't you think?"

"Well, that's just it," Denny said heavily. "You see, that's what he did in 'Nam. He was the explosives man. They even had a nickname for him in his outfit. They called him The Fuse."

Howie put down the battered canvas top of his car in order to cleanse himself with the rush of fresh air. He drove fast on the two-lane highway back to his cabin, his ponytail dancing in the wind. His green backpack lay next to him on the passenger seat, weighed down by a last-minute item that he had begged from Jack to take on the climb tomorrow: a revolver loaded with five bullets in the chambers, a snub-nosed Smith & Wesson .38 that was almost exactly like the one he had found by Aria's Jeep, only newer. Howie had been surprised at the extent of Jack's arsenal of handguns, which he kept hidden from Emma in a metal toolbox in his back pantry behind a burlap sack of potatoes. Jack had three automatics and two revolvers stashed away, along with boxes of ammunition. After some discussion, he gave Howie the Smith & Wesson because it was the smallest of the lot and the simplest for a gun novice like Howie to use.

"I'm trusting in your good sense, Howie," Jack had said sternly while he stood in the pantry loading the bullets into the chambers. "I got a little worried about you, frankly, back at Snider's house."

"It was only a transitional moment, Jack," Howie assured him, insincerely. "I'm my old self again. Honest Injun."

But Howie was not his old self, and as he took the gun, he knew he had crossed some invisible line within himself, joining a world of violent possibilities. The gun now lay in his day pack, a potent, malignant presence. Howie didn't know how this was all going to end, but he was in a mood to do battle and he was glad to be armed.

He pulled into his driveway alongside half a dozen police vehicles, marked and unmarked. A small army of FBI field agents had arrived at the site to sift through the wreckage and the area surrounding the blackened skeleton of Sheriff Snider's car. It was Jack who had convinced Captain Gomez to invite the Bureau to investigate the bombing, since bombings were an area of FBI expertise; Gomez, a little huffy, insisted that the New Mexico State Police would retain jurisdiction of all other aspects of the case. As Howie arrived home, a team of evidence gatherers in white lab coats were working through his front yard, some of them sprawled beneath the chassis of the car, others on their hands and knees crawling through the sagebrush and wild roses that Howie had planted in front of his house. Howie approached the yellow tape, which surrounded the entire front of his house.

"Hey! I live here!" he shouted. "I've got to go in and get a few things."

A grim-looking FBI woman walked his way. "You can't come in here," she said.

"I've got to. My Ph.D. dissertation is inside there, not to mention my toothbrush."

"I'm sorry, but this is a crime scene."

"Hell with that!" Howie said calmly. "It's still my home, humble though it might be, and I need a few things."

Howie became aware that he was being photographed by someone a few feet away. It was Heather Winter with a press ID on a cord around her neck, snapping way with a Nikon. Howie turned back to the lady FBI agent. "Look," he said, "my name is Howard Moon Deer. Why don't you phone Special Agent Neimeyer. I'm sure he'll vouch for me, tell you that I'm a very cooperative sort of guy who isn't going to remove any evidence." This was a bit of name-dropping. S.A. Neimeyer was Jack's old friend, in command of the Bureau's Denver office, and Howie knew him as well.

"Well, all right. I know who you are, Mr. Moon Deer. But don't touch anything yourself—I'll send in someone to help you. A bomb investigation is all about recovering very small particles."

So Howie got an escort, a young guy named Ned who was wearing a spiffy FBI Evidence Recovery Team T-shirt. Howie pointed, and Ned gathered what he wanted: a duffel bag from the top of his closet, a change of jeans, underwear, socks, a heavy sweater, a pair of shorts, Rockport hiking shoes, a rain parka, toothbrush, toothpaste, and dental floss. Next he pointed to his own laptop computer, which he had set off to one side on a kitchen shelf on Thursday night in order to work with Aria's, as well as three boxes of 3.5-inch computer disks (research notes) and three separate drafts of the dissertation itself. One day he might revert back from his current man-of-action mode and become once again scholar Moon Deer, man-of-thought; meanwhile he had Ned gather all the academic papers and computer paraphernalia into the duffel bag along with his socks and underwear, feeling strangely distant from the doctoral thesis that had once seemed such an important part of his life.

What else was there in this blasted-out cabin that he cared about? Howie's eyes roamed his small living space, past books and CDs until he came to a framed photograph of his parents, a picture they had sent him recently from a trip to Disney World. It had been their first trip out of South Dakota, and they both looked elderly and frail, two displaced Indians standing among the palm trees. The photograph had moved Howie to a surprising degree, so he had framed it and put it by his bed; he who knew too well what it was like to be a displaced Indian, out of context, a stranger in a strange land.

Howie stood for a moment looking at his parents. His father was wearing a cap with PARIS written across the front, which Howie had sent him from France several years ago; his long white hair fell in two separate braids down his back, his old Indian face was as deeply lined as the rugged earth. His mother looked more tentative, a round little woman, shrinking with age—probably she was intimidated at finding herself in such a strange place as Florida.

Howie felt unbearably sad to have disappointed them as he had, going off to school and never coming back except for brief, strained visits, sometimes in the company of Anglo girls from Vassar and Sarah Lawrence—they might just as well have been from Pluto, as far as his parents were concerned.

He had Ned put the photograph in the duffel bag on top of the three most current drafts of his dissertation, and he walked quickly from the cabin, throwing the bag into the trunk of his car. He felt suddenly rootless and free; his few valuables had just gone mobile.

Then he looked up and saw that Heather Winter was standing next to him, just as he knew she would be.

19

Howie sensed that flirting had been a more gentle art, once upon a time back in a more romantic pre-postmodern era.

"You look like shit, Howie," was what Heather said to him. Yet, strangely, he understood that she *was* flirting. It was the speculative way she regarded him through her round rimless glasses, a big waiflike question mark in her eyes. She was dressed in her usual refugee chic: purple tennis shoes today, baggy camouflage brown-and-green jungle pants with an old Nirvana T-shirt hanging loose on top. With her Nikon camera and press credentials around her neck, she seemed poised to cover the latest fashionable war, wherever it might be—Africa, the Middle East, even arty New Mexico.

"I haven't been sleeping much," Howie explained. "What are you doing here, Heather?"

"I convinced my editor to let me write something about the car bombing and how the investigation was coming," she said. "I told him we were friends and that you would give me the whole scoop," she added optimistically.

"Well, okay. I'll tell you what I can," he said dutifully.

She brought a small notebook and a pen from the baggy pockets of her jungle fatigues. "Shoot."

"Please, Heather, *shoot* is the wrong word. I was asleep last night about midnight when I woke and found Sheriff Snider standing next to me with a gun. . . ."

"Slower," she told him, scribbling as fast as she could. "Do you sleep naked, incidentally?"

Howie raised an eyebrow at her.

"I'm trying to get the atmospherics," she told him. "If you were naked, you see, you would be a lot more vulnerable."

"I was undressed," he agreed.

"Go on."

Howie went on. Basically he was sympathetic with Heather's desire to be more than just an intern on the newspaper. She made him think of a younger version of Aria—scrawnier and badly dressed, but the same scrappy, ambitious drive. So Howie spent the next ten minutes going over his account of the previous night while Heather struggled to write fast enough to get it down. Occasionally, she repeated a sentence to make sure she had it right; she didn't want to misquote him, which was admirable. Finally she closed her notepad and stared at him.

"You really thought you were going to die?" she asked.

"I did. For a few minutes, anyway."

"What was that like, Howie? Did you think about your childhood, or get some gigantic flash about the meaning of life?"

"Are these more atmospherics for your article?"

"No, I'm just curious. For myself."

"Well, it was strange. I could barely swallow, I was that terrified. But at the same time, there was part of me that felt very calm. Very connected. And then . . . no, I don't think I should tell you this."

"Go ahead," she insisted.

"It's sort of embarrassing. I started thinking about food."

"Food?"

Howie shrugged. "I'm a very oral person. I started wishing I had time for just one really great meal."

"This is fascinating . . . and what would your last meal be?"

"Fried chicken," he said without hesitating. "Mashed potatoes, gravy, and corn on the cob with lots of melted butter . . . I know, educated people don't eat that heart attack cuisine anymore. But it was something my mother used to make on special occasions when I was a kid. We were very poor, you know, and we didn't eat like that often. So these dinners . . . well, they were like the sum total of all happiness, all bliss. That ultimate childhood feeling of being snug and well cared for."

"And *that's* what you thought about, when you thought you were going to die? Fried chicken?"

"You made me tell you, Heather."

"No, I think that's very profound," she said, nodding seriously. "Cosmic chicken. So what are you going to do now, Howie?"

"Right now? Get some sleep over at Bob and Nova's spare room. I have to get up around four in the morning tomorrow to do some male bonding with the guys. We're going to climb San Geronimo Peak and get in touch with our inner-warrior, and all that."

"Isn't that dangerous?"

Howie shrugged. "There's a pretty good trail up there."

"That's not what I meant. Gary Tripp went on one of those male-bonding weekends, and no one ever saw him again."

"Gary's one of the things I'm trying to learn more about."

"Look, Howie—why don't you come over to my place for dinner tonight. I have this really great tofu recipe. Tofu loaf with cashews and a banana-cilantro sauce. At least I can set you off with a good healthy meal in your stomach."

Howie did his best not to gag. Tofu loaf sounded bad enough—but a banana-cilantro sauce? "Uh, no, Heather, thanks—but I think I'd better just make an early night of it."

She frowned. "Howie, it's not just dinner. There's something I need to tell you about Aria."

"Tell me now."

"I can't. It's complicated. But it's something you need to know."

"Heather . . ."

"Honestly, Howie. I know how much you want to find out what happened to Aria, but those men, they look nerdy but they're dangerous, they really are—Aria probably found that out the hard way. So if you're going to go with them, at least go properly prepared."

"And you can properly prepare me?"

"I can tell you something very important that you ought to know."

Howie didn't like this. Dinner with Heather was the last thing he was in the mood for. While he stood trying to think of some suitable excuse, she took out a notepad and wrote down her address.

"I'm subletting an apartment just down the road from the newspaper. You won't be sorry you came, I promise."

"What time?" he asked reluctantly.

She had an unexpectedly pretty smile when she was triumphant. "Seven."

Howie spent what remained of the afternoon running around doing chores. He drove over to Bob and Nova's to arrange for someone that Bob knew to come and fix his windows this weekend while he was gone. While he was in a broken glass mode, he phoned Jack to see if his window still needed repairing as well, but apparently Emma had already taken care of it. Then he took a shower and did a few minutes of yoga and tai chi in a heroic attempt to reduce his stress level. Finally he drove back into the center of town.

Heather Winter lived on the second floor of a small apartment complex that wrapped around an inner courtyard. She answered the door wearing a psychedelic tie-dye apron over her jungle fatigues and rock T-shirt, a costume that was exhausting even to look at. But the aroma drifting from the kitchen took him back to his childhood; Howie had no idea that tofu loaf could smell so much like real food.

Then he walked inside and saw that it wasn't tofu loaf at all. This was serious. Heather had made him fried chicken, mashed potatoes, gravy, and corn on the cob.

"What do you want? A breast or a leg?" she offered.

"Either," said Howie politely. She gave him a breast. Heather didn't have a dining room table, so they ate on big cushions on the living room floor, their plates on their laps, two candles burning between them, an open bottle of Chianti near their feet. Heather looked too young to drink, and in fact, she was only twenty years old. Howie wondered vaguely how she had scored the bottle.

"So what is it you have to tell me?" he asked finally.

"It's about Aria. You know, Howie, there are a lot of things I like about Aria. But she was never the right person for you."

He suppressed a sigh. "I'm not sure I really want to talk about this."

She gave him a steady look. "She wasn't faithful to you."

"I know that."

"You *do*?"

"Of course. She was sleeping with Lou Snider. Is that what you wanted to tell me?"

Heather's mouth fell open. "Doesn't it *bother* you?"

"Well, sure it bothers me. But in this case, it wasn't romance, it wasn't even sex. It was work. She was using Lou Snider to break a story."

Heather was shocked at his attitude. "You think that's all right?"

"I'm not a hugely judgmental person," he admitted. "Anyway, I should have seen what was going on, but I was sleepwalking. It's my fault for letting our relationship drift."

"Bullshit!" Heather exploded. "I mean, to sleep with a guy like Lou Snider to get a story . . . Howie, *I'm* ambitious too, but I sure wouldn't do *that*!"

Howie was not certain how to respond. In his mind, there wasn't any comparison between Aria Waldman and Heather Winter. Of course, it was terrible what Aria had done. Aria was beautiful, ambitious, cunning, complex, and vastly flawed; but despite her many failings, she fascinated Howie, whereas Heather did not.

"So how do you know about her and Lou?" he asked.

Heather peered at him unhappily. "I found them together once about a month ago, after hours in the office. It was maybe nine o'clock, and I'd come by to get some work I'd left behind. Aria and Lou were making out near her desk. He was all over her, but she was laughing and sort of pushing him away. Naturally, I asked if she needed any help, but she said she was okay. I couldn't figure it out. Then the next day she came into the office and said, let's have lunch. That's when she told me the story. She said she'd slept with Lou one time earlier in the spring, and now she was just luring him along. . . ."

"Wait a second. She told you she slept with Lou only *once*?" Howie interrupted.

"That's what she said. She went on about it, how she had flirted with him for a few months, then she gave in just one time, to give him a bite of the apple—that's how she put it. And now she was keeping him on a string by saying how confused she was, that she really wanted to be with him, you see, but she had to resolve the thing with you first. She asked him to be patient, and all that bullshit. To wait a little while longer until she was free."

"She said she slept with him only *one* time?" Howie repeated, shaking his head in amazement. He had imagined it all quite differently, the two of them sneaking off, gleefully giving him the horns every chance they got.

"Isn't once bad enough? My God, she was a total tease, Howie! And she did it just to get a story. I'm no prude, but I was shocked,

I really was. I asked her, what about Howie? And you know what she told me? She said she liked you, you were sweet, but no man was going to stop her from fulfilling her destiny . . . I mean, talk about pretentious bullshit!"

Howie nodded dumbly, trying to absorb this latest incarnation of Aria Waldman.

"So why didn't you tell me this when we had lunch on Wednesday?"

"Because I didn't know you well enough. Anyway, Aria told me all this in confidence. But then, when you said Snider had beat you up, it's why I believed you. I suppose he was jealous about *you,* as crazy as that sounds. So I realized I'd been awfully unfair. I'd been accusing you of beating up Aria when you were actually *her* victim. She didn't love you, Howie. Not like you love her."

Howie shook his head. "I don't know" was all he could manage to say on the subject. He was truly dumbfounded by who loved whom at the moment, or what any of this meant. "Well, thanks for dinner," he said finally with a yawn. "I'd better be getting on the road."

"Howie, look, you're exhausted. You can't sleep at your cabin tonight anyway. So why don't you stay here."

"Heather . . ."

"No, let me finish. I have like this *huge* bed. So it wouldn't be any big deal, you know. Just a strictly platonic thing. I know you have to get up early, but I've got a good alarm clock."

He knew this was a bad idea. All through dinner he had sensed that Heather Winter would probably not abhor the idea of having sex with him if he made the proper moves. To be truthful, Howie was tempted. He was tired and discouraged, and a shot of female comfort would be . . . well, comforting. As the Chianti level went down, he had glanced at her from time to time and saw that she wasn't entirely as scrawny as he had first imagined. She was a small but graceful person. A bit silly, yet he had come to like her— not romantically, not lustfully, but as a pal.

So couldn't pals have sex? No, not in this situation, he told himself firmly. He decided he'd better stand up and say good night quickly before his amoral hormones tempted him anymore.

"I should go."

"Don't be silly. I'll sleep on the couch, okay? Christ, Howie, look at you—you're so tired, you'll probably wreck your car."

He *was* exhausted. "Well . . ." *Say no,* said his brain. But his mouth, a rebellious creature, said yes.

Heather set the alarm for three-forty-five in the morning, a frightful hour to go off climbing a mountain with the guys, but there it was. Howie stripped down to his underwear and climbed wearily into her bed. He was glad he had decided to stay; he was so tired he wasn't sure he would have managed the twenty-minute drive to Bob and Nova's. *Tomorrow I'm going big game hunting,* he told himself. *Gotta get rested for this. Tomorrow, one way or another, I'm going to find out what happened to Aria!*

A few moments later, when he was nearly asleep, he felt Heather slip into the bed and curl up next to him. Somehow the couch had been forgotten. He sensed she was naked.

"If you want to Howie, it's okay," she said. "I mean, if it would help you sleep any better."

Howie's mouth wasn't the only rebellious part of him. But this wasn't right; it would be shoddy and second-rate, lust for convenience. A strange thought came to him, unbidden: *It's not what a warrior would do.*

"Better not," he told her. "It wouldn't be fair to you. Not while I'm still obsessing on Aria."

"You just have to work her out of your system, I guess."

"I guess," he told her sleepily.

Heather turned away. Howie felt her rear end against his own, cheek to cheek. He didn't hear her when she began softly to cry, for he had just drifted off to a dreamless place where none of this really mattered.

PART TWO

STUMBLING MAN

1

"Stop licking my toes!" Jack told Katya, pulling back his left foot. Wearing sandals had been a mistake this morning. Katya was a very friendly dog, also an extremely expensive one—a $25,000 dog, better educated than many two-legged Americans.

Nevertheless, she was driving Jack nuts at the moment. The sad fact of their relationship was that Jack Wilder was a self-described "cat person" and had never much cared for dogs; except for the accident of blindness, their fates would have never crossed.

Jack and Katya had been joined together during an intensive two-month Orientation and Mobility program at San Rafael Guide Dogs for the Blind, a training center north of San Francisco. Katya had done a lot better in the program than Jack, but then she had been raised for this destiny since earliest puppyhood: the first two years of her life spent in special training with a family in Sacramento, followed by six months of postgraduate work in San Rafael before the school had decided to pair her with one of their more difficult students, a wounded policeman, recently blinded, who showed no great interest in being alive, much less in adjusting to his new situation. Jack hated every minute of his Orientation and Mobility training—the sense of being helpless in a dark world where he knew nothing, where he had to start all over again like a slow and backward child. He was accustomed to being an extremely competent person; he had succeeded in every endeavor in his life up to now. So it was humiliating to trip and bang into things and trust his fate to a German shepherd, a dog who in this new realm of blindness seemed much more clever than he.

In the end, Jack had settled down enough in San Rafael to get through the program. Then he and Emma and Katya and their two cats had moved from California to New Mexico—a good move, a fresh start, an environment that was so different from his old life that a new life could gradually be born. Nevertheless, for a number of years he had disdained Katya's help, demoting her to a simple household pet, preferring to get about clumsily on his own, working out all sorts of intricate ways to navigate his world. But Jack had a strong practical streak, and there came a time, after walking into enough trees and traffic, when he understood that it was self-defeating not to use all available tools. By this time Katya had become spoiled and lazy, as well as slightly stout on Jack's cooking—a fate shared by everyone in the Wilder household eventually—and she was not quite the dog she once had been. But, still, they managed. More or less.

Thump . . . thump . . . thump, went her tail.

"Stop that," said Jack sternly.

She put her long nose into Jack's lap, hopeful of his affection. He scratched her downy ears for a moment and then pushed her away. "Lie down!" he commanded in a voice that had once bent a big city police department to his will. Katya sighed, dribbled some doggy saliva on his lap, and then slunk reluctantly to the floor, resting her chin on Jack's right foot.

It was Saturday morning, and Jack and Katya were in the Special Access Room of the San Geronimo Public Library, where Jack had come to use the Kurzweil reading machine—a device closely related to a photocopying machine, where you put a normal printed page onto the glass and a computer turned the text into synthetic speech. It was stilted, robotic speech, like listening to a talking alarm clock—Jack greatly preferred braille, a system of touch reading and writing in which raised dots represented the letters of the alphabet, but many documents still weren't available in braille. Emma, who worked at the library, had managed to convince the town to spring for the expensive reading machine in order to assist the estimated thirty-eight severely visually impaired citizens of San Geronimo County. Emma had become passionately involved in a good many local causes, and at the moment she was upstairs giving a two-hour seminar to a handful of volunteers in the adult literacy program. The library was an old house on Don Orlando

Street that had been bequeathed to the town by a genteel old lady of refined taste. As a library, the converted home was quaint but inefficient, a warren of small rooms on two separate floors connected by squeaky stairs.

Jack sat with earphones on, listening to old issues of *The San Geronimo Post*. Before going upstairs, Emma had set him up with every issue she could find that mentioned Chamisa Mall, but still this was a difficult way to get information. The problem with the reading machine was that it read indiscriminately, everything on each page. So Jack got local basketball scores whether he liked it or not, as well as car wrecks, the weekly ski report, letters to the editor, the works. But it was because of the indiscriminate nature of the machine that Jack came across an interesting article he might have missed, an exposé of a councilman who had used his town credit card to pay for personal items—gasoline for his private car, beer, cigarettes, and a night at a local motel with a woman who turned out to be his secretary, not his wife. The article had been written by Aria Waldman, and it resulted in the councilman, Dave Corazon, being forced to resign over the issue. Jack was impressed by Aria's reporting, but didn't she have any fear at all? The Corazon family were major power brokers in San Geronimo. The patriarch, Joe Corazon, was the head of the county water district as well as Corazon Motors, the largest auto dealership in town—the same Joe Corazon who, according to Aria's laptop notes, had accepted a bribe from Karma Konstruction. It was admirable to be such a crusader for truth, but Jack had to wonder if she actually understood the risk she was taking.

As for the Chamisa Mall story, Jack found the article depressing, entirely too similar to the angry debate he had seen in northern California over logging and the spotted owl. The environmentalists opposed to Chamisa Mall were mostly wealthy Anglo newcomers from the top of the food chain, as Howie would put it. They were self-righteous and insensitive to the fact that the quaint town they wished to preserve was also a very impoverished place for the majority of the Spanish and Native American inhabitants. The average family income in the San Geronimo valley was a little over $15,000 a year, far below the national norm, so Chamisa Mall represented an opportunity for jobs and money. But, of course, few of these poor people had any experience with what a huge shopping mall could do to a small, rural community. They did not understand how quickly the paving over of fields into five-thousand-car parking lots could marginalize everything they valued, their traditional way of life. And so it was a complex issue; unfortunately, the rhetoric on both sides was shrill and intolerant, and left no room for complexity.

Jack listened as long as he could, then he removed his earphones and turned the Kurzweil machine off. He hadn't learned much about Chamisa Mall, but he was bothered by Aria's story exposing Dave Corazon's misuse of his municipal credit card. Revenge, after all, was one of the classic motives for murder, along with love, hate, and jealousy. Jack sensed that he and Howie had been looking with too narrow a focus at the men's group, the Warrior Circle, as the sole probable cause of Aria's disappearance. The Corazon family certainly had a motive to wish her permanently gone. Not only had Aria seriously offended them, but her continued curiosity might wreck the entire Chamisa Mall deal, costing the family the loss of a lucrative business opportunity.

"Damn!" Jack said aloud to Katya. He wished he still had a large police force at his disposal; he would have sent squads of detectives on all sorts of errands. But there was only himself and Howie, and Howie was off climbing a mountain at the moment. The FBI was on the case now, thanks to the car bomb, but Jack hated to sit by helplessly on the sidelines. He opened up the crystal on his braille wristwatch and checked the time. Emma had nearly another half hour to go in her literacy program upstairs, and after that she was supposed to spend two hours at the checkout desk. Jack felt extremely frustrated.

"I hate this," he confessed to Katya. "I feel so impotent."

This was a serious confession, and Katya responded by placing her furry head on his lap. Jack had to admit that even though he was a cat person, his two cats at home really wouldn't give a damn were he to be so unwise as to admit his fear of impotency to them. Katya, on the other hand, seemed to care. You could talk to a dog. He scratched her head, then he reached down her body and felt for the small doggy backpack she wore—Howie had bought this for Katya as a present last Christmas. Jack opened the zipper. There were only three items inside, but they were vital ones for a blind detective: a cell phone, a miniature tape recorder, and a folding white cane that had a rubber handle on one end and a plastic tip at the other.

"Well, Katya, I don't know about you, but I'm getting discouraged just sitting here. What do you say we go get ourselves into a little trouble?"

She wagged her tail with enthusiasm. Jack used the cell phone to make a call. Then he unfolded the white cane, took hold of the business end of Katya's harness, and together they set forth into the black, unseen world.

2

The street was loud and clamorous, a confusion of overlapping smells, impressions, and potential dangers. Jack held on to Katya's rigid harness with his left hand and used the white cane in his right hand to sweep ahead of him from side to side, as though he were using a metal detector. A volunteer at the library checkout desk had pointed him in the proper direction and told him the number of intersections he would need to cross along Don Orlando Street in order to reach the downtown plaza. Still, even with a guide dog, a cane, and directions firmly in mind, he was fairly new at this; the moment he was outside the safety of the library door, he felt totally vulnerable. For Jack, taking a ten-minute walk along a city street was a perilous adventure.

He knew he was passing through the historic, touristy part of San Geronimo. Cars were stalled in heavy traffic along the narrow streets, radios playing, their tailpipes blowing thick clouds of exhaust into the air. Jack moved down the crowded sidewalk tapping his white cane back and forth, sensing the human crowd as it scurried out of his way. He could hear mothers as they grabbed their children, sometimes nearly flattening themselves against cars and buildings, as though bumping into a blind man might be contagious, causing some leprous contact to themselves. Jack had come to enjoy his position as an untouchable. "Out of my way, kiddies!" he intoned soundlessly under his breath. "Here comes Blind Jack the Ogre . . . out of my way!"

Katya's rigid harness was his joystick to traverse a sightless world; if he pushed forward on the harness, Katya would walk faster, when he pulled back, she slowed down. Occasionally Katya simply stopped in her tracks, causing the harness to become an immovable object, keeping Jack from going anywhere at all. If there was danger, she was trained to back up, pushing him out of harm's way. If she simply stood still, it meant that there was some obstacle in their path, perhaps a curb. Then it was his job to listen for the traffic flow and feel with his cane for what was ahead. Crossing a street was a partnership between dog and man, though Katya would refuse any command that would lead her and Jack into danger; she had been trained specifically for "intelligent disobedience," as they called it in Orientation and Mobility training. Ultimately, you had to put all your faith in the dog and allow the animal to make the final decision as to where it was safe to go. But this was hard for Jack. As a cop for many years, he had seen the worst that life had to offer and he had never entirely put his faith in anyone—with the single exception of his wife, Emma. So how could he give all his trust now to a German shepherd?

Then there were the distractions, people who did not understand that what he and Katya were doing was a difficult high-wire act requiring serious concentration.

"Oh, what a lovely dog!" came a voice nearby. It was a woman, a young woman from her voice, who had stepped from the shadows of the crowd to pet Katya's head. Katya was a sucker for affection, and Jack could feel the vibrations through the harness of her tail wagging in vigorous delight.

"What's his name?"

"*Her* name is Katya. And please don't pet her—she's working right now."

"Oh! . . . I'm sorry!" said the young woman. And she disappeared forever back into the shadows from whence she had come. But now Katya's concentration was broken; Jack could feel a slackness of intent.

"Hop up, Katya!" he told her sternly, the command for a guide dog to refocus and get back to work. But she still wouldn't cross the street. "Katya, I feel the curb—now, let's get going! I'm not in the mood to stand here forever."

But she wouldn't budge. Jack listened once again for traffic, and it seemed safe for him to continue. Why wouldn't she move? Jack was a willful man, accustomed to trusting his own judgment. He pushed forcibly on the harness, becoming irritated. *"Go!"* he commanded. But she refused, she just stood there like a rock.

"Excuse me, but you're trying to walk your dog into a parked car," said a voice at Jack's side. It was a woman, but she sounded much older than the one who had petted Katya earlier.

"There shouldn't be a car blocking this intersection," Jack said grouchily, annoyed that Katya had been right and he had been wrong.

"It has Texas plates," the woman explained dryly. In San Geronimo this explained a lot. "Where are you trying to go?"

"To the bus stop at the far end of the plaza. I'm trying to get to Corazon Motors, the Ford dealership on the south end of town."

"You want to buy a car?" she asked ironically.

Her voice carried a hint of old money, a particular patrician arrogance. Jack sensed he had run into someone as opinionated as himself. He smiled. "A car wouldn't do me much good. I have an appointment with Joe Corazon."

"Really? Joe is a son of a bitch. He also happens to be the son of a bitch who runs this town—not the mayor, not the town council, not any of our elected officials. Just Joe. The right tactic with Joe is that you have to pretend to pay him homage, then he's a real pussycat, he'll take care of you."

"I'm not going to pay homage," Jack told her. "I'm going for information."

"Well, then, Commander Wilder, perhaps I should drive you there. As it happens, you've just missed a bus, and the next one doesn't go for nearly an hour. You're lucky I came by."

He raised an eyebrow at her. "You know me?"

"San Geronimo is a small town, and I have lived here practically forever. You don't exactly cut an anonymous figure, Commander."

"I'd be pleased to accept a ride. Thank you."

"I'm Dorothy Lange, by the way. I've met your wife several times . . . would you like a hand to guide you? Or do you prefer to trust your lovely dog?"

"A hand, please. It will be faster."

The hand that took hold of Jack's left arm was birdlike but firm. Jack raised the estimate of her age up another decade. This was an old lady, perhaps in her seventies. Jack had to smile. With some luck and the unexpected kindness of strangers, a blind man could cover a lot of distance in this world.

*   *   *

Joe Corazon spoke in a surprisingly high, hoarse tenor. His voice was damaged. Too much shouting? Too many cigarettes? Jack's impressions of the world were limited and often came from indirect suppositions. Jack imagined a large, overweight man, his high voice in contrast to a bass body. A florid man, most likely, with several double chins and pudgy fingers with rings on them. But that was only a guess, and for all he knew, Joe Corazon was small and wiry, a tight little jockey of a man. The elderly lady who had given him a ride here had called Joe the son of a bitch who ran this town. If so, he was surprisingly polite and well-spoken.

"It's so very nice to meet you at last!" said Joe. "Would you like a beer? Perhaps a soda? You know, I've been hoping our paths would cross for quite some time." He lowered his voice delicately. "Kit Hampton was a close friend of mine."

Jack nodded. Ex-Senator Kit Hampton, a local celebrity, had been murdered a year earlier, and Jack and Howie had solved the case. Jack accepted a Coke and a bowl of water for Katya, for it was turning into a hot afternoon. He wondered how Joe was dressed. Was he wearing a gaudy sports shirt with a gold chain around his neck? But no, that was more a certain California type; here in New Mexico, an important man would dress more conservatively. There were times when Jack wished he could have his sight back for a few seconds just to see whether his guesses were right or wrong.

They were sitting in an office off the main showroom. There was a chemical cleaning smell in the air that made Jack think of carpets in hotel corridors. Jack was sitting in an armchair of squeaky synthetic leather; Joe was across from him behind a desk. Outside in the distance, Jack could hear a salesman pitching a used car to a dubious customer. Like most Anglo immigrants to New Mexico, Jack had little connection with the old Spanish community, a proud and sensitive people who kept themselves aloof from newcomers. He wasn't certain exactly how best to proceed, but sensed it would be wrong to get down to business too quickly. So Jack let the conversation drift. They spoke about different things. The wet summer and how the old-timers were saying they would undoubtedly have a lot of snow this winter as well. How Emma was getting on with her job at the public library. Joe had met Emma several times, apparently—Jack was not entirely surprised to learn that Joe Corazon was on the library board. Joe expressed the hope that the town would be able to build a new library one day, keeping up with San Geronimo's growth.

Finally, almost as an afterthought, he said gently: "Well, Jack, I can see we're going to be friends. Now, what can I help you with? I sense you have a problem, and it's my pleasure in this life to be of some help to my friends when I am able."

"It's my young Native American friend, Howard Moon Deer," Jack explained. "He's the one with a problem. His lady friend, Aria Waldman, disappeared this past Tuesday night. It's quite strange how it happened. He found her car a hundred feet from his house. The engine was running, there was opera playing on the stereo, but there was no sign whatsoever of Aria. She's simply vanished, and I'm trying to help Howie find out what happened to her. He's very upset."

"I can understand that," Joe agreed. There was a warm note of sympathy in his voice. "As a matter of fact, I know Aria Waldman just a little. This may sound unkind—and I certainly hope she turns up safely. But I think perhaps your Indian friend may be better off without her. Of course, if he's a young man, he won't understand this right now. But time will open his eyes."

"You don't like Aria?"

"It's not that exactly. From my limited contact with her, I don't either like or dislike her. But she struck me as very pushy. Very ambitious. Which is laudable, I'm sure, but she lacks . . . how can I put this? A certain sweetness of femininity. This will make me sound very old-fashioned, yet it is difficult for me to imagine how a man could be happy with a woman like that. For me, a woman should be a well of serenity where a man may go to draw inspiration when he is tired and discouraged. Don't you think so, Jack?"

Jack smiled vaguely. "I think that particular well of serenity ran dry some years ago, Joe."

"Well, perhaps in your culture, but not ours . . . no, I take that back. Things are changing, even here," he said with a sigh. "Our young men join gangs, they treat women badly, and the young women are promiscuous and treat them badly in return. But with my generation it was different. I suppose I cling to the old ways."

"Did Aria Waldman come to you investigating a story?"

"Oh, yes. She came with a tape recorder in hand and a most unattractive expression on her face. She did not come as a friend. She wanted to know about this real estate project that's been proposed, Chamisa Mall."

"What did she want to know?"

"*Know?* Oh, I think she believed she *knew* everything! Mostly she came to lecture me. You will excuse me for saying this, but like so many of you Anglos who have arrived recently, she seems to want San Geronimo to be some quaint and backward little village where rich people can come on vacation, or perhaps buy a second home. She doesn't appreciate that this is a very poor county, and we need jobs, quaint or not. My people have been in this valley for more than four hundred years, but what we're looking for now is a future, not a past."

So there it was, the cultural divide, the eternal pro-growth/anti-growth squabble. Jack decided to leave it alone.

"What exactly did she ask you about Chamisa Mall?"

Joe Corazon sighed. "Besides running this small automobile dealership, I am the current president of the town water board, you understand. No business can build here without water, and for that they need different types of permits, depending on the size of their operation and water needs. A huge project like Chamisa Mall would naturally require a great deal of water, and they are proposing four deep wells to supply their needs. This is what the Waldman woman came wanting to know about. We—the water board, that is—have given our initial approval for the wells, pending the report of the state engineer. Aria suggested—rather rudely, if I may say—that I accepted a bribe in exchange for this approval."

Jack tried to look suitably shocked.

"These people who want to build this mall, Karma Konstruction. Did they in fact approach you with some sort of . . . gift?"

"Naturally, they *approached* me, Jack. I know one of the men quite well, Chuck Hildyard, the local real estate agent. We've had long discussions about water in this valley, Chuck and I. After all, this is a desert, and water is a vital concern for us all. But, of course, he wouldn't dream of trying to influence me in any undue way."

"The figure I've heard quoted is $20,000, Joe. That's supposedly what Karma Konstruction slipped to you under the table for the water board to give its approval."

Joe laughed merrily, not offended in the least. "My goodness, $20,000! You know what I'd be doing, Jack, if I had so much money? I'd be in Acapulco right now, lying on the beach! Believe me, I wouldn't be here working like an idiot selling cars."

"Yes, of course," Jack agreed pleasantly. "Yet, you have a very large family, Joe. I believe you have several relatives who run construction companies and building supply yards—surely your family will benefit personally from this shopping mall?"

"I sincerely *hope* so!" Joe said heatedly. "Believe me, I hope we *all* benefit in this town!"

"But doesn't that give the appearance of conflict of interest?"

The high, hoarse voice became very quiet for a moment. "You know, I spent a number of years in Chicago when I was a young man, Jack. I went to college there—yes, I have traveled widely, and I have had a chance to observe what you Anglo people would call municipal corruption. Politicians filling their pockets in exchange for various favors and city contracts. You know how it goes. But it's quite different for us in this small corner of the world. Here we don't grease our own palms, we don't fill our pockets. But let me tell you what we *do* do—we help our friends and our families. You Anglos are a lonely people, each of you out only for yourself, one against the other. But we, on the other hand—we live through our relationships to one another. We are a very old community here, one that was well established when your Pilgrims were just arriving at Plymouth Rock. So to answer your question, Chuck Hildyard offered me nothing for myself—and indeed, I would accept nothing from such a man. But he did suggest that if Chamisa Mall received a green light, a local contractor would be put in charge of the construction. A cousin of mine. A particularly close and favorite cousin, I should add."

"I see," said Jack.

"No, Jack, in this instance, I'm afraid you probably *don't* see. We're talking about two different cultures, two opposing world views."

Jack had more understanding of this issue than Joe Corazon imagined. A good deal of business was conducted by feudal relationships in California as well; Chinatown was certainly a community where carefully tended friendships counted for everything, not to mention Hollywood. But Jack wanted to move to another question.

"Can you tell me anything about the land where Chamisa Mall

is going to be built? My friend Howie drove me out there on Thursday and described an old house set in an apricot grove."

"Yes, that's the Donald Hicks place. Hicks was an artist who moved out here from the East Coast in the seventies. He died slightly less than three years ago."

"So Karma Konstruction bought the land from his heirs?"

"It wasn't quite that simple. The site where the mall will be built is thirty acres in all, the last big parcel of undeveloped land within town limits. The way I understand it, these California people were able to pick up a fifteen-acre parcel on the north of the Hicks place, and a ten-acre parcel to the south. That left Hicks in the middle with his house and apricot grove. But he refused to sell."

"And then he died," Jack observed. "How did he die?"

"He committed suicide, I'm sorry to say. Very sad, but you know these artistic types. After his death, it turned out he didn't own the land after all. It belonged to a big drug company back East, Xerxes Pharmaceutical in Bridgeport, Connecticut. I don't know the details—I have no idea what sort of arrangement Hicks had with them to be living there, or why a pharmaceutical company owned a small house and fruit orchard in San Geronimo. But that's how Chuck Hildyard and his Karma backers got the missing five acres that they needed. They bought it from Xerxes."

"Do you know how much they paid for it?"

Joe was silent for a moment. "I don't know for certain. I wouldn't want to give you any wrong information."

"I appreciate that. How about a rumor, then? Or just a guess?"

"This is something the Waldman woman told me. She threw it at me as if it must indicate all sorts of terrible corruption."

"What did she tell you?"

"She said that Karma picked up the five acres for one dollar."

"*One dollar?* For five acres of prime commercial land? You're joking?"

"Well, maybe this corporation back East wanted to get rid of it. A tax write-off, who knows? Or perhaps Aria Waldman had her facts wrong—I'm only telling you what she told me. In any case, Karma will have the expense of tearing down the house and getting rid of the trees."

"You said you were friends with Chuck Hildyard. Did you ever ask him how they managed to pick up those vital five acres virtually for free?"

"Now, I didn't say I was *friends* with Chuck, I told you I knew him quite well. There's a difference, and in this case I didn't feel I knew him well enough to ask what he paid for a piece of land. It really isn't my business."

Jack sat very still in thought. A suicide, a pharmaceutical company from back East, the absurdly low price of one dollar paid for a piece of land that would complete the jigsaw puzzle of a multi-million-dollar development deal. None of this felt right to him at all.

"I'd like to find out more about Donald Hicks," Jack said finally. "Did you know him?"

"No, I'm afraid I can't help you there. I know a few of the artists in town, but I never met Hicks."

"Can you tell me who any of his friends were? Someone who might know why he killed himself?"

"Sorry, I just don't travel in those artistic circles, Jack. But you might try some of the galleries. Or the San Geronimo Art Association. There's a busybody old woman named Dorothy Lange who's head of the art association—she may be able to tell you something about Donald Hicks."

"Dorothy Lange? An old woman? She gave me a ride here this afternoon."

"Well, there you are—life in a small town! You see how it is. Everyone is connected with everyone else. That's why I always say, we must help each other. We must all be friends."

A pleasant sentiment, pleasantly said. Though in the mouth of Joe Corazon, Jack had the feeling it was intended as a threat.

3

Half an hour later, Jack was sitting in a shaded patio at the home of Dorothy Lange, the head of the San Geronimo Art Association. He had phoned her from Corazon Motors, and she encouraged him to come right over. An employee at the car dealership gave Jack and Katya a ride to her address, a quiet, residential neighborhood not far from the historic district.

There was a drowsy, midday, late-summer peacefulness hanging over the old woman's house and garden, a slowness of time. Jack had settled into a deck chair with a glass of iced tea on a table by his side, and Katya lay snoring near his feet. Overhead a stately old tree rustled in the afternoon breeze sending down speckled patterns of light and shade, which Jack sensed obliquely as heat and coolness on his skin. He spoke briskly, an attempt to rally against the suffocating heaviness of day.

"I'm very interested in Donald Hicks," he told her. "Did you happen to know him?"

"Why are you interested in Donald?" she fired back.

"It's actually Chamisa Mall that I'm trying to find out about. The other day, my assistant took me to where the mall is going to be built. He described the Hicks house, the apricot orchard. It seems like a lovely old property, very evocative. So I'm trying to figure out why Hicks should kill himself in such a pretty spot. And how the land came to be owned after his death by the Xerxes Pharmaceutical Corporation in Bridgeport, Connecticut, and then literally given away to the people who are developing the shopping mall."

"What do you mean by that, literally *given* away?

"I'm not positive of this information, but it appears that the people who are planning to build Chamisa Mall paid precisely one dollar for those five acres."

Jack heard her catch her breath. "Are you mad? Even four years ago, that land was worth a quarter of a million dollars, possibly more!"

"Well, this is the mystery I'm trying to solve. I understand that Donald was an artist. I was hoping that as president of the Art Association you might know his story."

"Yes, I knew him," she said after a moment. "Donald was my friend. But it's not a very pleasant story, I'm afraid. Frankly, I've been waiting for someone to come along asking the questions that you've been asking—it's rather disturbing, I think, that no one has."

"Please, go on."

"Well, Donald arrived in town in an old VW bus back at the tail end of the great hippie invasion. It was 1975, I think, perhaps 1976. There were all sorts of young people showing up in San Geronimo back then. I suppose they were escaping the cities, looking to play cowboys or Indians, or find God in the desert in a burning bush. Who knows? Most of them were awfully silly and pretentious. As a whole, it seemed just another sort of conformity to me. Counter-conformity, I suppose you could call it. But Donald . . . he was different. For one, he was quite a bit older than the others, a rather meek-looking man with short hair, almost bald. And then he had very interesting eyes. Brown eyes that were extremely watchful. He had some money too, unlike a good many of the drifters who came here with a vague idea of living off the land. He bought the Wyman place, as it was known then, a beautiful old place. In those days, there weren't any strip malls or gas stations, no Wal-Mart nearby. It was all open country, orchards and fields with only a narrow two-lane road going by."

"It sounds very lovely," Jack murmured dutifully.

"Oh, it was! I had a gallery in town at that time, a sort of cooperative, and one day Donald came in with an armload of really exquisite watercolors. He was a shy man, very quiet generally, but he got excited whenever he spoke about art. I liked his work immediately—he did landscapes mostly, but stylized, very impressionistic. He had a wonderful sense of color and a delicate hand. Quite amazingly, he had never shown anything in a gallery before, but now he was looking for someone to exhibit his work. Naturally, I agreed to put him in the co-op."

"Did he talk at all about his past? Where he had come from?"

"Well, yes, eventually, but only in a rather general sort of way. He had been a businessman, apparently, somewhere on the East Coast. One of those people who spend all their lives doing things they hate but believe they must do—make money, raise a family, hold down a steady job, be a responsible member of society, all that idiocy. What Donald *really* wanted to do, of course, was chuck the whole thing and become an artist. He put it off for a long time, but one day he finally got the nerve to be the person he wished to be. He dropped out of his old life and came to New Mexico to live out his dream. Anyway, that was the story he told me. . . . Would you care for more iced tea?"

"No, thank you. And then?"

"And then the years went by, he lived very quietly in his pretty little house in his apricot grove, and he painted every day. He didn't have many friends or make much of a splash in town. *I* thought he was first-rate as an artist, but commercially speaking, he was rather out in left field. On the one hand, he didn't paint the sort of Southwestern scenes that sell to the tourists. And on the other, he wasn't avant-garde or flamboyantly bohemian—he didn't wear the right clothes or hang out with the trendy people, so that crowd didn't take any notice of him either. It seems these days an artist has to spend an enormous amount of time promoting himself so people will take notice, but Donald simply didn't bother. Mostly he painted, and that was it. He was quite slow and painstaking, so he didn't have a huge output. A few of his works sold, but not many. I bought one or two of them myself—I would show them to you, if you could see. Fortunately, Donald had a small income, so he was able to live simply and continue painting. All in all, I think he was happy in his quiet way, doing what he wanted to do. Until Chamisa Mall came along and decided to bulldoze him out of existence."

"Yes, I'd like to hear about that," Jack encouraged.

"Well, the town changed, you know. Twenty years can roll by quickly in a little place like San Geronimo. The south end of town started to build up with motels and gas stations. The two-lane road that used to ramble by his property turned into a four-lane highway. Then a Wal-Mart was built nearby. Pretty soon, Donald and his five acres of apricot trees were surrounded by the worst kind of growth. Some California company managed to buy up the land on either side of him, and then they started to put the squeeze on Donald himself, hoping to drive him out. The tragedy was that those two lots next door had been for sale for years, but Donald never quite had the money to buy them up and protect himself."

"Tell me, Dorothy—do you know the name Karma Konstruction?"

The old woman laughed joylessly. "Yes, that was them. Those were the people who squeezed poor Donald out of existence. Karma Konstruction, indeed! These hippie entrepreneurs—or New Age, or whatever they call themselves now—they're even worse predators than the old predators, the money-grubbers who at least did not pretend to be advanced spiritual beings while they robbed you blind . . . I'm sorry, that was an unintended slur."

"Quite all right. I'll just turn a blind eye to it," Jack assured her. "Back to Karma Konstruction, do you know Chuck Hildyard?"

"That nasty little shit!" the old woman swore unexpectedly. "He's their front man, a small-time real estate developer here in town. He's put together a few shoddy subdivisions and some condos up at the ski resort, nothing very big. I'm not certain how he maneuvered himself into the big time. It must be lucrative for him to represent this obscene shopping mall no one wants."

"Some people seem to want it," Jack observed. "Would it surprise you to know that Karma Konstruction, although it was apparently incorporated in California, is in fact a group of local men from San Geronimo?"

"*Nothing* would surprise me when it comes to *those* people!" she declared archly. "My Lord, I suppose they don't want anyone in town to know who they are—the cowards!"

"I gather it was Chuck Hildyard who approached Donald to make an offer on his land?"

"Yes, it was Hildyard. That's how it started—he used to stop by Donald's house, pretending to admire the paintings, and then make his little offers. You have to understand, Donald only owned five acres, but for Karma they were crucial, since they were right in the middle of where they wanted to build. This was almost four years ago. Hildyard began by offering $75,000, I believe. Donald laughed and said no. So the offer was raised to $95,000, then

$110,000. But Donald kept saying no, that he loved his little spot and had no intention of selling. Over the next six months, Hildyard kept raising his offer until it got up to $350,000 plus stock in Chamisa Mall. But Donald wasn't interested."

"You said earlier the land was probably worth a quarter of a million dollars," Jack said. "So with stock in the shopping mall, and an offer that was $100,00 above market value—this was a pretty good deal. Why didn't he just sell and move someplace farther out of town?"

"I've told you that Donald was shy and quiet. But he was also extremely stubborn in his own way. I always had the impression that he had been pushed around entirely too much in his past life, and that he had made some sort of vow to himself never to be pushed around again. Frankly, Chuck Hildyard took entirely the wrong tactic. The more Hildyard pushed, the more stubborn Donald became. Then the offers stopped, and Don thought he'd beaten them. But it turned out to be only a lull in the storm. About six months went by. And then one day Donald came over to my house, and he looked absolutely awful—pale, ten years older, just dreadful. I said, 'My God! What's happened, Don?' But he didn't answer. He only stared at me like a dead man, it was truly terrifying. Then he asked if I would agree to be the artistic executor of his estate. He wanted me to take care of his paintings and watercolors. He was talking a little wildly. He said he didn't care if I sold them or gave them away, as long as they found their way eventually to people who liked them. He told me his life was a mistake, but his art—this was the only good thing he had ever done and he didn't want it to have been in vain. As you can imagine, I was extraordinarily upset to hear him talking like that. I kept asking him, 'Donald, what's wrong? What can I do to help?' But he wouldn't tell me. And then a few days later, he killed himself."

"How did he do it?"

"He hung himself in the orchard, from one of the large apricot trees," Dorothy said crisply. "So the predators won. And now it looks as though we're going to have this terrible shopping mall after all."

Jack sat quietly. He felt the old woman watching him, waiting for him to draw some moral conclusion from the tale.

"They blackmailed him, I suppose?" Jack asked finally.

"That's what I've always thought. When Donald refused to sell, they started looking for some leverage. They found something, I guess. But whatever it was, he preferred suicide to giving in. What I hate is that the bastards got his land anyway!"

"Do you have any idea what kind of leverage they might have had on him?"

"Not a clue. As I say, he was always quite vague about his pre-San Geronimo past. I remember once I pressed him for details, because frankly I'm an extremely nosy person. He became very serious and said I must never ask such questions again. He had been a sleepwalker, he said. A dead soul trapped in hell. But now he was reborn in a new life in New Mexico, and he had no wish to speak about the past."

"Do you suppose he pulled a Gauguin?" Jack asked. "Simply abandoned a wife and family back East?"

"Possibly," Dorothy agreed. "If so, I'm sure they didn't deserve him. An artist needs to be true to a higher calling, doesn't he?"

"Artists are people, and they have responsibilities like everyone else," Jack answered. "Did he ever mention Xerxes Pharmaceutical Corporation in Connecticut?"

"Never. Though corporations in general, yes. He could get very worked up on the subject. This was the great evil of our time, he used to say. The corporate mentality. And, of course, I agree completely. These corporations—it's positively cancerous how they gobble up everything that's small and decent. They're like locusts destroying everything in their path. And they certainly got Donald in the end, poor dear. You know, sometimes I wake up in the middle of the night thinking about this, wondering how they did it, how they drove a decent man to suicide. You'll find out, won't you, Jack? By God, we'll make those little bastards wish they'd never been born!"

Jack smiled. Dorothy Lange was an odd combination of patrician old lady and bomb-throwing anarchist. "I certainly intend to try," he assured her.

4

After dinner on Saturday night, Jack sat on the porch swing in the garden while Emma washed the dishes inside. The wind had come up, and there was a smell of rain in the air, the usual evening storm approaching. Jack heard the long, low growl of distant thunder—from over the mountains, he imagined, though thunder was often hard to pin down. He wondered how Howie was doing on his camping trip. Poor Howie was a very indoor variety of Native American and wouldn't enjoy getting wet.

He heard the kitchen screen door open and Emma's footsteps on the flagstone path. They'd had a fight earlier, most unfortunately. Emma was angry because Jack had disappeared from the library this morning without leaving word where he was going. In fact, it was a mix-up—Jack had told the volunteer at the checkout desk to tell Emma that he was heading out on some errands and she shouldn't worry. But somehow she hadn't gotten the message. Then, after Jack left Corazon Motors, he had been hot on the scent of his case and frankly he had forgotten to give her a call. *You forgot to give me a call, Jack? There I was, worried crazy, imagining you run down by a car! I was phoning the goddamn hospital, Jack, to see if you were there! And you forgot?*

All this was very hard. Jack replied bitterly that he had been a cop for over twenty-five years and he had never needed to ask his wife's permission before when he was on an investigation. Emma replied, most reasonably, that it wasn't a matter of permission, only common courtesy. He had to face it, circumstances had changed. He couldn't just go off like that anymore and not expect people to worry. It didn't help much that Jack knew he was wrong—certainly he should have thought to give Emma a quick call before heading off from Corazon Motors to Dorothy Lange's house. Yet he hated every part of it. His lack of freedom. His dependence on his wife.

"I brought you a glass of wine," Emma told him, joining him on the swing with a peace offering. "Not that you deserve it."

"I'm sorry," he said, belatedly. "It was thoughtless of me to leave you worrying."

"I'm sorry too. I didn't mean to scold."

"It's hard for both of us, my blindness. You're doing a heroic job, Emma—I know what I put you through."

Suddenly it started to rain. A few tentative drops fell, then the sky cracked with thunder, and in a second it was pouring, a real cloudburst. Jack took Emma's hand, and they ran laughing inside the house.

"I'm soaking!" she cried. "I love it! Do you want to take a hot bath?"

"Together?"

"Mmm . . ."

They were lying in bed upstairs an hour later when the phone rang. At their age, sex wasn't quite what it once had been many years ago. It was stout sex now, no longer sleek or supple. Yet tonight it seemed to Jack incredibly sweet, like a rainbow after a storm. To be with someone as long as he had been with Emma, through a lifetime of changes, and a career come and gone.

The phone keep ringing. Jack said hell, let the machine take it. Let all the world fade away except for you and me, honey, and a nearly finished bottle of pinot noir. But later when Emma was in the bathroom brushing her teeth, Jack's curiosity got the better of him. He walked downstairs to where the answering machine rested on a living room shelf. The message was from the FBI, Special Agent Kevin Neimeyer saying that Jack should call back as soon as possible.

"Hey, bubba!"

"Kevinsky, my friend."

This sort of buddy cop talk seemed increasingly shallow to Jack, but he did it anyway. A long time ago—sixteen years was it?—Jack and Kevin had been holed up together on a very boring stakeout in a San Francisco hotel room with lots of time for bullshit and male bonding. Now the friendship was getting a little thin, yet they kept up the pretense.

On Wednesday, Jack had given Kevin the serial number of the .38 revolver Howie had found near Aria's car. At that point this had been considered a low priority investigation, and they'd heard nothing in return. Then on Friday, after the FBI had been invited into the case, Jack convinced Captain Ed Gomez to send the actual gun itself, as well as the three empty cartridges by special courier to the Bureau's crime lab in Washington. The package had gone to Washington with a special request for urgent priority from Kevin. It was early, but Jack was hoping for some results.

"So what gives?" he asked.

"I got the lab report, Jack. Documents ran the serial number on the weapon while F and T did ballistics on the shells." F and T was the Firearms and Toolmarks Unit at the crime lab. "Latent Fingerprint and DNA had a go at everything as well. But let me start with Documents—your gun has a bit of a history, though probably nothing that's connected with your present investigation. It's an old revolver, as I'm sure you realized. Manufactured in 1959. In 1964 it was used by a woman named Louella Anne Hancock in Lubbock, Texas, who wounded her husband, a Baptist minister, as he came sneaking home one night at four a.m. after being with another woman. The lady convinced a jury that she thought it was a burglar breaking into her home at that hour . . . sounds like quite a story there, huh?"

"A real Texas ballad," Jack agreed. "What else?"

"The .38 remained in Texas for the next twenty years. It was registered at different times by a high school principal, a country-western singer, a lady who ran a massage parlor in Dallas, and a state senator. Then in 1984 it disappeared, reported stolen by the state senator. The thing dropped out of sight for about a decade, and then, lo and behold, two years ago a fourth grader brought it to class loaded, a little show and tell at Oñate Elementary School in—guess where?—San Geronimo, New Mexico. Does that ring a bell, Jack?"

"Yes, I remember hearing about the incident. It caused a brief bout of soul-searching among the adults. A few wild-eyed liberals went so far as to suggest that gun control might be in order. Let me take a guess, Kevin—the .38 was confiscated by the San Geronimo Sheriff's Department?"

"You got it. It should have been destroyed, of course. But confiscated weapons in small-town sheriff departments tend to take on a half-life all their own, which is why the serial number was left on our computer . . . so okay, on to F and T. Here's what they found. All three of the cartridges were fired by the same .38. The gun you submitted for analysis."

"All *three*?" Jack queried, wanting to be quite certain of this point. "The cartridges were *not* found together, you know—two of the shells were picked up in the San Geronimo Wilderness area near where Gary Tripp disappeared, and Howie came across the third one down in the desert."

"Right. I'm aware of that. Nevertheless, Jack, they were examined very carefully under a microscope, and all three came from the Smith & Wesson that you were so kind to send me."

"Sorry, I don't mean to belabor the point, but this is very interesting. Now, make my day and tell me the lab picked up a few latents belonging to Sheriff Louis Snider."

"That I can't tell you, Jack. There were no latents belonging to your missing sheriff on either the gun or the cartridges. Howie's prints were all over the gun, of course, and a few of yours as well. The lab brought up only one print that might be interesting to you. It was on the cylinder, and they were able to get a match on it from a driver's license application. It belongs to a Charles L. Hildyard of San Geronimo. Do you know him?"

"You bet. He's a real estate developer, and a member of the men's group I'm investigating."

"One more item. Just for the hell of it, they ran Charles L. Hildyard through the computer to see who was touching your gun. He has a sheet. A conviction in 1981 for flying bales of marijuana from Mexico to southern California in a single-engine Cessna. The pilot was a man named Michael Ballantine. They were doing low-level runs into a small airstrip south of Palm Springs. Both men cooperated and named names higher up, so they got off with light sentences."

"I know Michael Ballantine. He calls himself Misha, and these days he's a TV producer of sorts. He's in the men's group too."

"Well, well! Seems like you got yourself a men's group from hell!" Kevin laughed. "Better watch that fire in the belly stuff, Jack. This fire sounds like it could be dangerous!"

5

On Sunday, Emma Wilder had arranged to throw an afternoon garden party to stir up interest in the San Geronimo adult literacy program. As a rule, Emma was not a social creature, and there were few actual parties ever thrown at the Wilder residence—dinners, yes, but generally for no more than two or three of their friends. Today she had invited nearly forty people to stop by the house beginning at two o'clock. It was going to be quite a bash. She had invited all the volunteers in the literacy program, as well as a number of local teachers, writers, and politicians, including the mayor and his wife.

Jack had known of the impending garden party for more than a month. Emma had reminded him of it at strategic intervals—two weeks ago, one week ago, then mid-week on Wednesday, a sort of countdown to prepare him for the invasion. Of course it had still entirely slipped his mind. Now on Sunday morning, he was flabbergasted to discover that on a busy day, when he had serious matters to investigate, forty people were about to descend upon his house and garden. Emma was exasperated, but she knew her husband too well to be surprised. She requested only three things of him: that he make up a batch of sushi, his famous California rolls for hors d'oeuvres (he had in fact agreed to do this a month ago); that he mix up a few gallons of his equally famous sangria for the punch bowl; and that most of all, he stay out from underfoot while she cleaned the house and got on with the preparations. Fortunately, Emma had already bought all the ingredients for sushi and sangria, so Jack only had to do a few hours of kitchen work and then he could (please!) disappear.

Jack was astonished that anyone could think of garden parties at such a crucial moment in an investigation. Nevertheless, feeling like a martyr—for Emma's sake—he set himself in motion on Sunday morning cooking up a big pot of sushi rice, making the sticky vinegar dressing, cutting sheets of seaweed, and preparing the various ingredients that would go into the center of the rolls. Jack had learned to make sushi from a famous *itamae-san,* a sushi chef in San Francisco whose daughter had been kidnapped—Jack had rescued the daughter, and sushi lessons were his reward. Here in San Geronimo, blindness had slowed down Jack's gourmet pursuits only briefly, until he figured out that organization was the key to sightless cooking. Now he had his kitchen set up in such a way that everything was located in an exact, prearranged position within easy reach—each pot and pan, spice and herb precisely where he wanted it. When he got going, he was like an orchestra conductor, his arms in motion, his hands reaching high and low for different ingredients. Only occasionally did he have to stop and sniff and taste, to make certain he was using salt rather than sugar, or rice vinegar rather than the usual balsamic vinegar he preferred for green salads.

Jack got the rice going—making good sushi rice was a delicate operation, particularly at an altitude of seven thousand feet. But once the water had boiled and he turned down the flame on his gas range to a simmer, he used the kitchen phone to call information for the number of a retired detective he knew in Connecticut, Charlie Leighton, who had once been in the New Haven police department.

Jack wasn't even certain Charlie was still alive, for he was quite a bit older than Jack. But information had a listing, and after five rings Charlie picked up the phone.

"Hello?" The man who answered was suspicious and creaky, and had the voice of an isolated old person.

"Hey, Charlie . . . it's Jack. Jack Wilder."

"Jack . . ."

"Jack Wilder," Jack repeated hopefully.

"Oh, hey . . . Captain Wilder! Well, my goodness, imagine hearing from you!"

Captain had been Jack's rank the last time he and Charlie had spoken, years ago. Jack did not correct him; rank was the least of his worries at the moment.

"How are you doing, Captain? My goodness, I sometimes think of that homicide we worked on together . . . when was that?"

"A long time ago, Charlie. I'm retired now too. Emma and I are living in New Mexico."

"Are you? I've always wanted to visit the Grand Canyon there, but I never quite got around to it."

"The Grand Canyon is in Arizona, Charlie," Jack commented. Then he immediately felt bad for saying it. "It's close, though. Just the next state over," he delicately added.

"Well, I don't get around too much anymore," Charlie said wistfully.

Jack suppressed a sigh, fearing this call had been a mistake. Charlie must be pushing eighty by now—he sounded like an old eighty, by today's standards, probably feeble in health from all the years of bad cop food and stress. It was depressing to be two retired cops talking over the long-distance wire, Jack in his kitchen, Charlie in front of a TV set, which Jack could hear blaring in the background.

"Look, Charlie, the reason I called is this. I'm doing some P.I. work these days. . . ."

"Is that right?"

"Yes, I am. And I was wondering if you still had any contacts with your old department? I'm trying to find out all I can about a Xerxes Pharmaceutical Corporation down in Bridgeport, and a man by the name of Donald Hicks who has some sort of connection with them, though I don't know precisely what. He may be a past employee."

"Newport, you say?"

"*Bridgeport*," Jack repeated patiently. "Bridgeport, Connecticut."

"My son-in-law's the chief of police down in Bridgeport."

"Is he?" Jack tried to sound optimistic, though he wasn't at all certain old Charlie had his ports right—Bridgeport, Westport, Southport, they probably all sound the same after a certain age: the port of no return. Nevertheless, Jack spent the next ten minutes painstakingly repeating the precise information he wanted, as well as the names, Donald Hicks and Xerxes Pharmaceutical Corporation. Charlie Leighton had been a very good detective a long time ago, one of the best, and Jack hoped he had just a few good brain cells left.

"I know it's Sunday," Jack urged, "but this really is a matter of life and death. There's a young woman who's missing, and we're trying to locate her before it's too late."

"I'll get on it, Captain. I'll phone my daughter-in-law right away."

But wasn't it his *son*-in-law he was going to call? Jack went over it all again, trying to be patient. Of course it wasn't Charlie's fault that he was old. The problem was more Jack's, that he didn't have any other contacts in Connecticut. He was blind and out of the loop and retired, just like Charlie.

"Anyway, if you can help me with this, Charlie, I'd sure be grateful. But if it's too much of a hassle . . ."

"Oh, no, Lieutenant, I got this covered for you. My goodness, it's been ages since I've had a bit of detective work to do! And it's great to hear your voice. It sure has been a long, long time. . . ."

Lieutenant! Jack hung up the phone in despair, worried that if they reminisced any farther back in time, he'd be a young officer in uniform once again, walking a city beat.

By mid-morning, several of Emma's women friends had arrived to help with the preparations for the garden party. Jack did his best to stay out of the way. He made up a dozen sushi rolls filled with avocado and imitation crab flakes; a second dozen that were filled with asparagus, smoked salmon, avocado, and green onion; and a final dozen "reverse rolls"—the rice on the outside—with avocado, smoked salmon, asparagus and very thinly cut strips of red pepper. Each roll would eventually be cut into six pieces, but Jack would do that later, right before the party got under way, because he didn't want the rice to get dried out.

Jack had always found cooking a restful meditation, a way to set his hands in motion while his brain ran free. As his hands worked with the sushi, his mind was occupied with a very different problem. He was trying to imagine how it could be that a revolver might fire two cartridges in the mountains near Bear Lake, and then nearly two months later another shell from the same revolver be found on the desert near Aria Waldman's Jeep? Possible scenarios arranged themselves in his mind, but he still didn't have enough information to come to any conclusions.

Later, he mixed up a big bowl of red wine and brandy for san-gria; he cut the fruit, oranges, grapes, apples and strawberries that he would add to the punch at the last moment. Then he took his cell phone, and he and Katya fled the increasingly frantic pre-party household for a quiet, shaded corner of the garden where there was a wooden bench. Charlie Leighton was just too old to be trusted, so Jack spent the next hour tracking down Kevin Neimeyer to re-quest that FBI agents in Connecticut become involved in checking out the Xerxes/Donald Hicks/Chamisa Mall connection, whatever that might be. Kevin complained that it was Sunday, his day off—he was on his cell phone at the moment kayaking down a Colorado river with his son. Nevertheless, he would try.

At two o'clock, people began to arrive. Soon there was a sum-mery crowd nibbling and drinking and wandering through the Wilders' garden. There was no place now for Jack to hide, and he did his best to be sociable. Two elderly women, avid mystery readers, managed to corner him and ask him to settle an argument they were having—what was the difference between a latent fin-gerprint and a patent fingerprint? Jack explained that a patent fin-gerprint was one that could be seen by the naked eye, while a latent print needed some kind of chemical agent to make it visi-ble. "Dusting a print," they used to call it, though these days mod-ern police departments used everything from superglue to lasers to bring invisible prints to life.

Jack was holding forth on these esoteric matters—starting to enjoy himself just a little, if the truth be known—when the cell phone in his shirt pocket began to beep. To his surprise it was Charlie Leighton. Jack walked off into the bushes to get away from the sea of voices and make certain he was hearing Charlie cor-rectly. It was astonishing, but in just a few hours, the old detective had managed to find out everything that Jack needed to know about the odd connection between Xerxes Pharmaceutical and Donald Hicks.

More precisely, it was Charlie's son-in-law, the Bridgeport po-lice chief, who had gathered the information by making a phone call to a top executive he knew at the pharmaceutical company, and from old police reports.

To begin with, Donald Hicks was not the San Geronimo artist's real name. He was Richard Weinstein, and for eighteen years he had been an accountant for Xerxes, a quiet, methodical man who worked his way up the corporate ladder to become the company comptroller, the man in charge of the payroll. One day in 1974, Richard Weinstein did not show up at work, and when an outside accounting firm was called in to go over the books, it was discovered that exactly $200,000 was missing. The police were summoned, but the quiet, methodical accountant had vanished, leaving behind not only his job but also a wife and family.

Then a year later, the case took a more violent turn. A post office worker in Manhattan's East Village believed he recognized Weinstein from a wanted poster, though he wasn't absolutely certain. The suspect was living as an artist under the name Pablo Monet, not a very convincing pseudonym. An NYPD detective was sent to investigate; he arrived at Monet's studio on Avenue B and Sixth Street, but the suspect panicked and shot the detective dead the moment he walked in the door. From fingerprints and other evidence, the NYPD concluded that the perp was indeed the missing Richard Weinstein. But the accountant vanished once again, this time apparently forever.

Twenty years passed and the case was virtually forgotten. Then one day the CEO of the Xerxes corporation received a phone call from a real estate developer named Chuck Hildyard in New Mexico. Hildyard wanted to know if there was still a reward being offered for the capture of Richard Weinstein; if so, he might have some valuable information for them. Of course, $200,000 is very small change for a pharmaceutical company, and there was, in fact, no reward being offered. But the CEO was opposed to embezzlement as a general principal; he believed a stand should be taken, and so he worked out a deal with Mr. Hildyard. If Richard Weinstein was indeed found and apprehended, Xerxes would agree to give Hildyard any land that might have been purchased with the stolen money, once this property had been properly reclaimed by Xerxes.

It was a complicated and dirty way to get five crucial acres, but the strategy proved effective. A moral ending, perhaps, for an American story: the bad were punished, and there would be a Sears and JC Penny in San Geronimo after all. Only Richard Weinstein, alias Pablo Monet, also known as Donald Hicks, had hung himself in his apricot orchard rather than surrender the artistic life that he had stolen for himself twenty years earlier.

Jack turned off the cell phone, frowning deeply. He was not greatly surprised by the Hicks story, for everything Dorothy Lange told him had suggested blackmail and some old secret that Hicks was running from. But it was vicious just the same, and the bodies were starting to add up. Jack meditated darkly as images swirled in his head. The dead and the disappeared. A Cessna filled with bales of marijuana from Mexico. Bullet shells scattered on the land. A secret circle of men, some of whom had been friends since serving together in an elite squad in Vietnam. . . .

Jack's head jerked up toward the unseen mountains to the east. He felt a sudden surge of anxiety for Howie's safety on San Geronimo Peak with a group of self-styled warriors who played an exceptionally bloody game.

6

The assault on San Geronimo Peak began at dawn Saturday morning from an unpaved parking lot at the base of Forest Trail 141, eight thousand feet above sea level.

There were three separate trails that climbed San Geronimo Peak, the second highest mountain in New Mexico. Howie was dismayed to see that the men's group, being warriors, had chosen the longest and most dangerous route. Forest Trail 141 would take them on a steep, grueling climb above tree line and then across a narrow windswept ridge that traversed several lesser peaks—Mt. Williams and Mt. Hart—to arrive at the North Crevice, a final deadly ascent of rock and scree that claimed a climber or two every few years. The general plan for Saturday was to climb up the west face of Mt. Hart and then duck down a short distance over the other side to make camp at Bear Lake, the spot where Gary Tripp had vanished earlier in the summer. On Sunday, according to the schedule, they would make the ascent up the North Crevice to the summit of San Geronimo Peak, spend an hour or two on top in triumphant meditation of their virility, and then descend the treacherous East Face, a terrifying drop nearly straight down to the ski resort that lay below on the northeastern slope of the mountain. This was the quick way down—very quick, if you didn't watch out. If all went well, a friend of Zor McCarthy's would meet them with a van in the ski resort parking lot at seven p.m. on Sunday evening and ferry them back to the bottom of Trail 141, where their cars were waiting.

Howie was not happy about any of this. Among other worries,

he had a phobia about heights, a queasiness of stomach that overcame him while staring down terrifying mountain chasms; he could visualize too clearly his broken body sprawled across the rocks below, a buzzard pecking at his liver. He knew it was unmanly to worry about such things, but he worried anyway—particularly when he discovered they were not bringing the ropes and clamps and picks that climbers generally used in the North Crevice.

"Don't worry!" Misha said laughingly in the parking lot, amused by the worried expression on Howie's face. "This is a matter of my . . . my . . . *mind* over matter." He took a deep breath to steady his stutter, then began again: "A mountain is a spiritual challenge, after all—so don't worry about ropes. What you need to concentrate on is your attitude."

Misha was wearing a Gore-Tex windbreaker with lots of zippered pockets, Eddie Bauer shorts, and state-of-the-art hiking boots; with his trim beard and a cap over his bald head that had the logo of a major Hollywood studio on the front, this was a portrait of modern man about to tackle nature. "Human beings create such unnecessary limits!" he explained. "They say to themselves, 'Oh, I can't be a millionaire, not me, I'm not lucky enough!' Or, 'I can't fly, because that's what birds do, not people.' But all these limitations are only thoughts, and when we stretch our thoughts, suddenly we *have* no limits. It's so incredibly simple!"

"Believe in miracles, and there *are* miracles," Denny echoed.

"This is the warrior's journey, Moon Deer—to expand our minds," Misha continued. "To say to ourselves, '*Yes,* I can be a millionaire! Yes, I *can* fly!'"

"I still think we should be taking ropes," Howie insisted stubbornly.

The other men—Zor, Denny, and Shep—were standing nearby in the parking lot, all in various states of Gore-Tex chic. Unfortunately, Lou Snider was not making the climb this weekend, as Denny had predicted; this was disappointing, but the others seemed determined not to let it get in the way of their own metaphysical experience. As for Chuck Hildyard, the one warrior Howie had not yet met, apparently he had climbed up to Bear Lake yesterday afternoon on his own. He had been feeling a deep need for spiritual solitude and wanted to have a night on the mountain alone to meditate, cleanse his aura, and work on himself. Chuck was going to prepare the Spirit Circle as well as the Medicine Drum, and would greet them tonight at Bear Lake.

The worst part of all this, as far as Howie was concerned, was the fact that they were taking no food along, only a few oranges for "lunch" this afternoon, and then nothing for the rest of the weekend. No candy bars, no trail mix, no potato chips, *nothing*—only a small water filter, which Denny had brought along, a gadget shaped like a bicycle pump that made it possible to drink from high mountain streams without having to worry about elk poop and catching germs from big horn sheep. (Strangely enough, the contamination of elk poop and big horn sheep was the one part of this venture Howie did *not* worry about.)

"Food is one of those imaginary limitations, I suppose?" Howie suggested sadly.

"How right you are!" Misha agreed. "And when we fast, we rid ourselves of all those impurities that keep a warrior from being in touch with his true power."

"What *I* really like about fasting," Zor said happily, "is that after a few days you never have to take a crap."

"Okay, enough talk! Let's climb this goddamn mountain!" Denny cried, leading the charge over the parking lot and into the trees.

The first part of the trail was too steep and narrow for conversation, rising sharply through a thick forest of aspen and fir, following alongside a fast-moving stream. Howie soon worked up a good sweat even though the sky was dark with clouds—not a good omen when the afternoon thunderheads started building this early in the day. As he climbed, the metal butt of the .38 revolver that Jack had given him protruded uncomfortably into his spine from the inside of his backpack. Occasionally Howie tried to jiggle the pack, without being too obvious, hoping the gun would settle into a better position. But no matter what he did, the gun kept pressing against his back, a small but irritating burden.

By mid-morning the path widened, and the ascent was not so steep. The group spread out along the trail, with Denny and Misha far in the lead, out of sight, and Shepherd Plum somewhere in the rear. Howie found himself walking alongside Zor McCarthy, the solar architect. As Sensitive New Age Guys went, Howie found Zor the easiest of the group to take. Maybe it was because Zor had a ponytail, like Howie. Just two ponytail guys. Though of course Howie's ponytail was black and traditional to his culture, while Zor's hair was blond and counterculture. Walking side by side, they got talking about the lost continent of Atlantis and the wonderful, pollution-free technology they had way back then. Zor's particular interest was shit.

"What was really incredible, back in Atlantis, is that everything got recycled," Zor assured him. "They had houses that would do everything for you—it's where I got my inspiration for totally self-sufficient solar design. I mean, you take a shit—why waste all those fabulous nutrients? So in my houses, your morning dump gets solar processed in the special shit fryer and turned into compost that is carried automatically into your indoor garden, and this is where you grow all your food. You see what I mean? It's just so beautiful to have your food growing right there in your living room! All your vegetables and maybe a fishpond for protein—and you know, fish makes great fertilizer too. So you eat, you shit, your shit creates new food, and you eat again—a great big circle of life!"

Yes, but not exactly French cuisine, Howie thought to himself. Still, it was a long walk, and he could get into a rap like this. Howie even launched forth onto his dissertation for a while, "Philosophical Divisions at the Top of the Food Chain"—Howie's thesis that the true division in American culture was based on who ate what. Iceberg lettuce versus arugula and baby green. Those who ate "prawns" and those who ate "shrimp." White bread versus whole wheat—this was the great American divide, as Howie saw it, a more profound divide than Republican versus Democrat. Zor got the concept right away, which was more than Howie could say for his dissertation advisor at Princeton.

After an hour of this, Howie brought the subject around to Sheriff Lou Snider.

"So why did Lou flip out like that? I mean, what's his problem, Zor?"

"Hey, it's shamanism, man! It's what can happen when you start tapping into all that universal energy. We're talking powerful stuff here, like trying to ride a thunderbolt. And some riders, you know—they just can't hack it. But I feel for Lou. Deep inside, he's still a brother."

"Brother or not, he screwed my girlfriend," Howie mentioned sourly.

"Did he? Well, Lou did stuff like that, of course. All that competitive male jive, like who's the king of the harem. Personally, I find it's a lot easier just to not have girlfriends anymore. I'm saving all my universal energy for the big push to enlightenment. I'm hoping to fly soon, you know."

"Fly?" It was the second time this morning that the subject had arisen. "Are you speaking metaphorically, or are you planning to buy yourself a Cessna like Misha?"

"Oh, no, no! I mean really *fly*. Warriors can do that. Didn't you ever read Carlos Castaneda?"

"Those Don Juan books?" Carlos Castaneda was an anthropologist at UCLA in the sixties who met a *brujo* in Mexico named Don Juan who supposedly taught him all sorts of shamanistic magic. "Didn't someone prove that Castaneda made up all those stories? Magicians taking peyote and flying—it was all a clever hoax, Zor," Howie suggested gently.

"Oh, no! . . . hey, man, this is *real*! The corporate establishment, of course, they don't want people to know we all have unlimited potential, that we can do anything we want, even fly. I mean, how could Exxon sell gasoline if everyone got wise to the secrets of the universe? You dig what I'm saying?"

Howie dug, more or less. It was crazy, of course, like sinking intellectually into some New Age swamp. But then there were a lot of people who believed a lot of things, including the idea that the earth had been literally created in six days, and on the seventh God rested. Was this any less crazy? It was all part of a growing wave of antiscience that threatened to overwhelm the millennium.

"Hey, I'm going to fertilize that tree over there—it looks like it could use some nourishment," Zor said, pulling down his pants and moving off the trail. Howie was sorely tempted to walk off on his own, but he forced himself to wait for Zor.

He would keep asking questions until he discovered Aria Waldman's fate. He wasn't certain why he owed this to her; but he knew he did.

Looking back, Howie had to point to "lunch" on Saturday as the time when things really went over the top. Around noon, Howie walked out of the forest onto a grassy meadow with a small stream running past. He saw Misha and Denny up ahead kneeling by the stream refilling their water jugs, pumping water through their small filtering device.

"We're going to stop here and re-center," Misha said when Howie reached them. "Here, let me fill your canteen."

"I'll just dunk it in the stream," Howie told him.

"Don't be foolish! There are all sorts of bacteria in these streams," Misha said sharply. "Give me your canteen, Moon Deer—you need to drink a lot of water at this elevation, particularly since we're fasting."

"You gotta be on constant guard against impurities," Denny mentioned vaguely, gazing up at the threatening sky.

Personally, Howie wasn't convinced that a fast-moving stream at this altitude was going to poison him, but it seemed simplest to go along with the general paranoia. He took a final swig from his water bottle, then handed it over to Misha to refill. Meanwhile, Zor and Shep wandered in from the trail, they had their water filled as well, then everyone sat in a circle. Overhead, a black thundercloud slipped past the sun, allowing a short burst of sunshine to brighten the meadow where they sat.

"I did that," Shep announced, pleased with himself. "I made that cloud go away so we could sit here in the sun."

Howie began to laugh, thinking this was a joke. But then he saw that Shep was perfectly serious. "You think you can control the weather?"

"Naturally, we can control the weather," Misha interjected. "Isn't that what your Native American rain dances are all about? Modern man has lost the ability to do a lot of things, but that doesn't mean they can't be done. It's our path as warriors to re-claim our natural talents."

Howie raised an eyebrow but decided to let it pass. Denny had the oranges in his pack, five plump oranges, one for each warrior, and he passed them out with solemn ceremony. This was the last solid food they would eat until they emerged from the wilderness late tomorrow night. In silence, each man peeled his orange and chewed thoughtfully, segment by segment. Howie did his best to eat slowly, savoring every burst of juicy flavor. He devoured the pulp, the stringy parts, even a seed or two. After hiking all morning, his stomach was already growling for something more solid. A burrito. A tuna sandwich. A bag of blue corn tortilla chips . . . he tried to concentrate on the task at hand: *I'm not here to eat, I'm here to find out what happened to Aria.* It was a struggle to get a straight word from any of these guys, but this afternoon he planned to hike alongside Misha and do some serious male bonding. And then tonight, he would finally meet the real estate agent, Chuck Hildyard. . . .

"I see you're re-centering, Moon Deer," Denny said with a dippy smile.

"You bet," Howie told him, flashing a smarmy dippier-than-thou smile in return.

"Shh!" said Misha, raising a finger to his lips. "Meditation time."

The five men fell into a profound silence, each with his eyes closed, sitting in the circle on the meadow while the sun drifted in and out of the clouds. Howie felt a strange surge of peacefulness, though he struggled against it; he was not here to feel peaceful. He sat in a quasi-lotus position, his palms resting upward on his knees. The mountain meadow was very beautiful, high above the cares of the town far below. The stream nearby gurgled and sputtered. *Don't go all Zen here, for chrissake! This is not the time!* Howie told himself urgently.

A butterfly fluttered by and landed briefly on Howie's left knee. It was an iridescent fairy being with wings of multicolored velvet. As Howie watched, the butterfly winked at him and flew away. This was getting a little strange.

Then he heard soft laughter. It was Shepherd Plum, giggling to himself. Denny meanwhile was grinning like a Cheshire cat. A cloud of butterflies flew between Howie and the sun.

"It's starting," Zor said softly. His eyes seemed particularly bright.

"*What's* starting?" Howie asked. His mouth was dry, and he felt an unreasonable surge of fear.

But the others only laughed. Gentle laughter, tinkly as broken crystal. Wise looks passed between them.

"What's *starting*?" Howie demanded, trying not to panic. He took a long swallow of cold mountain water from his bottle.

"I think we need to move now," Misha said. "Coyote-That-Sings is waiting for us at the Spirit Circle. . . . Owl Dancer, let's top off the water bottles."

Owl Dancer, apparently, was Denny Hirsh. Some very weird transformation was taking place.

"Give me your bottle, Moon Deer," Owl Dancer said.

Howie handed Owl Dancer his plastic bottle and watched as the water passed from the cold mountain stream, through the filter of the water purifier, and into Howie's jug. Howie laughed suddenly because the water sparkled so delightfully.

It was really the most insanely beautiful water he had ever seen.

7

The sky turned black, then caught fire. The thunder god spoke in his big booming voice, and at last fat drops of purple rain began to fall, plip-plop, on Howie's head. He opened his mouth and caught a few diamond droplets on his tongue. This was turning into some afternoon.

The men were scattered above tree line, following a trail that rose and fell over a green swell of endless alpine meadow. Howie understood that he was not his usual self when he found himself singing ecstatically: "The hills are alive! . . . with the sound of Proz-ac!" He sensed he had the lyrics slightly wrong, but what did it matter? The sound of music was just as sweet whatever the words, a melodic roar of butterfly wings all around him. Man, I'm one stoned Indian! he thought to himself. It was the water, of course. Something in that little bicycle-pump filter. Howie even had a pretty good idea what that something was.

Most of all, he just wanted to lie down and roll in the gooshy grass. Roll down the mountain. Roll a stone. Roll a joint. Roll over Beethoven all the way into town. Nevertheless, he was straight enough to know he'd better not roll anywhere. Walking was the thing. A person needed to keep upright in a situation like this. A long walk into the purple plip-plop of acid rain.

None of this was right, and Howie struggled to get a grip on himself. Fortunately, he knew what LSD was, and this gave him some grip on what was real and what was not. It was many years since he had taken any psychedelics. Back when he was a sophomore at Dartmouth, he had briefly fallen in with a crowd that thought it was a lot more interesting to drop acid on Saturday nights than get drunk on kegs of beer and barf and get into fist-fights and crash cars. At least with acid, you saw God in His universe from time to time, and sex was fascinating, if a little rubbery and strange. But this was a long time ago, only a phase; like the rest of his crowd, Howie had matured and gotten on with the important things in life, like finding obscure subjects to research, and convincing banks to give him credit cards so he could get into debt.

"You spiked the water, asshole!" Howie managed to shout at Denny the Owl Dancer, as Denny passed by on the trail.

"White Lightning!" Owl Dancer cried happily. "Osley's original formula. We're gods, Moon Deer! All of this, everything you see—it's only a vision of your own godlike imagination!"

"You should have asked me," Howie grouched. "You should have given me a choice."

"Hey, it's your movie, Moon Deer! Enjoy it!"

The sky opened up with rain. This was indeed a serious predicament to find himself, stoned silly above tree line in a thunderstorm at somewhere between ten and eleven thousand feet in the company of a bunch of raving SNAGs. If he could just hang on for another seven or eight hours, he knew he would be his ordinary self again. But a lot could happen in seven or eight hours. There was a flash of lightning close by, followed by a terrifying crack of thunder. Imaginary lightning, perhaps—Howie was as solipsistic as the next man. Nothing was real, but thinking made it so. Even so, imaginary lightning could turn a guy into a strip of blackened bacon if he didn't watch out.

Better get a grip. Calm down. Chill out. Howie hurried after Denny up the trail.

Up hill, down dale. High in the mountains. Howie felt like some just-born baby, all wide-eyed, agog and agaggle. He did his best just to keep going and not stop too often to sniff the flowers or examine the intricate veins in rocks. He was soaked through with rain before he thought to stop and get his raincoat from his pack. Talk about closing the barn door when the cat was out of the bag. He kept reminding himself that this was only a drug. Face it, a better drug than television—at least it delivered quality entertainment.

But it would end, he wasn't really crazy, he only had to survive long enough to see it out.

Yet the afternoon seemed to last for all time. Howie straggled in the rear, dreaming awake. Fortunately, the universe above tree line was open to his X-ray vision, and he could make out the other hikers above him on the trail. In snakelike fashion, they went up, up, up. Howie kept walking. That's what a person did in this world: you walked and walked and walked. And sometimes you thought about things. What Howie thought about was Aria Waldman. With a flash of X-ray insight, he saw very clearly that he had never known her, not even when he thought he did. He had fallen for some Aria Waldman doll of his own imagination, a creature whose purpose on earth was entirely wishful thinking, to satisfy his own bio-psychosexual needs. But it had nothing to do with the real Aria Waldman, whoever she was. He had been seduced by a self-created mirage. What a farce it was! Poor Aria, for her part, had fallen for an illusionary Howard Moon, some ghost of *her* own desires. It was like the two of them had been locked in some strange shadow play where nothing was real. These, at least, were Howie's psychedelic thoughts on the matter, which he was able to grasp at the moment in a kind of breathless, gossamer intricacy where everything seemed, at last, to make sense.

"Aria Waldman!" he shouted to the sky. "I never possessed more than a ghost of you anyway! So I release you now into the ether!"

There was a white zap of lightning. BOOM! cried the Thunder God. This was powerful stuff, and a lot cheaper than paying for psycho-counseling.

"However!" he cried, screaming out a codicil to the heavens: "Even though I can't possess you, I'm going to find out what the hell happened to you!"

Another flash. Another boom. This was fantastic! Meanwhile the line of men continued to go up, up, up. They crossed a high mountain ridge, then they went down, down, down, back into the trees. After a while, the lightning stopped, the air grew cool and misty damp. The rain stopped as well but the dark clouds continued to glower and spit. Without warning, the endless afternoon was ending. It was sunset now. The sky cleared enough overhead to catch fire from the exploding west, nature's big orgasm of the day. Howie was thirsty, but he didn't dare drink from the altered state of his water bottle. He found a stream, a silvery ribbon through the woods that climaxed in a quaint little waterfall. He got down on his hands and knees, and lowered his face into the rushing water. He resisted the temptation to take off his clothes and swim away like a trout.

When Howie finished drinking from the stream, he stood up and saw that he was alone in the darkening forest. For a moment he felt like Hansel and Gretel without a bag of bread crumbs to his name. Then he saw a flame ahead of him through the trees, the flickering light of a bonfire. The sacred fire, was it? The magic circle? Howie was surprised there was no one beating a drum. Remind him never to get involved in a men's group intensive weekend ever again! Nevertheless, these men were company, and Howie figured at a time like this they were better than being alone.

He walked the short distance through the woods and came into a circular clearing with a bonfire in the center. But there was something wrong with the fire. He looked more closely, and his heart began to pound: there was an inert human body stretched out upon the wood, flames licking at the hands and legs. Misha, Zor, Denny, and Shep stood together, staring in horror. Shep was whimpering, not a manly sound. Denny kept saying, "Oh, my God! . . . oh, my *God!* . . ."

Howie forced himself to walk closer. The body on the fire was already partially consumed. Blackened skin like burned paper. A horrible smell hung thickly in the air. A barbecue sizzle of burning flesh. Was it just another hallucination? If so, Howie had seen this particular hallucination before. He was quite sure the burning corpse on the funeral pyre was the large man with the secretive, bovine face, the giant with whom he had wrestled on the hillside behind Aria's house for possession of the laptop computer.

"What?" Howie managed.

"It's Chuck," Zor said, his voice a stunned whisper. "We found him like this."

"*This* is Chuck Hildyard?"

"Was."

"Then, the fire . . . did you?"

"None of us. It was going when we got here. Chuck was lying there."

Howie's mind was racing. Shouldn't they try to get the body off the pyre? But the flames were leaping higher, engulfing the figure.

Howie's brain felt like Swiss cheese, but he knew there was a log-ical deduction to be made. The fire could not have been going long. The chances were it wasn't set by lightning. And so if none of them had killed Chuck Hildyard and set him alight, it could only mean . . .

Just then a rifle shot roared through the woods with a logic all its own. Howie heard the mosquito whine of a bullet pass inches from his head. All the men screamed and scattered, warriors no longer.

Howie crouched behind a tree, clutching his .38 revolver. Clearly, he was not the only one who had come hiking this week-end with a pistol in his day pack. Guns were going off all around him, a small stereophonic war. The tree seemed to him particularly thin and narrow under the circumstances. Howie double-cocked the hammer, pointed the revolver, closed his eyes, and pulled the trigger. It made an impressive bang, yet it all seemed basically fu-tile. He didn't know who he was shooting at or what was going on.

The night had already fallen, a moonless night that was so dark Howie feared he was already dead and lying in his tomb. He couldn't see any of the other men, friend or foe. He was by him-self about forty feet from the bonfire—the flickering light through the trees was his only point of orientation.

He heard footsteps running his way. Howie double-cocked his gun. "Who is it?" he screamed hoarsely, standing and pointing his weapon.

"It's Denny!" Denny arrived out of breath behind Howie's tree, a pistol in hand. "Goddamn!" he cried. "This is *mondo* scary, man!"

Howie was suddenly angry, so angry that except for a strange iridescent glow that seemed to hover around Denny's head, Howie felt reasonably sober. Six or seven hours had passed now since the LSD lunch, and the world was starting to resume a more solid ap-pearance. Denny was peering into the darkness, listening intently to the gunfire in the distance, when Howie raised his own pistol to the back of the restaurant owner's head.

"Drop your gun, Denny."

"Moon Deer, for chrissake!"

"I mean it. Drop the gun. I've just reached my bottom line. I've been jerked around by you guys as much as I intend to be. Are you reading my aura?"

"Yeah, yeah. Loud and clear."

"All right. Now, what the hell's going on here?"

"Christ, *I* don't know what's going on. It's Lou—he's followed us up here somehow, and now he's out there with a rifle. He's flipped out, that's all."

"Why has Lou flipped out? Tell me exactly."

"He thinks everyone's against him. His feelings are hurt. He thinks we tried to kill him. Like supposedly *we* told Chucky to plant that bomb in his car! But it's his own fault for opening his mouth to Aria Waldman. For chrissake, she was a reporter, and he told her *everything*!"

Howie pondered this. "So Chucky wired Lou's car with a bomb, and you're saying Lou got even by roasting Hildyard on a funeral pyre?"

"I guess so. I don't know."

"Who told Chuck to set the bomb? Was it Misha?"

"I told you, I don't know, Moon Deer. Everything's been real strange ever since the Donald Hicks thing. Hicks was our albatross, you know. Everything was going great up till then. We were a perfect circle, like totally in touch on a spiritual plane. We were manifesting money like crazy, we were real warriors. And then this one guy, Donald Hicks, wouldn't play ball. We tried everything. We offered him a ton of money for his land, we even offered to let him into the group. But he wasn't interested, so we leaned on him a little. Old Lou set to work. He got hold of the guy's fingerprints, ran them through some computer, and found out that Hicks had a past-and-a-half—he was no saint, believe me, he had shot a cop back in the seventies. But, still, it was a bitch when Hicks had to go and hang himself in his goddamn apricot tree. Ever since then it's like there's been a curse on us. Nothing's been the same."

"What happened to Gary Tripp?"

"I don't know. He and Shep had a big falling out, and then Gary just vanished one night not far from here. It was really spooky, I swear to God."

"Do you think Shep helped him vanish?"

Denny sighed and shook his head. "Anything's possible."

Howie tried the big question. "So tell me about Aria. What happened to her?"

"You keep asking me these things, and I keep telling you—I don't know!"

"Better improvise then, Denny. Or I'm going to pull this trigger, I swear to God."

"Look, all I know is that Lou thought Chucky killed her. And Chucky, he thought Lou did it. It was totally crazy the way they were carrying on. Last weekend—I guess it was a few days before Aria disappeared—Lou showed up at Chucky's house raving mad. He said the San Geronimo D.A.'s office was conducting a secret investigation into corruption in the sheriff's department and that he'd just heard Chucky had gone to them volunteering all sorts of information, saying Lou was on the take from some of the drug dealers in town. Chucky said it wasn't true, he'd *never* turn against a brother warrior, but they almost had a fistfight over it."

"Did Lou say how he had found out about this secret D.A.'s investigation?"

"He said Aria told him. That she had a lady friend who was the D.A.'s secretary and sometimes leaked things to her. Chucky and Lou had this huge shouting match for about half an hour, and then Lou stormed off. So you can see how much bad blood there's been between them."

Howie could also see a possible motive for Chuck Hildyard to kill Aria. It was a growing club of suspects, all the people who might have cause to celebrate Aria Waldman's permanent disappearance.

"What do you think, Denny?" Howie asked. "Who killed Aria? Was it Hildyard, or Lou, or Misha, or did you all do it together?"

"It *wasn't* the group, believe me—we're not *that* crazy. If you want my honest guess, Moon Deer, it was Lou, and that's why he's flipping out. I mean, he was really stuck on Aria Waldman—this part I know for a fact. So he told her too much, more than he should, and then he realized this was absolute suicide, so then he had to get rid of her. But it made him crazy, it drove him over the top. And that's why he's acting in this *mondo* bizarre fashion . . . oh, shit! Listen to that!"

Two shots had just rung out less than twenty feet from where Howie and Denny were crouching.

"It's Lou, I bet. He's trying to circle around behind us," Denny said, peering out into the darkness. "Moon Deer, you gotta listen to me. Lou was in 'Nam, he knows about bush fighting, so you and me are dead unless you let me pick up my gun and we get ourselves into a defensive mode here."

Howie jammed the muzzle of his revolver harder into Denny's neck. "If Lou killed Aria, what did he do with her body?"

"I don't know!"

"Make another guess, then."

"Okay, okay! I think Lou was waiting for her on your road that night, when she was driving away from your cabin. Either he shot her then, or he drove her away somewhere else and did it. But my guess is he took her body way out in the desert. There are a lot of empty miles around San Geronimo where a person can disappear."

Howie let his gun hand relax while his imagination took in this possibility. Aria's body—her warm body fresh from his bed—thrown into some sandy hole in the desert. While Howie was imagining, Denny decided to take his leave.

"Look, Moon Deer, I'm going to pick up my gun now, so don't shoot me, okay? You *need* me, honestly. Together we have a chance against Lou. Otherwise we're dead meat."

Denny reached for his automatic and then lurched forward into the night. Howie let him go. A moment later, he heard a flurry of gunshots not far away in the woods. There was angry shouting and then nothing. Howie sank down wearily behind his tree. As far as he could make out, when push came to shove, New Age guys were awfully much like Old Age guys. Underneath the latest haircut—ponytail or crew cut—it was remarkable how nothing much changed from one stoned age to the next.

8

The night was cold, and Howie was soaked through from the purple rain of the afternoon. When the drug wore off, he felt entirely exhausted and discouraged. He searched in his backpack for his heavy sweater, but found that it was soaked as well. He did his best to stay warm by curling into a fetal position on the damp ground, clutching himself as tightly as possible. The temperature had plunged close to freezing. He couldn't imagine how he was going to survive until morning. There were no human sounds anywhere around him; for all he knew, he was the last man alive. He supposed this should make him feel like the king of the mountain, but he only felt lonely and afraid.

Time passed. Howie wasn't certain if he was falling asleep or dying; he felt himself fading, yet it was pleasant to give in to such an irresistible summons. He was lying on the ground in a tight ball, his hands shoved between his legs for warmth, when he heard footsteps nearby.

"Who's there?" he cried.

A figure drifted closer in the velvety darkness. Howie was astonished to recognize him—it was an old Indian, his great-uncle, Horace Two Arrows, who had died when Howie was thirteen. An apparition, certainly, but why not? If warriors could fly, why shouldn't the dead walk?

"Hey, Moon Deer. What'cha doing, boy, getting yourself all tangled up with these crazy white men? This is no place for an Indian."

Howie rubbed his eyes. "You got that right, Great-Uncle," he told the apparition. "I guess I wanted to see what the world was like outside the rez."

"Well, so you saw it, then," Two Arrows said laconically, sitting down next to Howie. He took a pouch of tobacco from his shirt pocket and began rolling two cigarettes, one for Howie and one for himself, just as he always used to do when Howie was a kid. Two Arrows was a lanky, leathery old man who had never done a whole lot of talking. Yet Howie had been close to his great-uncle as a boy. They used to go fishing together. Often in the afternoons they would sit together in Two Arrows' ancient '52 Ford pickup truck, going nowhere, just sitting, while Howie read aloud from one of the Hardy Boy mysteries that he checked out of the library at the nearby town of Red Creek. Howie had always been a bookish child, even at the age of nine or ten, and his great-uncle was the only one of his relatives who seemed to approve. Hour after hour, Howie read to him the fabulous adventures of Frank and Joe Hardy, and their fat friend Chet, while Two Arrows sat with his wrinkled old hands on the steering wheel, staring at the South Dakota horizon. Sometimes at the end of a book, Two Arrows would nod and say, "That was a pretty good yarn, all right."

There was something very comforting about Howie's great-uncle. In fact, the only other time in his life that Howie had slept outside in the cold without a tent or sleeping bag had been when he was nine years old and his great-aunt had just died. After the sun set that night, Howie had found Two Arrows sitting at the edge of a field, leaning against a tree with a can of beer open in his hands.

"You'd better come inside, Two Arrows," Howie had told him. "It's going to get cold tonight."

"You go inside, boy. I think I'll stay here for a while."

"Then I'll stay too."

"Well, suit yourself."

So Howie had sat next to him, snuggling closer when he became cold. Sometime during the night, it began to rain. But his great-uncle just wrapped his arms around Howie and had kept him safe and warm. It was the deepest, most comforting sleep that Howie could ever remember. Safe and warm. A sleep so profound that when he grew up and found himself from time to time in distant beds in foreign lands, lonely and unable to sleep, all he had to do was think back to that evening, his great-uncle's arms around him.

Then, wherever he was, he'd be comforted; he'd drift off like a small boat slipping from shore into dark, peaceful waters.

All night long, Howie felt his great-uncle's arms around him and in the morning he woke to find himself in a cold, misty forest. He stood up, stretched and yawned.

"Great-Uncle!" he called. For the dream had seemed so real.

Just then, there was a commotion in the trees above his head. He looked up in time to see a bald eagle spread its wings and take off from a high branch. As Howie watched, the eagle flew into the sky, circled Howie three times counterclockwise, and then disappeared into the rising sun.

"Whew!" said Howie, slapping himself. "No wonder I quit taking psychedelics back in college!"

In the light of morning, Howie saw that he had slept not far from a small, oblong mountain lake, hardly more than a pond. He supposed this must be Bear Lake. Everything was remarkably serene after the terror of the night, birds chirping in the trees, not a warrior anywhere in sight, dead or alive. Howie felt like the last person left on the planet.

There was a chill in the morning air, and he warmed himself by the still glowing embers of Chuck Hildyard's funeral pyre. There were a few charred bones and a blackened Rolex watch to commemorate the real estate developer's death, but Howie didn't let them disturb his enjoyment of the fire's remaining heat. He was on his haunches, his hands over the glowing embers, when a figure wrapped in a gray blanket wandered into the clearing. Howie bolted to his feet, his heart beating fast. The figure was ghostly, the hooded blanket concealing its face.

"Great-Uncle?" Howie whispered.

"Well, well. Have you found your Dream Guide, Moon Deer?" the Indian asked slyly.

He recognized the voice. It was a TV producer, not an Indian spirit.

"Misha, for chrissake! What happened to everybody?"

Misha threw the blanket back from his head. It was the same shiny, bald head. The same well-trimmed beard. But Misha's eyes were altered, they were large and strange.

"Everybody?" he repeated vaguely, squatting close to the embers. "They have metamorphosed, I'm afraid."

Howie did his best to translate this in his mind. "They're dead?"

"They wimped out, anyway. . . . Lou's dead," he added after a moment. "I found his body not far from here at the top of a knoll. Some very brave warrior shot him in the back."

Howie took a moment to absorb this. Life, death, the Whole Banana. Should he beat his chest to celebrate the fact that his rival was dead, the guy who had screwed his girlfriend? But he felt nothing, neither glad nor sad, only empty.

"And the others?"

Misha shrugged. "Who knows? Chuck and Lou were the only serious ones. The others don't count."

"Everybody counts," Howie said dutifully.

"Don't give me that humanist bullshit! Only the brave count, Moon Deer. Those who are willing to risk everything, stand or fall on the roll of the dice, and not weep about it one way or the other. I've lived the big life, at least—I can honestly say that. But the show is over."

Howie was trying to decode this statement when the producer stood up and began walking away from the clearing. His hiking boots were wet and made little squishy sounds as he stepped down. Howie hurried after him.

"Misha! For chrissake, where are you going?"

"To the summit, of course. That's what we came to do, isn't it?"

"You're kidding? You can't still be planning to climb the Peak?"

"You want knowledge, Moon Deer? You want to be a man of power?" he taunted. "Then you'd better come with me."

There was a note of self-mockery in Misha's voice, and Howie didn't know if he was serious or not. But Misha was heading quickly up the trail, and Howie had to run to catch him.

"Misha, listen to me. Your brain is still fried on LSD. You're not thinking rationally. Tomorrow you'll wake up, and you'll be your old self again. Let's just turn around and hike down this damn mountain and get some help."

Misha paused long enough to turn and give Howie a contemptuous look. "There is no help, I'm afraid, not for what ails me. So to hell with it, I'm going all the way to the top. You can come with me, or turn around and wimp out with the others—the choice is entirely yours."

"Hold on a minute!" Howie called, because Misha had turned

and was walking away again. "You've got to answer some questions first. What happened to Aria?"

Misha chuckled, but he did not stop. "You'd better come with me, Moon Deer, if you want your answers. A warrior climbs a mountain so that his eyes will see."

"I want to know about Aria now."

"At the summit," Misha turned for a moment and said in a strange, mocking voice: "Everything will be revealed at the place where the earth meets the sky."

The day passed in numb mindlessness. Several times Howie stopped in his tracks, determined to turn around. But each time his curiosity got the better of him, beating out his fear and doubt by a very thin millimeter. He kept moving despite torturous blisters on his feet, climbing into the sky. In the morning the sun blazed down on them. In the afternoon the clouds came up, and there were the usual thunderstorms, very dangerous above tree line. But Misha paid no attention to any of it: sun, wind, rain, or lightning. Nor would he answer any questions or even respond when Howie spoke. He just kept walking up the trail toward the summit of San Geronimo Peak.

"Misha, this is crazy—let's stop and rest awhile," Howie pleaded in the mid-afternoon. "We're going to die up here, for chrissake!"

But Misha acted as if he hadn't heard him. The man was unstoppable. He went up the North Crevice like Santa Claus going up a chimney. Howie struggled somewhat more, but he was determined not to be outdone by a middle-aged television producer. In the late afternoon they climbed through the very heart of a cloud, a mist so thick it was impossible to see farther than the end of one's arm. Then without warning, Howie stepped through to the far side of the cloud and found himself in dazzling sunlight. It was late now, almost sunset, and below his feet there was a soft pink carpet of clouds stretching forever toward the setting sun. Howie felt like an angel newly arrived in a Renaissance painting. The wind was howling. A second later the fog blew in around him, and he was enveloped once again. Then he climbed out of the clouds a final time and saw, a dozen feet above him, Misha standing on a small promontory of rock at the very summit of San Geronimo Peak, one long finger outstretched to the glowing red ball of sun on the western horizon.

"Take a peek at the crack of doom," Misha said as Howie approached.

"I'm sorry?"

"The twilight horizon—it's the opening between two worlds. You see before you the crack between light and darkness, life and death, heaven and earth. It is said, Moon Deer, that a man of power can fly through the open crack of the universe at just this time of twilight and seize hold of his godhead. Shall we give it a try?"

The producer seemed larger than life as he stood on his promontory of rock, wrapped in his gray blanket. He spoke with a new authority, without a trace of his old stutter. Nevertheless, the new Misha worried Howie even more than the old.

"Whoa, wait a second, Misha! You promised to tell me about Aria first."

Misha turned to him with a slow smile. "She really yanked you around, didn't she? That's no way to be a warrior—to stand there like some idiot with your wanker out just waiting for some lady to yank you. She used you."

"That's not true," Howie said with forced patience. "What could she use me for? I'm not a big shot like you, I don't even own a Cessna. There wasn't anything I could give her, except love."

Misha seemed to ponder this. "Come closer," he said. "I'll whisper this in your ear."

"Just tell me, Misha."

"All right. Here are the facts. She was a witch. A witch needs to suck a man's vital juices in order to survive. You gave over to her your courage and your power, which she wanted for herself. She filled herself up on you, like a car at a filling station, so she could putt around and do her errands for another hundred miles or so. There's only X amount of energy in this universe. Sometimes a deer must die for us in order that we may eat. In shamanism, we say the deer gave away. That's what you did to Aria, Moon Deer. You gave away, but you didn't do it consciously so that you could gain power from your act of sacrifice. And she ate you up alive."

Howie considered this briefly. Was there any twisted truth in what Misha Ballantine was telling him?

"So you're saying that love is just another snack on the food chain?"

Misha grinned. "You figure it out," he said. "Personally, I'm about to move on to a whole new playing field . . . look to the horizon, Moon Deer. Do you see it? Look closely at the exact line between day and night."

The sun was sinking into a fluffy red paradise of clouds. At this elevation, from the craggy summit of San Geronimo Peak, the setting sun sat in the midst of a vast horizon of exploding light. Higher in the heavens, the sky was a darkening violet; lower, the colors were red and orange and gold. Between them was a subtle line that was becoming more definite as the sun sank.

"You can come with me, if you're man enough," Misha said with a facetious grin. He went on in his mocking voice: "In a few minutes, we'll see if all this shamanism bullshit means anything or not. At the precise moment when the sun sets, we'll jump into that line between day and night. Aren't you curious to see if we'll fly away and turn into sorcerers?"

Howie's mouth went dry as he finally understood why Misha had come to the top of this mountain.

"You're kidding, I hope," Howie said cautiously. "Listen to me, Misha—you don't need to go all Roman here and fall on your sword." But Misha only smiled enigmatically. Howie tried to get him talking: "You never believed any of that New Age jive, did you? The whole thing was only about money all along—maybe Zor and Denny and the others were believers, but you were only in it for the cash."

"That's not entirely true," Misha replied. "Put it this way—it's easy to believe all sorts of rubbish when things are going well. Anyway, it was good when we were a real circle of friends, all of us together. Ironic, isn't it?—when the money was flowing, we all thought there was a lot more to it than just making money. But the gig's up now. We're busted, Moon Deer. Whoever shot Sheriff Lou in the back finished us off right and proper. The cops will investigate that to death and come away with all our secrets. So we can say bye-bye to Chamisa Mall."

"It's only a shopping center. No reason to commit suicide and jump off this mountain."

"Only a shopping mall!" Misha laughed. "No, I'm afraid it's more than that, my friend! It's every cent I have in the world, plus a lot of money I *don't* have. I'm in debt up the proverbial wazoo, I'm afraid. And I know what jail's like. I'm not going back."

"Come on, a tough guy like you!" Howie tried. "Come down off that precipice, Misha. Look, you'll get out of jail, and you'll still be young enough to be a millionaire all over again, if that's what you want. It's more of a manly challenge, to make and lose a few fortunes."

"But I've done that, Moon Deer. I've done it all. I've gone through two fortunes already. This was going to be the third magic try. No, I've struck out—three chances at bat are all you get in this game. And let me tell you something. In America, a man of power needs cash. You can't be a mover and shaker without it. Frankly, I'm not prepared to be a frightened little schmuck without a dime. I'd rather take my chances on the crack between heaven and earth. Who knows? Maybe I'll turn into an eagle and fly away? Not much time now," he said, scanning the horizon.

"Hey, let's slow this down a little," Howie cautioned. "You need to tell me more about Aria. Remember, you promised. You said everything would be revealed if I came to the summit with you."

"Did I promise that? Well, you'd better ask your questions fast. The sun is sinking, pal."

"What happened to her?"

He shook his head ruefully. "Who would have thought we'd be done in by a nosy reporter? I tell you, that piece of skirt beat us up bad, Moon Deer! She turned Lou against us. It was like taking the cornerstone from a foundation—the whole damn building collapsed. I don't know for sure what happened to her, but I hope she suffered a little."

"Bullshit! You know. You're no dummy, Misha. You *must* know."

"Well, for what it's worth, my guess is that Lou killed her. Poor Lou was a tortured man. But I suppose we all end up killing the things we love, don't you think?"

As he spoke, Misha's eyes remained fixed on the western horizon. The sun was sinking fast, a half orange ball that seemed to be melting into a puddle of gold. Howie thought desperately of ways to restrain him. Unfortunately, he couldn't see how. Misha was standing in a dangerous place on the very edge of a precipice a few feet above Howie's own position; any attempt to grab hold of him would surely send both of them plunging to their deaths.

"If Lou killed her, what did he do with the body?" Howie asked urgently. "Come on, I climbed this damn mountain with you. Tell me."

"Poor Lou," Misha answered vaguely, keeping his eyes on the sun. "Once your dreams are dead, you might as well be dead yourself . . . look! Do you see it now?"

Misha pointed to where the last rays of sun had just sunk into the molten clouds. With a flourish, he threw open his arms and allowed the gray blanket to fall to the ground. Except for his muddy hiking boots, he was stark naked underneath. To Howie's astonishment, Misha had a huge erection that was pointing upward at about a forty-five-degree angle to the sky. Howie wasn't sure if this was some Krafft-Ebing abnormality of the criminally insane, or whether the man had really become so in tune with his fierce inner masculinity that he had discovered the secret of the eternal hard-on.

"You know, I *do* believe I'm going to fly, Moon Deer. Just watch how it's done!" He opened his arms in supplication to the west. "I am Silver Bear here to greet you!" he cried in a booming voice to the sky.

"Don't!" said Howie in a hushed voice. "Look, let's talk about this some more. You can't fly, Misha, honestly. You're a TV producer, not a bird. And a shopping mall isn't worth killing yourself over."

But to Howie's horror, Misha began flapping his arms like wings. He flapped three times. "I am White Eagle!" he cried.

Howie had one final desperate idea how he might restrain the man. He made a lunge to grab hold of the only handle, so to speak, which protruded from Misha's body—his erect penis—hoping to wrestle the man to his senses before he could jump. It was an unappealing plan for Howie, and he was too late; perhaps his aesthetic reluctance made him slow. Misha Ballantine was already in motion. He took three running steps and jumped off the precipice toward the far horizon, the line in the sky between day and night.

"I am . . . *White Eagle!*" he called a final time as he sailed out into nothingness.

Howie almost believed Misha might turn into a bird and fly away. But he was not completely surprised when the TV producer plummeted like a stone back into the clouds below. An instant later, out of sight, Howie heard the final strains of "*Eeeaagle!*" turn into a fading scream.

9

Four in the morning was not that different from four in the afternoon for a blind man, except for a predawn scent in the air and the deep quietude upon the land. Early Monday morning, Jack Wilder woke with a pervasive sense of worry. He lay for a time in bed listening to the first subtle changes that marked the passage of night into day.

Jack was worried that Howie had not reported in Sunday night as he was supposed to. Before going to sleep, Jack had set off all the alarms that he could think of. He phoned the ranger station at the foot of the mountain, San Geronimo Search and Rescue, and also Captain Gomez to say that Howie and his group of campers on the Peak had not returned when they were expected. Everyone was concerned, for missing people were a serious matter in these mountains, but there wasn't much that could be done at night. Most likely the campers were fine, said the ranger at the station, for they weren't greatly overdue. But if the group hadn't appeared by morning, a search for them would be launched.

Jack opened the crystal of his braille watch and felt for the time. It was four-seventeen; there was more than an hour to wait until first light. He was closing the crystal impatiently when the bedside phone rang. He reached quickly and grabbed the receiver before the second ring.

"Yes?"

It was Howie, full of astonishing tales to tell.

* * *

Howie was asleep on the ground at the entrance to the ski resort parking area, leaning against a sign that said SKI SAN GERONIMO!, when Emma and Jack arrived in the Wilders' Subaru station wagon. Dawn was just breaking, and this catnap was the last sleep Howie would enjoy for some time.

"Let's find breakfast," Howie said when Emma tapped him awake. He had been dreaming of the *baguettes* he used to eat during his year in Paris. Bread and jam, cheese and fruit, and strong coffee that you drank from a bowl.

"Talk first, breakfast later," Jack said, taking a hard line.

So Howie talked. He talked while Emma drove them into town, starting with the last part of his adventure first: How he had climbed down from the very top of San Geronimo Peak in the dark, waiting first for the sky to clear, then making an extremely slow descent, inch by inch along the steep north slope of the mountain with only moonlight to guide him, down to where the ski resort lay. While he talked, Emma drove them to Juanita's, an early morning greasy spoon on the edge of town. Howie ordered two breakfast burritos—tortillas stuffed with eggs, beans, chorizo sausage, and smothered with melted cheese and green chile—a high-fat feast that would cause any veggie-fascist to stand Moon Deer against a wall and shoot him dead. With a pot of coffee, a large glass of orange juice, and a side order of pancakes, Howie was persuaded to start his tale in proper order, this time from the beginning. The hike, the water filter containing lysergic acid, the bonfire, and all the nasty little secrets of male bonding gone bad, like Chuck Hildyard going to the D.A. to rat against his old Vietnam buddy, Lou Snider.

An hour later, Howie repeated his story to Captain Gomez and as the day progressed, he repeated it again and again—to the head ranger, several FBI agents, and the head of San Geronimo Search and Rescue. He was starting to feel like a talking fool. Then in the early afternoon, when Howie's tongue was thick with exhaustion, Captain Gomez wanted to hear it all over again, this time with several other New Mexico State Police bigwigs present—it seemed that Howie was such a good talker that they had come up from Santa Fe just to hear him. By mid-afternoon, reports were coming in by radio from the mountain itself. Search and Rescue found the body of Sheriff Lou Snider not far from Bear Lake; meanwhile, the FBI contingent was collecting various firearms and bullet casings from the ground while a forensic expert was gathering burned bone fragments from the remains of the bonfire, which Howie had described to them. By late afternoon, the body of Misha Ballantine was located at the bottom of a steep precipice, several hundred feet straight down from the summit of San Geronimo Peak; his flight had been a short one. Then, while Misha's body was being evacuated by helicopter, three weary hikers wandered into the small mountain community of Rio Blanco on the eastern slopes of the wilderness area: Denny Hirsch, Shepherd Plum, and Zor McCarthy. The three men had been lost in the woods for many hours; they were cold, hungry, exhausted, and suffering from various stages of exposure. Yet, being modern men, they had the presence of mind to refuse to utter a single word before consulting with their attorneys.

Howie was stunned at how this had all turned out; all the warriors were dead or they had wimped out, as Misha would have said. Meanwhile, all sorts of important people and official machinery had been set in motion. Howie was aware of a great whirl of activity around him, but finally, toward evening, there came a time when he was no longer necessary to this whirl. Even Jack didn't seem to need him—Jack had closeted himself with Captain Gomez and a number of important-looking officials to discuss the early forensic reports that were coming in from the mountain. One of the FBI agents collected Howie's .38 revolver and conducted a test for gunpowder residue on both of his hands; apparently they were conducting similar tests on the different warriors, alive and dead, and searching for shell casings and bullets at the crime scene in order to figure out who shot whom and with which gun. At last—weaponless, talked out, and no longer needed—Howie was driven home by a state trooper. His modest cabin had never looked so inviting to him. His front windows had been repaired over the weekend, and all signs of Sheriff Snider's bombed-out car had been removed from his front yard. Inside, everything was snug and orderly. Someone had been busy cleaning here, and he soon figured out who that someone was. There was a vase of wildflowers on his worktable with a note from Nova: "Welcome home, Howie. With a tenant like you, who needs tornadoes? A good thing we love you!"

At the moment, he was too exhausted to love anyone in return. He took a hot shower, and then he collapsed into bed. There was still light in the sky, but in Howie's body and soul, it was long past midnight. Sleep came nearly the instant he closed his eyes.

The phone was ringing. Howie lay in bed with his eyes still closed, unable to move, overcome with a deep melancholy. It was starting to hit him now, the sadness of those who had died. Misha, Lou Snider. Even Chuck Hildyard, whom he had only met briefly in life, and Gary Tripp, whom he had never met at all. And Aria, of course. Aria, whose crusade for the truth had started a crazy downward spiral of destruction. Though maybe, as Denny suggested, the destruction began earlier still when the Warrior Circle destroyed Donald Hicks for five acres of land. If the men's group had ever been idealistic, greed won out in the end. It all seemed such a waste.

Howie listened to a series of electronic beeps as his answering machine processed the incoming call. Finally he opened his eyes. His bedside clock said 9:47. He looked out his window and saw that it was morning. He had slept for nearly fourteen hours. Groggily, he yawned, stretched, and got out of bed. Nothing was going to hurry him today. He took his time grinding fresh coffee beans in his Braun grinder. He put them in a crisp white filter and set the coffee brewing. Only then did he press the play button on his answering machine.

It was Jack: "Okay, enough sleep already! Give me a call. We have an appointment with the district attorney at eleven-thirty."

District Attorney Jed Peterson was a baby-faced pudge of a man with a body that looked as if it had been stuffed full of milk and white bread for the past forty years. He wore a bristly mustache in an attempt to appear vaguely grown up, but it only made him look like a very large preschooler with a mustache. He had thinning mouse-colored hair, eyeglasses with tortoiseshell frames, huge corduroy pants, a plaid shirt, suspenders, and a string tie. He sat coatless and self-important behind a large desk in his office at the San Geronimo County Civic Center. Howie studied the man with some fascination. Scientifically speaking this was a classic specimen of *genus mid-americanus,* the Cookie Monster who had won the American West from Howie's ancestors. *Wasicu* was the word the Lakota people gave to the paleface who invaded their land: He-Who-Takes-the-Fat.

"Commander Jack Wilder, well, well!—I've been hearing about you for several years now. Glad we finally had a chance to meet!" the D.A. said warmly. His tone was simultaneously folksy and profane. "And you must be Howard Moon Deer. Ed Gomez came by earlier this morning to give me a full report of what's been happening up on the Peak. My God, a men's group! I thought guys who went in for stuff like that were supposed to be gentle. Getting in touch with their sensitive side, and all that."

"Not the Warrior Circle, it seems," Jack mentioned. "These men wanted power."

"Hell, it looks like we've got ourselves a bad sheriff too. A bad *dead* sheriff! And a reporter who's vanished. . . . I've met Aria Waldman, of course. A very smart young woman. Incidentally, Ed has a major search under way, a lot of people looking for her."

"It's about time!" Howie muttered.

"I'm afraid this is all going to be extremely traumatic for the town and county of San Geronimo," the D.A. continued with a sad, officious shake of his head, ignoring Howie's comment. He lowered his voice: "And now there's something new and troubling. I just had a phone conversation with one of those FBI guys. They're flying in some of their science people from Washington. There's a lot more work to be done, of course, reconstructing exactly what happened up there. But they're saying Lou Snider was shot in the back at close range with a shotgun. The only problem is that so far they've recovered a whole bunch of weapons—some were lying on the ground, one or two they picked up from the three guys who wandered into Rio Blanco. But not *one* of them was a shotgun. You see what this suggests, don't you?"

Jack frowned. "It suggests there was another shooter up there, someone we haven't accounted for yet."

"You bet your bingo card!" said the D.A. "Of course, they could still find the gun somewhere in the bushes, maybe even at the bottom of the lake—I gather they've brought in some serious metal detectors that can probe just about everywhere. But so far, *nada.* . . . Did you hear a shotgun go off up there, Howard?"

"There was a lot of firing, I don't know. The first shot, though, the one that made us all scatter—I remember thinking it must have come from a rifle because it was so loud."

"Well, they *did* find a rifle up there, a Remington M760 Gamemaster. Apparently that gun belonged to Lou. But, like I say,

Lou himself was killed with a shotgun, not a rifle. So unless we find that weapon, we got ourselves a mystery." The D.A. smiled at Howie. "*You* didn't kill ol' Lou with a shotgun, did you, Howard? After all, I understand he was messin' with your woman."

Howie's mouth opened in surprise. "The only gun I had on me was the Smith & Wesson I gave to the police yesterday. Anyway, I wouldn't have been able to carry a shotgun up there without everybody seeing it—all I had was my day pack."

"Of course, some guns can be disassembled and carried quite compactly," the D.A. said smoothly.

"A shotgun?" Jack asked. "Even broken down, it's still hard to imagine it could be carried secretly in a small day pack . . . Howie, did any of the men have larger packs?"

"No, we weren't carrying much. Everybody had day packs pretty much the same size as mine."

"Well, there you are," the D.A. said. "If none of the men could have brought a shotgun along, we get back to the idea that there was an unknown shooter up there. Someone we don't know about yet."

"What do Zor and Denny and Shep have to say about this?" Jack asked.

D.A. Peterson shook his head. "Those guys are terrified. So far they're not talking, not a word. Which leaves us with just a few loose ends."

"Speaking of loose ends," said Jack, "it's come to my attention that your office was actually investigating Sheriff Snider. I'd like to know more about that. Specifically, why you started looking into him, and what you've found out."

The D.A.'s face went professionally blank. "Who told you there was an investigation?"

"Denny told me on Saturday night," Howie said. "Apparently, it's one of the main reasons Chuck and Lou were at each other's throats. Lou believed that Hildyard had come to you, telling all sorts of lies about him."

"Really?" asked the D.A.

"I imagine you're reluctant to name your informant," Jack said, "but it would be very helpful for us to know about this."

The D.A. stared at Jack for a moment in silence. Then he shook his head. "But there was no investigation. *Nada.*"

"What do you mean, no investigation?"

"Just what I said. Nothing. No one came to me from the men's group, not Chuck Hildyard or anybody else. I wasn't investigating Lou Snider. I wish I had been, believe me! Maybe some of this mess could have been avoided."

Jack nodded. "I see!"

"You do? Well, I don't see at all, myself. I wish you would explain it to me, Commander. What's happened in this damn town, anyway? A bunch of our finest citizens get involved in some crazy men's group, our sheriff goes berserk. . . . I'm not exactly thrilled to be the district attorney of San Geronimo at this moment in time. I'm sure you can understand that."

Jack managed to look very understanding. Yes, he too had weathered some storms in San Francisco; no, it wasn't easy to be a city employee in times of municipal madness. After a few moments of packaged empathy, Jack said a quick good-bye and got himself and Howie out of the D.A.'s office.

"Let's stop and have a brief chat with Peterson's secretary," Jack said quietly to Howie as they were walking from the office.

"What for?"

"Howie, just lead me to her, please, and you will see what for."

Howie shrugged, reversed course, and led Jack to a desk in an anteroom outside Jed Peterson's closed door, where a matronly Hispanic woman sat behind a computer. The black plastic name-plate on her desk said MARILYN HONDO.

"Can I help you?" she asked politely, looking up from her work.

"Yes, you can. Do you know Aria Waldman, by any chance?" Jack asked her.

She seemed puzzled by the question. "Why, yes. Aria comes by every now and then. We were in a step-aerobics class together."

"And you talk about some of the cases here?"

The woman was immediately defensive. "I can assure you, I haven't told her anything I'm not supposed to. Aria's a friend, but she's also a very sharp reporter."

"Did you tell her that the D.A. was investigating Sheriff Lou Snider?"

"I did not!" she protested angrily. "I don't know what you're talking about—as far as I know, there hasn't been any sort of investigation like that. And if there had been, I certainly wouldn't have spoken about it to anyone outside this office."

"Then you didn't say *anything* about Sheriff Snider to Aria?"

"I told you, not a thing. Why should I? There wasn't anything to tell."

Jack smiled. "Thank you. There must be a misunderstanding."

Jack took hold of Howie's arm and kept smiling as they walked from the building out into the parking lot.

"Finally!" he said. "This damned case is starting to make sense!"

"You think so, Jack? It seems to me things are more confusing than ever. Why should Snider believe the D.A.'s office was investigating him, when there wasn't any investigation?"

"It's a Zen riddle, isn't it?" Jack said, his smile widening. "What's an investigation that's not an investigation? Think about it, Howie."

"Aria lied?"

"That's right. Aria lied. She was the one who told Snider that Chuck Hildyard was selling him out to the D.A., yet we find now that it wasn't true."

"But why? Why should she tell Lou Snider something like that?"

"Keep pondering, Howie. And I'm sure you'll arrive eventually at the one inescapable conclusion."

10

_____

The San Geronimo Post came out once a week, every Thursday morning. By Tuesday afternoon, the paper was already in high gear, building to the semifinal phase of weekly hysteria of putting the paper to bed. Nevertheless, Don Jolly, the editor, dropped everything when Jack telephoned, agreeing to see them immediately. He hoped to get a firsthand account of the biggest story to hit San Geronimo in a long time. Murder wasn't entirely unknown in the community—San Geronimo averaged two a year—but this case promised to be spectacular, involving important businesspeople, the county sheriff, even a missing reporter from the *Post*.

Don Jolly met Jack and Howie in the reception area and ushered them to his small office overlooking Don Orlando Street and a slice of the New Wave Café across the street.

"We're going crazy around here, Jack, totally nuts . . . God, I hope Aria's all right, I can't tell you how worried we all are . . . sit down, sit down. Listen, do you mind if a few of my people sit in on our meeting and take notes? So far we've only received the official jive from the state police."

Don was a nervous man who spoke faster than any human being ought to speak. He was young for the job, in his mid-thirties, with short red hair and an earring in his left lobe. There was a gee-whiz cub-reporter quality to Don that Howie found grating. They had met a number of times during the past year while Howie was dating Aria, but Don was generally doing five things at once and it wasn't easy to get beneath his surface hysteria.

". . . Here, let me get you guys some coffee," he was saying.

"Howie you take yours black . . . you do too, Jack? . . . let me just use the phone a sec . . . Robin, get Heather and a tape recorder and come into my office immediately . . . no, *drop* that, this is more important . . . now, where am I?"

It was exhausting to share a room with so much stress and motion. Jack settled into an upholstered armchair, crossed his legs, and took charge of the situation: "Don, sit still for a minute and listen to me—we're in a hurry, and I know you must be too. So I tell you what. Why don't you allow me to give you the rundown on what happened this weekend on the Peak while Howie uses the time to do a little research."

"But I'll want some quotes from Howie, of course. He was there . . ."

"Don, believe me, at this point, I can probably quote Howie better than he can quote himself. I can also give you some insight into what the state police and the FBI are doing. So let's let Howie get on with more urgent business. I'd like you to give him Aria Waldman's personal employment file, whatever you have on her—her original job application, her social security number, who to call in the case of an emergency, all that sort of thing, which I'm sure you have somewhere."

The editor frowned, and a good deal of his boyish gee-whiz quality disappeared. "Whoa, whoa, whoa! All our employee files are strictly confidential—I can't possibly show you *that*. Anyway, I don't see that where Aria went to high school has much bearing on her present situation—I mean, that's the sort of stuff you'd find in her file."

"Don, to be honest, you're probably right, the file may not be at all helpful. But at this point she's been missing for a week, and we're getting desperate. There's a possibility that someone, maybe some*thing* from her past has come back to haunt her. Maybe it's the reason for her disappearance, maybe not. It's a slim chance, but we're looking at everything. Naturally, I can understand your reluctance to open a confidential employee file, but in this case it's literally a matter of life or death."

Don held up his hands, the image of helplessness. "Jack, I just can't do it! Aria could waltz in here tomorrow and sue the pants off me!"

Heather Winter and a tall, middle-aged man walked into the editor's office at this moment carrying notebooks and a small tape recorder. Heather was dressed in black: a short black skirt, a baggy black T-shirt, and her black Doc Marten boots. She had done something frizzy and 1930-ish to her hair. She gave Howie a brief sideways glance.

"Hey, Howie."

"Hey, Heather," he answered.

"So you can't let us see the file?" Jack was asking.

"No way, José. Absolutely can't do, amigo!" Don replied.

Jack stood up from his armchair. "Well, we'd better be on our way then," he said. "Howie, give me a hand."

"Wait a sec! You're not leaving, are you?" Don cried.

"I'm sorry, but finding Aria Waldman is our only priority. If you can't help us, we'll just have to keep looking elsewhere."

The editor's eyes became small slits. He had not quite been aware of the quid pro quo nature of Jack's visit until this moment. "Hold on here, let's think about this," he said. "If I let you see Aria's file, you and Howie will give me an exclusive statement, right? About your investigation and exactly what occurred this weekend on San Geronimo Peak?"

"Not an entirely full statement," Jack admitted. "But full enough for your readers. And I will make the statement, not Howie. I have more experience with what may be said and what must be kept from the public, at least a little while longer, so as not to compromise the ongoing investigation. Let's not forget that a woman's life is at stake here."

Don considered this for a moment. Then he nodded and quickly wrote a note on a pad of paper. He handed it to Heather. "Okay, you're on, Jack. Heather, give this to Judy in the business office and stay with Howie while he reads the file—he can take notes, but I don't want Aria's file to be photocopied."

Howie followed Heather Winter through the hall to a small office in the rear of the building. A young Native American woman was working at a computer on a cluttered desk in a room full of filing cabinets and plants. A fluorescent light buzzed overhead. The woman had long black hair, thick glasses, and a round, almost Eskimo face. There was a placard next to her computer that said, in bold letters, JESUS IS LORD. Lord of what? Howie wondered. Cyberspace?

"Don wants you to let Howie have a look at Aria Waldman's personal file," Heather told the woman, handing over Don's note.

"I'd better just check," the woman said, scrunching up her nose in a humorous gesture, trying to be nice about it. But she buzzed Don Jolly's office just to make certain the note was genuine before she stood up and began searching through the huge metal filing cabinets that stood behind her desk.

While she searched, Heather turned to Howie: "So what was it like before everyone started shooting one another? Did you beat on drums and do a lot of male bonding?"

"You bet. I'm a real man now," he assured her.

"Are you? What *is* a real man these days, I wonder?"

"Oh, strong. Sensitive. A good dancer. Someone who can change diapers or wrestle a grizzly bear, depending on the situation. We have to be very versatile, you know."

"And carry a gun as well, it appears?"

"Certainly. A warrior never knows when things are going to get hot."

"That sounds like the same old bullshit to me," Heather commented.

"Well, it is," Howie admitted. "But that's another thing a guy has to do well. In the modern world, we're often called upon to be sincere yet full of bullshit at the same time."

Heather laughed. "Sorry, Howie, but you'll never make it."

"No?" He was a little hurt.

"Not you. You've got a face a woman can read like an open book."

Howie took Aria's file to the small reading room where he had been the last time he was here. Heather settled herself on a chair next to him, peering over his shoulder while Howie studied Aria's job application form.

The application was dated September 12, 1996, almost exactly a year before Howie had met her in the hot tub at Bob and Nova's house. The information she had supplied was sparse. Date of birth: 11/3/69. Current address: P.O. Box 2141, San Geronimo, NM 87502. Marital Status: Single. SS #: 349-01-8164. Education: Smith College, Northampton, Mass, class of '89. Graduated from the Columbia University School of Journalism, NYC, '92. As for jobs held during the four years after leaving Columbia and arriving in New Mexico, Aria had listed only *The San Francisco Chronicle,* July '92 through '94. Position: copy editor. Supervisor: Marcus Quigley. Salary: $2760 per mo. Aria had never mentioned to Howie that she had lived in San Francisco, just one more thing she hadn't told him. After leaving the *Chronicle* for "personal reasons," she listed only "freelance journalism, etc." in the further space provided for her employment history. This was a big etcetera. She had provided no personal references, simply leaving the spaces blank, and there was no mention whatsoever of the supposed husband in Santa Fe, the marriage Aria always blamed for getting her off her career track. In case of emergency, one might call her mother, Mary Waldman, in Ft. Lauderdale, Florida, at a phone number she provided—again, she had never made any mention to Howie that her mother was in Florida. He took quick notes, recording the brief statistics of this revised life.

"This is awfully bare," Howie mentioned. "Would Don really hire someone with so little history?"

"For a dinky little newspaper in New Mexico? You got to be kidding, Howie! She graduated from the Columbia School of Journalism—that alone would be enough for Don to give her a chance. Most of the people who apply for jobs here, it's lucky if they've graduated from some junior college somewhere and know the difference between an adjective and an adverb . . . and here, look at this. She gave Don an article of hers that was published in *The New Yorker.* That's probably what really made him wet his pants. . . . "

Along with the application form, the manila file contained five pages that had been photocopied from the June 3, 1996 issue of *The New Yorker.* The article—"Desert, Wind, and Sky," by Aria Waldman—was about racial tensions in New Mexico's tri-cultural population, Hispanic, Anglo, and Native American. Howie read the first paragraph, which seemed breezy to him but well-written. None of it, neither this article nor the job application explained the central question, however. The very question that had brought Jack and Howie to the *Post* this afternoon—why Aria had apparently lied to Sheriff Lou Snider, her lover, saying that the D.A.'s office was running an investigation on him.

"Can I take this with me?" Howie asked, holding up the magazine article.

"You're not supposed to. Remember what Don said."

"He said no photocopying. He didn't mention anything about an

old *New Yorker* article that I could probably find in the library anyway."

"Then find it."

"I don't have time. Anyway, you should help me, Heather. I'm
a guy on a quest," he added with a hopeful smile.

Heather turned her light gray eyes on him. "You know, maybe
you're better at bullshit than I thought. Go ahead, I guess. I'm only
an intern here—I'm going back to school in September, so what
does it matter to me?"

"You're going back to California, then?"

"Of course I'm going back to California," she told him, turning
away. "What's to keep me in New Mexico?"

11

A state trooper was waiting with a car outside the newspaper building. They wanted Howie up at the crime scene near Bear Lake for more questioning as to who did what, where, and when; a helicopter was standing by in a nearby parking lot to fly him quickly up the mountain. Jack said he'd go along for the ride, since he'd like to better visualize where the shooting took place.

By helicopter, it took a little over twenty minutes to reach Bear Lake, a journey that had been an entire day's hike. It seemed unfair somehow, the triumph of technology over personal effort. Howie didn't like the way the wingless metal insect bobbed up and down on the air currents, though Jack and the pilot hardly seemed to notice. Occasionally the helicopter dropped like an elevator in free fall, with Howie's stomach left behind somewhere up at the penthouse. He closed his eyes and prayed. It always astonished him how quickly he got religion whenever he was flying and the ride got rough. What had Misha said? *A warrior can fly, Moon Deer! . . . You just need to stretch your limits.*

The helicopter came down in a meadow near the lake, and Howie gradually unclenched his fists. A young FBI science nerd, Agent Thompson, met them under the whoosh of the rotor blade and led them to a knoll on the far side of the lake where a cutout cardboard figure had been laid out on the ground, a crime scene reconstruction to show where Lou Snider's body had been found. Howie was relieved the actual body had been removed, yet there was something almost more terrible about the cardboard silhouette. Nearby a small army of forensic experts were combing through the grass and trees, still searching for spent bullets, empty shells, and other evidence. One agent was sitting in a branch halfway up a tree, removing a slug with a knife.

"We think Snider got up here sometime mid-afternoon on Saturday," Agent Thompson was telling them. Agent Thompson was a somewhat goofy-looking guy with glasses and big ears, and he seemed to enjoy the intellectual challenge of imagining bloody deeds. He pointed across the meadow over a rise. "We found a place over there where he must have been hiding, waiting in ambush. The grass was flattened enough to suggest that he spent a few hours there. We recovered an orange peel and three orange pits—we've already sent the pits to Washington, of course, for a DNA analysis."

"You can do a DNA analysis from orange pits?" Howie asked, astonished.

"If he put them in his mouth and spit them out, we can," Agent Thompson said. "Bascially, you need some sort of body fluid. Semen. Sweat. Blood. Vaginal fluid. Urine. In this case, saliva. From there it's like a fingerprint—the DNA code doesn't mean anything in itself unless you get a match. So the lab will take a scraping from Snider's body, probably from the inside of his mouth, and then they'll try to match up the orange pit with him. But if the DNA code is different, if someone else spit out that orange pit, and if it doesn't match any of the other men—then we'll have compelling evidence that there really was an unknown shooter up here."

"So you believe there was someone up here you haven't accounted for?" Jack asked.

"Yes, I do. For several reasons . . . by the way, Mr. Moon Deer, do you mind if one of our technicians takes a scraping from *your* mouth?"

Howie sighed. This all seemed very depressing to him, the cardboard figure, the crisp efficiency of science. Nevertheless, Howie said "Ah" when a technician came over with a small wooden scraper to remove a few loose cells from inside his mouth, taking a bit of the genetic blueprint he came from. Meanwhile, Jack was having a splendid time discussing such things as blood splatter, the various angles at which bullets had traveled and been found, and the subtle conclusions an expert might infer from this evidence to indicate that a yet-unknown person was involved in the carnage.

Howie couldn't concentrate on their esoteric reasoning; he was overwhelmed by so much death.

All in all, the afternoon was a bust, for Howie and for the various law enforcement personnel who did their best to question him as to the precise chronology and movements of the different men during the gun battle. All that Howie could honestly show them was the tree where he had hidden while guns were exploding around him. Except for his brief encounter with Denny Hirsch, he hadn't seen a thing. Agent Thompson and the others were very understanding; anyone sane would be hiding behind a tree at a time like that. And yet Howie couldn't help but feel a hint of contempt in their manner toward him. They seemed to be saying: a real man, a warrior, would have gone forth in a burst of gunfire and glory, no matter what.

Well, the hell with them! Howie didn't buy any of it. Still, when the helicopter took off for the return trip to town, he felt dissatisfied with himself.

Heroes don't hide behind trees, a voice seemed to whisper.

It was already early evening when Jack and Howie were dropped off back at the *Post* building. Howie drove Jack to the library, where they met up with Emma, who was just getting off work. Emma and Jack went home in her car, leaving Howie in town to find his own dinner somewhere. Howie was perfectly capable of playing hunter-gatherer, of course—probably he would duck across the street to the New Wave Café. Yet the prospect of a bachelor meal depressed him tonight. Jack had Emma, Bob had Nova, everybody had someone . . . so why not him? What did Howie have? Just a vanished woman whose memory was turning into a phantom.

Jack had taken Howie's notes containing Aria's social security number and her abbreviated employment and education history. Brief as it was, Jack planned to run this information by his old FBI friend in Denver. The social security number was particularly promising, for it could unlock a credit history, tax records, old traffic warrants, the entire official docket that shadows each individual as he or she skips blithely through the American dream. Maybe some of this would add up to who this disappearing woman, Aria Waldman, really was. And most importantly, why she had lied.

As for Howie, after he said good-bye to the Wilders in front of the library, he found himself in a funky mood. Jack had suggested a number of areas of investigation, but for the first time in ages, what he really felt like doing was getting drunk—stupid, falling-down drunk, blasting his brain cells with anesthesia. But he knew this was a bad idea. In the end, he decided it was better to find a cozy nook inside the library, which was open tonight until ten o'clock. Howie liked libraries; they soothed his bookish soul and made the world appear orderly and sane, all those passions and facts and fantasies lined up alphabetically from A to Z. He would find a quiet chair and read Aria's *New Yorker* article on racism in New Mexico.

Inside the library, Howie found himself confronted with a choice of two different tables where he might sit. At one table, there was a hairy young Anglo man with a bad complexion reading the latest issue of *Rolling Stone*. At the second table, there was an attractive woman, mid-twenties, long blond hair—an arty, intellectual type of blonde who was sitting with a book of poetry open in front of her. W. H. Auden, he observed. Gravity worked on Howie's decision. Not that he was interested in any more romantic foolishness—God knows, he was burned, and he was through with the mating game. But nevertheless, he sat down at the far end of the pretty woman's table, rather than at the table of the hairy Anglo guy. He opened his green day pack and then cursed aloud. The blond woman gave him a brief worried glance and then looked quickly away. He felt like an idiot. Somehow he had given Jack the photocopy of the *New Yorker* article along with his notes on Aria's employment application.

But all was not lost. The San Geronimo library kept several years of old *New Yorker* issues, and fortunately, Howie remembered the date of the magazine that interested him: June 3, 1996. He left his day pack on his chair, went to the magazine section, and soon found the issue he wanted. Feeling more pleased with himself, Howie sat down with the magazine and glanced through the table of contents. But to his surprise, there was no article listed by Aria Waldman, nothing at all on tri-cultural problems in New Mexico. He looked at the date on the cover once again to make certain this really was the June 3, 1996 issue. It was. Then he read through the table of contents more closely. Aria Waldman and her article were still not there.

This was strange, but not inexplicable. Magazines make mistakes, perhaps Aria's name had inadvertently been left out of the table of contents. For the next twenty minutes, Howie turned laboriously page by page through the June 3 issue, looking for Aria's article. Finally he found an ad and a cartoon that he recognized. The ad was a small box for an inn in Vermont that Howie had noticed earlier running alongside the second page of her article. Only now, where her article should have been, there was a John Updike short story. Of course the Vermont inn might have run the same ad in several different issues. But on the next page, Howie recognized the cartoon: A very New Yorkerish kind of businessman was lying in bed, saying to his wife, "Hypochondriacs get sick too, you know." In the version Howie had read earlier in Aria's file at the *Post,* a single column of her article had run down the page to the left side of this cartoon. But in the version he had before him now, the column along the left side of the page was no longer Aria's article—it was a continuation of the Updike story.

At last Howie put down the magazine, stunned. It was clear that Aria had pulled off a clever fraud to get herself hired as a reporter on *The San Geronimo Post.* She had simply done a little cutting and pasting, making a montage of her article onto the *New Yorker* page and then photocopied the resulting artwork to make it look as if she had been published in the June 3 issue. Perhaps Aria's article had been published in some minor magazine somewhere, or she might have taken her unpublished manuscript to a print shop and had a *New Yorker*-like mock-up made. Either way, he had uncovered one more of her astonishing lies.

Howie stood up like a sleepwalker. He returned the issue to its proper rack in the magazine section and then wandered outside the library into the night. He was standing, dazed and unhappy, debating what to do next, when he became aware that he was not alone. The intellectual blonde from the far end of his table was nearby on the sidewalk, studying him.

"Are you all right?" she asked with concern.

"Sort of. I've just had a bit of a shock."

"Really?"

The woman was more than pretty; she had such a kind and sympathetic face that Howie found himself spilling his emotional beans. "It's the damnedest thing!" he told her. "A lady I was seeing simply vanished last week—exactly a week ago, as a matter of fact. And since then I've learned that she was cheating on me, lying—in fact, hardly anything she told me was true. It's a weird sensation, like the floor's fallen out from under my feet. The latest shock is only a small thing, I suppose. She claimed an article she wrote was published in *The New Yorker,* she even had a fake mockup made. But when I looked in the real *New Yorker,* it wasn't there."

"How strange."

"Well, it is." Howie studied the woman more closely. She wore thick eyeglasses that gave the initial impression of bookishness. It was hard to say exactly where her beauty lay, yet Howie was certain she was lovely. Milky skin and passionate eyes, she had a decidedly poetic glow to her. She wore no makeup, her long straw-blond hair was pulled back from her face in a simple ponytail. Yet the simplicity suited her. San Geronimo was a small town; how was it he had never noticed such a pretty woman before?

"Are you, uh, from around here?" he asked clumsily.

"I wish!" she laughed. "I've never been to New Mexico before. I just drove into town a few hours ago. . . . I'm from Iowa," she added, apologetically.

She *was* a mirage, he decided. Perhaps an afterglow of LSD that had not entirely worked its way out of his system. Howie wished he could touch her to make sure. Hallucination or not, he was probably studying her too closely, for suddenly her eyes flashed and she looked away. In the light of the streetlamp, Howie had a sense that she was blushing. It had been a long while since he had seen a woman blush.

"Actually, I've had a shock recently too," she said. "Sort of like yours."

"Have you?"

"It's my husband—he teaches literature at the University of Iowa. Last Wednesday . . . well, I came home unexpectedly, and I found him with a graduate student we both know on our living room floor. They were, you know . . . in flagrante delicto."

"I'm sorry," Howie told her. He liked her Latin.

"Well, I was sorry too! And I felt so insanely stupid because I hadn't ever suspected a thing."

"I know that feeling. Feeling stupid," he assured her. "It's part of the cuckold experience."

"I just stood there with my cello, gaping at them."

"Your cello?"

"I'm in a string quartet. I guess I didn't tell you that. I give private cello lessons as well. That's why I was home early, actually. One of my students had canceled."

"I see. So you had your cello."

"And you know what I did? I just turned around and left them on the floor together. I got in my car, and I started driving, and I haven't stopped since. I drove up to Canada, and then I started down here—through Montana, Wyoming, and Colorado. I pulled into San Geronimo this afternoon. To be honest, I don't know why I'm here or where I'm going next, but I know I don't feel like going home yet."

"I can understand that," Howie told her.

"Can you? I left my two children there. I'm twenty-eight years old, and I left everything to drive off nowhere! I'm not sure I understand myself."

As she spoke, Howie did a terrible thing in his mind: he took off her glasses and her clothes as well, and placed her on a giant clamshell, her long blond hair more or less covering the intimate areas. Botticelli could have done her justice, and if he was ever in Iowa, might be inspired to paint the birth of a lanky, slightly freckled corn-belt Venus.

She laughed suddenly, shyly. "Anyway, I don't generally go around telling strangers my deepest secrets. But, well . . . your shock was awfully similar to my shock."

"Shock therapy," Howie agreed. "It's not a whole lot of fun to be betrayed, is it?"

"No, it isn't. And frankly I'm in the mood for a drink," she said determinedly. "Is there a bar around here you could recommend?"

Howie was no fool. He was lonely, upset, and thirsty; the woman in front of him was beautiful, intelligent, and the cello happened to be his favorite stringed instrument. He seized the moment.

"Look, why don't we have a drink together? I know a place down the street where they have good margaritas."

"Great!" she said. "I tell you, after all that driving, I'm in the mood for something stiff!"

12

After dinner, Jack took the cordless kitchen phone outside into the garden. He sat in the deepening twilight on the double swing that was hanging from the huge branch of a cottonwood tree. Rocking gently with his toe, he dialed the home number of his friend in Denver, Special Agent Kevin Neimeyer. Jack was aware that he was using up favors fast with all his old law enforcement buddies.

"Kevin. I hope you don't mind, but I have another favor to ask you."

Was that a small sigh of impatience? If so, Kevin did his best to cover it up. "I don't mind at all, Jack. Listen, I'm at the dinner table—hold on a sec while I move to my office."

Jack felt guilty about disturbing Kevin's dinner, but not guilty enough to suggest he call back another time. He gave Kevin Aria Waldman's social security number, which he had memorized earlier, and also the dates of her graduation from Smith and Columbia. Kevin promised to get on it right away; he'd probably have the scoop on the social security number within an hour.

"Great," said Jack. "I owe you another one, old buddy."

"Nonsense," said Kevin. "No one's keeping score here."

But that wasn't true: Jack was keeping score and knew he was deeply in debt. After hanging up with Kevin, he tried the second number he had memorized, Aria's mother, Mary Waldman, in Ft. Lauderdale. The phone rang three times, and then a recorded voice came on the line, an operator saying he had reached a number that was no longer in service. He tried the number a second time to make certain he hadn't misdialed, but the operator's message cut

in on him again. It seemed that Mary Waldman had joined the vanished.

An hour later, Jack was brushing his teeth in the upstairs bathroom when he heard the phone ring.

"It's Kevin," Emma called from the bedroom. "Shall I have him
call back?"

"No, I'll be right there."

Jack spat out toothpaste and made his way along the upstairs
corridor to the bedroom, feeling ahead of him for Katya, who had
a perilous habit of stretching herself out in strategic places along
his path. Emma was already in bed with a book propped up in her
lap. She handed him the phone and went back to her reading. A
few minutes later, she glanced up and saw that Jack was nodding
to himself in satisfaction, holding the phone to his ear. He looked
to Emma like a chess player who had just figured out some particularly difficult move.

Howie had never seen a naked woman play the cello before. He
found it almost unbearably erotic. Maybe it was the way she held
the instrument between her long legs. It was nearly two in the
morning, and he lay sprawled out on a creaky bed in a cabin at the
Lone Coyote Motel while his blond corn-belt Venus played a Bach
suite for him on the cello. Her name was Claire, and she played
wonderfully well. The Lone Coyote was a sleepy old motel on the
edge of town, a grouping of rustic wooden cabins beneath the
shade of cottonwood trees. The blue neon light of the motel sign
glowed through the cheap cotton curtains of the window, shining
electric patterns onto their naked bodies.

The gods had certainly smiled on Howard Moon Deer tonight.
Claire wasn't accustomed to drinking, and after two rounds of
margaritas at the Hacienda Bar, she had looked up at him with star-
tlingly lovely blue-gray eyes. Emboldened by tequila, she popped
the big question: "Just out of curiosity, do you have any sexually
communicable disease, Howie?"

"No, I have a clean bill of health. How about you?" She shook
her head with a sweet, radiant smile. And that was that, the start of
modern romance. They piled into her car, kissing like teenagers,
passed by Ortega's Liquors, where they bought three bottles of
cheap Spanish champagne, then continued on to the Lone Coyote,
where Claire had a cabin. Sometime after one in the morning,

Howie crept naked outside to her car to fetch her cello, which she
fortunately had in hand when she stumbled across her husband's
infidelity back in Iowa City—a thousand years ago, she assured
him, another life entirely.

"I'm wild about the cello," he confessed passionately, kissing
one of her long legs while she played.

"I'm wild about you," she confessed in return. And the Bach
Suite No. 1 for Unaccompanied Cello got interrupted in the middle of the gigue for a different kind of music.

They drank much too much. "Let's get married," he told her at
close to three in the morning, when the third bottle of champagne
was nearly empty. "Let's have a whole flock of children."

But this made her sad, and she started crying. "I'm already married!" she sobbed. "I already have children!"

"Ah, well," he said. And held her while she cried.

They both passed out not long after that. In the morning he woke
up with his mouth dry as cotton, but Claire was gone. There was a
note on the dresser weighed down by an empty Freixnet bottle:

Howie! What can I say? You were the perfect romantic
stranger! You've made it possible for me to go back to Jim
and the kids and face reality once again. Think of me sometime. I kiss your sleeping eyelids good-bye.
                            XXX,
                                 Claire

Howie stood by the dresser, staring at the note. For a few minutes he wasn't certain whether to feel bitter or amused. A perfect
night, yet she had become one more disappearing woman in his
life. This wasn't quite the role he would have chosen for himself,
the romantic stranger in a sleazy motel who had plugged a few
leaks so she could return to "Jim and the kids."

"Well, what the hell!" he decided, sitting back down on the bed
and laughing as hard as his dry mouth and hangover would allow.

Howie had a three-mile walk from the Lone Coyote back into
the center of town, where he had left his car. It was a golden morning with a snap in the air, a crisp hint of autumn to come. Howie
didn't mind the walk. It was good to stretch his legs and clear his
head. He had to admit, getting laid last night with a lovely stranger

had improved his opinion of himself. He no longer had that squashed roadkill feeling of being cuckolded by Aria Waldman, just as he had most likely erased in Claire the sight of her husband on the living room floor frolicking with a graduate student.

So it wasn't great love. He had used her, and she had used him. But at least they would both have the ego-restoring memory of a perfect night. Howie walked along the highway full of jaunty optimism, humming Bach as the morning traffic passed him by. He felt free as a butterfly. The only thing missing in life was a good cup of coffee, and he did something about it as soon as he reached Don Orlando Street. He ducked into the New Wave Café and ordered a double cappuccino and a bear claw at the counter, a power breakfast, with enough caffeine and sugar to jump start any day. When it was ready, he took his cup and claw outside to the garden, looking for a quiet table. The New Wave was full of its usual morning crowd—flamboyant arty-types with progressive hairstyles, as well as some more humble souls who worked in the nearby stores and often didn't bother with much of a hairstyle at all. Howie sat down at the one vacant table that always seemed to be waiting for him: *their* table, where he used to sit with Aria. But this morning he only smiled, immune to the pain. *I'm cured of her,* he thought. *My God, I'm really cured!*

To his surprise, he saw Mary Jane Tripp a few tables over sitting with her three young children. Well, well! She was having breakfast with a man, a contractor Howie knew, a guy named Jim Harding who had gone through a bad divorce a few years back. Apparently, guys named Jim had all the luck with women these days, but this was okay with Howie. He watched them with a vague wistfulness without regret. Jim and Mary Jane had that look of brand-new intimacy, of a first breakfast after a first night. Such was the triumph of the birds and the bees, a happy ending for them all: she had gotten herself a new man, Jim had found a replacement woman, the kids even had a temporary father.

Howie was filled with a bittersweet sense of love, motion, time, and loss. He too was in motion. Sitting here at *their table,* he pondered his own loss, how spending the night with Claire had put a closure, a final punctuation mark to his emotional attachment to Aria. He was glad to be free, of course, yet he felt a certain nostalgic sorrow. It was strange, almost cruel, how a lifetime carried you along. How you might care so horribly much for someone, and then simply move on. Howie raised his cappuccino cup in a toast to departed love. *Frankly, my dear, I really don't give a damn!* he said inwardly to Aria Waldman, wherever she might be. Then his expression froze, and his half-raised cappuccino cup fell from his hand with a clatter. Less than a dozen feet away, on the far side of a low barricade that separated the café garden from the street, Aria Waldman herself was standing on the sidewalk looking fresh as a flower in the morning sun.

The patio was separated from the sidewalk by a low wall of planters. To get outside, Howie disentangled himself from his cappuccino, stood up with a stupid expression on his face, jogged through the interior of the restaurant, and came out the front door onto Don Orlando Street. By the time he had accomplished all this, Aria was gone, vanished again. He looked up and down the street, bewildered. And then he saw her several shops down, gazing into the window of a store that sold Oriental carpets and musty little knickknacks. Aria was more suntanned than when he had seen her last, dressed in vacation clothes. She could have been a tourist in her beige shorts, sandals, and loose Guatemalan blouse.

"Aria!" he shouted, trotting down the street toward her. She turned, saw Howie, and smiled determinedly. "Aria! For chrissake, where have you been?"

"Oh, the Big Island," she answered casually. "It was lovely."

The Big Island? Howie was so confused he tried to imagine briefly where in New Mexico such a big island might be.

"Hawaii?" he managed finally. "You've been in *Hawaii* all this time?"

"It was very spur of the moment, I must confess. Suddenly it seemed like a great idea to get away from San Geronimo."

Howie was so flabbergasted, he didn't know where to begin.

"Aria," he said as calmly as he was able, "you left your car by my house with the engine running and a gun on the ground. Jack and I have been looking all over for you, not to mention the state police. We've all been frantic."

Her face expressed concern. "I'm sorry, I honestly am. I didn't mean to cause any worry, but I just had to get away. I flew back into Albuquerque yesterday and only got home last night."

Howie was getting angry. "Sorry doesn't begin to cut it, I'm afraid. What the hell happened that night at your car? Nobody just disappears like that!"

"Look, Howie, I came to your cabin Tuesday night intending to break up with you. You're a nice guy, but I just don't have time for this."

"Oh, I see. You thought you'd have one more tumble and call it quits? Well, why didn't you, then?"

"Because I couldn't!" she exploded, full of exasperation. "Goddamn it, it was just too hard . . . or maybe I went weak, I don't know. But it was a mistake. I *should* have broken up with you that night, for your sake as well as mine. So let me do it now, okay? We're finished, Howie. Just forget about me. Whatever I've done, it's none of your business any longer. It's better you don't even know."

This was a weird twist for Howie: to free himself at last of Aria Waldman, as he had just done, and then have her pop back into his life to break up with him belatedly. Frankly, now that she was here, he *did* really give a damn. It didn't seem fair somehow.

"Look, this *is* my business," he assured her. "I made it my goddamn business by nearly getting killed a few times trying to find out what happened to you."

Tourists walking up the street were starting to give them curious glances, for they were having their quarrel too loudly. She lowered her voice: "Damn you, Howie! I never asked you to get involved in this. But if you really must know, an investigation I was doing was starting to come up with a lot of dirt on some important people here. Too much dirt, really. So I got frightened and thought it would be wise to vanish for a while, and do it with, well . . . a slightly dramatic flair. Enough drama so that certain people would know I was truly gone."

"And what about the gun?" he asked. "You still haven't explained that."

She looked away, refusing to meet his eyes. "Howie, I can't tell you. You just must believe me that I didn't do anything wrong."

"*Believe* you? Aria, my God—you went to bed with Lou Snider! You lied to me, you lied to him, you lied your way from start to finish in this entire business. So give me one good reason I should believe anything you're telling me now, including your supposed trip to Hawaii?—which is pretty damn convenient, seeing you were gone while a whole bunch of people were busy dying."

Aria shook her head sadly. She opened her mouth to say something, but then stopped herself. When she did speak finally, her tone was mechanical, strangely empty of life: "I flew into Los Angeles from Honolulu Tuesday afternoon on United flight 1216. On the Big Island, I stayed at the Kona Surf Hotel. Check it out. You're a detective."

"And Snider? What about him?" he pressed bitterly.

"Well, what about him?" she repeated in the same dazed voice. "I'm sorry, but I'm a free woman and that's just the way things go. I've never wanted to hurt you, but if you start snooping into my private life, I guess you deserve what you get. So let's say good-bye before things get even more unpleasant. Okay?"

Howie stepped backward, stung speechless.

"I never told you that I loved you, Howie. Remember that," she said in a strangled voice, close to tears. "I never promised any kind of future for us. I was honest about the things that count!"

She turned abruptly, and he watched as she walked quickly down Don Orlando Street away from him. Halfway down the street she broke into a run. From her body language—a body he knew too well—Howie was certain she was crying. He thought he should probably run after her with the many questions that still needed to be answered, but at the moment he could only stand frozen in place, a vein throbbing in his temple, too upset to press farther down the road of hard suspicions that were starting to float unbidden through his mind.

13

Howie pulled into Jack's driveway. He slammed his car door and hurried up the path toward the house. Then he saw Jack in the shaded part of the garden, sitting at his redwood picnic table with a cordless telephone in hand and Katya dozing at his feet. Howie changed directions and charged toward him.

"Guess who I just saw!" Howie challenged.

"Aria Waldman, I imagine," Jack answered mildly, turning his dark glasses toward Howie and putting down the telephone.

This stopped Howie with his mouth open. "You're not a whole lot of fun to surprise, Jack," he said at last. "Where do you think she's been all this time?"

"Somewhere suitably far away, I imagine."

"She says Hawaii. She told me she stayed at the Kona Surf Hotel on the Big Island. She even gave me her flight number back to Los Angeles last night, just in case I wanted to check."

"I think we can assume she's telling the truth. It would be a stupid lie when we can check it so easily. But we'll make some phone calls anyway."

"Personally, I wouldn't trust her if every hotel in Hawaii swore she was their honored guest! Here's something else. I found out last night that she didn't publish that article in *The New Yorker*—that thing we found in her file is a cut-and-paste job from a photocopy shop."

"She didn't go to the Columbia School of Journalism either, Howie, though she *did* graduate from Smith, I'm sure you'll be happy to know. Magna cum laude. A bright young woman. But her name isn't Aria Waldman, it's Rebecca Weinstein."

"Oh, great! I never slept with anyone named Rebecca before. Now it seems I have!"

"You're talking rubbish. Sit down, Howie."

"I don't feel like sitting down. I feel like standing."

"Suit yourself. Are you calm enough to listen to me?"

"I'm calm, Jack. I'm like an iceberg standing in your garden."

Jack shook his head and sighed.

"Well, what do you expect?" Howie cried bitterly. "I feel like an idiot the way she's twisted me around. What really gets me is last night I had a fabulous time—I spent the night with a very nice woman, thank you. I thought I was through suffering over goddamn Aria Waldman. And then I see her this morning, and I'm so churned up I feel crazy. How could she do that to me? Run off like that, leaving her car in the middle of my road so I'd think something horrible had happened? And the worst of it, I'm sure she's involved in all these deaths somehow. I don't have a clue why, or how she did it, but she's manipulated me and everybody else for some reason. . . . I mean, goddamn it, Jack! The lady jerked me around, and I don't even know why!"

"Are you through ranting? If you'd like, you can try punching your fists against a few of my trees."

"You think that'd help?"

"Nothing's going to help, Howie. Except the truth."

Howie's sigh was so long and deflated, he sounded like a tire going flat. He slumped down onto the bench across the table from Jack. "Okay, so tell me. What's the truth?"

"I've already told you everything of importance. Her name is Rebecca Weinstein."

Howie shook his head blankly. "Is this supposed to mean something to me?"

"No, not yet. I haven't had a chance to fill you in on a few of the leads I've been investigating while you were off having fun in the woods."

"Fun?"

"That was an attempt at humor. Now, shut up and listen to me. There once was a man named Richard Weinstein who was an accountant at a big pharmaceutical company in Connecticut, a rather colorless, nebbishy man, as far as I can gather. But then in 1974 he surprised everyone, and it turned out he wasn't so colorless after all. One night Weinstein didn't return home to his wife and family, and the next day he didn't show up at work either. When the pharmaceutical company went over their books, they discovered their nebbishy accountant had embezzled $200,000. A year later, he was spotted in the East Village living the life of an artist, but when an NYPD detective went to investigate, our Mr. Weinstein shot him dead. So now it was murder, not just a financial crime, and at this point Richard Weinstein disappeared forever, becoming one of those many unsolved footnotes in the annals of crime . . . are you following me so far, Howie? If so, you might try a logical deduction about now, just to let me know your brain cells haven't entirely turned to mush."

"Richard Weinstein became Donald Hicks?"

"You got it. I suppose artists are born in all sorts of ways. Hicks reinvented himself, he showed up in San Geronimo in the mid-seventies, bought himself a nice little house with an apricot orchard and would have lived happily ever after had it not been for a group of guys who called themselves the Warrior Circle and wanted to build a shopping mall on his land. Of course, a big part of Sheriff Snider's unofficial job was digging up dirt on people, so with some effort he was able to find out who Donald Hicks really was."

"It wasn't so hard. Snider just ran Hicks' prints through some computer . . . at least, this is what Denny told me," Howie said.

"Well, there you are. And that's pretty much the whole story. The Warrior Circle only wanted the land, they offered a deal, but Hicks decided to hang himself instead. Maybe he was tired of running, maybe he thought these men would never leave him alone once they got their hooks in him, maybe he simply hated the idea of his orchard turning into a Foot Locker and JC Penny. He seems to have been a uniquely stubborn man."

"Okay. But what's Aria's connection to all this?"

"Howie, you're slow today. She's Richard Weinstein's daughter. Rebecca Weinstein."

"Ah!" said Howie. And then as the implications sank in he gasped, "My God!"

"That's right. This has been about revenge, from start to finish. She came to San Geronimo, she got herself a job as an investigative reporter on the local newspaper, and she set about to do some digging herself. Then, when she was satisfied that she knew what had happened, she ruthlessly destroyed the men who had destroyed her father. Poetic justice, don't you think?—a men's group brought down by one angry woman?"

Howie's world had gone topsy-turvy once again. "Rebecca Weinstein," he said, mulling over the sound of the name on his tongue. He wondered if people called her Becky. "But if her story checks out and she really *was* in Hawaii this past week, then she has an alibi. She couldn't have killed anybody."

"Not directly, no. But she did it nevertheless. Indirectly. She set all the men against each other, and they obliged her by responding pretty much as she'd planned. It's possible, of course, that she may have committed one actual murder back in June—Gary Tripp, our musician turned Hemperware tycoon. Gary's disappearance is what set everything in motion, like giving a nudge to a house of cards and then standing back while they all fall down. After that, all the men were extremely nervous and ready to believe the worst about each other."

Howie was shaking his head. "I still don't see how she could do it. It's impossible!"

"No, it isn't. Remember, we're talking about a very smart and determined woman here. Lou Snider was her point of entry into the Warrior Circle. I wouldn't be surprised if she studied the group for some time before concluding that Snider was the weak link, a strange, lonely man who was at an age where he might fall hard for a beautiful young woman. Not only did she get vital information from Lou, she used him to plant all sorts of destructive seeds. Like telling Lou that Chuck Hildyard was cooperating with the D.A.'s office in a secret investigation of the sheriff's office—she simply made that up. Or the notes she left on her laptop making it clear that Lou was talking his head off. Frankly, I think she left her laptop deliberately for Chuck Hildyard to find. You interfered with that plan, Howie, but obviously she had planted some other clues as well. We've probably only scratched the surface of her various plots and plans. My guess is that the photograph of Shepherd Plum in drag that was sent to Plum's wife came from her. The way I see it, there were a whole bunch of these little salvos that she fired into the men's group, hoping that just a few of them would explode in their faces. Basically, it was a campaign of misinformation designed to set them all against each other. Remember, these guys had committed a number of crimes together, including blackmail and bribery of public officials, so they could go to prison if they weren't careful. Once Aria scattered her seeds of destruction, it was every man for himself."

"Did she put the bomb in Lou Snider's car?"

"Well, it's possible, though my guess is that Chuck Hildyard did that—he was the explosives expert, after all. The FBI lab is still in the midst of their investigation, but I've heard from Kevin that they're saying it was a sophisticated device. They recovered a minuscule fragment of the timer, I understand—it came from a VCR, the clock that records your favorite TV show when you're out of the house. It turns out that Snider was scheduled to give a talk that night at a statewide sheriff's convention in Albuquerque. The meeting was planned to end promptly at ten-thirty p.m., so if he had stuck to his schedule the bomb would have exploded while he was in the car driving home on I-25, halfway back to San Geronimo."

"I guess it's lucky for him that he decided to come to my house and kill me instead!" Howie mentioned sourly. "So what about the revolver I found by her Jeep?"

"I think that was meant to make Lou Snider believe that Chuck Hildyard was involved in Aria's disappearance. The gun had been confiscated by the sheriff's department after a fourth grader brought it to school, but the FBI lab found a latent print belonging to Hildyard on the cylinder. This is only conjecture, but let's say Lou gave the revolver to Chuck some time ago, for personal protection or whatnot, then it's found at the Jeep. . . . "

"Found by me?"

"Why not? Of course, you were supposed to turn it over to the cops like a good citizen. Or the cops could find it themselves if you missed it. Either way, it would come to Lou's attention—he would recognize the gun and think that Chuck had been involved, that he had made Aria disappear because she knew too much. Aria was tracking these men very closely, remember. She could have stolen the gun from Hildyard's house one day when he was off playing golf—who knows? But I'm sure she realized that Lou Snider was an unstable and violent man, and that if she lit his fuse in just the right way, he'd end up blasting that men's group to hell and back."

"She's good at lighting a guy's fuse," Howie said heavily.

"Yes, I think she is. Incidentally, the two shells that were found up near Bear Lake last June came from that same revolver, as did the shell you picked up in the desert. I'm not sure what this means, but I sense something very devious."

"So what about the unknown shooter?" Howie asked. "The person your FBI friends think was up at Bear Lake with a shotgun? If Aria was in Hawaii, who's our extra player, Jack?"

"Well, here's where it gets tricky," Jack said with a thin smile. He was enjoying himself, which Howie found annoying. "Now that Aria's back, all the vanished have returned, except for one. Which player in this drama do we have left unaccounted for, Howie?"

"Jack, I'm really not in the mood for games."

"Think, Howie."

"Gary Tripp? But he's dead. . . . "

"Is he? Remember, Gary's body has never been found, Howie. Now, I'm not sure what his motive might be, but if he made it down alive off that mountain back in June, I can imagine some interesting possibilities. I don't have this entirely in focus yet, but it's a fascinating twist, don't you think? And basically, unless our unknown shooter is someone totally from left field, who else could it be?"

Jack might be enjoying himself, getting his teeth on such a fine puzzle, but Howie was full of a growing agitation. It wasn't pleasant to discover that the woman he once thought he loved had manipulated the deaths of two men, maybe more. Yet he couldn't help feeling a certain sympathy for her. She was a crusader, after all, avenging the death of her father and exposing a corrupt and particularly noxious shopping mall development. Howie couldn't bear his own moral ambivalence. Was she a monster or someone who simply had the nerve to seek true justice? He wanted emotional completion, to either hate the woman or give her a medal.

Howie stood up restlessly from the picnic table.

"I've got to go, Jack. I need to think about this."

"Howie, sit down. We've got a lot to do."

But Howie was already walking away on the path toward his car. "I need some time alone. I'm sorry, Jack."

Jack stood up and shouted after him: "Goddamn it, Howie, where are you going?"

He didn't answer.

"Look, Howie, stop for a second. We're going to confront Aria soon enough, but we're not ready yet. We need more time to gather evidence first. So stay away from her . . . Howie, do you hear me?"

"*You* may not be ready to confront her, but *I* am!" Howie shouted back, lowering himself into the bucket seat of his car.

Jack listened as Howie started up the growly old MG engine and drove away, his tires crunching gravel as he sped off onto the pavement. Left on his own, Jack sat down again at the picnic table. A weary smile came to his lips. He knew he was a manipulative son of a bitch, and he wasn't proud of it. Like Rebecca Weinstein, Jack Wilder understood the power of indirect action. He had deliberately riled Howie up in order to send him off with the proper mindset on what he hoped would be a final fact-finding mission.

14

Howie drove fast on the curving highway east of town into the foothills. He was headed toward Aria's A-frame . . . no, it was Rebecca Weinstein's A-frame, he reminded himself. This would take some getting used to, her new identity. Howie sensed Jack was right; he should stay away from her. But he couldn't help himself. The thought of her reeled him in like a fish on a line. He only hoped she was home, and alone.

He downshifted into her driveway and came to a stop alongside her powder-blue Jeep Cherokee, which had a cracked windshield but otherwise had apparently survived Sheriff Snider's final ride, as well as the Big Bang, having been parked at the side of Howie's cabin the night of the explosion. It was a shock to see her car back in use; she must have reclaimed it this morning from the state police, and answered a lot of questions in the process. Howie hoped she was still in a question-answering mood. He stepped from his car and stood in the driveway studying the house, letting his eyes travel upward from ground level, up the wooden steps to the second-floor sundeck. At first he saw no one, but as he continued to stare, Aria came out the sliding glass door from the living room, carrying a huge cardboard box awkwardly in her arms. She was dressed in a ratty old T-shirt and cutoff jeans, hard at work.

"I guess you're moving out, now the job is done," Howie called up to her.

With a grunt, she set the box down on the deck, then walked to the railing to peer down at him. "Go away, Howie," she told him warily. "Haven't we said too much already?"

"No, I don't think so . . . Rebecca."

Her expression didn't change. "So now you know. But you still shouldn't have come here."

"Rebecca Weinstein," he continued. "Daughter of Richard Weinstein, an accountant who stole two hundred thousand bucks from a huge drug corporation so he could become an artist in New Mexico. You know, Rebecca, I guess I'm here because I'm trying to decide the moral of this tale. I really don't know whether your father was a hero or just some scumbag."

Her face became flushed, as Howie had intended. "Then you'd better think it over," she said angrily. "Listen to me. With a big pharmaceutical company, it's *all* stolen money. These companies couldn't give a shit who lives or dies as long as they get to gouge the public. My father was a sweet, gentle person, and he couldn't bear it anymore. He bailed out, that's all. So what if he took some of their money?"

"A shame he had to kill a cop in New York to get away with it."

"Well, too bad! They should have left him alone, those bastards! If you come around collecting money for gangsters, that makes you a gangster too, as far as I'm concerned. Anyway, Dad had no intention of exchanging one prison for another."

"So how old were you when he left? Five? Six? It must have left a scar."

She shook her head and sighed.

"Come on, tell me your sad story," Howie urged. "People like you always have a sad story to justify what you do."

Her eyes flashed. "What do *you* know about sad stories? I was five when my father left. One night my daddy didn't come home, like daddies were supposed to do, and after that everything changed. My mother had to get a job, we moved out of our nice house in Westport into a crummy little apartment in Bridgeport. I was put into day care, Mom started drinking, suddenly my life was not so warm and wonderful anymore."

"How did you find your father in San Geronimo?"

"I didn't. He found me. He just showed up one day about a week after I graduated from college. It's funny, I recognized him instantly. And, of course, he knew me—I was the one thing from his old life that he regretted leaving."

"Weren't you angry at him? After all, he abandoned you."

"Well, I was angry for a while. But it was hard to stay angry after he told me why he'd done what he did. I guess I've always liked Robin Hood more than Sheriff John. Anyway, Dad had been miserable with my mother, living in Westport, working at a job he hated. Everybody has a right to be happy, Howie. Everybody has a right to be free."

"Not if you have to kill and steal in order to do it," Howie told her.

She shrugged. "Well, there are all kinds of justice. Aren't there?"

"You tell me, Rebecca . . . Aria—whoever you are. What kind of justice did you deal out to Lou and Chuck Hildyard? You killed them to get even for what they did to your father. Indirectly, perhaps, but you did it. You destroyed that entire men's group."

"Did I?" she said vaguely, with a thin smile. "No, I think they destroyed each other. I might have urged them on a little—like cheering on a cockfight. I'm not admitting anything, I'm only being theoretical, you understand. But those roosters are responsible for their own violence, Howie. Not me."

"You got them going, though. You planted all the lies that set them against each other. Jack says you're guilty of conspiracy to commit murder, and he's planning to get you for it too," Howie told her, doing some creative lying himself.

Aria had wandered down the wooden steps from the sundeck. Now she sat on the third step from the bottom, hugging her bare legs and regarding Howie with her green eyes.

"Look, I didn't mean to hurt you, Howie," she said, more softly than she had spoken before.

He laughed bitterly.

"But I had an agenda, and it didn't include you in my life," she went on. "Let's say for the sake of argument that maybe, just *maybe* you're right—that I decided the vicious bastards who drove my father to suicide shouldn't get away without punishment. Howie, I don't know if I can make you understand this, but my dad was this little Walter Mitty sort of guy, not exactly a seasoned criminal, and I adored him when I was little. After he took their money, Xerxes made life absolute hell for my mom and me—they thought my mom must have been in on the deal and was stashing the money somewhere. For years they sent private nvestigators, thugs basically, by every few months to intimidate her. These guys would show up at our apartment. Sometimes they'd even be waiting for me outside my school—just a little more pressure, you see. That's when my mother started drinking. God, Howie! You can't imagine how evil they were! As soon as my mom would get a new job, they'd call and inform her employer in these very official voices that she was the object of a major criminal investigation and they'd better watch the cash register. I remember Mom started dating this nice man, a high school math teacher, but they called him too and told a bunch of lies about her. It was the end of that romance, believe me. Sometimes there would be these phone calls late at night. 'Just tell us where your husband is, Mrs. Weinstein, and we won't bother you anymore.'"

Aria took a deep breath. "So I hated them," she said on the exhale. "And when I was old enough to understand, I thought it was cool what Dad had done, taking money from those greedy shits. He beat them at their own game. It appealed to my sense of poetry and for a few years, after Dad got in touch with me, it warmed my soul to think of him out here in New Mexico doing his beautiful watercolors and paintings. Then a whole bunch of bad things happened in my life all at once . . . do you want to hear about this Howie? Or am I just babbling on for nothing?"

"I'm listening."

"Well, I was raped," she said in a mockingly bright tone. "How about that? I was living in Hartford, and one day I was riding my bicycle through a park around dusk. I stopped to check the pressure on one of my tires when two guys came jogging by . . . joggers, for chrissake! They dragged me into the bushes and took turns at me for about an hour. When they were done, I went to the cops, but they weren't too interested. I mean, sure, they filed a report, but that was the end of it. You're probably saying, big deal. Plenty of women get raped in this country, and hardly anyone ever gets brought to trial. I was just another statistic, so who cares?"

"I'm not saying that," Howie told her. "I'm sorry."

"Well, so was I. *Very* sorry. But the reason I'm telling you this has to do with my state of mind, how someone resolves to do something that's not so pleasant. It's a number of things, you see, not one thing at all. About two weeks after I was raped, my mother died in a car accident. Then a month after that, I found out

that my father was dead—my letters were getting returned, so I fi
nally called the San Geronimo post office and someone told m
he'd died. I phoned a few galleries in town, trying to learn the de
tails, and that's how I heard it was suicide. I just couldn't figure
out. I knew Dad had been happy in New Mexico, and it didn
make any sense to me that he would kill himself. So I kept dig
ging—I pretended I was an art collector, that I owned a few Don
ald Hicks paintings, and I was looking for information about h
estate. One of the galleries gave me the name of Dorothy Lang
the head of the Art Association, saying she might be able to te
me something. So I called her. She said she didn't have any ide
why Donald might hang himself, except he was getting pressure
recently by a shopping center development to sell his land. It wa
the first time I heard that awful name, Chamisa Mall. I just kne
in my bones that they were responsible somehow. . . ."

Aria/Rebecca had been growing visibly more upset as she tol
her tale. She took a deep breath, and when she spoke again, he
voice was harder, angrier, more brittle:

"So, okay, I cracked, I really did! I was just so goddamn angr
I mean, I'd been raped, my mother was dead, my father had hur
himself . . . I was tired of all the slick evil bullshit in this worl
Howie. I remember there was one night I knew either I had to ki
myself too, or I had to fight back. Well, I fought back. I put ever
thing, my sanity included, into this one job of finding out exact
what happened to Dad. I changed my name and came out We
and made up a few credentials so I could get a job on the loc
newspaper. Being a reporter gave me a chance to poke around a
find out what I wanted to know."

"And you found out?"

"Damn right I did! I found out how a bunch of jackals hounde
my dad until they discovered his secret. You know, at first Dad re
fused to sell his land to them on principle—he loved his orchar
and he hated to see a huge shopping mall come to San Geronim
But in the end—I found this out from Lou—he only wanted to b
left alone. He agreed to take their final offer and just move some
place else and start all over again. But they only laughed at hir
Once Lou had discovered the big secret, they figured they cou
turn Dad in and work out some deal where they'd take that lar
for free as a reward from the drug company. Dad was too old t

run, he didn't want to go to prison, so he decided that ending his life was the only way out."

"All right, so these warriors were pretty nasty. But it still doesn't justify what you did," Howie told her.

"You don't think so? Then tell me what *you* would do, Howie, if a group of guys killed somebody you loved and they got away with it, all in a very legal manner? Are you trying to tell me you wouldn't have done *anything*?"

Howie shook his head. "I don't know. It seems to me that your father set up his own bad ending when he stole and killed all those years ago. None of this is right. Not what he did. Not what the men's group did. And not what you did either."

"But what did I do?" she asked. "Nothing, really. I didn't shoot anyone, I didn't even raise my voice. *They* did it, Howie. To each other."

"Christ, Aria!—you were screwing Lou Snider! For *information*! Don't you think that was pretty damn shoddy, sleeping with the enemy?"

She smiled grimly. "Howie, I wasn't playing games. I only slept with Lou once, but I would have done it again if I had to. I would have done anything that was necessary. And it was pathetic, really, how easy it was to string him along . . . a middle-aged cop who thought of himself as a big Romeo. Poor old Lou! He didn't tell me everything about the Warrior Circle, but he told me a lot."

"So what was *I*?" Howie threw at her. "How did *I* fit into your plans?"

"That's the point. You *didn't* fit, Howie."

"Then why did you get involved with me?"

She gazed at him steadily. "Why? Because I liked you. I was lonely, I had come a long way from home to do something extremely difficult, and there were times when I craved a normal life and some friendly human contact."

He shook his head. "You only used me, like you used Lou Snider. You left your Jeep outside my cabin so Jack and I would investigate—I see that now. That gun on the ground with Hildgard's prints on it was part of the bait too. You wanted me and Jack to pressure the men's group from one end, while they tore themselves apart from the other. It was all designed to make them start going after each other, each of them thinking everybody else was the traitor."

She shrugged. As Howie watched, she seemed to change, covering any tenderness that might have been left inside her. "Well, you'll never know for sure, will you?" she taunted.

Howie laughed harshly. "Oh, I *know*! You're the queen of destruction, I really have to hand it to you. Did you expect in your wildest dreams that your crazy sheriff would kill Chuck Hildyard for you, just because you made him believe that Hildyard had killed you? But I guess you paid him back for that piece of misguided chivalry—somehow you killed old Lou, didn't you? You know, I'm really curious how you managed that, shooting Lou in the back with a shotgun long distance from Hawaii? Jack thinks that Gary Tripp was involved somehow, but that seems a bit farfetched to me. So you've got to tell me, Rebecca. I'll bet it's your crowning bit of cunning. Your pièce de résistance."

She stood up from the stairs, regarding him coldly. "I wish I could say it's been good seeing you again. I'm sorry you're so bitter, I really am. But I think I've told you everything I intend to, so you'd better go. Unless, of course, you want to help me pack. Frankly, it's time I got out of this shitty little town."

Howie felt a heavy weight of sadness press down upon him. "I came looking for you when I though you were in trouble," he told her. "I was your friend."

"Well, that's your misfortune, isn't it?" she replied. Her face had become an ugly mask, no longer a person Howie recognized. He stepped closer to her, blood rising in his head, a great darkness shrouding his heart.

"Go ahead, hit me," she offered. "Probably I deserve it."

Howie paused. "No," he said. "I'm not much into vengeance. Just look what it did to you."

She glared at him defiantly, and Howie stared right back, studying the hardness in her face. Maybe there had been something in her once, the warmth and intelligence he had fallen for. But sometimes people choose the wrong fork in the road, and then there was no going back to what might have been. Rebecca Weinstein had chosen hatred and revenge, and it had changed her utterly.

She stood on the stairs, uncomfortable at the way he was studying her. "Christ! Go away, Howie. Leave me alone!"

"Just one more question. Last Tuesday night when you left you

Jeep near my cabin and made your grand exit—how did you get to the airport?"

Her smile was genuine. She had worked this all out so carefully. "Easy. I had my mountain bike in the back of the Jeep and a rental car waiting for me in town. I carried the bike all the way to the highway so I wouldn't leave tire marks on your road. And then *poof!* . . . I just disappeared!"

15

Howie got into his car and drove in a zombielike trance from her driveway onto the road. His hands were shaking so badly on the steering wheel, he was afraid he'd have an accident. As soon as he was out of sight of the A-frame, he pulled onto the shoulder and stopped to take a few breaths of air and steady his nerves. There was a scenic view here, from the foothills down into the desert, the wide stretch of valley that was San Geronimo. He turned off the ignition and listened to the wind through the pines and the gurgling death of his engine.

No one was around, and he felt so forlorn that he let himself cry. Sensitive New Age Guys seemed to cry at the drop of a hat these days, but for Howie it was still a little embarrassing, an act requiring a watershed of emotion. It felt good and salty, and he hoped the jays in the trees weren't taking any photographs. He cried for lost love and lost innocence, and because he felt very dejected at the moment, an ugly man in an ugly world.

Well, at least now it's truly over! he thought with weary satisfaction as his tears sniffled to a halt. The whole affair had clearly been a case of mistaken identity from start to finish. He had loved a shadowy projection, not a real person—not entirely his fault, of course, since she had consciously concealed everything from him, her real name and past and what she had come to San Geronimo accomplish. As Howie wiped the last tears away from his eyes with the back of his hand, he took some consolation from the fact that knowledge had set him free at last. Yes, he had said this himself before, but now he really meant it. Thank God, he would never have to run after Aria Waldman again!

Just as Howie was arriving at his long-delayed personal liberation from misguided love, he heard thunder not far away, a deep booming explosion, then slow reverberation as the thunder echoed and died. He looked up to the sky, but there was not a cloud in sight. While he was gazing upward, there came a second explosion, a bass thud that was followed by a series of high treble cracks. This wasn't thunder; it was gunfire, and it was coming from the direction of Aria's A-frame.

Howie turned on the ignition and jammed the accelerator to the floor so hard that he flooded the engine. Now the MG wouldn't start. He shouted four-letter expletives, jumped from the car, and ran as fast as he could back down the road, around the bend, and up the driveway to the house. The sound of gunfire grew louder and sent his adrenaline into such a dizzying overdrive that for the moment he did not appreciate the irony: that here he was, back in the loop, running after Aria Waldman one more time.

Howie ran as fast as he could, and he arrived out of breath at the bottom of the wooden steps to the sundeck. The powder-blue Cherokee was still outside the garage, but the house was enveloped in a heavy midday stillness, not a sign of anyone in sight.

"Aria!" he shouted. Then remembered: "Rebecca!"

But there was no response to either name. Howie dreaded climbing the steps. The silence was thick and unnatural. Even the birds in the surrounding forest had ceased their usual chatter. Howie's heartbeat thumped in his ears.

"Rebecca!" he called again.

"Goddamn it, go away!" she hissed back at him finally from somewhere inside.

"I'm coming up." Howie flung himself up the stairs two at a time, running with his head down, trying to make himself the smallest target possible. In his haste, he stumbled through the living room door, falling onto his hands and knees across the carpet.

"Howie! I never asked for any clumsy knight in shining armor to save me. This is my battle, and I'm doing fine."

"Who's shooting at you?" he demanded, catching his breath.

She shook her head, disgusted. "God, you're persistent!"

She was kneeling beneath an open window at the rear of the

house with a small semiautomatic pistol in her hand. The living room around her was still a mess from being ransacked last week. There were plastic bags full of garbage on one side of the room, as well half a dozen cardboard moving cartons that were half-full. Howie's eyes came back to the woman he had once loved. He saw there was blood running down her arm from her right shoulder.

"You've been hit."

"Not badly. I ducked at just the right time to pick up a moving carton. I never thought I'd have my life saved by a cardboard box!"

"Where'd the shots come from?"

She gestured to the steep hillside at the back of the house, to a spot about thirty feet away, where the ground rose up nearly parallel to the rear window. Howie crawled to where she was crouching and then stood cautiously to peer out the window. He didn't see anyone.

"It's Gary, isn't it?" he asked. "Jack was right—we still have one warrior up and fighting. Somehow Gary Tripp survived that night in June up in the mountains, and now he's having the last word after all."

She shook her head.

"Goddamn it, I'm tired of being jerked around! Tell me!"

"It's not *Gary,* for chrissake. And I though you were smart! Haven't you figured it out yet?"

Howie's mouth fell open.

"Well, bravo!" she said sarcastically, watching the light of understanding come at last into Howie's eyes.

Just then a movement of dark clothing on the hillside caught his eye. A figure had broken from the cover of a large piñon and was scrambling quickly toward higher ground. Howie hesitated only an instant before bounding out the door to the sundeck. He kept his head low and ran down the steps in pursuit of the unknown shooter, the last dangling end to this whole mystery.

It was a woman—that was all he could make out before she disappeared into the woods, a blur of feminine form. Howie ran with all his might to catch her. When it came to chasing women, he suspected he must be the all-time champion running fool.

Howie had been on this hillside before. This was déjà vu with a vengeance, now that he was again at his personal mountain of manly endeavor. There was daylight now, which was an improvement, but he was still slapped by low branches as he ran. Scratchy, thorny things tore at him. The hill was steep and densely wooded, but he pulled and clawed his way forward. He could hear footsteps somewhere above him trampling through the undergrowth, but he could not see through the thick foliage.

She was armed, and Howie had no clear idea of what he would do if he actually caught her. Still, he mindlessly kept going. He panted until his lungs felt like they were about to explode. He raged forward like an angry bull high into the hillside above the A-frame house. Finally he had to stop and catch his breath.

The palm of his left hand was bleeding, cut from one of his many falls. He stood with his palm in his mouth, sucking the wound clean, tasting his own blood, listening for footsteps. But now there was only silence above him. Had she managed to escape? He wasn't certain but after Howie caught his breath, he proceeded more slowly, as quietly as he was able. Every few feet he stopped to listen. There was nothing. Nobody. More than half an hour went by in this slow progress up the hill, a few feet at a time, then stopping to listen. At last Howie came out upon level ground at the top of the long rise. But there was no one here.

He kept walking across the top of the hill, moving with Indian caution, just in case she was nearby, lurking in ambush. Many years ago, his great-uncle Two Arrows had shown Howie how to move through the woods as a hunter, walking on the balls of his feet, feeling his way carefully. He moved like that now, remembering Two Arrows' lesson, passing soundlessly across the level forest until he came to the far side of the hill, a sharp precipice from which there was a vista to the east. The land fell off into a canyon, and on the far side of the canyon there were more foothills that gradually ascended into the true mountains.

Looking down, Howie saw a paved road in the canyon far below. It was the same road that snaked past Aria's house, though he had never been this far on it before—her house had always been his destination. There was a stream running through the canyon and an old car, a dusty Volvo station wagon, was parked on a narrow pull-off. He recognized the station wagon and remembered the rear bumper was covered with stickers, though he couldn't see them from where he stood. ARMS ARE MADE FOR HUGGING—that was one of the slogans, he recalled. A nice New Age sentiment, very gentle. A pity, in this instance, that it was such a lie.

Howie froze, sensing movement nearby. His eyes traveled more sharply downward, closer to the hill on which he stood. Mary Jane Tripp was standing directly beneath him on a ledge about fifteen feet below, her back to Howie, a shotgun cradled in her arms.

Howie wondered how many women might kill their husbands if they thought they could get away with it. He had the outline of Mary Jane Tripp's crime pretty well figured out, though few of the details. Meanwhile, she was so close, he was afraid to breathe.

Could he jump her? Perhaps. Howie and Mary Jane stood together, one above the other, in a frozen tableau. His mind was racing. He had an absurd image of Misha Ballantine on the summit of San Geronimo Peak, flapping his arms like an eagle before taking off into the great beyond.

A warrior can fly, Moon Deer! You only need to stretch the limits of your imagination!

In this case, Howie would need to fly approximately fifteen feet and land exactly on target. Not a huge distance, but one in which he could still break his neck, or hers, or overshoot the mark and get blasted with a shotgun for his trouble. Anyway, he was sick of violence; Howie was suddenly quite certain that this was not what being a man was all about. He, at least, was a man of thought. He believed in the power of ideas, and he had an idea now—a tricky idea, but he thought he'd give it a try.

He spoke very carefully: "Don't move. Don't even twitch. I have a gun, and it's pointed at the back of your head. I don't want to kill you."

Mary Jane froze beneath him. Her shoulders seemed to turn into a block of stone. Was she going to spin around and shoot him?

"I *don't* want to kill you," he said again, more sternly, his scariest voice. "Listen to me carefully, Mary Jane. Don't do anything suddenly. Very gently, toss the shotgun over the cliff . . . do it now. Don't make me pull the trigger."

She hesitated. Howie wasn't certain if she was going to buy his lie. But then with both hands, in a gentle underhand throw, she tossed the shotgun outward into empty space. The weapon fell with a clatter to the rocks below. Howie quickly climbed down the steep incline to the ledge where Mary Jane was standing, sliding the last five feet. She turned to face him. Her long brown hair framed her face—a pretty woman, but with eyes long dead.

"You don't have a gun," she said dully. "You tricked me."

"We've had enough guns, I think," Howie said. "You killed Gary. Then you had to kill Lou and go after Aria, didn't you? Because they found out."

She nodded numbly. Every human has a certain amount of struggle and fight in their fiber, but Mary Jane had used all hers up. Tears filled her ravaged eyes.

"You can tell me all about it," Howie told her. "On our way into town."

16

In the weeks that followed, Howard Moon Deer had dreams nearly every night that he was flying. Recently, though, his dream flying had become a huge effort. His wings were too heavy. Not so easy to toss and turn in your bed, flapping with all your might, always pulled downward to the hard, unyielding earth.

September arrived, a beautiful month in New Mexico, dry and clear and golden. For quite a long time, Howie had been bothered by the various official people who insisted on talking with him, but as soon as he was able, he went camping by himself in the mountains of Colorado. He was talked out, exhausted, as empty as a person could be. As far as he was concerned, there really was no more to say about anything. Not only was the case over, he sensed his youth was somehow over too.

In Colorado, autumn had already come to the high mountains, transforming the shimmering aspen to gold. Howie looked up one afternoon from his campsite to see a single golden leaf as it was plucked loose by the wind. The leaf floated lazily in the blue sky, falling gently downward to the ground. *There go I!* he said to himself gloomily. Then, as he was watching, another motion caught his eye, much higher in the sky: It was an eagle floating directly above him. He stood to get a better view, but in a second the huge bird was gone.

Probably he was mistaken, he decided. There were so few eagles left, even in these remote mountains. It must have been a buzzard or a hawk.

From the ledge on the hill behind the A-frame house, Howie had driven Mary Jane Tripp to collect her three children at a friend's house in town. Then he went with her to the bus station and helped put her kids on a Greyhound to their grandmother in Texas. This was the deal she struck with Howie, and it seemed to him a reasonable one. She was just a shell of a person now, her will collapsed, but she managed to spare a final though for her children. If he would help get Indiga, Sativa, and little Bud safely to Texas, she would answer his questions and allow herself to be delivered to the state police.

Her story was intricate but not, at heart, complex. Early in the summer, in the cover of night—the night following the full moon in June—Mary Jane's husband, Gary, had returned home on a stolen motorcycle. He was frightened, cold, hungry, and had an astonishing tale to tell. The camping trip with his men's group had turned into a nightmare. High on peyote, Gary had been splashing his face in the waters of Bear Lake when a masked figure came up behind him and pressed a gun to the back of his head. It was a Native American "power mask," one that could be bought in any of the local craft shops. The mask that approached him now was a stylized dog, that he recognized could only belong to Dog-Running-Free, or Lou Snider as he was known in normal life. The figure gestured him from the lake into a nearby stand of trees and Gary believed he was about to die. But then came a fortunate accident. In the darkness under the trees, wearing his clumsy mask, Lou Snider had stumbled—whether from a branch, a rock, or uneven ground, Gary couldn't say. But he knew this was his chance to run for freedom if he was going to live. He took off into the forest as the dog-masked figure fired his gun at him, two shots that missed wide.

And so Gary escaped. He spent the night shivering in the trees, then the following day he climbed down the eastern slope of the mountain to the ski resort, just as Howie had done months later. He waited until dark to hot-wire a motorcycle in the parking lot and drive home, arriving at the ranch not long after his kids had gone to sleep. Once home, Gary broke down and told his wife everything, all his fears and woes. He believed that Lou Snider had nearly supernatural powers, and he was terrified the sheriff warrior might show up any minute to finish what he had begun. Gary admitted to Mary Jane that the Circle had good reason to be furious with him, for he had betrayed the warrior's notion of brotherhood and honor; he had been stealing money from them, paying less than the full amount that was due to the group's common fund from his Hemperware business. Over the past few years he had siphoned off approximately $40,000.

Gary believed himself marked for death. He wasn't certain what to do in the long run, but for the present he decided he'd better go into hiding. He had Mary Jane pack up their 4-wheel drive pickup truck with supplies—food, water purifier, sleeping bag, tarp, warm clothes, a Coleman stove, and the family shotgun—then she drove him to a lean-to on a stream in a remote corner of their eighty acres where they had camped before. He hoped that if he stayed out of sight for a few weeks, Lou and the others might conclude that he had died up on the mountain and ease up on trying to find him. Then he would come up with some new plan. Unfortunately for Gary, his wife was busy making her own plans as she drove him across their land, bouncing torturously up and down the arroyos.

It seemed to Mary Jane that her husband, in a sense, was already dead. Lou Snider had shot at him up on the mountain, and wasn't it a pity the two shots had missed? Or *had* they missed? Who was to say exactly what had happened up there in the dark? Mary Jane hadn't loved her husband for a long time, perhaps never. She had been seventeen and impressionable when they met, and he forty-one and world-wise; now she was twenty-seven and he was fifty-one—an old man by her standards, and their marriage had taken on quite a different appearance. She was no longer impressed that he had been a famous musician many years ago. He had always bullied her. He pretended to be such a liberated New Age male, but all the liberation was for him, not her. She was only the cook and house cleaner and breeder of children. Worst of all, he had a bad temper, particularly when he was trying to meditate and the children made noise. Once, in a fit of irritation, he had slapped Bud so hard that Mary Jane had had to take the child to the doctor, saying he had fallen while playing a game.

None of these accumulated resentments in themselves would have added up to homicide, had not this odd opportunity presented itself. As Mary Jane drove, she pondered her options, and she really couldn't see a single obstacle in her way. It would be a pleasant murder, coolly planned, not passionately spur-of-the-moment. Without Gary, she would have the ranch all to herself. There would be no one to tell her what to do, no one to treat her in a condescending manner like she was a dumb child. Perhaps eventually she'd meet a man closer to her own age, someone sexy who did not have a bad temper, and who did not steal the covers at night, as Gary always did. She would be rich. She could travel. She wouldn't have to answer to anyone.

Mary Jane and Gary reached the lean-to close to midnight, and she helped him unpack the camping supplies from the rear of the truck. The last item was the shotgun, which she carried to him with the barrel pointed at his chest.

"Don't point that thing!" he told her irritably. "God, you're stupid!" he added with a sigh.

She had been wavering until that moment. More than the irritation in her husband's voice, it was his superior, condescending tone that decided her. "Let me have it," he commanded, reaching out his hand.

"Okay," she added. And she pulled the trigger.

That was the easy part. She buried Gary in a shallow grave near where she had shot him, then she drove the camping gear back to the house and went about determinedly pretending that her husband had simply never come home that night. Several weeks went by before the first surprise came: Zor McCarthy appeared at the ranch and told her that the Warrior Circle held the paper on her property, as well as her husband's business, and that they would give her a few months to leave. She knew nothing about mortgages and "paper"—she had always assumed that she and Gary owned the ranch outright. Then came the second shock: Sheriff Snider started coming by, clearly suspicious, bullying her, implying that he knew exactly what she had done, wanting to look around. It was in hiding her crime that Mary Jane's passions were finally aroused, for she was terrified of Lou Snider.

Wasn't there anyone to help her? Yes, it seemed there was. In mid-July, around the time that Lou started paying unwanted visits, she had a new visitor, Aria Waldman, the reporter from the local paper. Over a cup of coffee, Aria confessed that her real name was Rebecca Weinstein and that she was the daughter of Richard Weinstein, a man whom Gary and the Warrior Circle had driven to suicide. Aria's plan was to expose the Warriors in the newspaper, and she was hoping that Mary Jane would tell her anything she had overheard about the group. Meanwhile, Aria warned Mary Jane to be on guard against Lou Snider; the sheriff was virtually certain the young wife had killed her husband, and he was determined to get her. Aria explained, woman to woman, precisely how she had gotten this information from Sheriff Snider—in bed. She knew the sheriff better than anyone, she said. Lou was a brutal man, unstoppable, a crooked cop, capable of anything—he might even harm Mary Jane's children if he thought it would help him find out what he wanted to know.

"But I didn't do anything!" Mary Jane lied, terrified. "Gary died on that camping trip. I never saw him again!"

"It doesn't matter if you're innocent," Aria replied. "He *thinks* you're guilty. And with Lou, that's enough."

Aria came to the ranch again on the weekend before she fled to Hawaii. She told Mary Jane that she had heard from Lou that the men were planning another of their male-bonding intensives for the following Saturday and Sunday, the first such weekend since Gary's disappearance. According to Lou, they were going to spend Saturday night at Bear Lake. It wasn't hard to find Bear Lake, Aria said. She even drew a small map.

"You know, I've been thinking of doing something really terrible," Aria confessed. "You'll have to tell me what you think. I hate Lou, I really do. I want to break off with him, but I'm terrified of what he'll do if I leave him. So I've been thinking . . . well, if I hiked up to the lake on Friday with a shotgun, and hid out in the trees . . . God, it would be so damn easy to pick him off, and no one would ever suspect it was me! There's so much intrigue going on in that men's group, all of them at each other's throat—the cops would think one of the guys had done it." Aria spent quite a long time telling Mary Jane her plan, even using the map she had drawn to show the places she thought would be good to hide. "It's so tempting!" Aria confessed, shaking her head. "I could be rid of Lou forever!"

"So are you going to do it?" Mary Jane asked in a trembling voice.

Aria shook her head. "No, I want to, but I don't have the nerve. I've decided I'd better just run instead. I have a ticket for Hawaii on Wednesday morning, and I'm never coming back here, believe me—I just dropped by to say good-bye. And by the way, *please,* don't tell Lou where I'm going, will you? I didn't even come by here today. We'll keep each other's secrets, okay?"

As Aria was leaving, she passed on one more secret, just between the two of them: Lou didn't have a shred of actual evidence that would stand up in court, but he was convinced that Mary Jane had killed her husband. Early the next week, as soon as he got back from his Warrior Circle weekend, Lou was planning to come by the ranch and force Mary Jane to confess—Aria didn't know exactly what he had in mind, but the sheriff was a man who believed himself above the law and he could be extremely brutal. So Aria just wanted to drop a friendly word of warning. Woman to woman.

"But *Lou* was the one who shot Gary!" Mary Jane cried. Then, in confusion, realizing she had said too much, she tried to cover up. "I mean, I think so, anyway."

"You're probably right," Aria agreed. "But that only makes Lou more dangerous. You know what really happened up on that mountain, don't you? And that's why Lou is never going to rest easy until he's dealt you out of the game."

Mary Jane still thought she might come out of this on top, if only she could keep the ranch. Thinking herself very clever, she did a curious thing: she went to Jack Wilder for help. She was certain that Wilder & Associate would find out what had nearly happened. What was *supposed* to have happened, at least, and *would* have happened except for an unlucky stumble that no one needed to know about—that Lou, acting on behalf of the others, had shot Gary by Bear Lake. Mary Jane was a wistful, dreamy woman, not entirely realistic. Indeed, she had almost convinced herself that Gary hadn't really come home that night, terrified, seeking a safe place to hide. She was certain that Wilder & Associate would discover the proper motive, that Gary had been stealing money from the Hemperware business, and the men's group had killed him over it; Jack and Howie would prove this and then surely, once the men were convicted of murder, she would be left in possession of her eighty-acre ranch. She even had the clever idea that perhaps the case would not need to come to trial, which might be risky. It would be enough for ex-police Commander Jack Wilder to frighten the men sufficiently with a possible murder prosecution, and they would be eager to settle with her out of court.

Of course it all would work better if Sheriff Snider weren't

around to tell his part of the tale. Best of all, perhaps Sheriff
Snider's death could be arranged in such a way that it would be
blamed on the other men, the bad men who were trying to steal her
ranch. Aria Waldman had believed this was possible—she had almost decided to do it herself, and Aria was a smart lady who had
gone to college. So why couldn't Mary Jane use Aria's discarded
plan? Then she wouldn't have to worry about the scary sheriff anymore. Aria had adroitly taken her own diagrams and maps away
with her, but Mary Jane was certain she remembered very clearly
how it all went. Growing up in Texas, she knew how to use a shotgun. She wasn't so stupid that she didn't understand, after thinking
it over, that Aria was trying to push her to do a dirty deed that Aria
didn't have the nerve to do herself. But why not? Aria would certainly never tell! She couldn't, or she would be implicated herself.

Mary Jane found a friend in town to look after the children for
the weekend, and then she went hiking to Bear Lake with a shotgun. But it turned out to be more complicated than Aria had told
her, for Chuck Hildyard had been camping solo since Friday night,
and on Saturday afternoon Lou Snider suddenly appeared on his
own as well. From her vantage point, hiding behind a knoll, Mary
Jane had watched as Lou shot Chuck Hildyard and then put the
body on the stack of wood that Chuck had prepared for the evening
bonfire. After that, things got very weird. Toward evening, Lou lit
the bonfire and then hid himself a short way off in the woods.
When the rest of the men arrived, all hell broke loose. It seemed to
Mary Jane that everyone was firing guns at everyone else. She was
about to give up on her plan and sneak away when to her astonishment, she saw Lou standing hardly a dozen feet from where she
was hiding, his back to her. Would one more gunshot really matter? Wasn't this a blessing in disguise that all the men were trying
to kill each other? Who was to worry about one more explosion?
And so she crept a little closer, and she shot Lou in the back.

Mary Jane had managed to rid herself of Lou Snider, her main
threat, and she was starting to think she would triumph. But the
planet didn't stand still; as soon as she plugged one leak, another
occurred. She thought Aria Waldman had disappeared to Hawaii
forever—didn't she say she was going to do that? But then to her
horror, after spending the night with a nice man, a contractor who
was awfully sweet to her children, she saw Aria on the sidewalk
outside the New Wave Café, where she was having breakfast.

Mary Jane understood very well that Aria would put two and two together when she learned the circumstances of Lou Snider's death. Originally, Mary Jane had believed Aria could never expose her without exposing herself, but thinking it over, she saw that this was not a guarantee. What had Aria done, really? She had simply said a few things, dropped some hints. No, it was not a good idea to leave someone alive—a reporter!—who knew that she was a murderer. Anyway, Mary Jane had become a little hardened by now, and one more death did not seem significant.

So there it was—as much, at least, as Howie was able to learn from Mary Jane's semi-garbled account while he drove her first to pick up her kids, then to the Greyhound bus, and finally to Captain Ed Gomez. Mary Jane obviously knew a good deal more about the Warrior Circle than she had admitted to Jack. She told Howie, for instance, that she knew about the hillside behind Aria's A-frame from overhearing Chuck and Gary plotting possible ways to rid themselves of Aria, if that was ever deemed necessary. Mary Jane was a borrower, and she borrowed Chuck's planned route, parking her car farther up the road and approaching the A-frame overland from the hillside to carry out her unsuccessful attempt to shoot Aria. Howie spent hours repeating all these admissions to Jack, who listened with many sighs and shakes of his head.

As for Aria, she had a good attorney, and she wasn't talking at all now beyond a very simplified, bare-bones account of her actions. Yes, her father was Richard Weinstein, and she had come to San Geronimo to find out what had happened to him and to expose Chamisa Mall—but only in a thoroughly legal manner, as an investigative reporter for *The San Geronimo Post*. Personally, Jack wasn't buying it. He believed that the figure in the dog mask who had approached Gary with a gun at Bear Lake on the full moon in June had been Aria, not Lou. For a woman of determination, it would not have been difficult to get hold of that .38 Smith & Wesson, and the maps she had drawn for Mary Jane proved that she knew the area well. It was Jack's theory that Aria had hiked up into the mountains on her own to watch and wait for some good chance to get Gary alone. Probably she had stumbled and missed deliberately; if Lou had been the masked figure, the chances were that at least one of the two bullets would have found their mark. Knowing that she had missed, Aria would have become suspicious when Gary never surfaced; probably she was the one who had urged Lou

Snider to go after Mary Jane Tripp, just as she had set Mary Jane against Lou.

The object of all this, of course, was to further her grand plan of indirect action, to create enough fear and loathing and confusion among all the players that they would conveniently destroy one another, saving her the trouble and mess, not to mention the danger of getting caught. Perhaps Aria had been improvising all along, trying this and that. She could not have known how it would all turn out, if she had truly been the one in the animal mask at Bear Lake on that full moon in June. But she could be fairly certain that with a mask that pointed to Lou, and a revolver with Chuck Hildyard's fingerprints on the cylinder, she could cause some serious mischief.

Howie, for his part, kept quiet about the admissions she had made to him on the stairs outside her A-frame. He felt in some obscure way that the conversation was privileged and shouldn't be used against her by strangers in court. As the legal case progressed, he maintained a strictly neutral position: if Aria was convicted for conspiracy to murder, so be it, but he wouldn't help District Attorney Jed Peterson make the case against a woman he had once loved. Neutral or not, the conspiracy angle proved too subtle for the legal brains of San Geronimo. Jack had expected the worst all along. It was one of the quaint charms of rural New Mexico that criminals who could afford a decent defense attorney almost always walked.

Aria was no exception. She was held for several days as a material witness, but she still hadn't been charged by the time Howie left for his Colorado camping trip. As for Zor, Denny, and Shep, they had been released pending a grand jury inquiry and at the moment they were all claiming complete and utter innocence, conveniently blaming every possible wrongdoing on Chuck, Lou, and Misha. In New Mexico, this could all take quite a few years to sort out and come to trial. None of it mattered much to Howie, this white man's justice. He was glad to remember at such times that he was a Sioux. These people were interesting, sometimes funny, often tragic. But when push came to shove, they were not his people. They were not his tribe.

Howard Moon Deer turned his back on it all.

17

Howie returned to San Geronimo from Colorado on a Friday afternoon, the second week in September, a clear and golden day. There were eighteen messages stacked up on his answering machine, the world waiting in ambush. Refusing to oblige, Howie put off listening to his messages until the following morning. He pressed the play button and then sat down with a cup of coffee, staring out his back window at San Geronimo Peak in the distance.

The third message was from Heather Winter, and it had been left last Tuesday: "Hey, Howie, it's Heather. I was just calling to say good-bye. School's starting up again so, well . . . I'm heading back to Berkeley. I sold my car for five hundred bucks, and I'm taking the bus this afternoon. I guess you heard about Aria. The D.A. couldn't figure out any way to deal with her, so he let her go finally while you were gone—she flew to Hawaii, though she's supposed to come back if they want her for more questioning. Maybe you'll be going to Hawaii too now. . . . "

There was a pause on the tape, and then Heather started again: "Anyway, Howie, I have to find an apartment and all that boring stuff, but I'll send you my address as soon as I get one. You're always welcome to come crash on my floor if you ever get a city urge . . . or any kind of urge at all, to tell the truth. . . . " There was a longer pause, then softly: "I love you, Howie. But I guess you know that." Then the phone went dead.

For Howie, this message from Heather was painful. He suspected she found him interesting mostly because she could not have him. Such was the human comedy, everybody wanting what they couldn't have. But Heather was wrong about Howie chasing Aria to Hawaii. Time and distance had finally accomplished what all of his rational thoughts and insights had failed previously to do. He was over Aria, at last. Though he was wise enough to be happy that she was thousands of miles away, just in case. . . .

The remaining messages on the machine spanned a wide range, from reporters to Howie's mother, up in South Dakota, who had somehow heard of his latest escapade and was calling to see if he was all right. The last message was from Jack, inviting him for dinner tonight, tempting him with a particularly rich Greek dish, moussaka, which he knew Howie loved. Jack was trying to cheer him up, of course, and Howie phoned back to accept the invitation, feeling it would be churlish to refuse. Clearly it was time to pretend at least to rejoin the living world, even though Howie suspected he was in fact emotionally dead inside.

In the late afternoon, he drove into the center of town to the one wine shop where he could pick up a few bottle of retsina, Greek wine to go with the moussaka, a small way to let Jack and Emma know that he appreciated their efforts. He parked near the plaza, bought two bottles of the resinated wine, and was putting the bag into the trunk of his car when he heard a Bach cello suite coming from someone's radio or CD player not far away. It was the famous opening Prelude from Suite No. 1 and it made him smile, remembering his night at the Lone Coyote Motel with Claire, the passionate, cello-playing blonde with the cheating husband in Iowa. He hoped she was doing okay back in mid-America, and that her creep of a husband had come to his senses.

Howie was slipping behind the wheel of his car when the Bach cello music in the distance paused, did some tuning, then started again on the second movement, the Allemande. This was not a recording. The music was live, and it was coming from the plaza. Howie listened more closely. Whoever was playing, played superbly well.

"It *can't* be!" he muttered.

Howie left his car, slung his green day pack over his shoulder, and walked toward the plaza to investigate. The music swelled in volume as he drew closer, the deep guttural resonance of the cello soaring and falling, penetrating the narrow ancient streets of San Geronimo. In the plaza, Howie saw that a small crowd had gathered around a solo player who was sitting on a bench beneath a large shade tree. There was no mistaking that long blond hair. It was Claire!

Howie found himself grinning from ear to ear, full of a strange surge of happiness. He was stepping forward into the crowd that had gathered around her when he noticed two young children, a dark-haired boy and a blond girl, who were standing together with a tip jar. Howie paused, his smile frozen in place. He had been fantasizing about a carefree return to the Lone Coyote, but this made matters a good deal more serious.

"Hey," Howie said, approaching the kids. "Is that your mom? She sure can play the cello!"

"She was in the Iowa String Quartet," the boy said solemnly. He was eight or nine, handsome and serious. "But we left Iowa," he added unhappily, "so she just plays on the street now."

"I bet you miss Iowa?"

"I miss my dad," he said darkly.

"Of course, you do."

"We're going to live in a tepee!" the little girl said happily. She was younger, perhaps seven, and as cute as she could be.

"A tepee!" Howie laughed.

"My mom bought it in Oklahoma," the boy said. "It's on the top of our van now. I don't know where we're going with it, though. California, maybe. My aunt lives in Santa Cruz."

"Indians live in tepees," said the girl.

"I know. I'm an Indian," Howie told her.

"You *are*?"

He assured her that, yes, he was indeed an Indian, even though he had never lived in a tepee. He turned back to the boy.

"So you're heading to California, huh?"

"Maybe. Mom says she wanted to look up a friend here in San Geronimo, and then she'd know whether we're going to California or staying in New Mexico. Personally, I think it's nuts," he said sullenly, old beyond his years. "I just want to go home."

"Yeah, I can understand that," Howie said. "What's your name?"

"Jonathan," said the boy.

"Well, Jonathan. Let me tell you something from my own experience. Home is a very wonderful thing. But sometimes home isn't what you've left behind in the past—it's what's lying ahead of you in the future, waiting to be found. Do you understand what I'm saying?"

But the boy didn't understand. How could he? Howie had been kneeling by the two children. He stood now and looked over to Claire, who was concentrating on her cello and hadn't seen him yet. Apparently she had returned to Iowa only long enough to break up with her cheating husband, collect her children, and head out upon the open road with nothing but a tepee for a roof and her cello to make a living. She was radiantly beautiful, a feast for Howie's sore eyes. It was mind-boggling, really: such innocence and foolhardy courage. And, dear God, she played the cello like an angel, with almost unbearable passion, as though the fate of the world hung upon every note! Howie was deeply moved. But the responsibility of a woman who had just left her husband, and two young children in tow!—was he brave enough for that? It still wasn't too late to turn and walk back to his car and pretend he had never seen her.

"Aren't you going to give us a tip?" the little girl asked in a high childish voice, holding up the jar.

"Sure, you bet I am," Howie told her.

It was very scary, but Howie took the leap. Maybe it would work out, maybe not . . . but he was a warrior, after all, and this is what warriors did: they took scary chances. He got a yellow legal pad from his day pack and made a map of the road to his cabin, drawing a tepee in the backyard, a very pretty tepee with ribbons flying from the tops of the poles. Then he folded the map and dropped it into Claire's tip jar.

Walking back to his car, Howard Moon Deer started laughing for no reason at all, except he felt suddenly alive again. Foolish, certainly. Still looking for love, at the mercy of lust, full of wild and unfounded hope. But what the hell. He had placed his bet on the great Indian roulette wheel in the sky, and it would be interesting to see how it turned out.

Don't miss the next thrilling
Howard Moon Deer
and Jack Wilder mystery,
Red Moon
coming soon from Signet!

1

Howard Moon Deer was looking out the window, watching the first snow of the year fall on the old adobe wall, when their client appeared in the Spanish courtyard below. As clients go, this one appeared top-of-the-food-chain: early thirties, tall, handsome, and finely tuned. His long blond hair was pulled back tightly from his aristocratic face in a clean, polite ponytail. Everything about him suggested privilege and progressive sensibilities, except for his clothes. He was dressed oddly in black leather boots, jeans, a black turtleneck sweater, and a long black cape. The cape was trying hard to be very Toulouse Lautrec, but the effect, as far as Howie was concerned, was more Bela Lugosi.

"Offhand, I'd say our new client is either a vampire or an artist," Howie said to Jack Wilder, who was sitting in a rocking chair across the room. "Let's hope it's the former. Personally I'd rather have my blood sucked dry than listen to another misunderstood New Mexico genius telling me how great he is."

"He's early," Jack said grumpily, feeling beneath the crystal of his braille wristwatch.

"The snow's early, too," Howie replied, apropos of nothing. It was still October, the day before Halloween, and already three or four inches of fluffy virgin whiteness had floated down gently from the sky. Meanwhile, their client in the courtyard below seemed lost. His gaze traveled questioningly across the nameplates on the ground floor of the small office complex. Eventually he noticed the brand-new sign pointing upstairs to WILDER & ASSOCIATE, PRIVATE INVESTIGATIONS. Jack and Howie had recently moved their business from Jack's kitchen into what passed in the small northern town of San Geronimo for a professional building—a refurbished old adobe home in the historic district downtown. Unfortunately, it just about took a detective to find the office.

Howie stepped back from where he was spying at the window. He didn't want it to appear that clients were such a rare event at Wilder & Associate that one gaped at them idiotically. He listened as heavy boots thumped up the outside stairs. A moment later there was a knock.

"Glad you could find us," Howie said, opening the door with an efficient smile. "Come in. I'm Howard Moon Deer, Jack's assistant."

"I'm Robin Vandenberg. I phoned earlier," the man said, stamping his feet to shake the snow from his boots. His voice was gentle and airy. He studied Howie quickly, absorbing the fact that Howie was an Indian with long black hair in a braid down his back, probably not his idea of a private eye.

"Let me take your things. . . . Hey, nice cape!" Howie said, managing to keep a straight face.

"Well, it's very theatrical, of course—wearing a cape," Robin replied modestly. "But I found it at a flea market in London last year, and it's strange how it changes the way I feel about myself when I wear it. It makes me feel like I'm a swashbuckler in an old movie. Like I can do anything. It's my magic cape, I suppose. So I wear it at difficult moments in my life, when I need just that small extra bit of courage. Like today."

"Is that so?" Howie didn't quite know how to respond. He took the cape, shook the snow from it on the landing outside, then hung it on a pair of antlers mounted on the wall by the door—no relative of mine, Howie liked to say.

Up close, Robin Vandenberg had a poetic face. Dreamy blue eyes. A finely sculptured nose. A clear, boyish complexion complete with rosy cheeks. He wore a small gold ring in his left earlobe: nothing too flashy, but just the right amount of hipitude. All in all, such a pleasantly nice, upbeat sort of person, it was difficult to imagine why he was here—in an office where few pleasantly upbeat people ever came.

Jack, meanwhile, had moved from his rocking chair to stand behind his antique wooden desk, an impractical piece of furniture with too many drawers and cubbyholes. The twin lenses of Jack's dark glasses fixed themselves in the direction of their client.

"Commander Wilder, I can't tell you how grateful I am that you found time to see me," Robin said politely, peering about the office.

"Just call me Jack," he replied gruffly. "I've been retired for years. Please, have a seat."

Robin debated between a big wooden platform rocker and a smaller spindly rocker. One of Jack's interior design eccentricities was that every chair in the room was required to rock. The office was very homey for a detective agency. It was a low-ceilinged room with adobe walls, a kiva fireplace, and a clutter of comfortable furniture. Katya, Jack's German shepherd guide dog, was stretched out luxuriously on an expensive handwoven Navajo rug in front of the fire. As Robin settled into the platform rocker, his expression became very solemn.

"You know, I've always been fascinated by blind people," he said unexpectedly. "But how do you manage it? Being a blind detective, I mean. Aren't there difficulties?"

Jack smiled thinly. "There are always difficulties, Robin, even if you can see. I have Howie's help, of course, but nevertheless, I only accept certain cases where I feel I can be useful. So perhaps you should get to the point and tell us why you are here."

"It's my stepfather, Sherman Stone," Robin began. His voice had become unexpectedly hard, no longer so sweet and boyish. "Do you know him?"

"The artist? I know *of* him, but we've never met."

"As an artist, he's very talented. I won't deny him that. But as a human being, the man is impossible. He's like some sort of dangerous child. He's cruel, he's vain, he's totally self-absorbed. And I have reason to believe he's planning to kill my mother."

Robin Vandenberg paused for dramatic effect. Jack said nothing, but only continued to wait and listen. Ex-police Commander Jack Wilder was very good at waiting, and even better at listening.

Robin took a deep breath and continued. "He wants to get his hands on my mother's money, of course. I'm hoping you'll find out exactly what he's up to. I need hard facts. Something I can take to my mother to open her eyes before it's too late."

Jack cocked his head slightly to one side and smiled vaguely, inviting all sorts of confidences and true confessions. Jack Wilder was a big man with a slow, melancholy manner. Comfortably stout, in his mid-fifties, with curly gray hair and a well-trimmed

gray beard—Howie liked to joke that if Jack got rid of the dark
glasses and let his beard grow, he could always get a job as a department store Santa. A dangerous Santa, however. You might not
want to sit in his lap.

"Perhaps you should tell me a bit more about your family situation," Jack murmured after a moment.

"Well, you know my mother, I presume? Barbara Vandenberg . . . ? Barbara Vandenberg Stone is how she likes to be known
these days."

"Again, I've never met her. But I know the name, of course."

The name Barbara Vandenberg was literally everywhere in the
small, arty town of San Geronimo. Babs, as people called her, was
the richest woman in the county, an oil heiress, a collector and a
patron of the arts. There was a Barbara Vandenberg Scholarship
Fund which sent the best graduating student each year from the
public high school to the college of his or her choice. There was
also the new Barbara Vandenberg Performing Arts Center, and
even a Barbara Vandenberg wing of the local Native American
Arts and Crafts Museum.

"My mother's from Texas," Robin was saying, relaxing into his
family history. "She met my father, Richard Vandenberg, when she
was at Vassar and he was finishing up at Harvard Business School.
They married a few years later, after Dad got his seat on the New
York Stock Exchange. He invested a lot of my mother's inheritance in the market and it made Mom . . . well, very wealthy. They
lived in New York primarily, but summers they came out here to
New Mexico. They loved San Geronimo. The light, you know.
Dad was something of a painter. . . . He was also an expert on Native American folklore," Robin added, turning toward Howie with
a hopeful smile.

Howie smiled back. His best go-ahead-and-study-me, see-if-I-
care smile. Howie was taking notes, seated in the early American
walnut rocking chair, a chair that was fiendishly—and uncomfortably—puritanical in design. It rocked, but did not roll.

Robin cleared his throat and his brief smile faded. "Of course,
neither of my parents had much time for children. They were so
busy being rich and cultured and wonderful—know what I mean?"

"I'm not sure," Jack said delicately.

"Well, it doesn't matter now. In some ways, it's extremely lib-
erating to have parents who hardly know you're alive. As long as

we were decorative at parties, Mom and Dad left Pooh and me pretty much alone."

"Pooh?"

"That's my older sister. Her real name's Penelope, but everyone's always called her Pooh. So that made us Pooh and Robin, you see. Which is fairly pukey, I admit, but there it is. I changed my name in college for a while, but when I came home, everybody kept calling me Robin, and after a while I just gave up."

Jack nodded with encouragement. "So you and Pooh are the only children?"

"That's right. I'm thirty-three and she's four years older. She was planning to come with me today, by the way, but she had some work she couldn't get out of."

"What does she do?"

"She runs an art gallery in town. The New Vision."

"All right. Now about your father and mother—did they divorce?"

"No. Dad died. He had a heart attack about twelve years ago . . . frankly, it came as a surprise to everybody that he even had a heart. My mother closed up the Manhattan apartment and moved into the San Geronimo house permanently. And here she remains, a big fish in a small pond."

"And where did you grow up, Robin? Here in New Mexico?"

"No. I went to boarding school for a while in Santa Fe. But mostly I lived in New York, spending my summers in San Geronimo. Then a few years ago, I had a loft in SoHo and I just got sick of city life, all the traffic and pollution. I had a sort of . . . a meltdown."

Jack raised an eyebrow. "A meltdown?" he questioned.

"Well, a spiritual collapse, I guess you could call it. Nothing *too* serious," Robin said with a self-conscious laugh. "Anyway, whatever it was, it all got cured when I moved back to New Mexico. I bought forty acres in the mountains here north of town. It's very primitive, but I really love it. I built a tree house, actually. My bedroom's fifty feet up in the air."

"Really? A tree house? That must be quite something. Tell me, are you an artist?"

"Oh, no! God forbid!" He laughed. "Actually, I'm a carpenter. That's what I like to think of myself as, anyway. Someone who builds simple, useful things. And I volunteer a few days a week at an alternative preschool near where I live. Frankly, I enjoy being with children a lot more than I enjoy the company of grown-ups. I guess I'm not very ambitious. Normally, I don't even come into town very much. But this thing about Sherman and my mother really has me worried."

"All right. Tell me about Sherman and your mother. What kind of relationship do they have?"

"The first thing you have to understand is that my mother is sixty-seven-years old. Sherman is much younger, he's just turned fifty-two. The age difference in itself doesn't bother me—after all, men often marry women who are much younger, so why shouldn't a woman do the same? But Sherman is the wrong man to be married to anyone, no matter what the age. For starters, he's monstrously selfish. He only cares about himself and his painting."

"When did they get married?"

"Three years ago. Just six weeks after they met at some art opening."

"And you believe he married her for money?"

"Well, naturally. He jokes about it, even. How every artist should get himself a rich wife. He's very open about it."

"And your mother puts up with this sort of joking?"

"Well, she adores him. It's very strange, really. The man's totally self-indulgent. He generally starts off the morning with a joint, and by noon he's drinking red wine—extremely *good* red wine, I should add, since he married my mother! And he's not exactly what you'd call faithful. Frankly, when it comes to sex, Sherman seems to believe it's still the 1960s. But he has a weird charisma and he's very handsome, I suppose. He's beguiled her, he truly has."

"Does she know he's unfaithful?"

"Yes. I think so, at least. She would have to be blind not to know. . . . Oh, I'm sorry!"

"That's quite all right, Robin. So she doesn't care that he sleeps with other women?"

"Oh, I think she *cares*. But it's the deal they have. It's the price she pays for being married to a very charismatic artist who's fifteen years younger. She hates boring people, you know, and you can't accuse Sherman of being *that*. She says he makes her feel totally alive."

"And yet you're telling me he's planning to kill her?" Jack mentioned, guiding the conversation back to its beginning.

Robin nodded. "There was an incident a few weeks back in early October. Someone took a shot at Mom as she was walking by herself in the woods. The bullet only missed her by a few inches—it broke off a branch not far from her head. She was furious. She assumed it was a hunter, of course."

"That seems a reasonable assumption, walking in the woods in the fall," Jack agreed. "Did she see anyone?"

"No. We all warned Mom to wear brighter clothes during her walks, and I pretty much forgot about the incident. But then a few days ago, my brother-in-law overheard a very strange conversation at a bar called Pinky's Hacienda. It's a biker dive on the south end of town. A big drug scene. There are some pool tables and they have awful live music on the weekends. It used to be mostly an Hispanic hangout, but recently some counterculture types have started going there. The tattooed and pierced set. Pooh's husband, Frank, goes there sometimes to play pool and hang out with his friends—Frank's an artist, too, you know. Frank Cobb. Anyway, he was at Pinky's one night last week when Sherman staggered in and sat near him at the bar. Sherman was shit-faced, really carrying on."

"How about your brother-in-law, Frank?" Jack asked. "Just for the record, how sober was he?"

Robin smiled. "Probably not very. But when it comes to excess, Frank can't hold a candle to Sherman. Sherman's the party animal of all time. God knows what he was on that night. Out in the parking lot, just as Frank was getting ready to drive home, he happened to overhear Sherman having a conversation with some guy—it sounded like he was trying to hire him to kill Mom. What he said exactly was that he would pay $25,000 to anyone who would help him get free from his golden cage. That's how he put it."

Jack scowled. "It's hard to believe he'd seriously discuss murder in a public place like that. You said earlier that your stepfather jokes about marrying a rich wife. Could this be just another example of his odd sense of humor?"

"Well, yes. Very possibly. Still, serious or not, Sherman made the offer. Frank heard him."

"All right. Who did he make this offer to?"

"Well, that's the problem. Frank was sitting in his car, facing the wrong direction. Like I said, he was getting ready to drive home and he didn't actually manage to get a good look at the person Sherman was talking to. But the whole thing worried him. He decided to sleep on it, but he woke up the next morning and he was still worried. So he told Pooh, and Pooh phoned me. And we've been figuring out what we should do about it ever since. I mean, yes—Sherman gets drunk and he says outrageous things. But you can't go around offering people $25,000 to kill your wife, even if you're half-joking about it. We decided to hire you to see how serious the threat really is. Particularly after the incident in the woods."

Jack nodded. "Tell me something, Robin. In the event of your mother's death, how will her estate be divided?"

Robin shrugged. "I don't know precisely. I presume her various charities will get a big chunk. As for the rest . . . my mother is a romantic. She's one of those women for whom the man in her life is everything, almost like a religion. Pooh and I will get something, of course. But I'm afraid Sherman will get his hands on most of her fortune . . . and to answer the question you're probably thinking, yes, I *do* care about the money. Pooh and I both care. It's our birthright, after all. It's not easy to grow up with rich parents, so you might as well get something out of it when they die. Like an inheritance."

Robin fell silent and for a few moments there was no sound in the room except for the logs crackling in the fireplace. Jack appeared to be lost in thought. Howie paused with his pen raised above the notebook. Katya, still sleeping by the fire, let out a small snore.

"Look, I sense your hesitation to get involved in murky family matters," Robin said finally. "How about just giving me a week of your time. Go see my sister's husband, Frank—I'll give you his address. Talk with Sherman, meet my family, make up your own mind. If you decide that Sherman was only drunk that night at Pinky's and his $25,000 offer wasn't to be taken seriously . . . well, it's not a great situation, but if Mom puts up with it, I guess there's not much for us to do. But if you believe he's really trying to hire someone to kill my mother, we've got to stop him."

Jack leaned back speculatively in his rocking chair. From the semi-sour look on his face, Howie was almost certain he would decline the case. It was unpleasant to meddle in family matters when money was at stake, and the allegation that Sherman Stone was trying to hire a hit man in a loud voice outside a crowded bar seemed a little thin. As for the mysterious bullet, hunting season was a dangerous time to be walking in the woods.

"Look, I'll write you a check for a thousand dollars," Robin said quickly, feeling a 'no' in the air. "All I want at the end of the week is your judgment whether the case is worth pursuing or not. If at that time you're convinced my stepfather doesn't pose a danger to my mother, I'll let the matter drop. But if you believe there's any chance this isn't a joke, you'll owe it to my mother to protect her life and expose him. Okay?"

Jack nodded slowly. "All right, Robin. One week. Unless Howie and I discover some justification to continue the investigation. Please write your check to Wilder & Associate."

Howie watched from the window as Robin Vandenberg walked away across the snowy courtyard, disappearing into the bleak, wintry day. Howie couldn't quite put his finger on it, but there was something unsettling about their new client. . . .